Praise for *The Washington Lawyer*

"*The Washington Lawyer* is a thrilling tale of intrigue and revenge at the highest levels in the American government—told from an insider's point of view. The action is nonstop, from the gripping prologue to the satisfying end. Not to be missed!"

—Joan Johnston

inful

"Archeologist p   twin
sister, congressi   vhile
away for the w   was
never one of th   ds to
Washington to   in a
tangled web of   :ople
will go to keep

   Fast paced a   )wer,
murder, and in   belly
of Washington

ullen

Mom

"Rich with international intrigue, *The Washington Lawyer* bristles with insider details, heart-stopping action, and memorable characters. This is Washington politics at its most revealing, told by a top attorney who knows where the truth—and the bodies—are buried."

—Gayle Lynds
New York Times best-selling author of *The Assassins*

"Morals, ethics, values, and integrity often go out the window when temptations come your way. What happens when two men let their greed and desire for wealth and power overtake their moral compasses, and find that one simple indiscretion leading to one wrong choice can bring down your entire world? . . .

Once again author Allan Topol delivers a plot and storyline that will keep readers in suspense from start to finish . . . When the truth is revealed whose damage control wins out? Find out when you read this five-star novel."

—Fran Lewis
Author, creator and editor of *MJ* magazine, and host on Red River Radio Show and World of Ink Network

Also by Allan Topol

FICTION
The Fourth of July War
A Woman of Valor
Spy Dance
Dark Ambition
Conspiracy
Enemy of My Enemy
The China Gambit
The Spanish Revenge
The Russian Endgame
The Argentine Triangle

NON-FICTION
Superfund Law and Procedure (coauthor)

THE WASHINGTON LAWYER

A Novel by

ALLAN TOPOL

SelectBooks, Inc.
New York

This edition is published by SelectBooks, Inc.
For information address SelectBooks, Inc., New York, New York.

First Edition

ISBN 978-1-59079-266-7

Library of Congress Cataloging-in-Publication Data

Topol, Allan.
  The Washington lawyer / Allan Topol. – First Edition.
      p. cm.
  Summary: "In the high-stakes world of Washington politics, hotshot lawyer Andrew Martin is put to the test. When longtime friend Senator Wesley Jasper calls, with explosive news–a sex tryst at Martin's beach house in Anguilla has gone horribly awry–Martin must decide how far he'll go to secure his nomination for chief justice"– Provided by publisher.
  ISBN 978-1-59079-266-7 (pbk. : alk. paper)
  1. Adultery–Fiction. 2. Scandals–Fiction.
  3. Washington (D.C.)–Fiction. 4. Political fiction.
  I. Title.
PS3570.O64W37 2015
  813'.54–dc23
                    2014030930

Manufactured in the United States of America

10 9 8 7 6 5 4 3 2 1

Dedicated to my wife, Barbara, my partner
in this literary venture

Acknowledgments

I have enormous gratitude for my publisher, Kenzi Sugihara, who founded SelectBooks. Kenzi read *The Washington Lawyer* in a weekend, and his enthusiasm for the novel gave me a huge boost. This is our third novel together and it has been a pleasure working with Kenzi.

All of the people at SelectBooks have been wonderful: Nancy Sugihara and Molly Stern in the editing of my manuscript, and Kenichi Sugihara as the Marketing Director.

My agent, Pam Ahearn, added critical advice on key story elements as well as editorial insights. Again, it has been terrific working with Pam.

A special thanks to my wife Barbara, who added valuable insights and suggestions on draft after draft. She particularly helped me shape the characters as what was known in our house as "the sisters book" gradually became *The Washington Lawyer.*

Anguilla

Sunday, November 10

Life could never be better than this, Senator Wesley Jasper thought. He closed his eyes and leaned back in the chaise on the sand at Shoal's Bay. It was eleven in the evening, and above the deserted Caribbean beach a full moon, in a cloudless star-laden sky, peered down on the island of Anguilla. What a way to spend the long Veteran's Day weekend. He was sated from the food, wine, and most of all the mind-blowing sex with Vanessa Boyd. But then tomorrow . . . Oh well, all good things have to end.

"Hey, I'm not losing you, am I?" Vanessa said.

"Just relaxing," he replied, opening his eyes, "after that wonderful dinner."

"Don't forget what happened before dinner."

"Are you kidding. I could never forget that. I still have the taste of you in my mouth."

"Wes, you're an amazing lover."

"You mean for a guy my age?"

"Nonsense. You've ruined all of the thirty-something-year-olds for me. After this weekend, why would I want one of them? They don't know what it takes to satisfy a woman the way you do."

Jasper wanted to believe that the gorgeous blonde—definitely natural—former runway model meant it, but deep down he knew she was flattering him. Still, he enjoyed hearing her say it. He felt younger with her. Maybe next week he'd color the gray starting to form at the temples of his coal-black hair.

He watched her reach into her purse on the small table that held a bottle of red wine and two glasses.

1

She pulled out a half full pack of cigarettes and fished around inside, cursing, "Dammit. I brought four for the weekend. There's got to be one more joint in here somewhere. I did such a good job concealing them to avoid a customs search that I can't find the sucker."

He cringed at her words. In his position, the last thing he needed was to be busted for drugs; and Anguilla had a zero tolerance policy.

"Aha, success," she said pulling out the joint carefully.

She crossed over to his chair. He moved his bare feet to give her room to sit between his legs, facing him. The only sound came from the gently lapping Caribbean against the beach. As she leaned over to light the joint and her long hair cascaded over her face, he saw the tops of her breasts and the protruding nipples beneath the thin yellow sundress with spaghetti straps. He felt himself becoming aroused again. God, he hadn't been like this in twenty years.

She took a deep drag on the joint, closed her eyes, and blew out the smoke. Then she held it out to him.

"Sorry, I don't do that."

"Creep."

With one hand she held the joint. With the other, she stroked the white cotton slacks covering his crotch. When she finally finished the cigarette, she lifted a wine glass and took a long sip.

"Great wine," she said. "I intend to learn something about wine. That's one of my projects for this fall. That and making a decision about graduate school or law school for next year."

"Your hand feels so good. You've got a fabulous touch. To think you used that same hand to blast tennis balls at me this afternoon."

"Very funny. Most of the time I was trying to get my racket on the ball and hang in there. You were doing all the blasting."

"Well, I've been playing longer. A lot longer, I'm afraid." He recalled being on the Yale tennis team. Despite their twenty-year age difference, he was in better physical shape from regular exercise. Unlike most men in their mid-fifties, Jasper didn't have a protruding gut.

She moved her hand up to his face and caressed his cheek, then down to his left arm and to his hand. She fiddled with the gold band on his third finger. "Where does your wife think you are this weekend?"

He pulled back and sat up. For three days he had banished Linda from his mind. Now reality returned with acute clarity. He had a wife who was in Denver visiting her mother. He had a son, and a daughter in college almost Vanessa's age. Ah well, they wouldn't know. They wouldn't be hurt.

"Argentina on business. Ever been there?" he asked, eager to change the subject.

"No, but I'd love to go. Will you take me someday?"

"Sure."

"When will you leave your wife and marry me?"

She said it in a matter of fact tone. No intro or lead-in, as if she were calmly placing a live grenade on the chair. But her words hit him like a ton of bricks. He viewed Vanessa as a sexual play toy. Regardless of how good the sex was with Vanessa, he couldn't possibly leave Linda for her. Wesley Jasper loved his position in the Senate as the powerful chairman of the Armed Services Committee. He was facing a tough reelection battle. Trading Linda for a committee staffer would finish his political career. Besides, he had his family, children whom he loved.

He carefully weighed his response. He had to play this carefully. By going public, Vanessa could make trouble for him. He'd seen it happen to other colleagues. He had to put this genie back into the bottle until after the election. He'd worry about it then.

When he didn't respond, she added, "In May when we were in Paris, you said that you would marry me, but you wouldn't say when."

"That's right. I will leave Linda, and we will get married. It's just that the timing's not good right now with my reelection coming up next year."

Her face hardened. "I'll wait another year. That's all."

Her words conveyed a veiled threat.

"What do you mean?"

"I've been lied to by other men about marriage. This time I have an insurance policy to make sure you keep your word."

"An insurance policy?" He was stunned.

"When we were in Tokyo in July and sharing a suite in the Okura, I was in the bedroom when you held your top-secret late night meeting. You know what I mean?"

His heart began pounding. "You were asleep in the bedroom. I was reading in the living room. There was no meeting."

"Don't lie to me." She sounded indignant. "I hate it when men do that."

"I don't know what you're talking about."

"Before the trip, I overheard you scheduling the meeting. So, I planted a recording device in the living room. I now have a CD with the recording of your meeting. I listened to it again a few days ago. I have no doubt that if I delivered it to the *Washington Post* you'd lose a lot more than your political career. You'd go to jail for a very long time."

Jasper was furious. He couldn't believe she'd done this. What an ungrateful little bitch! After all he'd done for her. He'd taken her to Paris and Tokyo. And the gifts he'd given her—a Chopard watch and a Bulgari bracelet. My God! Now this!

"So when are we getting married?" she asked again.

His heart was pounding. Keep control, he cautioned himself. He had to find a way to placate her.

"Right after the election, I'll divorce Linda. I promise. We'll be married before Christmas. We'll come back here for a honeymoon or anywhere you'd like. In thirteen months you'll be Mrs. Wesley Jasper." He said it with conviction. Another false promise from a politician accustomed to making them.

She stared at him for a long moment, then added. "I can wait a year. But just so you know, and don't forget, I have that recording."

"I would do it even if you didn't have it."

She leaned over and kissed him. "I'll be a good wife for you."

"I'm sure of that."

She stood up. "We'll have great sex all the time. Now that we've settled that, I'm going for a swim."

She sashayed toward the water, her feet bare. About ten yards away, she unzipped her sundress and let it fall to the sand. She wasn't wearing any underwear. As she bent over to pick up the dress, she paused for a minute, her legs spread, letting him admire her from the rear, the way he had most enjoyed sex with her this weekend. Certain he was watching, she laughed easily, picked up the dress and threw it back over her head. It landed on his face. The scent of her still fresh.

He tossed it onto the sand. This wasn't working out the way he had expected. He thought about that movie with Glenn Close—the one where she killed the bunny.

He watched her walk into the water. When it was up to her waist, she dove in and swam out in smooth strokes. He followed her blonde head, getting smaller and smaller under the moonlight. Then he stood up and walked along the beach. He saw his whole life crumbling and disintegrating. From the bluff above the beach, close to the villa they had been using for the weekend, he heard a noise. He pivoted and saw a small native boy, maybe ten or twelve, tossing a ball to a dog.

He shouted at the boy. "Get away." The boy and the dog disappeared.

After another minute, Jasper pulled off his clothes, racing toward the water. He dove in and swam out to Vanessa.

Israel

At five on Monday morning, the sun was already beating down on the dig. Allison Boyd, dressed in khaki slacks and a pale blue polo shirt, with her brown hair up in a ponytail, stood with her hands on her hips watching backhoes excavate the stubborn, rocky soil. Three Israelis worked nearby with picks and shovels. Allison was extremely pleased.

The thirty-four-year-old archeology professor from Brown University had, with incredible persistence, overcome so many obstacles to get to this point. First, there were all those much older stuffed-shirt male professors, her peers in the United States, England, and Israel, who had dismissed the idea of discovering a town from King Solomon's time in this location. But Allison's development of a groundbreaking new dating technology that could establish relics were from Solomon's time, not the Omride Dynasty, caught the attention of British philanthropist Moses Halpern. He traveled to Providence to tell Allison that he believed in her work and admired her persistence, and he was willing to fund her search for the town. She believed this would be a major breakthrough.

The site work had begun three months ago, and then was shut down for two weeks because an official in the Religious Ministry claimed they were digging on holy ground. Allison and her Israeli partner, Zahava, went over that official's head and got the order reversed thanks to the intervention of a former general, now an archeologist, who told them, "I admire the commitment to the project the two of you have."

That work stoppage order was now a distant memory. They had moved lots of earth. Allison was hopeful they would find something. If they didn't . . . well, she hated to think about that possibility—the money and time wasted—the damage to her reputation and that of Zahava, whom she had dragged into this.

She and Zahava were chugging bottles of water and watching the backhoes when Zahava asked Allison, "How'd you happen to become an archeologist?"

"When I was a little girl my father told me I had too much curiosity. I always wanted to know what was happening. No, it was more than wanting to know. I had to know. If a family member was ill, I leaned on other relatives to tell me what was wrong and if they would recover. I'd press my parents about our family history and their backgrounds. Digging up facts excited me. In school I thought about being a journalist—an investigative reporter—because they dig up stories. But writing wasn't my strong suit. The summer I was ten years old we took a trip to New Mexico, visiting the remains of indigenous communities. The guide told us how the people lived in caves on the sides of hills and how their society functioned. But what I saw in those caves spoke to me louder than the guide. I became hooked. I loved it," she bubbled. "I still do. What about you?"

Before Zahava had a chance to answer, Allison's assistant Jonathan raced up the rocky mound toward them. "Look at this," he said bursting with excitement.

He was holding a black metal object. Allison placed it on a table and examined it under a microscope. The sun was reflecting off the metal. *It might be a piece of a spear or other weapon from King Solomon's time,* she thought.

Although so many had argued against her, telling her she was stubborn and pigheaded, she was convinced they were in the right place. Now she had a substantial object. But she cautioned herself not to get too carried away. They would need a lot more study of this metal and much more digging before any definitive conclusions could be reached.

Zahava was looking over her shoulder. "What do you think?" Zahava asked.

"It's too soon to draw a conclusion," she responded.

Zahava turned to Jonathan. "Tell them to shut down the backhoes and use only shovels for now." Jonathan raced off.

"This does look promising," Zahava said to Allison.

"That's a good way to put it. We still have a long way to go."

"Let's take a look for ourselves."

Zahava walked quickly toward the location where Jonathan had found the object, with Allison two steps behind. Suddenly, Allison felt a powerful jolt in her body as if she were struck by electricity. She had an incredible pain in her stomach, causing her to double over, gasping for breath.

Zahava spun around. "What's wrong?"

"It just hit me. A blow to my stomach."

"You better sit down." Zahava led Allison to a chair under an olive tree.

She bent over to ease the pain.

"We should get a doctor," Zahava said. "Call one to come here. Or I can take you into town."

The pain was easing. Allison gave a sigh of relief.

"Let me call a doctor."

"No need to. I'm feeling better."

"At least rest for a while."

"Okay. I'll sit here. You go to Jonathan and the others."

Even as the pain abated, Allison had a sick feeling. She knew what caused it. Something terrible had happened to her twin sister, Vanessa.

Allison didn't want to tell Zahava because her colleague, the quintessential rational scientist, would have laughed at her and told her she was being ridiculous. But Zahava wasn't a twin. She didn't understand about twins. Allison had gotten jolts like this twice before, precisely when something had happened to Vanessa.

The first time was when they were twenty-two. Allison was playing field hockey, in training for the US Olympic team during the year she took off from archeology, after getting her undergraduate degree from Maryland and beginning graduate school at Brown. She had to call time-out and go to the sidelines. An hour later, she received a call from a hospital in Switzerland, telling her that Vanessa had broken her leg skiing.

What was it now? Vanessa had to be in trouble.

It was 10:30 now, Sunday night in Washington, DC. Allison didn't even know whether Vanessa was there. When they had spoken a few days ago, her sister was vague, no, evasive about her plans for the Veteran's Day weekend. Allison replayed their conversation in her mind the last time they spoke. Allison had asked:

"So what are you doing this weekend?"

"A little of this and a little of that."

"Will you be in Washington?"

"I don't think so."

"The weekend starts tomorrow."

"I'm not as organized as you are."

Vanessa plainly didn't want to tell her. "Listen, I'm not judging you and I won't. That's not why I'm asking. I'm just worried about you."

"Allison, you live the way you want, and I'll do what I want. In Israel, you should hook up with an Israeli soldier. They're tough. You could run each other ragged doing your judo and end up in bed. When I was on a shoot once in Tel Aviv I met this guy, a colonel or a captain. He stayed hard all night."

They both laughed. Allison never pressed Vanessa about her weekend plans. She was sorry now. Vanessa could be anywhere in the world, and Allison had no idea with whom. *Damn, damn, damn. I should keep better track of her. I can't let her get into trouble again.*

Frantic with worry, she took out her cell phone and dialed Vanessa's cell. The call went into voice mail. She tried Vanessa's apartment in Washington, but just received more voice mail.

She made up her mind to keep trying both numbers every half hour until she reached Vanessa.

Washington

Andrew Martin ate a piece of Saint-Nectaire on dark bread as he sipped some of the fabulous 1990 Clos de la Roche from Dujac, the third spectacular wine he had served this evening, and looked around the dining room of his Foxhall Road house. He could barely control his excitement. This was one of the best days of his life. This morning's Sunday *New York Times* had reported that Chief Justice West had prostate cancer and was planning to retire shortly. While he felt sorry for West, Martin was thrilled that the article named him as one of the people being considered for chief justice.

It wasn't official, but Martin, the powerful Washington lawyer, knew that when the *Times* carried an article beginning, "*The New York Times* has learned that . . . " it was generally conveying information from an official leak by the Braddock Administration. This was a trial balloon to gauge public reaction. Being on the Supreme Court had been Martin's dream from his first year at Yale Law School. Now it might be a reality. And being the chief justice certainly elevated the prize. He closed his eyes for a second and imagined himself sitting in the center of the bench with four black clad justices on each side of what would become known as the Martin court.

When he opened them, he turned his attention to the elegant dinner table. Martin was seated at one end; his wife, Francis, of thirty five years, looking lovely and radiant in a lavender Valentino sheath, sat the other end of the table of eight. The three other couples, no one sitting next to a spouse, were Secretary of State Jane Prosser and her husband, Philip; the Speaker of the House, Hugh Dawson, and his wife Louise; and Drew and Sally Thomas from New York. Martin's friendship with Drew spanned more than thirty years, since the first day they'd both arrived at Queens College, Oxford, on a Rhodes scholarship. Drew now ran a successful private equity firm.

Drew tapped a spoon on a glass to gain everyone's attention. "To enhance Andrew's candidacy to be chief justice," Drew said, "he needs a song. Now Andrew, you've argued in the Supreme Court forty-eight times and won forty of them."

"Actually, only thirty-nine," Martin said.

"Don't nitpick. So when you enter the court to take your seat on the bench, the other justices will sing . . . "

Taking the cue, Sally, Drew's childhood sweetheart, a good-looking, vivacious gray-haired woman who had aged gracefully, began singing to the tune of Hello Dolly, "Well, hello, Andrew, it's so good to have you back where you belong . . . "

The others laughed. "Hey. That's great," Louise said. Then in good spirits from the free-flowing wine, they all joined Sally in the singing.

"You're looking swell, Andrew . . ."

"Bear with me everybody," Martin said after they finished the song. "I desperately want to talk about something else. That's a prerogative of the host, to change the subject. Isn't it, Drew?"

"Absolutely."

"Good. Francis and I saw Verdi's Luisa Miller at the Kennedy Center last evening. It was fantastic. Anybody else going?"

"We have tickets for Tuesday," Jane said.

Hugh added, "Did you know that Verdi's parents were dirt-poor peasant farmers?"

As the discussion about Verdi continued, Martin stole a quick look into the mirror along the side wall above the black marble topped credenza. He looked damn good for fifty-eight. Hadn't gained a pound in the last thirty-five years. Still a hundred and seventy-five on his six-one frame, thanks to lots of exercise. And he had the same sandy brown hair.

"Wrong." Drew spoke up. "They kept a little inn combined with a village shop. But what always struck me about Verdi was that he was rejected by the conservatory in Milan."

"Ah, but with talent you always succeed," Hugh said.

"Not always, unfortunately," Philip retorted.

"Speaking of music," Louise said, looking at Francis, "Andrew told me that you performed on the violin several summers at Aspen. What was it like?"

"It was so long ago."

"Please tell us."

Francis gave a tiny nod to a tuxedo-clad waiter in the corner of the room, who then began clearing the Limoges plates with the cheese and salad course. Next would be a cold Grand Mariner soufflé that Francis had made.

As Francis began talking, Martin felt a vibration in the vest pocket of the jacket of his Lanvin suit. What the hell? Then he remembered. Concerned that he'd miss a call from Arthur Larkin, the White House Counsel, about the chief justice nomination, Martin had broken his rule of never leaving his cell on during a meal. He yanked the phone out and glanced at caller ID. It was a number he didn't recognize with a 202, Washington area code. It might be Arthur. He better take it.

Not wanting to interrupt Francis, he quietly left, walking rapidly toward the study. "Hello," he said.

Expecting it to be Arthur, he was startled to hear another man shouting, shrill and hysterical. "She drowned. Goddamn it. She's dead."

He recognized Wes Jasper's voice. But his brain was fuzzy with alcohol, his feelings caught up in the euphoria of the evening. Jasper . . . where was he? Why would he be calling?

"Andrew, it's Wes. You've got to help me."

Slowly, it came to him. Thursday Jasper had called and asked to use Andrew's house in Anguilla for the weekend. "Just a short getaway, he had explained." Andrew assumed Wes and Linda would be flying down. So he'd said, "Sure." Now Jasper must be calling him on a cell phone with a Washington area code. What was Wes telling him now? Linda had drowned. "What happened?"

"Andrew, weren't you listening. She's dead. She drowned. And I'm fucked! Don't you understand? Don't you get it? Totally fucked."

Martin felt in a fog. If Linda drowned, why was Jasper fucked? "Now calm down, Wes. Go back to the beginning. Tell me what happened to Linda."

"It's not Linda!" Jasper was shouting. He sounded delirious. "Linda's in Denver visiting her mother. The woman's name is Vanessa."

"Who's Vanessa?"

"She came down here with me."

"Why'd she do that?"

"For Christ's sake, Andrew. Why do you think? Focus."

"Where is she now?"

"On the bed, in the master bedroom of *your* house. I carried her up from the beach."

What in tarnation is this? "You're sure she's dead?"

"How stupid do you think I am?"

Martin took some deep breaths.

"You have to help me," Jasper pleaded. "You're my best friend. You have to help me."

While Martin tried to think of what to say, Jasper kept ranting. "I'm screwed. If this comes out, my reelection is in the toilet. My marriage will be history. My kids will never talk to me. I might as well go out and drown myself."

"Stop." Martin commanded.

"Then *you* tell me what to do?"

"Call the Anguilla police. Tell them what happened. I assume it was an accident."

"Of course it was an accident. She was swimming and went out too far. Stupid, crazy bitch. I almost drowned trying to save her."

"Tell the police all that."

"You don't get it, do you? I can't go to the police. I'm a senator. It'll all be on TV. I'll be ruined. You know that's what'll happen."

Jasper, he was sure, had been drinking. "You have to do it, Wes. It's the only way."

But then as the mess sunk in, Martin began to see ramifications. Disclosure in the media, he realized, could have a devastating effect on his becoming chief justice. He could imagine the Post's headline: "SUPREME COURT NOMINEE RUNS CARIBBEAN LOVE NEST FOR INFLUENTIAL SENATORS."

No, there still was only one right way to handle this. "You must go to the police."

"That is not an option. *You* have to find a way of making this go away. You're my friend. You can't let me be destroyed for one little indiscretion. You know I'm right. Friends help each other when one gets into trouble."

Martin didn't know what to do. If stone sober, he thought, finding a way around this would be almost impossible. But with his mind clouded with alcohol, he felt as if he'd been submerged into a tank.

"Please help me." Jasper raved on. "We've been friends forever. Don't let me go down."

Hearing the sounds from the dining room, he wanted to tell Jasper he'd call him back. But he couldn't do that. Wes had been his friend for decades, and Wes sounded too miserable. But should Martin be responsible for Jasper's life going up in smoke? It was his own damn fault.

"You've got to do something."

The only right thing was for Jasper to call the police and report the drowning. But that would ruin Jasper's life and most likely derail Martin's Supreme Court nomination.

Martin stopped dithering and decided. "I'll help you. I'll take care of it."

"Oh my God, I'll be grateful forever."

"Does anyone else know what happened?"

"Not a soul."

"Stay where you are. I'll call Gorton. He'll tell you what to do."

"Thank you so much."

Martin had to get back to the dinner, he realized. But first, he had to call Gorton, a mover and shaker on the island whom Martin had befriended over the years.

He called Gorton at home, waking him. "I need your help," Martin told the groggy-sounding Gorton. "The man using my house is a good friend. The woman he's with drowned tonight. And she's not his wife."

"Oh my."

"Yeah. Right now they're both in the house. This could be bad for him. And very bad for me."

It was a blessing, Martin thought, that his closeness with Gorton enabled him to make this call.

"What do you want me to do?"

As if preparing to leap off a high diving board, Martin took a deep breath. "Move the woman's body to another location. Make certain no one will be able to tie my friend or me to her death."

There was no response.

"If this worries you and makes you too uncomfortable, you shouldn't do it. Please tell me."

Finally, Gorton said, "I'll do it."

"I'll be seriously grateful. My friend's waiting for you at the house with the body."

Saying those last words made Martin cringe. Feeling lousy, he put away the phone, returned to the group and slipped into his chair, all shook up. Francis was staring at him.

Sally sitting next to the him, said, "No rest for the weary. The price of fame."

Thank God Philip, on Sally's other side, asked her, "Do you have children?"

She launched into a tale of her children and grandchildren. Martin tuned them out. On the table he noticed a glass of sauterne as well as the dessert. He had no appetite for the cold soufflé, and as he picked up the wine glass, his hand was trembling. Perspiration dotted his forehead. His striped shirt felt soaked under the arms. Why in hell did Wes use his house with another woman? Jasper certainly led Martin to believe he was going with Linda. Wes, he recalled, slept around at Yale. But that was thirty-five years ago. He put down the sauterne and drank ice water to steady himself.

At that moment, it was as if a cloud covering Martin's eyes suddenly lifted. He could see clearly and understood what he had just done—committed the greatest blunder of his life!

He had an acute sense of right and wrong. The rationalization he had been feeding himself about his friendship with Jasper and helping a friend disintegrated. That couldn't possibly justify what he had done. It was wrong! Wrong! Wrong!

As for the impact on his nomination to be chief justice, if he hadn't agreed to help Jasper and instead had called the Anguilla police, the consequences for Martin might not be so bad. He had let a longtime friend use his house. Unknown to Martin, he took a woman there who accidentally drowned. Martin couldn't be blamed for that, particularly if he had called the Anguilla police. Sure, Jasper would be hurt, but Wes had played a high-risk game, taking this Vanessa to Anguilla. In life there are no free fucks.

But if the story of what Martin had done, arranging for the movement of Vanessa's body, came out in the press, then Martin's chief justice nomination would sink faster than a heavy rock in a pond of water.

I made the wrong decision.

In his anguish, his legs shaking, Martin thought about trying to undo it. He could race into the study and call Gorton back to tell him not to do a thing. Then he'd call Jasper and tell him he changed his mind. Martin's cell phone would show the number Jasper had used to call him. He'd give Wes the choice of calling the Anguilla police or doing it himself. Yes, that's what he should do.

But he couldn't get himself to move to undo what he had done. It's too late, he told himself. Everything is already in motion. *I'll have to live with the consequences.*

An hour later, their guests had gone. Francis came up to him with a huge smile. "Everybody was so complimentary. They all had a great time. Drew called it an evening he'd never forget."

"The food was incredible. Especially the lamb."

"You don't think I overcooked it?"

"Nope. Perfect. And they loved hearing you talk about performing at Aspen."

Isabella and Juan, he noticed, were picking up dishes and straightening furniture.

Francis kicked off her shoes. "Who called?"

Martin couldn't bring himself to tell Francis about Jasper's call. He was so ashamed of what he had done that he couldn't possibly let anyone know about it. Not even Francis.

Their marriage was based on the mutual respect and admiration they had for each other. What he had done was so stupid that he was afraid she'd think far less of him. He couldn't bear that. Not right now.

Looking away, he said, "A client from the Midwest. His son shot and killed someone. He wanted to know what to do."

"What did you tell him?"

"Go to the police. I put him in touch with a local lawyer."

He hated himself for lying to Francis, which he had never done before. But he had to. He felt like a boat pulled away from its mooring in a storm.

*   *   *

Though it was almost two in the morning, Xiang Shen was fully awake in his Connecticut Avenue apartment watching *Seven Days in May,* one of the endless in a stream of American movies that the insomniac, with the title of Assistant Economic Attaché at the Chinese Embassy, watched most nights.

Xiang particularly liked political thrillers, although he would watch just about any drama or action film. Hitchcock and James Bond were among his favorites. He couldn't explain his obsession with American movies. Perhaps it was the forbidden fruit. Most of them would be blocked from showing in China. Or, more importantly, they portrayed the sense of freedom that Xiang longed for. And they also helped him pass the long and lonely night hours.

Five years ago, Xiang was assigned to the Chinese Embassy in Washington by Liu Guan, who was Deputy Director of the MSS, the Ministry of State Security, China's premier intelligence agency. As part of his briefing, Liu told the thirty-year-old Xiang, "Your assignment in the United States is highly sensitive. You are prohibited from dating American or foreign women. You can only date women working at our embassy who have a security clearance equal to yours. The honey pot is the oldest trick in the book. I won't risk you falling into it."

At the time, Xiang thought that Liu's edict was absurd. He was merely passing on to Beijing information about United States military plans and capabilities which appeared in the print or electronic media in the United States. There was nothing confidential about his work. He didn't have access to secret information. What could he possibly pass along to a woman in bed?

Still, he had learned from instructors in training that disobeying any order of Liu meant certain and severe punishment. The deputy director was known for brutality in dealing with enemies of the state, a category he defined to include those who didn't follow his orders.

When Xiang had arrived in Washington, a healthy thirty-year-old with strong sexual desires, he systematically went through the available pool of eligible embassy female employees in six months. Only four he decided were worth dating. Two he slept with, both unsatisfactory experiences. So he decided to wait for sex until he returned to China on periodic visits.

In Washington he spent time in the gym where he could press 250 pounds, and he ran four or five mornings a week. His six-foot frame had filled out. Xiang could have been on the cover of a men's fitness magazine.

After two years, Liu gave Xiang his title of Assistant Economic Attaché and assigned him to cover the American Congress, obtaining information from any source, not merely the media, about actions in Congress that could affect China, either militarily or economically. As part of his work, Xiang attended a myriad of diplomatic receptions and cocktail parties where women often flirted with him. Occasionally Xiang was on the verge of asking one of them to come home with him. Before he uttered the words, Liu's stern face and harsh voice appeared in his mind. He deflected their advances and went home where he took a cold shower and watched American movies. All the while cursing Liu. He wasn't having any fun, his job was boring, and he didn't believe anything he did was helping China, which was why he had originally joined the MSS.

All of that changed five months ago when Liu was appointed director of the MSS and summoned Xiang to Beijing where he informed him about Operation Trojan Horse. "You and our ambassador in Washington will be the only two in the United States who will know about Operation Trojan Horse. But you will have the critical role in this operation. Extreme secrecy is essential. Trojan Horse is the most important intelligence operation in our country at this time."

Xiang had replied, "I'm honored to be a part of it."

"If you do a good job in this assignment," Liu had told Xiang, "the possibilities for you in Beijing are unlimited."

Liu had also snarled, "I am concerned that you may be too young and immature for this assignment. But no one else has your knowledge of the United States and the nuances of American life. So I am forced to take a chance on you."

"I appreciate your confidence."

"I don't have confidence. And I will tell you that if you fuck it up, I will personally direct the torture until you beg to die."

Xiang was so terrified that he could barely walk out of Liu's office.

However, after the next two days of briefing about Operation Trojan Horse and his role, Xiang realized Liu hadn't been exaggerating. The Operation was critical for China. At thirty-five, Xiang was thrilled to be on the cutting edge of his country's paramount intelligence operation.

Seven Days in May ended. Xiang glanced at his wristwatch. It was two fourteen in the morning. He'd order *Vertigo* and watch it for about the twentieth time. It was his favorite movie of all time. And he knew why. More than the brilliant screenplay and Hitchcock's mastery of suspense, there was Kim Novak, who reminded Xiang of Kelly Cameron, his one and only love, fourteen years earlier when they were both students at Carnegie Mellon University. He could still remember every detail about the beautiful Kelly. He loved her long blonde hair, her warm smile, her perfectly rounded breasts, the way she walked—and her insatiable desire for sex. Beyond all that, she had a sharp, analytical mind. She challenged him intellectually as no one else had ever done. And she was fun to be with. He had been enraged when Liu had ordered him to break off his relationship with Kelly at the end of their junior year, but he had no choice.

From time to time over the years he had thought of Googling Kelly. She had been a brilliant computer major, easy to locate. But he had been too frightened to do it. Security officials at the embassy constantly monitored the Internet usage of employees and calls on office phones as well as embassy-supplied cell phones. And Kelly had told him that following graduation, she intended to utilize her computer expertise to enter a career in law enforcement. "I want to do something good for my country to safeguard our democracy." If it reached Liu that Xiang had been trying to locate Kelly . . . there would be serious repercussions for Xiang and his parents in China. For only himself, Xiang might have been willing to risk it. But he loved his parents too much to put their lives at risk.

While Xiang was waiting for the movie to load, one of the cell phones on his desk rang. He recognized the distinctive "Ping . . . Ping . . . Ping." That was the special phone dedicated to calls with Senator Jasper.

Xiang answered and said, "Yes."

He hoped the senator remembered not to identify himself. And he did.

"Tu—Tu—Tuesday," was all the senator said, sounding hysterical, and ended the call.

Xiang, who had created the code, knew exactly what the senator meant. Tuesday, at five in the morning, Jasper wanted to meet on a path in Rock Creek Park, which was generally deserted at that hour. If anyone passed by, Xiang and Jasper would look like two joggers who had a chance encounter in the park.

From Jasper's urgent request for a meeting in the middle of the night and the sound of the senator's voice, Xiang feared that Operation Trojan Horse had been compromised. Xiang pondered his options. Liu had told him that if there ever was a threat to Operation Trojan Horse, Xiang was to call him immediately and without explaining what happened on the phone, announce that he would be flying to Beijing for a briefing.

But until he spoke to Jasper, Xiang told himself that he had no idea what had happened or how serious it was. No point alarming Liu until after the Jasper meeting. For now, he'd have to operate on his own. Besides, notifying Liu was only a last resort. The spymaster didn't tolerate failure, and he never took responsibility himself. Xiang had observed how savagely Liu dealt with underlings whom he charged with failing to perform up to his high standards. "We have a zero tolerance for failure," Liu lectured agents. Those words, "A zero tolerance for failure . . . A zero tolerance for failure . . . " reverberated in Xiang's brain. They sent a shiver up and down Xiang's spine.

His meeting with Jasper was twenty-seven hours away. He turned back to *Vertigo*. He doubted if he'd sleep at all until he learned what had happened to Jasper.

*   *   *

Lying in bed, Martin glanced at the illuminated clock on the bureau. It was 3:11 a.m. And he hadn't slept at all. Francis was snoring softly, burrowed under the down comforter.

He never had trouble sleeping. But this night was like no other. He had been wrong. Wrong, wrong, wrong. The enormity of what he had done hit him like a wall crashing down on him.

He should have made Jasper go to the police. Or called them himself. Gorton? What the hell was he thinking? This went against his whole life. He counseled a million clients that you don't try and cover up illegal or embarrassing situations with lies. You've got to play it straight—not just because it's the right thing, but because in the end you'll get caught.

Damp with perspiration and trying not to wake Francis, he got up, put on a robe and went downstairs. In the den he sat in the dark, staring into space. His body shook from time to time. He thought about other mistakes he'd made. Once during a lawsuit, he failed to produce a critical document, which a client had concealed. Another time, when relying upon an associate, he mischaracterized a legal precedent. Both times, as soon as he became aware of the error, he'd notified opposing counsel and the court and faced the unpleasant consequences. He could still call Anguilla to rectify this.

But then he'd be destroying the marriage and career of one of his best friends. And the death had been an accident.

No, c'mon. He realized he was kidding himself. This wasn't merely about Jasper. Martin would have to pay, too. If the media got a hold of it, they'd crucify him. They would claim he didn't merely lend his Anguilla house to a friend. He lent it to the powerful chairman of the Senate Armed Services Committee which dealt with legislation affecting Martin's clients. He was using his house to buy influence. Arthur and Braddock would cut him from the short list for chief justice at the first sign of trouble. Jasper and Vanessa were standing in his way. If he hadn't asked Gorton to move the body, he'd have been doomed.

But he could be wrong. Maybe he'd have been alright if all he did was let Jasper use the house. Wes was his friend. Martin could honestly say he didn't know Jasper would be with another woman. His big fuck-up was making that dumb ass call to Gorton. Jesus, what was he thinking?

Lights came on. He turned and noticed Francis, in the doorway, staring at him. "What's wrong?"

He realized now that he had to tell her. She was his partner in everything. He couldn't bear keeping it from her. And he needed to tell someone to get it out. As if that would somehow purge the wrong.

"I made a mistake before. A terrible mistake."

"That phone call?"

"I wasn't thinking. Too much wine. Later when you asked me about it, I was still shocked. But that's no excuse for lying to you."

"Who called?"

"Wes Jasper. Thursday he asked if he could use our house in Anguilla for the weekend. I assumed it was for a trip with Linda. With all this Supreme Court stuff and the dinner party going on, I forgot to tell you."

"What happened?"

"He didn't go with Linda. He went with another woman. Some Vanessa. I don't know who she is."

"Our house." Francis sounded irate. "He used our house for screwing around."

Then the name Vanessa clicked for Martin. He remembered at the office of the Senate Armed Services Committee Jasper introducing him to a drop-dead gorgeous woman, a Vanessa.

"She may have worked for Jasper's committee. I'm not sure. Anyhow, she drowned."

Francis seemed too stunned to speak.

"It was an accident. Jasper said he nearly drowned trying to save her."

"Noble of him. Idiot! Is he so out to lunch he forgot about his wife, his children?"

"Thanks to me. They may not find out."

"What'd you do?"

"Called Gorton and asked him to move Vanessa's body. Then helped Jasper leave Anguilla. He shouldn't be tied to her death."

"You didn't! You didn't really do that, did you?"

"Honey, it's our house. If it came out, I was afraid it would have destroyed my chance for an appointment to chief justice."

"Oh Andrew, this is awful! It's so unfair to have this happen to you with all of the great things you've accomplished. You just made an impulsive decision to help your best friend who put you in a terrible position. And the woman was already dead before you did anything."

"I know, but . . ."

"Come to bed. There's nothing we can do about it now."

Israel

Allison and Zahava were watching three men and two women sifting through the dirt. "I found something!" Dora cried out in excitement. She clutched what looked to Allison like a pottery fragment, raising it high over her head.

"Let me have a look."

Before Dora handed it over, the cell phone on the belt of Allison's khaki pants rang. She checked caller ID. It was not a number she recognized. A 264 area code. Where's that?

Allison walked away from the others.

"Is this Allison Boyd?" a man asked in a British accent.

"Yes it is. Who's calling?"

"The name's Har Stevens. I'm the police commissioner on the island of Anguilla in the Caribbean. I found your name and phone number in the wallet of a woman named Vanessa Boyd. Are you related to her?"

Oh my God. What happened? Her knees felt wobbly. She took two steps to a chair and sunk into it. "She's my twin sister. Has something happened to her?"

"Unfortunately, Miss Boyd, I have to inform you that your sister drowned."

"No!" Allison shrieked. "No! . . . No!"

Zahava rushed to her side.

"I'm very sorry. But, I didn't have anyone else to call."

"Oh, Vanessa. Oh, Vanessa," Allison placed the phone in her lap and cried. When she picked it up again, tears were streaming down her cheeks. "What happened?"

"Your sister must have gone swimming at night. Her body washed up on the beach. People from her hotel called."

"What about the man with her? Did he drown too?"

"As far as I can tell, she came to Anguilla herself. That's what they told us at the hotel."

Her face red with anger, Allison shot to her feet. "No way. Vanessa would never go to a Caribbean island for a vacation herself. And damn it, she's an excellent swimmer. You made a mistake. It's not my sister," she screamed. "I should kill you for doing this."

"I'm sorry, Miss Boyd, but the photo on her passport clearly matches. And we found a Chopard wristwatch with her initials on the back. She had a scar on her left leg at the ankle. Did your sister have one there?"

Allison felt as deflated as a helium balloon that had struck a spike. Some Washington bigwig had given Vanessa that watch last summer. The scar was from Vanessa's skiing accident.

"She's my sister," Allison managed to stammer as she collapsed back into her chair.

She thought of their blood oath, taken as twelve year olds. Always stick together, no matter what. "Vanessa, Vanessa," she mumbled. And she wept what felt like a torrent of tears.

It was her fault, Allison thought. She should have moved to Washington. She could have gotten a teaching job at one of the universities in the DC area and shared an apartment with her sister. Then this would never have happened.

"What about the body? Where shall we ship it?"

Allison recalled her uncle's funeral last year. "Blake's Mortuary on Main Street in Oxford, Ohio."

"We'll do that. And I want to tell you how sorry I am, and so are the people of Anguilla."

Allison hung up, put her head in her hands, and cried again. She couldn't believe it. This all seemed like a terrible dream.

Looking sympathetic, Zahava touched her shoulder.

In a fog, Allison said, "I have to call my mother."

"Would you like me to call for you?"

She dreaded making the call, but she knew she had to do it herself. Pushing the buttons on the cell like a robot, she doubted she'd be any comfort to her mother.

"I have bad news."

"What happened? Is it Vanessa?"

"A policeman in Anguilla just called. She drowned." Allison couldn't continue. As the word "drowned" came out of her mouth, she broke into sobs.

"Oh no, no, Allison, no."

After a time, she forced herself to finish. "They're shipping the body to Blake's."

Her mother was now shrieking and moaning.

Allison waited until her sobs quieted. "I'm in Israel now on a dig. I'll get the first plane out. I should be there Tuesday morning."

*   *   *

On Zahava's recommendation, Allison booked a plane to New York, three hours after they'd arrive at Ben Gurion Airport. "You'll need the time," Zahava told her, "between our endless security checks and the miles of walking." At JFK she'd connect to Cincinnati.

Now, she was standing in a long line, moving slowly toward the El Al ticket counter, astounded at the high ceiling and vastness of the spanking new state-of-the-art terminal. In the polyglot of humankind around her, a few were pushing and shoving. But most were patiently keeping their places in line. There were Christian church groups, Muslims, and school children. She saw bearded Hasids, American Jewish tour groups, Asians, and the diversity of Israelis with every imaginable skin color from Ethiopian to Scandinavian. There can't be another place like this in the world, she thought.

Damn it, this is taking a long time. I hope I make my plane. Her mind turned back to Vanessa. Last year she'd read a book called *The Black Swan* about significant, traumatic events people never see coming, never in their wildest imagination. Vanessa's death was a black swan. She wouldn't have guessed it in a million years. They came into this world together. Allison always assumed they would leave the same way. Maybe if they were older, Allison might have conceived of one of them going first. But not at thirty-four.

A part of Allison died with that call.

The line was moving at a snail's pace. Too restless simply to stand in line, Allison decided to call the *Washington Post* and have them run an obit. Vanessa lived in Washington. She'd worked for a major committee on the Hill. She had friends in the city. They had to know about her death.

She took out her phone, called the obit editor, and recounted the information. He said they'd probably publish it.

An hour later, approaching the last of several security checkpoints, another thought struck her. Suppose this wasn't accidental. Suppose the man Vanessa was with killed her. A nut case? Or both high, carried away during kinky sex?

What really happened? She had to find out.

Almost at the glass booth, manned by armed guards, she noticed the sign. "NO CELL PHONES BEYOND THIS POINT." Hell, she still had a couple more minutes, she thought. And there was something she could do, even before the funeral.

She checked the contacts on her iPhone and dialed Sara Gross, her former schoolmate and friend, now a doctor in Oxford, waking her in the middle of the night in Ohio. "I only have a minute."

She told Sara about the call from Anguilla.

"We can talk on Tuesday morning, but when Vanessa's body arrives will you examine it?"

"Of course. What am I looking for?"

"Anything you can tell me about how she died."

After a pause, Sara said, "I'll do that."

Allison realized that she hadn't given Sara any guidance, but she didn't know what she was looking for. Still, Sara was smart. If Vanessa's body disclosed any evidence about her death, Allison was confident Sara would find it.

Washington

Leave it and move on, Martin chided himself. But easier said than done. He felt it like a twenty-pound weight hung around his neck.

He was usually able to compartmentalize. But not today.

Suddenly he remembered it was Veteran's Day, a holiday for some in Washington. But not for him. He had tons of work at the office.

Francis was still sleeping. He trudged downstairs, brewed a pot of coffee, had some cereal, and headed to the office.

Three hours later, Martin was sitting behind his green leather top desk in his corner office overlooking Pennsylvania Avenue, twelve floors below. He lifted the china cup and swallowed the bitter black coffee as he watched lanky Paul Maltoni, clutching a legal pad and pen with his curly black hair as unruly as ever, come into the office and sit in front of his desk. Paul was Martin's star associate, who had been with the giant law firm Martin had founded and headed for eight years.

Martin felt a common bond with this brilliant young lawyer who, like Martin, came from a modest background and rose to the top of his class at Yale Law School as a scholarship student. Martin expected Paul to become a partner in another year.

"We have a big new case," Martin said. "And I need you to work with me on it."

"Sure, Andrew. What's it about?"

"Global Media wants us to challenge the proposed FCC Rule calling for a Board of Censors to review and to cancel television shows for undue sex or violence. The so called 'decency regulations.'"

"As a violation of free speech?"

"Correct. And we'll also have some procedural issues relating to the rulemaking. They decided to fire their current lawyer."

"I'd love to work with you on that."

"You'd be perfect for it, but . . ." Martin hesitated. "Look Paul, you're an excellent lawyer, but you love working on lots of things. Sometimes too many. You have to learn to say no."

Paul looked chagrined.

"This is a discussion we've had before," Martin added softly. "So if you don't have time, it won't be good for me and it won't be good for you."

"I am busy now, but not overloaded."

"Okay, but we'll be operating on a tight schedule."

"I'll give it all the time it needs."

"I should have the background material later today. I'll . . ."

Martin's office phone rang. Hoping it was Arthur Larkin calling about the Supreme Court, he stopped talking and held his breath, waiting for Alice, his secretary, to answer. Seconds later, she buzzed on the intercom. "Arthur Larkin, White House Counsel, is holding for you."

Martin lifted the phone to his ear.

"Hi, Arthur. What's up?"

"Can you meet with me over here this afternoon. Say three o'clock?"

Martin looked at his calendar marked for a conference call at two thirty with his partner Janet Derby and people from Merck about FDA approval for a new drug application. Janet could cover it.

"That works for me. You want to give me a subject?"

"I'd rather do it in person," Arthur responded in his usual gruff tone.

"Fair enough. See you at the White House then."

Putting down the phone, Martin felt his body tingle. Well, there it was. Braddock wanted to consider him for chief justice. No, he couldn't count on that. Never mind what the *New York Times* said yesterday. Arthur might want to talk about something else—or worse—solicit Martin's view about who should be considered.

Swept up in what Arthur's call might mean, he'd forgotten about Paul, who was clearing his throat. "Okay, we're finished," Martin said. "Alice will send you the material when we receive it."

Paul left, and as Martin walked across to the cherry credenza, he studied the photo of Chief Justice Hall seated in a high-backed black leather chair with Andrew, standing beside him, holding out a law book. He still remembered Hall's note, "To Andrew, my clerk, my friend. With best wishes and my hope that you will one day sit in this chair."

And maybe, he would.

*   *   *

By the time he reached his office, Paul's stomach was churning. All he had overheard was that the president's counsel wanted to meet with Martin. Paul had read in the *Times* yesterday about Chief Justice West's resignation and Martin named as one of the people being considered to succeed West. He didn't think it was a coincidence. More likely, Arthur wanted his old tennis buddy to become chief justice.

Damn it, Paul thought. It was so great working with Martin. And so challenging. Somehow, Martin always found solutions—ways to argue cases that no one else saw. Paul would hate it if Martin left.

Also, there would be the personal impact for Paul. With Martin remaining at the firm, Paul was a certainty to make partner unless he peed on one of the oriental carpets. But with Martin gone, and other powerful partners viewing him as Martin's associate, it would be an open issue. Paul was well aware that law firms, like all organizations, were full of petty jealousies and resentments.

Paul thought about the first time he met Martin. After graduating from Yale Law and clerking on the DC Circuit, Paul had been working in a neighborhood legal services office in Washington. At its annual banquet at the Washington Hilton, the organization was honoring Martin for the contributions his law firm had made to the program. Two weeks before, Paul's father, who ran a small roofing firm in New Haven, had fallen off a roof. While the accident wasn't fatal, his dad would never work again. He didn't have disability insurance and Paul's only sibling, Gabriella, was a grad student in a PhD program in English at Columbia. That left Paul as the sole source of support for his parents.

After the banquet, Martin invited Paul for a drink at the Cosmos Club. Paul was surprised to hear that Martin knew all about his legal career, and also about his father's injury. Without beating around the bush, Martin offered Paul a job as an associate at the firm with a hundred thousand dollar signing bonus and said, "We'll even help you get a mortgage when you decide to buy a house."

As a law student at Yale, Paul would have viewed working at a large law firm as a sellout, but he had to help his parents. And it might not be so bad. He'd be working on cutting-edge legal cases, even if it would be for corporate clients.

So Paul made a spot decision to accept.

If Martin left, Paul should still make it. The partners all gave him outstanding reviews. Only Jenson had been critical. Paul sensed that Jenson was jealous of Martin, resented having to share Paul's time, and might want to strike at Martin through Paul. He'd been so pissed when Jenson once told him, "You're Martin's fair-haired boy." And Jenson, Paul knew, coveted the chairman position. So if Jenson moved up . . .

He chided himself. This isn't about you. Martin deserves it. Paul couldn't imagine anyone else with Martin's smarts. The whole country would benefit from his wisdom and judgment, instead of just the firm's money-grubbing clients.

Paul heard the office phone. "Caller ID," said Jenson's secretary, Grace. The environmental case he'd been working on with Jenson for two years flashed into his mind, settled last week on great terms. So what the hell's he want now?

"Will you come up here?" Grace said.

She sounds more like her surly boss every day.

"I'm on my way." Paul looked around for a yellow legal pad. Finding it wasn't easy. This office is a pig pen, he thought. He remembered when dating Vanessa, and he'd taken her here, she'd said, "How can you get anything done in a mess like this?" Nonplussed, he'd responded, "But I know where every piece of paper is."

He located a pad in a pile on an ancient wooden chair, standard issue for associates. Before heading up to Jenson's, he tucked in the tails of his blue button down, put on his navy suit jacket, and slipped a couple of pens into his pocket. His suit was Macy's. Martin wore Lanvin. One day Paul's suits would be Lanvin. And after he became partner, he'd spice up his wardrobe with some of those colorful shirts and ties, like Martin.

Feeling like Jimmy Stewart in *Rear Window* he looked across the atrium to see if that cute paralegal was in her office. She wasn't. He grabbed the crossword from this morning's *New York Times* and headed out.

To keep in shape, he took no elevators between floors. Only interior staircases. He found himself puffing as he climbed three flights and thought he better start running again and lifting weights. And find another woman. After a year, agonizing over Vanessa's break up with him was stupid.

On the twelfth floor, he walked along the stately corridor, an antique grandfather clock its only decoration. Jenson's office was at the corner diagonal to Martin's. He got no smile from Grace. "He's on the phone," she said, pointing to Jenson's closed door. "He'll buzz when he's ready." Paul always had to wait for Jenson, and it irritated him.

But the man had a brilliant legal mind. He had to give him that. Otherwise, Jenson reminded Paul of a toad. He was five eight, pudgy and bald, except for a ring of black hair mixed with gray around the side of his head. This crowned a tough looking face with a sharp nose and chin and a tight mouth with thin lips. From going on the firm's retreats, Paul knew that Jenson played at tennis and golf with no skill or style.

Unlike Martin, usually considerate of Paul's time and feelings, Jenson could care less. Paul thought Jenson went out of his way to be rude. Other associates told Paul he was the same with them and they all dreaded working for him. Jim, in the office next to Paul's, admitted he got so tense working for Jenson that he couldn't get it up with his wife.

Paul noticed the light go off on Jenson's line. Sullen Grace said, "He's ready for you now." As Paul walked in, Jenson curtly said "Hold on a minute while I make some notes on the last call."

Paul looked across at Jenson standing at the specially designed wooden lectern he used as a desk, with papers on the sloping front part and a computer on the flat rear shelf—something to do with his bad back.

Waiting, Paul glanced around at the football memorabilia from Green Bay Packers victories, including helmets and jerseys. Vince Lombardi, pointing his finger, targeted Paul from a picture on the wall.

Jenson was chomping on an unlit cigar while he made notes.

He put his pen down and took out the cigar. "The firm has a good opportunity. We've never worked for the State of California, but I cultivated their new attorney general at a conference last month. Today, he called me about a dispute they have with Nevada over Colorado River water. Nevada is planning to divert more than its allotted share before it gets to California to support growth in Las Vegas. He asked me to think about their legal options and to call him next week. If they like what we show them, he's promised a lot more work."

"Shouldn't they file in the US Supreme Court?" Paul said right back. "The Court has original jurisdiction of disputes between states."

Jenson nodded. "Precisely what I was thinking."

Now he's going to draft me to work on it. Damn it.

"Listen, our little star," Jenson said. "I want you to join on this, and prepare by early next week a first draft of California's brief as if they were filing in the Supreme Court. That'll impress this California AG. He's already sent me all the key documents. I can e-mail them to you."

Damn! Damn! Damn! "Mr. Jenson," Paul took a deep breath. "I'm willing to take this on, but I can't promise you a brief by early next week. By the week after next I can, for sure. Unfortunately, I'm already committed to other work for this week."

"For Martin," he added. He was frowning. "A big new matter for Global Media."

Jenson pursed his lips. "Fine, Maltoni," he said, piqued. "I'll get somebody else." He pointed the cigar at Paul for emphasis. The chewed down end was wet and falling apart. It smelled disgusting. Jenson flung it toward a wastebasket. He missed. He left it on the floor, and went over to the credenza where he opened a wooden humidor, extracted a fresh cigar, peeled off the wrapper, and shoved it into his mouth.

Paul felt like saying, "Look asshole, one week can't possibly matter since the case hasn't even been filed; regardless, you take your brief and shove it." But hell, wait a minute, if Jenson were to become chairman . . . Paul needed to work this out.

"I have an idea," he said. "I'll get Diane. She's a second-year, very smart and fast, to work with me. I'll do my best to make it next week, but to be safe, let's figure early the following week." Paul paused, then added, "I'd like to work on this case. And you know I can give you as good a brief as anyone."

Jenson didn't respond. Then he snarled. "Humph."

Paul sensed that meant he'd agreed.

"Okay," Jenson finally said, "But it better be a good brief."

"Have I ever given you one that wasn't? Those summary judgment papers I just did got us a great settlement."

"Alright. Alright. That's enough. Try for Friday. And it better be your work, too. Not just Diane's."

Feeling pleased, Paul charged down the stairs. He lined up bright-eyed Diane to help him.

Between Martin possibly becoming chief justice and Jenson, Paul saw his path to partnership as a minefield. But he would find a way to navigate through it.

Beijing

Liu Guan sat at the head of the polished rectangular table in the director's conference room adjacent to his large corner office in the Xiyuan headquarters of the MSS. The four men he had selected to be members of his select operations committee were the best people in the agency. He had divided up the world among them. Chang had Europe; Chu, Asia and the Pacific; He, Africa; and Peng, Latin America. Liu reserved for himself control over operations in the United States.

He took one final puff on his cigarette, blew smoke circles in the air, snuffed it out, and began talking.

"We are embarking on a new day for Chinese intelligence operations," Liu said. "Our old methods of relying primarily on our information coming from our scientists and engineers who travel abroad to conferences, as well as on information from foreign tourists, including ethnic Chinese, who happen to come to China for meetings, will still be utilized.

"But these will be secondary. We are now establishing an extensive network of agents in place in foreign countries, often as members of our embassy staff or as journalists. These agents in place will be charged with obtaining secret information in their host country and relaying it to Beijing. This change is consistent with our new status as the primary rival of the United States in the world order. We are on the verge of surpassing the United States economically and militarily within ten years.

"I want each of you to develop in thirty days a plan for installing at least ten agents in place within your assigned territory. Those will be the beginning of much more extensive networks of Chinese spies throughout the world. I won't tell you how to do it. Each of you should use your imagination and creativity."

Liu paused to push back his wire-framed glasses and to run his hand over his pencil thin mustache.

"Now are there any questions?"

Looking around the silent room, Liu felt the vibration in his jacket pocket of an electronic device, connecting him to his secretary. She was aware that this was an important meeting for Liu. She would not have sent him a text message unless it was critical.

Liu removed the device and glanced at the message: "President Yao wants you to come to his office as soon as possible."

Whenever Liu received a summons from the Supreme Leader, he dropped anything he was doing.

"This meeting is now over," Liu said. "I will be expecting each of your plans in thirty days."

The fifty–eight-year-old Liu marched back to his office. Though he was five foot ten, not a short man, he wanted to stand higher than most other men to gain a psychological edge, so at the MSS he wore platform shoes, which added another three inches, but they slowed him down. That wasn't a problem. He wasn't running any races within the MSS headquarters.

"Car ready?" he barked at his secretary.

"Yes, sir. Chou is out in front. He's arranged a motorcycle escort."

Xiyuan in the West Garden section of Beijing, near the Summer Palace, was only seven miles northwest of Tiananmen Square and the president's office. The late afternoon traffic in central Beijing was fierce, and the motorcycles with their sirens and flashing lights, indicating an important official, were essential for Liu's car to cut through the gridlock. Beyond that, Liu, the son of a wealthy Shanghai real estate developer, loved the trappings of wealth, the symbols of power that elevated him above the common man.

Ten minutes later Liu was in the back of a plush black Chinese-manufactured limousine with tinted glass windows forcing its way through traffic. He had no idea why Yao wanted to see him.

He had developed a close relationship with Yao Xiao when Yao was engaged in an intense battle to succeed Xi Jinping as Supreme Leader. At the time, Liu was deputy director of MSS. In return for Yao's promise to promote him to MSS director, Liu surreptitiously forwarded to Yao damaging information about the two other possible choices. Liu had no doubt that information about the corruption of one and the sexual proclivities of the other destroyed their chances.

Thanks in large part to Liu, Yao had gotten the prize: president of the People's Republic of China, the Supreme Leader. Foreigners rarely understood how powerful that position was in the world's most populous country. It was Mao Zedong who established the almost unlimited authority of the office. His successors, Deng Xiaoping, Jiang Zemin, Hu Jinto, and Xi Jinping brought their own personalities and styles to the position, but all followed the autocratic approach of Mao to a great extent.

As a reward, Liu had expected Yao to elevate him to director of the MSS as soon as Yao assumed the presidency two years ago.

But that hadn't happened until five months ago, and Liu was concerned that Yao would never have done it if Liu had not greatly benefited from his secret relationship with Andrei Mikhailovich, his Russian partner who had given him a great deal of his information.

During the year and a half Liu waited for the promotion, he fumed at the ungrateful Yao, who had to know that Liu's boss, the existing director, was incompetent. But that period of waiting taught Liu a bitter lesson: Yao couldn't be trusted to keep his word. He also observed Yao turning on other former backers. The man had some of Mao's qualities. Even after Liu was promoted to director of MSS, Liu had to be careful to avoid having Yao turn on him.

*   *   *

Yao was alone, seated behind a large red leather topped desk in his ornate office. He didn't come forward or even rise when Liu walked into the cavernous office. Instead, he motioned to the empty chair in front of his desk.

As he sat down, Liu was struck by the fact that the sixty-three-year-old Yao had aged perceptibly in the two years he had been in the president's job. He had creases in his face, bags under his eyes, and a sallow look. The pressure of the office was getting to him.

The desk was empty except for a bound document which Liu recognized as the top secret summary of the documents Xiang had obtained from Senator Jasper, which Liu had personally prepared for Yao—and only Yao.

The president pointed to the document. "In your summary, you have powerful and sensitive information about American military actions, including their development of a new generation of long-range missiles and their commitment to aid Japan in the event we attack over islands in the East China Sea. How accurate is that information?"

"Extremely. I prepared it from copies of American internal documents."

"Are you certain they were true documents? Not misinformation? The CIA is experienced at doing that."

"Quite certain."

"What's your source?"

Liu had an intelligence agent's reluctance to disclose a source, but Yao was the Supreme Leader. And he was now staring hard at Liu. Refusal to respond was not an option.

"US Senator Wesley Jasper from Colorado. He's the chairman of the Senate Armed Services Committee. He has been supplying the documents to my agent in Washington. I've code named it Operation Trojan Horse."

"Your agent recruited Jasper?"

"No. I did. At a meeting in Tokyo in July."

Liu expected a compliment, but deadpan Yao continued his interrogation. "How did you turn Jasper?"

"With money." Liu hoped Yao wouldn't ask him how much. The expenditures were enormous, but so were the rewards.

Yao didn't follow up. Instead he told Liu, "One of the documents you summarized refers to a 'Five-Year Plan for Asia and Pacific Deployment' being finalized now by the Pentagon."

"Correct."

"I want that five-year plan. Get it for me from Jasper."

"I'm not sure it's been completed."

"Then, as soon as it is. I must have that document."

Yao's eyes were boring in on Liu. The normally unflappable spymaster felt uncomfortable.

Leaving the office, Liu decided to call Xiang in Washington and order him to fly to Beijing. A face to face meeting would be better to impress upon Xiang the importance of getting the plan from Jasper.

Washington

For Martin, the last several hours passed like an eternity. Finally, it was time to leave for the White House. First, he stopped in the men's room, where he straightened the collar of his red and blue striped shirt with a matching silk tie, concentric blue circles against a red background. He looked damn good, he decided. But he had to give Francis credit.

Coming into their marriage, he refused to spend a cent more than necessary for clothes. He remembered growing up, before his mother contracted polio, her taking him to Pittsburgh to Joseph Hornes and buying him his first suit when he was twelve. He recalled her waiting until the final reductions on the end of the season sales. He knew money was tight, but he'd felt sorry when she showed the salesman a defect, convincing him to knock it down another twenty percent.

That was the way he always shopped until Francis dragged him kicking and screaming into Neiman's to buy an Italian suit. It cost more than a couple months of his initial salary at the firm where he began his career and where he spent several years before leaving to open his own firm with Glass. Now he wore expensive suits, shirts, and ties, but he still felt guilty spending a lot of money for them.

Riding down in the elevator, he thought: suppose someone had asked, "What would you give to be chief justice?" He would have answered, "Just about anything."

Martin decided to walk. He liked having his office building so close to the centers of power. This was a major factor, he recalled, in his decision to select this new building in the 800 block of Pennsylvania Avenue when they'd outgrown their prior space. The location with Martin & Glass plastered in large black letters across the front had to make an impact on clients. And it probably helped bring in the best lawyers.

Walking west along Pennsylvania, as he stopped for a red light, he thought about how the firm had grown in the twenty-eight years since he and Fred Glass had opened up near DuPont Circle. Now there were five hundred and twenty lawyers, two hundred and seventy here in Washington. They had offices in New York, Los Angeles, London, Paris, and Beijing. The firm was strong—almost an institution. It was sure to survive and thrive, even if Martin left and became chief justice.

The light changed. He stepped off the curb and winced. Damn left knee had been hurting for the last month. How much longer could he put off that surgery? He knew the cause: too much pounding in youthful basketball, followed by decades of jogging, skiing, and tennis. And he knew the solution was to replace the knee. But those operations never went as easily as the orthopods said. And, never mind their promises, you weren't really as good as new. So he took pain killers from time to time, iced it after sports, hobbled when it bothered him, and hoped it would magically go away.

He stopped at the guardhouse next to the opening in the black wrought iron fence separating the White House grounds from Pennsylvania Avenue. One of the soldiers inspected his driver's license, checked it against a list of visitors on a clipboard, and waved him through.

At the end of a twenty-yard walkway, he entered the west wing. In the entrance foyer were four armed guards. Again, his driver's license was examined, his face checked against the photo. Then he was passed through a metal detector.

"Follow me," an escort said. Fourth door on the right, Martin remembered. The last of a series of small offices off the navy blue carpeted corridor. It astonished him that the White House Counsel had an office the size of an associate at Martin and Glass. Washington, Martin thought. Office size doesn't matter. It's all accessibility. Arthur's office was only a few yards from the oval office. No one's closer to the president. Next to Arthur's office was another room. The president's "other office," Arthur called it. "Braddock's hideaway to escape for private time."

Martin walked through an open door. "Hi, Mr. Martin," Arthur's longtime secretary, Helen, said with a smile. She pointed to the closed door across the room. "He should be with you in a couple minutes."

"How's your daughter like Cornell?"

Helen groaned. "That's the trouble, she likes it too much. All I hear about are the boys." Helen paused to push back strands of long brown hair that had fallen over her eyes. "Sorry, I'm supposed to call them men. That and the parties. Not her classes or grades. Over Thanksgiving I intend to shape her up."

Martin thought about his daughters' freshmen years. Karen at Yale was nose to the grindstone without a word from him or Francis. Lucy's first year at Northwestern sounded like Helen's daughter. Tri Delt was all they heard about. He'd been amused and sympathetic, he recalled. But Francis also lowered the boom during Thanksgiving break. "If she were a boy, you wouldn't have cut her any slack," Francis had said.

Helen added sternly, "It's a rough world now, and you get only one chance."

Moments later, she led him into Arthur's office. Martin saw the White House Counsel sitting behind his desk looking his usual disheveled self. He was five foot six with a pear shape and thin gray hair ruffled and out of place from constantly running his hand through it. He had a tie loose around his neck. A couple of spots of food on his suit jacket. Gut protruding over the top of his pants with suspenders holding them up. It always amazed Martin that Arthur was such a good tennis player.

The office had space only for an L-shaped desk and chair with a small table behind it for a computer as well as a coffee pot. There were two wooden chairs for guests.

Martin didn't expect an opening greeting. Arthur never bothered with those. He sat down in his desk chair and pointed Andrew to one of the others. The eyes of the perpetually wired New Yorker were darting around the room. Then they zeroed in on Martin.

"Last Thursday, Chief Justice West came to see the president. The doctors give him a month to live. Two at most. He's ready to step down as soon as we select a replacement." Arthur paused. "It's too bad, but that's his situation."

Martin held his breath, eager to hear what was next.

"This'll be Braddock's first Supreme Court appointment. He wants to change the way the game's played." Arthur was shooting the words out in rapid fire. "He hates the idea that the nominee's views on issues like abortion have become a litmus test. Braddock wants to go back to the way it used to be, before all this bullshit started. When the president found the best lawyer or jurist in the country. Somebody honorable with integrity and high moral standards—a Holmes, Brandeis, or Cardoza."

Arthur stopped, letting his words sink in. "Personally, I think he's naive and idealizing the past. I've told him that, but he's the boss."

"I'm all for it. I applaud the effort."

"I figured you would."

Arthur pivoted in his chair and reached for a mug. "Can I get you a cup?"

This guy does not need caffeine, Martin thought.

"Sure."

Arthur poured two cups and placed one in front of Martin. The cherry wood desk top, Martin noticed, was already stained with the outlines of numerous other cups.

Arthur paused to sip his coffee, making Martin wait. "I want to put you on the short list for chief justice."

Well, here it was. He felt thrilled. "I'd be honored."

Arthur tapped his fingers on the desk. "You answered so quickly. Have you thought about it?"

"Yes. Ever since I clerked for Hall."

"Good. Let's talk about the selection process. One thing you have going for you is that you're a very fine tennis player. " Arthur flashed a smile. His effort at levity, Martin thought.

"Being serious, I have enormous respect for you as a lawyer. You have one of the country's great legal minds. I know that from our New York litigation. And you were brilliant last year persuading the court to require a recount in the Ohio senatorial election."

"Coming from you, those are real compliments."

"I mean them. And I'm amazed that you've argued in the Supreme Court forty-eight times and won thirty-nine of them. Phenomenal, given that so many of those arguments were against the United States, and they usually win. So in terms of legal ability, we don't have an issue. For Braddock, personal character will be the other decisive factor. We'll have to turn the FBI inquisitors loose. Your whole life goes under a microscope. Can you deal with that?"

Arthur was looking right at Martin, who thought about Jasper's call last evening, and the action Martin had taken. Still, he didn't flinch. "I have nothing to hide."

"Do you really believe that?" Arthur sounded skeptical and slumped back in his chair. He locked his hands in front of his chest and closed his eyes. It was a tactic Martin remembered Arthur using at depositions. Lulling a witness into over confidence. Then pouncing.

"I do. No personal issues that would be embarrassing."

Arthur's right eye was twitching. That only began, Martin noticed, when Arthur became White House Counsel. Proof, Martin thought, that the Washington pressure cooker topped the stress level in New York. Here, even at tennis, Arthur kept that beeper hooked up to his shorts. "The president has to be able to reach me twenty-four and seven." At first Martin had thought Arthur wanted to show off his importance. Later he realized it went with the job.

Arthur shot forward and leaned over the desk. "Don't crap around with me. Everybody has something. Tell me the worst now. I don't want to be surprised later on. What about the judge you gave a bottle of scotch to as a Christmas present before he decided a case your way?"

Martin thought again about Jasper's call last night and his call to Gorton. That was precisely what Arthur had in mind. If it ever became public, it would destroy his chances of becoming chief justice. And Arthur would be furious at him for not mentioning it now. But how could he? He'd be eliminated immediately. He had to take a chance it wouldn't come out.

"Sorry to disappoint. You can lay out my whole life."

"They all say that in the beginning."

"This time it's true."

Arthur snarled. "Could there be one virgin in the realm?" His tone was cynical. We may be tennis buddies, Martin thought, but for Arthur this was all business.

"I don't know about the virgin part."

"How about one truly virtuous man?"

"You could put it that way."

"If something comes out, President Braddock won't swing with you. We got killed two years ago over the Marian Lawlor appointment to DOD. Sticking with her for a long fucking miserable week after we received info about her ties to Winston Defense Industries. That'll never happen again. We'll cut and run. Throw you to the wolves at the hint of trouble. I mean something of substance that tarnishes you, not smoke that somebody blows your way. We'll hand you a shovel and tell you to dig your own grave. We'll be so far away that you won't even remember what we look like. Those are the ground rules. You better understand them."

Arthur's words didn't surprise Martin. As governor of New York, Braddock had acquired the nickname of Pragmatic Philip. Some said he was dull. He refused to take chances, playing it safe. He had emerged as his party's candidate as a compromise between two ideologues and was elected in large part by his promise to end the bitterness in America. "Let's have a period of calm." Preferring charismatic leaders who tried to lead with a bold vision, Martin had never been a big fan of Braddock's, but he didn't share his views with Arthur.

"Now let's talk about specific areas."

Arthur picked up a pen and pulled over a pad. Martin saw extensive notes on the first page.

Arthur glanced down at the pad. "You must have had some complaints filed against you with bar committees. Let's start with those."

Martin tried to think. "About twenty years ago I took a death penalty case, on appeal, pro bono for Roosevelt Taylor. It was down in Texas. I gave it a good shot, but lost two to one in the court of appeals. The Supreme Court refused to take the case. Taylor filed a complaint with the bar accusing me of malpractice."

Arthur smiled. "No good deed goes unpunished. So what happened?"

"They tossed it out."

"I don't care about shit like that. Anything real?"

Martin shook his head.

"What about clients you represented that would be embarrassing?"

Martin thought about it for a minute and said, "Nothing."

"Which foreign governments do you represent?"

"France, China, Brazil, and Australia. All longtime clients. I don't see any problems there. I'm a Washington lawyer."

"What about health issues? Anything that would affect your ability to do the job?"

"Hey, you can't be serious. You've seen me running around a tennis court for hours. I'm still going strong when you're ready to collapse."

"Okay, let's move on. People in this town usually get in trouble because of sex, money, or power. Let's talk about those."

Martin gripped the arms of his chair. He'd have to submit to this—grin and bear it. He took the initiative. "My sex life has been boring.

I've been married once. We still are after thirty-five years. I've been monogamous."

"Really?"

"Yes."

"No affairs?"

"No."

"Not even with one of those women on the tennis team at Kenwood who are always chatting you up? 'Oh hi, Andrew,'" he cooed.

"No."

"Somebody you met at a bar or on a business trip?"

"Nope."

"How about prostitutes?"

"Never."

"Gay relationships?"

Martin scowled. "C'mon."

"I had to ask."

"The answer's no, but you should drop that one from your repertoire." Martin's voice was sharp.

Arthur raised his hand. "Okay, don't get pissed. What about money?"

"Tell your FBI people to see Walter Cox at PWC in town. He does my taxes. Has all the records, including ten years of tax returns. I'll tell him to open up the books."

"What'll we find?"

"I filed and paid every year."

"Good for you. What else?"

Martin sighed. "I had one bad investment a couple of years ago in Florida realty. There wasn't much money involved."

Arthur winced. "I got burned myself big time with a dot com during the go-go nineties. We should stick to law practice." Arthur ran his hand through his hair. "Ever had any disputes with the IRS?"

"They disallowed $10,000 of the deduction I claimed on the Florida realty matter. No big deal. That's it."

"Will you be able to take a huge pay cut and live on the salary of the chief justice?"

"Absolutely. I've saved a lot from what I've made at the firm. I want to serve my country."

"And you want the power that goes with the position."

"Of course."

"Now let's return to the skeletons in your closet, the things you'd like not to read about in the newspaper, all the way back from putting chewing gum under your desk in fifth grade and feeling up Juliet, the girl with the big tits, in the seventh. Now's the time to put it all on the table."

Martin thought once more about Jasper's call and calmly replied, "I already told you there isn't anything."

Arthur sighed deeply, finishing his coffee and refilling the cup.

Wanting to shift the discussion away from himself, Martin asked, "Who else is on the short list?"

"Mary Corbett on the Second Circuit and Lance Butler from the Fifth Circuit."

Both formidable, Martin thought. Well respected federal appellate judges.

"It'll be one of you," Arthur continued, "unless all three go up in smoke. Anything to say about the other two?"

"They're both good people."

"I agree."

"What's your timetable?"

"All three of your names will be leaked to the *Washington Post* to run in tomorrow's paper. The president expects to announce his choice within two weeks. The next step will be an FBI investigation followed by an interview with the president. Okay, we're done. Keep your cell phone on whenever possible."

Walking along the corridor from Arthur's office, Martin felt like leaping into the air for joy and shouting "yes!" How far he'd come, he thought. The son of a steelworker in Beaver Falls, Pennsylvania, laid off when the mill slowed down and forced to scrounge for work in construction. He had a mother with polio and a sister killed by a gang in high school. These were unhappy times. Then with the help of a guidance counselor, he won the scholarship to Yale established for a resident of Western Pennsylvania. Things soaring after that—Oxford on a Rhodes and Yale Law with scholarships, loans, and part-time jobs. And now maybe he'll become chief justice of the United States.

Get a grip, he warned himself. He was still nowhere near being nominated. Butler and Corbett were tough competitors. The Senator

Jasper incident with Vanessa was a huge cloud on the horizon. And Martin couldn't let that interfere with his chances.

Though he hadn't been offered the job, Martin realized he had to alert the other members of the law firm's management committee before they read about him being on the short list in the press. He took out his cell phone and called his secretary. "Schedule an emergency meeting of the management committee this afternoon at six."

*   *   *

Martin walked down the polished wooden floor with its oriental runners to the Fred Glass conference room. He liked management committee meetings to take place there as a way of remembering Fred's instrumental role in starting the firm.

With his own departure now possible, Martin recalled dedicating the conference room two years ago. It was a month after Fred's death. Martin had asked Betty, Fred's widow, and their two children and six grandchildren to bring pictures of Fred to hang on the walls along with legal memorabilia of his accomplishments. They brought photos of a gigantic financing he engineered for New York State, shots of acquisitions for IBM, GE, Intel, and a stock offering for Aero Industries. They also showed his award from the president of Harvard for his fundraising. So now Martin might also be leaving. But the baby the two of them had spawned was powerful. It would thrive without its founders.

Martin never looked forward to these management committee meetings. Running an organization by committee is a plague. For years, with Fred's acquiescence, he'd operated the firm as a benevolent dictatorship. He could have strangled that group of young partners who, ten years ago, demanded a management committee elected by all partners. He felt like King John at Runnymede. He had to acquiesce or the firm would disintegrate. But, he'd nonetheless maintained the real power by operating as chairman.

Entering the conference room he checked his watch. Five to six. He looked around. Three were already here. On one side was Meg Worth, head of the firm's wills and estates practice. Good old Meg, stocky and solid in both appearance and outlook. She had pale blue eyes, rimless glasses, and a Dutch bob. In her mid-forties, she was always calm, always searching for the compromise.

Martin liked that she was a voice of reason. Next to Meg, was Tom Wilder, IP litigator and quintessential nerd. At fifty, he was a tall string bean with thinning black hair over a narrow face. His navy suit was rumpled. It probably had never been cleaned or pressed. Constantly tugging on his earlobe, he needed a shave, even at ten in the morning, but he was a technical genius. Recipient of a PhD from Cal Tech in near-record time, he tossed it all away and enrolled at Harvard Law. And what amazed Martin was that Tom could not only understand complex technical issues, but managed to explain them to a lay judge.

Across the table, was Michael Perry, Fred's choice as his successor to head up the firm's transactional practice. Short, with carrot red hair and intense gray eyes, he walked with a cane due to a congenital hip problem that couldn't be rectified by numerous operations. He never lost sight of the bottom line, which made him such an effective negotiator, giving on the less important issues and digging in on what counts.

And next to Michael, the empty chair. Waiting for Jenson.

No big surprise, Martin thought. The guy must have a hidden camera somewhere in here so he can always be the last.

Finally, Jensen strode in. "Can we get started?" he said. "I have an important dinner meeting with a client."

"We were waiting for you," Martin replied.

Jenson looked at his Rolex. "It's exactly six now."

Meg laughed.

"I'm glad our little exchanges amuse you," Martin said.

The others laughed as well.

Great camaraderie, Martin thought. "Okay. Down to business."

He saw their eyes turn toward him. They must have all read yesterday's *Times*. They had to know what was coming, why he'd assembled them on such short notice. "A couple of hours ago, I met with Arthur Larkin. He wants to place me on a short list for chief justice. I told him yes. The others are Mary Corbett, from the Second Circuit, and Lance Butler, from the Fifth. He'll be leaking our names to the *Post* for tomorrow's paper."

For a moment, there was silence. Martin realized they were each thinking about how his leaving would affect them and the firm. His view was that his being chief justice would add luster to the firm.

In that respect, it would be good for business and might even offset the loss of their largest rainmaker.

At last Tom said, "Congratulations. It's a tremendous accomplishment for you and for the firm."

Meg and Michael called out. "Here, here."

Jenson nodded without saying a word. Remaining silent, Jenson took out a cigar, rolled up the cellophane wrapper into a ball and tossed it to the far end of the table, then shoved the cigar into his mouth.

"Let's talk about some of the practical problems," Michael said. "Assuming that you leave."

The commercial lawyer, Martin thought, ready to raise business issues.

"We have to face the fact," Michael continued, "that we'll lose some clients. Lortech and Aero, for starters. And lots of others."

"That does not have to happen. It'll take hands-on attention. But if we designate committed partners to follow-up with each client, we should be okay."

"I think that's right," Tom said, tugging on his ear. "We'll have to select individuals to be the contacts with each one."

Martin said, "I'll draw up a client list and designate each one's new firm contact."

Jenson stopped chomping on his cigar. "You can do that to get the process started, Andrew, but ultimately, the rest of us will have to decide who becomes the primary contact. We'll be here."

"That's correct," Martin said.

"Alright," Jenson said, taking charge. "We now have a process for the client transition issue. First, Andrew draws up his proposed list. Then the four of us make the final decisions. Is everyone in agreement with that?"

The others nodded.

Jenson continued. "Now, next issue. Andrew, under the partnership agreement, you have an unfunded pension for life based on your last five years' income. So that's set. What about your recusal in cases involving firm lawyers?"

"I'll disqualify myself from any case involving a firm lawyer. Ethically, I think that's the way to go."

"I agree," Meg said.

"Are we finished then?" Martin asked.

"I have something else," Jenson said.

"Sure. What?"

"FYI, I've been working on the Attorney General of California. And it's paid off. We've been retained for the first of what I expect will be many cases. This involves a conflict with Nevada over water rights."

"That's great," Michael said. "If it's half as successful as Andrew's work for New York, we should earn a bundle."

"Agreed. I'm going all out. Paul Maltoni's helping me draft California's Supreme Court brief."

Martin was startled. Paul, he thought, was working for him on the Global Media FCC case. He considered telling Jenson he was wrong. But his pleasure in that would only make problems for Paul. The Global Media case was damn important. He hoped to hell Paul knew what he was doing.

Martin gathered up his papers and left. Though his knee was bothering him, he sucked up the pain and went for a walk along the mall. A stiff breeze was blowing. The temperature plunging.

"Hot chocolate?" a vendor asked. A couple of joggers passed.

After the management committee meeting, he was now more than ever longing to be chief justice. He loved being a lawyer, but he was ready for a change. Ready to move on to something new and exciting.

Meantime, he was still at the firm. He had to deal with the Global Media case. If I stay, I want to win that one, he thought. Before returning to the office, he stopped for a cappuccino at a small café.

Back in the office, he saw Meg sitting next to his secretary's desk.

"The brethren sent me as their representative. We're all sorry that we got a little carried away discussing practical issues. We want you to know how proud and pleased we are for you. We really hope you get it."

"I'm glad to hear you say that. We've been together a long time."

"And we genuinely do appreciate all you've done for us."

*   *   *

Xiang had run cross-country at Carnegie Mellon. He looked like a runner as he walked into his kitchen at 4:15 in the morning, dressed in running shorts, a plain gray sweatshirt to brace against the thirty degree temperature, and sneakers. He grabbed a cup of coffee and a piece of stale bread and headed out to Connecticut Avenue and then into Rock Creek Park.

It was still dark, with heavy fog covering the area—typical for November in Washington. The trail, filled with leaves, was deserted as he expected it to be. Xiang passed the tree with a large hollow hole in the trunk facing away from the trail which he used as one of the spots for Jasper to drop documents which Xiang later recovered. He continued running. Ten minutes before 5 a.m. he reached the meeting point. No sign of Jasper. Xiang sat down on a tree branch and waited for the senator.

Xiang recalled what Liu told him about Jasper when he gave Xiang the assignment four months ago. "The senator is extremely powerful as Chairman of the Senate Armed Services Committee and has access to his government's most sensitive military documents. Jasper is also badly in need of money. He faces a reelection campaign next year, and in American politics, which are so corrupt, money is everything. Besides that, he lost all his savings with a poor investment in a high-tech startup in Colorado. He has an expensive life style operating houses in Washington, Denver, and Aspen, and a mistress to whom he gives costly gifts."

Xiang felt nothing but contempt for Jasper, a man who had no control over his own destiny, and for the American political system in which offices went to candidates who had the most money.

In the thick fog, Xiang saw the senator approaching, precisely at five. Xiang stood up and looked around. No one else was in sight. Despite the cool morning breeze, Xiang noticed that Jasper was perspiring heavily. From tension, he guessed. The senator's face was also red from the sun. He must have been in a Southern resort.

"What happened?" Xiang asked tersely, wanting to get right to the point and wrap up their discussion as soon as possible.

"When I met with Liu in Tokyo in my suite in the Okura in July, a young woman on my staff at the Senate Committee on Armed Services overheard our conversation."

"She overheard your conversation?" Xiang was incredulous. "How is that possible?

"She was in the bedroom of the suite. Asleep, I thought. Liu and I met in the living room."

You fool, Xiang thought. You stupid, contemptible fool.

"What's the name of the woman?"

Jasper shifted awkwardly. "Vanessa Boyd."

"Your lover?"

"Yes."

"Now she's threatening to disclose what she heard?"

"Vanessa's dead. She drowned on the Caribbean island of Anguilla, Sunday night."

"And you were with her at the time?"

Jasper nodded weakly. "It was late at night. She had a lot to drink. Dumb bitch shouldn't have gone swimming. She accidentally drowned. I tried to save her."

"To your knowledge, did she tell anyone what she heard in Tokyo?"

Jasper shook his head. "I don't think so. She didn't tell me about it until a little while before she went swimming and drowned. I had no idea. I thought she was asleep in the bedroom at the Okura."

Xiang realized he was missing a piece. "So what's the problem? Vanessa's dead."

He was staring at Jasper, waiting for the other shoe to drop.

"She secretly recorded the Tokyo conversation." Jasper was speaking softly, barely above a whisper.

Xiang leaned forward, straining to hear.

"She made a CD," Jasper said.

Xiang was horrified. This was worse than he had ever imagined. Happily, he was not responsible for the problem. Liu should have taken precautions to make certain he and Jasper were alone in the Okura suite and there were no bugs. Liu had been careless, but Xiang couldn't dare tell that to Liu. He became apprehensive when he realized he would have to report all this to Liu. It could still come back to bite Xiang. Without a solution to the problem, Liu might shoot the messenger, particularly a subordinate who knew about his failing.

Xiang had a knack of always cutting to the bottom line quickly. Here, he realized that his only chance of saving Operation Trojan Horse and his own life was by getting his hands on that CD.

"Where's the CD?" Xiang asked.

Jasper looked chagrin. "I don't know. Vanessa only told me about it Sunday. She didn't have it with her in Anguilla. I looked through all of her things after she drowned."

"Have you searched her apartment since you've been back?"

Jasper shook his head.

No, of course not, Xiang thought. US Senators don't do stuff like that. They only fuck subordinates and then call for help, letting others do their dirty work.

Jasper provided Xiang with the address of Vanessa's apartment near DuPont Circle. Then he said, "When you look for the CD, remove her diary, calendar, and anything else that mentions me. I don't want to leave any evidence showing we were involved or that she went away for the weekend with me."

"Did you and Vanessa ever send e-mails to each other?"

Jasper shook his head vigorously. "Never. I made her promise when we began seeing each other that there would be no personal e-mails. Those are what usually nail men who . . ."

"Are fucking around."

"You don't have to put it that way."

Xiang was pleased he wouldn't have to deal with Vanessa's computer. "Anyone know she was going to Anguilla with you?"

"I asked her not to tell anyone. To my knowledge she didn't."

Jasper raised his right arm and pointed a thick finger at Xiang. His hand was shaking. "You have to find that CD. My whole life depends on it not falling into the wrong hands."

Your life means nothing to me, Xiang thought. But he did have to find that CD, not merely for Operation Trojan Horse, but because his own life depended on it.

"Did Vanessa live alone?" Xiang asked.

Jasper nodded.

"Good. I'll break in, search for the CD, and sanitize the apartment to eliminate any mention of you. But you'll have to find a way to do the same for Vanessa's office. I can't break into a Senate office building."

While frowning, Jasper thought about it for a minute, then said. "I'll do it myself. I'll get in this morning before the staff arrives. It's my committee. If anyone asks, I'll say I'm looking for a report.

"Oh and one other thing. If you don't find the CD but you find what looks like a bank vault key, then take it and give it to me. She may have locked the CD in a bank vault."

"Will do."

"If you find the CD or the bank vault key, call me on the cell and say 'positive,' If you don't say, 'negative.'"

They split. Xiang raced home, changed into a suit and tie, and put on a large, brimmed hat to conceal his face. He grabbed some tools and loaded them into a briefcase.

At 6:30, he left his car on New Hampshire Avenue and walked two blocks to Vanessa's apartment building, a modern tan brick ten story. Vanessa had an apartment on the penthouse floor, number 10K, Jasper had told him.

The sidewalk was deserted except for a young man walking a dog while looking at his iPhone. He didn't seem to notice Xiang.

As he approached the building, Xiang wondered if there was a guard on the desk in the lobby. If so, this could be dicey.

He opened the front door and looked around. There was a guard. A large black man, but his shaved head was down on the desk, asleep. As he passed the desk, Xiang noticed that the guard's face covered a civil engineering text book. Must be a student from Africa, he decided.

Xiang walked softly to the elevator. The guard never even looked up. Xiang took it to the tenth floor.

The corridor was deserted. En route to Vanessa's door at the end of the hall, Xiang heard a television playing through a closed door. In front of 10K, he glanced around, saw no one, slipped on a pair of latex gloves to avoid leaving prints, and went to work on the lock. The door clicked open in thirty seconds. His instructors had trained him well. Still no one in the corridor. He went inside and softly closed the door behind him.

The apartment was large. He entered the living room which was furnished expensively with ultra-modern pieces. White and glass predominated. The carpet and sofa were white. The coffee table was glass. The furnishings looked relatively new. He searched the living room first, then the dining room and kitchen on the left. No sign of the CD or a bank vault key.

Xiang was preparing to go to the other rooms when a copy of *Vogue Magazine* from fourteen years ago on the coffee table caught his eye. On the cover was a picture of a strikingly beautiful blonde. The caption read: VANESSA BOYD. AMERICA'S NEW SUPER MODEL.

Xiang sat down and read the profile. It contained a family photo of Vanessa, her twin sister Allison, and her mother, Claire, taken at a Paris show. Allison was an attractive brunette but nothing like the beautiful blonde bombshell Vanessa.

Xiang went to the other side of the apartment. He saw a study and two bedrooms. The larger was Vanessa's; the other one must have been a guest room.

He began in the study, sitting down at Vanessa's desk and opening the center drawer. Inside, he saw a bulky diary. Not wanting to waste time reading it, he placed it in his briefcase. He found a date book calendar. It had several entries including one for last Friday. "Anguilla with W.J." He tucked that in his briefcase as well. No sign of a CD or bank vault key.

Based upon what Jasper said, he ignored Vanessa's laptop.

He checked the side drawers. No CD. In one of them, he saw a stack of Verizon phone bills bound by a rubber band. Those might show calls with Jasper, he decided. So he took those as well. He leafed through Vanessa's bank statements. No point taking those.

He checked all the other drawers in the room. No CD. No key. He looked under the oriental carpet on the wooden floor. Nothing.

Next, he searched the small bedroom and didn't find a thing of interest.

He went into Vanessa's bedroom and looked in the large walk-in closet. He was amazed. He had never seen so many clothes, shoes, and handbags in his life. He looked everywhere in the closet, opening each bag and reaching inside, even opening zipper compartments. No CD. No bank vault key.

In the large bedroom, he saw on the bureau several pictures of Vanessa with a woman he now recognized from the *Vogue* article as Allison. One was taken on a boardwalk along a beach, possibly Rehoboth. He was struck by the fact that Vanessa, not all dressed up for a shoot but casual in shorts and tank top, looked pretty, but not drop-dead gorgeous as she did in *Vogue*.

He was also struck by how similar the twins looked when both were in shorts and tank tops.

Xiang began opening drawers in Vanessa's bedroom. He couldn't believe what he saw in the underwear drawer. Must have been two dozen silk bra and matching panty sets in different colors. All neatly arranged. He looked underneath for a CD or key and came up empty. He tried to restore them to the original arrangement.

As he did, his hand stopped on a pale yellow set. Yellow was his favorite color. He carefully removed the silk panties and held them up to his face, trying to draw in her scent.

It infuriated him that Jasper, that disgusting old fool, had been having sex with Vanessa. She should have had a younger man, someone like Xiang. He closed his eyes and imagined what it would be like to make love with Vanessa. He felt his cock stiffening. Later, he told himself as he slipped the panties into his briefcase.

He checked the two bathrooms. Nothing. Satisfied it wasn't in the apartment, Xiang pulled the hat down close to his eyes, took off the latex gloves, and left the apartment. Fortunately, no one was in the corridor.

He stepped out of the elevator and looked anxiously at the reception desk. It was deserted. Perhaps the African student had gone to the bathroom. He crossed to the front door and exited the building.

On the street, he walked at a normal pace toward his car. No one called to him. He was confident he hadn't been seen.

Back in his apartment, he placed the encrypted phone on the desk and waited for Jasper to call with the results of his search of Vanessa's office. With time to kill, he undressed and stretched out naked on his bed with the briefcase next to him. Merely pulling out Vanessa's yellow panties and fingering them gave him an erection. He wrapped them around his hard cock, closed his eyes, and imagined it was Vanessa's moist pussy. He touched himself lightly. That's all it took. His semen wet the panties. He closed his eyes and relaxed.

Thirty minutes later, Jasper called on the dedicated cell. "Negative," the senator said tersely.

That was bad news. Xiang desperately wanted that CD.

What to do now? Call Liu and fly to Beijing? Or continue searching for the CD here, hoping to avoid a disaster?

He paced on the living room carpet, trying to decide. Both held risks. If he told Liu now, Liu might blame him for not having better control of Jasper. But how could he have blocked this from happening? The fault was Liu's. The spymaster had made an amateur's mistake by not making certain his July conversation with Jasper wasn't being overheard or recorded. Liu would never accept responsibility. He'd find a way to blame Xiang.

But staying in Washington and not telling Liu was risky as well. To be sure, the CD might be buried somewhere and never surface. But if he didn't find the CD and it ended up in the media, Liu would severely punish him for keeping the information to himself. And at this point he had no way of finding the CD. Liu might have some ideas.

Neither was a good choice.

He was leaning toward calling Liu and flying to Beijing. At least that way he wouldn't be hanging out alone.

Then one of the cell phones on his desk rang. The secure phone Liu had given him.

Xiang raced over and grabbed it.

"I want you to fly to Beijing immediately," Liu said.

"Yes sir. I'll get the first plane."

Xiang was terrified. Had Liu found out about the CD? Had it already surfaced? Is that why he was calling?

After showering and hiding the yellow panties, he got back into his car and headed to Dulles Airport. While driving, he used his cell to book the first flight to Beijing.

He hoped he'd be returning to Washington.

*   *   *

At seven thirty in the morning, barefoot, Martin walked down the four cold flagstone stairs in front of his house. In the heavy fog, he could barely see the street.

After stopping to retie his robe, he picked up the morning *Washington Post* and *New York Times*. He was tempted to tear into them on the spot to see if they had any stories about the chief justice appointment. No, don't go crazy, he cautioned himself. A few minutes won't matter. Francis wasn't up yet. He'd sit down with coffee and do this calmly.

First, the *Times* said nothing about the Supreme Court. He turned to the *Post*. On the upper right-hand corner was a picture of Chief Justice West and an article quoting unnamed medical sources as stating that West's prostate cancer had metastasized and he would be stepping down as soon as Braddock selected a replacement. The article went on to name Corbett, Butler, and Martin as the three candidates on the president's short list.

Profiles of the three were on A-10. Martin flipped to that page.

"Oh . . . Oh," he said when he saw that his profile was written by Rick Potts, the *Post*'s legal affairs correspondent.

Martin knew that Potts disliked him because he refused to talk to Potts about legal matters he was handling. Martin strongly believed that when lawyers spoke to the press, it wasn't good for the lawyer and it wasn't good for his client. As a result, he never discussed his cases with any reporters. Potts took umbrage at that. And they argued about it from time to time, including once on an ABA panel.

As Martin read his profile, he realized that Potts was now getting even with Martin. The reporter depicted Martin as a greedy lawyer who charged clients excessive rates. He was, "The quintessential Washington insider and a wheeler-dealer . . . Lyndon Johnson appointed someone like that in Abe Fortas, and we all saw how it ended."

Martin was enraged, but he knew he couldn't do a damn thing about it. He just hoped Larkin and Braddock wouldn't pay much attention to Potts's profile.

Martin sipped some coffee and turned to the sports section. Nothing good there. Lots of agonizing about why the Washington lost to Dallas.

He flipped through Metro. On the obit page, a good-looking woman with long blonde hair caught his eye. "Vanessa Boyd, Senate Committee Staffer." His heart began pounding. Studying the picture, now he remembered Jasper introducing her in the committee's offices. A knockout. Jesus, she was the woman Jasper took to Anguilla.

His hand unsteady, he placed his cup down and began reading:

Vanessa Boyd, Senate Committee Staffer

by Harriet Olsen

Washington Post Staff Writer

Vanessa Boyd, a staff member of the Senate Armed Services Committee died Sunday while vacationing on the island of Anguilla. The cause of her death is not known. She was thirty-five.

Born in Oxford, Ohio, Miss Boyd was an internationally acclaimed fashion model. After retiring from modeling, she attended New York University and received a bachelor's degree in political science, graduating cum laude in 2003. That same year she came to Washington, working initially as a receptionist for Senator Linkletter from Ohio. Three years later, she began as a research analyst on the Senate Armed Services Committee, where she has worked since.

She is survived by her mother and father, Claire and George Boyd, of Oxford, Ohio, and a twin sister, Allison, a professor at Brown University.

Vanessa's obit worried Martin. He had hoped her death would pass without notice. He thought some more about what had happened Sunday night. Suppose someone who knew she was going to Anguilla with Jasper, maybe a fellow staffer, saw the obit. Would the staffer raise questions about how Vanessa died?

He started cursing himself. Moron. Imbecile. Stupid idiot. Sure, he had a lot to drink, but that didn't justify what he did. Was there some way he could undo it? Turn it around? Couldn't Jasper still tell the police in Anguilla what happened? He could concede that a mistake had been made. No harm done. It was an accidental drowning.

Yeah, but awkward, he realized. Still, far better for him and Jasper than if the facts got discovered by someone else and they were charged with a cover-up. But Wes could be a brick wall. Advising him in his two senatorial campaigns, Martin had nearly come to blows with Jasper. Once, he'd wanted to take a two by four and whack him.

He ran through the day's schedule in his mind. On Tuesday evenings Francis had her chamber music group at the home of the first violinist with the National Symphony and she ate with them. So, of course, she'd be there. Tuesday evenings were sacrosanct, he thought with resignation. It didn't matter what else came up. Even when Fred Glass had arranged an important client dinner with spouses, he had uselessly pleaded with her, "Can't you make an exception just this one time?" She not only refused, but they ended up in a shouting match, he recalled. "I must have my own life, Andrew. I'm not just your little helper," she claimed.

So Tuesday evenings he made plans for himself. During baseball season, he loved going out to watch the Nationals. He always bought the cheapest ticket and sat in the outfield bleachers with a beer and a hotdog, a carryover from his boyhood when all he could afford was a bleacher seat for the Pirates. If his father wasn't working, they'd go together. If not, he'd hitch a ride into Pittsburgh and go himself.

Francis laughed at him for not sitting in the expensive box seats the firm bought for client entertaining. But she didn't understand. It was a way of remembering his childhood. And sitting out there with a beer, even on a hot, muggy Washington evening, he tuned out his weighty legal problems.

No baseball in November, though. This evening he had planned to go to the Caps game against the Bruins. But the hell with that. He'd invite Jasper over for dinner. It wouldn't be easy, but one on one he'd persuade the senator to tell the Anguilla police.

He yanked out his cell phone. "Listen, Wes, you and I have to talk. How about my house for dinner this evening? Francis will be out."

"Not tonight, Andrew, I have something on."

"This is important, dammit."

"What are you talking about?" The man's voice had a snarly edge.

Damn you, don't turn hostile on me, Martin thought. You dragged me into this. "I don't think I should spell it out on the phone. This cannot wait. Issues we hoped were resolved may not be concluded."

"What in hell happened?"

"Take a look at the obit page in this morning's *Post*. And please come at seven thirty."

Francis walked in and poured a cup. "Anything about the Supreme Court in the papers?"

"You don't want to read the *Post*."

"Darling, give it to me straight."

He showed her the Rick Potts's profile.

"That stinks."

"I should have found a way to placate that asshole years ago."

"I doubt if it will carry much sway."

"I hope you're right."

"Maybe I'll go back to bed."

"Wait. There's more. The *Post* ran an obit on the woman Wes was with in Anguilla."

She closed her eyes and scrunched her face. "That won't go away. Will it?"

"I invited him here to dinner this evening. We can still straighten it out. If he gets obstinate, I'll put arsenic in his food."

"Better yet, cut off a certain part of his anatomy."

They both laughed.

"This isn't funny," he said. "Why are we laughing?"

"Because if we don't, we'll be crying."

Oxford, Ohio

Allison was driving a rental car along Route 27 from Cincinnati to Oxford over flat land past farms that looked desolate after the harvest. She took her eyes off the road for an instant to glance at the finger she'd pricked when she and Vanessa had sworn a blood oath to stick together. The grim, gloomy, gray morning matched her mood.

Approaching the city, centered around the university, the terrain became hilly. As she passed a sign, "Welcome to Oxford," she recalled things she and Vanessa did together for the first fourteen years of their lives. Making out with boys near the reservoir. Buying beers at Craig's Market after Vanessa told him, "Dad sent us," and drinking them behind the high school building. Hiding in the trees of the park to smoke Pall Malls and recite Ingrid Bergman's lines from Casablanca. Vanessa peeling off her clothes and swimming nude at night in Hueston Woods Lake with Allison as the lookout.

Midway across the Atlantic she'd begun to wonder if Mother—and that's what she insisted the girls call her, not mom—was responsible for Vanessa's death. Vanessa had always been gorgeous, but a perfectly normal girl. They were twins in spirit and personality.

Then at the age of fourteen all that ended. Allison remembered the two of them staying up all night, the night before Vanessa was leaving for New York to accept the position with the Premier Modeling Agency that Mother had worked so hard to get for her. This was the culmination of eight years of effort by Mother—enrolling Vanessa in every beauty contest, having her try out for TV spots, and paying for her lessons in learning how to walk and pose like a model. All the while Mother ignored Allison, the A+ student and athlete, while George, their father, stayed out of Mother's way in this and everything else.

Though the idea was Mother's, Vanessa was excited about going to New York. She was also nervous and scared. But Allison was worried. From stories and memoirs she'd read of washed-up former models, she knew what awaited Vanessa. Mother was robbing Vanessa of her youth, pushing her into a world of hell.

And what was it all for? Allison now asked herself, rain spattering the car. All because Mother had once been a runner up to Miss Ohio, and she was sick of her dreary life and job in the university's development department.

Allison turned left from Route 27 onto High Street, passing on both sides box-like red brick university buildings scattered across well-tended areas of grass. Then she passed the president's beautiful white wooden house and the hockey arena, finally entering the commercial heart of the city with banks, movie theaters, bookstores, and restaurants.

Stopping for a red light, she noticed the yellow brick building that had once been her Dad's store, its brown sign with white letters, "BOYD'S HARDWARE AND VARIETY. IF YOU NEED IT, WE HAVE IT," faded so badly as to be barely legible. When she and Vanessa were growing up, business had been good, but then Home Depot opened up outside of town, and Allison recalled Dad saying, "They're killing us on price," as his customers drifted away. Then she remembered coming back here to visit Dad after his first stroke when Mother had shuttered the store. Now workmen were tearing down the boards, and a sign in front proclaiming "OPENING JANUARY I UNDER NEW MANAGEMENT." Perhaps Mother had found a buyer.

Allison hadn't been home since Labor Day, she recalled. She didn't care much about seeing Mother; she had wanted to see Dad before she flew off to Israel. But with his second stroke, he "disappeared into another world," as Vanessa had said.

On the first step of the white colonial on a one-acre wooded lot Allison reached into her purse and pulled out a house key. Before she could turn it, Mother was standing there, her eyes red and bloodshot. Her face puffy. Allison tried to hug her, but never affectionate, her mother pulled away.

"I'm so sorry." Allison didn't know what else to say.

Mother began crying. Allison cried with her.

"She was an angel," Mother said. "An angel."

"Does Dad know?"

"I tried, but couldn't get through."

Allison dropped her black duffel and walked upstairs. She hoped somehow he'd speak. At least recognize her. She sat next to his bed. "I'm Allison, Daddy." He gave her a blank stare. She loved him so much. He had always been there with encouragement and support. "You can do great things, Allison."

She sat still and looked around. On the wall were his military medals. In high school in Oxford he had been a star halfback and was awarded a football scholarship to Ohio State. But it was during the Vietnam War and he was a patriotic American so he had enlisted in the Marines. Saving two of his wounded comrades, he took a bullet in his leg. He was awarded a Silver Star for gallantry in action and a Purple Heart.

He returned home and worked with his father in the hardware store. His football career was over. He saw no point in going to college. He had never been bitter. He was proud he had served his country.

After fifteen minutes, she left his room and wandered around upstairs. The door to Mother's room was closed. She stepped into Vanessa's, sobbing for what she'd lost, looking at the stuffed bunnies and Barbie dolls, gazing at the framed photos of Vanessa from *Vogue*, *Bazaar*, and *Elle*.

She cried, and she cried more.

When she was finished, she crossed to her own room, still cluttered with college leftovers and copies of some of her articles. She had taken all the athletic trophies with her when she moved to Providence. Downstairs she found Mother sitting on the sofa sipping vodka on ice in a water tumbler looking through a family photograph album. I have to try to get along with her, Allison told herself.

But sitting down next to her, looking at the old pictures did little to soothe Allison. On the left she saw Vanessa being crowned Miss Teen Ohio as a gold tiara was placed on her blond head. The whole family was standing next to her. On the right, Allison receiving a national honor society award with only Dad and Vanessa in that one.

They were always so close. Twins. How can anyone who isn't one understand it?

She remembered the two of them infuriating Mother by talking in an imaginary language, calling each other Alley and Van instead of "the beautiful names" she had given them.

The phone rang. It was Sara Gross, the school friend, now a doctor, whom she had called from the Israeli airport. "I'd like to come by and talk to you. When's a good time?"

"As soon as you can."

Thirty minutes later, Allison opened the door for Sara. She was wearing a white doctor's coat, her stringy brown hair hanging loose, her tortoiseshell glasses pushed up on her hair. She hugged Allison, then turned to the twins' mother, who put down the album and stood. Sara tried to hug her, but she pulled away.

"I'm so sorry, Mrs. Boyd."

She began crying again.

"Let's go outside," Allison said.

The rain had stopped. They walked to High Street, Allison noticing students, some rushing to class, loaded down with book bags. Others were hanging out on the corners, or going into a bookstore. As they walked along the sidewalk Allison said, "Listen, I really appreciate your help."

"C'mon. I owe you big time for teaching me how to dribble and shoot baskets. Without your help, I would never have made the team."

"Naw, you just needed more self-confidence. That's key in sports."

"Before we talk about your sister, how about you? You look exhausted. This is an incredibly tough experience. I want to prescribe something, to make it easier for you?"

"You mean drugs? Tranquilizers?"

"Just to help you through the next couple of days."

"Sara, you always accused me of being a health nut, and I haven't changed. I never take any medicine unless absolutely necessary."

"What about talking to your minister?"

"Phil Barnes is a moron."

"I could put you in touch with a counselor at the hospital."

Allison ran a hand through her hair. "How could a counselor help? With all the grief I feel? But don't worry. I'm tough, I'll survive."

"Speaking of which, how's the leg?"

"It hardly hurts at all. Those Olympics seem like so long ago."

"You were great."

Sara sighed.

Allison was eager to talk about Vanessa "So tell me what you found."

"Well, for starters, your mother wouldn't permit an autopsy. That limited my options. Still, I did what I could."

They were passing Ozzie's Restaurant. "Let's go inside," Sara said.

At eleven thirty, the place was only half filled, mostly with students, loud and raucous. Two women with babies in strollers in a corner. Sara led Allison to a table near the women. The smell of French fries in the air. The waitress in a short-skirted pink and white uniform, who looked to Allison to be about twelve, came over.

"Just coffee."

"How about some eggs?" Sara asked. "You look like you haven't eaten in days."

"I'm okay."

"Two orders of scrambled eggs with toasted English muffins," Sara ordered, then turned to Allison. "I can't imagine the pain of having my sister die."

"With a twin, it's worse."

"I still can't believe it."

"Now tell me what you learned."

"I took a blood sample for analysis. I examined her body and studied her medical records from Dr. Miller's office."

Allison somehow felt alarmed.

"Not to worry. He won't tell your mother. Well anyhow, Vanessa had a heart condition known as hypertrophic myopsy. Were you aware of that?"

Allison nodded. "But she never let that stop her from doing anything."

"Yes, that's the Vanessa Boyd I remember."

Sara pushed the glasses down over her eyes, reached into her purse, and took out some papers. "She also had traces of marijuana and some alcohol, but not a great quantity. Without an autopsy, I can't say whether any of these caused her heart to stop when she was swimming, or whether it was something else that caused her to drown."

"Such as?"

"A sudden swift current. A rip tide. Muscle cramp."

"Any bruises on her body? I mean evidence of a struggle? Like somebody forced her under the water?"

"You think someone killed her? That it wasn't an accident?"

Allison pounded her fist on the table. "The story I was given over the phone was total and utter bullshit." Allison was getting loud; the two young mothers were staring at her. One baby started crying. Sara motioned with her hand for Allison to keep it down.

"I know my sister. You know her, too. She'd never take a trip like that herself. She always attracted men like a magnet. She drew them to her and loved being with them, particularly the movers and shakers. She hated being alone. She wouldn't anymore go to Anguilla herself than I would fly to the moon. Some man had to be there. And he had to be responsible."

"Well, I looked and I didn't see any bruises. But that's not dispositive. Someone could have lured her into the water when she was too wasted to swim—or held her under without leaving any bruises. But there is one thing . . ." She hesitated.

"What?"

"I did see something suggesting Vanessa wasn't alone in Anguilla."

"What's that?"

"Irritation and inflammation on the inside walls of the vagina." Sara spoke in a clinical voice.

"You mean she was raped?"

"No. Probably just prolonged intercourse."

"Prolonged intercourse," Allison sighed. "That's Vanessa. At least that makes sense."

"Which means she may have gone there with a man, or perhaps met him in Anguilla."

"Either way, some scumbag man's involved," Allison's voice rose again. "Son of a bitch left her to die. He abandoned her on the beach where her body could've been chewed up by seagulls."

"I'm sorry, Allison. That's all I learned."

Allison said. "Wait till I catch the bastard. I'll strangle him with my bare hands."

Allison left Sara, then walked to the gray stone Blake's Funeral Home. The outside was dingy with peeling paint on the wooden front door, but a shiny clean black hearse parked in front.

Inside, steadying herself against a beam and looking at Vanessa in the open coffin, Allison thought Bruce must have worked hard. He'd restored the body to a good likeness. Had to be a tough job between the Caribbean climate and the lapse of time.

She sat down in silence, staring at her sister's body. At Vanessa's calm, still face, resting and at peace. In contrast, Allison was boiling with rage. Who did this to you, Vanessa? I swear to you he'll pay for it.

She asked Bruce, "What came with her body?"

"Wallet. Passport. Airplane receipt. Jewelry. I gave them to your mother."

"Cell phone?"

"Negative."

Allison planned to get them back at the house. She should have them.

"Oh, and a shipping ticket filled out by someone in Anguilla."

"May I see it?"

"Sure."

Bruce went into his office and returned with a wrinkled piece of beige paper. Allison studied it. "Har Stevens, Police Commissioner" was the signature. The man she'd spoken with. Under his signature was a phone number. She memorized it. As soon as Bruce left, she punched the number.

"Har Stevens here."

The voice and British accent, she remembered. "Mr. Stevens, this is Allison Boyd. We spoke yesterday."

"Of course. Vanessa Boyd's sister."

"I'm afraid I wasn't very coherent."

"Under the circumstances, it's only natural."

"Now I'm calling to clarify some matters."

"Unfortunately, I don't have any further information."

"I want to know what happened to my sister in Anguilla."

"Miss Boyd. I'm very sorry for your loss. From our investigation, we learned that your sister came to Anguilla by herself. She was staying at the Corinthian Hotel. I spoke to the hotel manager, who said she went swimming alone at night. Her body washed up on the beach in front of the hotel. Our first rate medical examiner concluded she drowned."

"Are you certain she wasn't with a man?"

"I did question the manager of the hotel on that myself."

"What's his name?"

"John Burt. But I've already told you what he knows."

"I understand that."

Allison realized she wouldn't get anything else from Stevens. She hung up the phone.

Damn it, she thought. If only she'd pressed Vanessa in their last talk about her plans for the weekend, she'd know something.

She was convinced Vanessa had gone with an older, powerful man. And he didn't want his name linked with her. So he left her dead body on the beach and ran. Protecting his marriage? His career? Both?

Allison recalled another time that Vanessa's affair with an older, powerful man ended in disaster. She had told Allison she was in Rome dating one of the wealthiest and most important men in the country. Then two days later, Allison received a call from the police in Rome, telling her that Vanessa, strung out on drugs and drunk, had been arrested for being nude frolicking in the Trevi Fountain with a man who had run away and wasn't identified.

Allison had immediately flown to Rome. She persuaded the police to release her sister, who was well known from the covers of fashion magazines, on the condition that Allison immediately take Vanessa to a clinic in Northern Italy for rehab, and she would have to remain there for a month. Allison readily agreed.

When Allison returned a month later, she took Vanessa for a week to Stresa. During that week, Vanessa poured out the full extent of her unhappiness to Allison. "Mother really pushed me into modeling from the time I was five. Sure, I thought it would be a glamorous life when she arranged for me to leave our house in Ohio and go to New York with the Premier Modeling Agency. And it was for a while. I should have quit years ago, but I was afraid of facing her. To overcome my misery, I started doing drugs, drinking far too much, and sleeping with men who were no good."

Allison developed the blueprint for Vanessa's new life. Quit modeling, go back to school at NYU, and get a degree. Vanessa wasn't a straight-A student like Allison, but she was smart. Even while modeling, she took courses at NYU and always managed to get Bs. In her new life, Vanessa swore to Allison there would be no more hard drugs. Only pot. And alcohol in moderation.

At Vanessa's insistence, Allison traveled to Oxford with Vanessa to explain to Mother that Vanessa was giving up the modeling life. It was an acrimonious discussion, with father on the sidelines as usual, and Mother calling Allison "a jealous spoiler." But Vanessa hung tough. And Vanessa began her new life.

She graduated from NYU with honors in government, planning to go to law school one day. In the meantime, she landed a good job in Congress. As far as Allison knew, she never did hard drugs again. Allison was proud of Vanessa and proud of how she helped her twin sister, who meant more to her than anything in life.

But now her sister was gone. And Allison couldn't bring her back. All Allison had now was a burning desire for revenge. She needed to find out whom Vanessa was with in Anguilla and destroy him.

Washington

Paul Maltoni sat across the desk from Andrew Martin and waited for the senior partner's reaction. By working until two in the morning he had a preliminary analysis of what it would take to prevail in a challenge to the FCC's proposed television decency regulations.

For the last fifteen minutes he had presented it to a dour-faced Martin, who had only asked a couple of clarifying questions—nothing to gauge Martin's reaction.

After leaning back in his chair and closing his eyes for a minute, Martin said, "A brief along those lines should work. Get started now. You'll need a full court press. Time's short. I'll want a draft in a week."

"You'll have it."

Pleased, Paul returned to his office and began preparing a detailed schedule for the brief.

Suddenly, Ray York, a friend and fellow associate of Paul's for the last eight years, barged into the office, waving a newspaper. "Hey, amigo, did you know she died?"

Paul looked up from his notes. "Who died?"

"You didn't see the *Post* this morning?"

"I was down here until two on a project for Martin. So who died?"

Paul's mind was cluttered with facts about the FCC decency regulations and Jenson's brief. "Who died?"

"That luscious piece you introduced me to last year at Warren Scott's fundraiser. I was insanely jealous."

Paul's mind cleared in a snap. "Vanessa Boyd died?"

"You got it."

He held out his hand and Ray gave him the morning Metro section.

Reading the obit, Paul was stunned. He couldn't believe Vanessa was dead.

"Why'd you break up with her?" Ray asked. "You told me you were going to marry her."

"It's a long story."

"At least you could have turned her over to me."

"You weren't her type," Paul said glumly.

"Okay. I've got it. You want to be alone right now."

"Yeah."

"Call me later if you want to drown your sorrow in a few beers this evening."

"I'll let you know."

Ray left the office and closed the door.

Paul was stunned.

He thought about the first time he'd met Vanessa. It was now a year and a half ago. Martin, who represented the Chinese government, was making an effort to block legislation authorizing an American arms sale to Taiwan. Paul, working with Martin, had prepared a report demonstrating that the weapons weren't needed by Taiwan, wouldn't be used defensively, and would only exacerbate US-Chinese relations. Martin had told Paul to take his report to the Senate Armed Services Committee.

Paul had learned from the committee counsel that Vanessa Boyd was the key staffer on the bill. So he went up to the Hart Senate Office Building to meet with her.

The receptionist directed him to a knockout, drop-dead blonde, whom Paul assumed was one of the member's mistresses stashed as a "secretary" in a committee office where answering the phone and smiling at constituents was the job description. To his surprise, the blonde was the staffer. Okay, he thought, this is going to be great, explaining these complex concepts to some airhead.

In fact, Vanessa knew more about the arms package for Taiwan than he did.

She also supplied him with data on the recent Chinese arms buildup, showing that the balance of power between China and Taiwan had been adversely affected by Beijing and the new arms were necessary to restore the balance of power. When he made his point about US-Chinese relations, she told him, "Senator Jasper and a majority of my committee members believe we have to be tough with China." In the end Paul said, "Will you please distribute my report to all of your members."

"Absolutely."

Then Paul, who always liked long shots, decided to try one with this gorgeous woman who was also smart and savvy. "What are you doing this evening?"

"Having dinner with you. Tell me where and when."

He couldn't believe it.

"Eight o'clock at Tosca."

"Good. I like Tosca. I'll be there."

Leaving her office, he had second thoughts. He was just a nerdy lawyer. Was she too much for him? A little voice, deep inside, said, "You're going to get hurt."

He ignored that voice. That evening, Paul had a fabulous meal, including great wine because, thanks to dinners he'd had with Martin on business trips, he had learned quite a bit about French and Italian reds. But even more than this, he later had the most incredible sex of his life. When he left Vanessa's DuPont Circle apartment at one thirty in the morning, he thought his dick would fall off.

He was wildly in love with her. They dated for about six months. She refused to move in with him, but they saw each other most weekends and traveled to Cannes and Paris, where she knew all the best places.

Then one day, without any warning, she broke it off with him.

"You're intelligent, fun to be with, and the nicest man I ever met, Paul, but I don't want to marry you. It's gotten too serious."

"Don't you ever want to get married?"

"I'm looking for something different."

"You mean a powerful Washington figure. Not an associate, or even a junior partner, in a law firm? No house in Bethesda with a white picket fence?"

"That's right. Let's go out to dinner, come back to my bedroom for one more fling, and part as friends."

Paul realized that arguing with her was hopeless. After that evening, he never saw her again.

Now she was dead. The only woman he'd ever loved.

He recalled that once when he was dating Vanessa he had met her twin sister, Allison, who was visiting her in Washington. The three of them had dinner together. He was amazed at how different the twins were.

He had to call Allison and tell her how sorry he was. He realized that he had Vanessa's parents' phone number in his contacts. She had called him from Oxford once when she was visiting there.

A woman answered, who called Allison to the phone.

"This is Paul Maltoni in Washington. Hopefully, you remember me. I had dinner with you and Vanessa a year or so ago."

"Sure. I remember."

"I read about Vanessa, and I wanted to tell you how sorry . . ."

"Oh, Paul, I can't believe it."

She began crying.

"What? What happened?"

"She drowned Sunday night . . . I got a call in Israel that she drowned in Anguilla."

"But she was such a good swimmer."

"Oh, Paul, it's awful. I'm back in Oxford."

He'd never heard anyone sound so lonely and sad.

"Is there anything I can do?"

"The funeral's tomorrow."

He made a snap decision. "I'd like to come. To be there for you. And to say goodbye."

"Oh, Paul. Would you?"

"Just tell me where and when."

"It'll be a graveside ceremony at ten in the morning in Oxford at 6200 Adams Road."

"I'll be there."

In a daze, Paul put down the phone. Beautiful Vanessa, gone. Drowned. He thought about his time with her at Rancho Valencia, north of La Jolla. She'd insisted on swimming in the Pacific. He'd never known such a good swimmer. How could she have drowned? Besides, if he didn't go to the funeral, he'd never believe she had died.

*   *   *

Martin stared across the dining room table at Jasper, who was pushing around the grilled salmon and butternut squash on his plate, and eating very little. On the other hand, he was hitting the sauce pretty hard. Jasper had two double scotches before dinner and three glasses of wine through the mushroom soup and main course. Martin had sipped only a little wine. He wanted to be stone sober when they talked about Anguilla. Jasper didn't usually drink this much. Martin was worried he was spinning out of control.

Still, Martin had to make sure to be alone with Jasper when they discussed Anguilla. So he confined their discussion to football and the stock market until they were finishing the salmon and he heard Isabella call from the kitchen. "Good night, Mr. Martin."

He heard the back door close. Time to get serious.

"Listen, Wes. I've been thinking about Sunday night."

Jasper drained the wine in his glass. "Send the bottle down here," he said, slurring his words.

"I don't think so. We have to talk."

He watched Jasper tense up, put down his fork, and clutch the arms of the chair. "Andrew, I'm sorry for involving you. But I had absolutely no choice. You know that movie with Glenn Close? Where she cooked the kid's rabbit?"

"*Fatal Attraction.*"

"Yeah. I felt like that guy."

"What happened?"

"Saturday, Vanessa was fine. We had a great time. Sunday too, during the day. Then in the evening, I don't know what it was. Maybe all the wine. But she decided to snort coke on the beach."

Jesus. This gets worse, Martin thought. *She must've kept the stuff in his house.* "Did you do that too?"

Jasper shook his head. "Shit no. Anyhow, she got crazy after that. Taking off her bathing suit and running into the ocean. I tried stopping her, holding her, but she pulled away. I had to chase after her. When she started floundering, I tried my Red Cross lifesaving, but I kept going under, swallowed a ton of water, almost drowned myself, but somehow managed to get her on the beach. Probably should have left her in the deep. Then we wouldn't have this mess."

"I've thought about this a lot," Martin said somberly. "And I'm convinced I made a terrible mistake. Did you a disservice."

"What do you mean?"

"I should have insisted you call the police."

"You sure tried. But, it's too late now."

"I don't think so. We can get on a plane first thing tomorrow. I know Dorsey, the governor. We'll tell him what happened. And he'll correct the records. Real simple and easy."

Jasper now was sitting up ramrod straight. "But these so-called corrected records will show that the girl was with me on the beach. That the two of us were staying in your house."

"Yeah. The truth."

"No, no." Jasper shook his head. "You might as well be putting a bullet in my brain."

"Sure, the Governor will know. But he'll keep it quiet."

"Are you kidding? Once they learn a US Senator was involved, it'll be too big not to spill right out. 'WOMAN DIES DURING TRYST WITH SENATOR.' You've seen it every year. 'STRIPPER WITH CONGRESSMAN GOES INTO TIDAL BASIN.' 'SENATOR NABBED IN MEN'S ROOM STING.'"

Jasper tapped his fork on the table. "You know how that press crap goes." Jasper was almost yelling. "And you know damn well, Linda hates this town. She'll toss my ass out of the house. Forget our twenty-seven years together. Call the *Denver Post*. My senate seat goes right down the tubes."

Martin felt stymied. Hell, he had just as much riding on this. Somehow he had to turn Jasper around. "Listen to me, Wes, no one from Dorsey on down will want that publicity. Anguilla lives on tourism. You think they want people hearing their beaches are fatal?" Martin shook his head. "No way. They'll change the records. That'll be the end of it."

"You can't guarantee that."

"Of course not."

"Well, then I can't take the chance."

"If you don't do this, you're exposing yourself to a much greater risk. Someone else may discover it. And you know damn well the cover-up can be a hellu'va lot worse than the deed."

"Who? Who could discover it?"

"I don't know. But these things happen. A friend, a relative?"

Was Jasper even listening?

"We've been friends since college," Jasper's voice was cracking. "Now I'm pleading with you to help me. You don't know Linda.

She can be vindictive. She'll go to the media. Get a sharp divorce lawyer. Clean me out."

Jasper lifted his glass, realized it was empty and put it back down. "Do you know how hard it is living on a senator's salary? Three houses. All heavily mortgaged." He seemed about to break down and cry.

Martin wanted to say, "You should have thought about these things before you flew off with this babe." But he needed to sound understanding. "Believe me, nobody's life will be destroyed. This is the only way to minimize the risk to both of us."

"You don't understand."

"Understand what?"

Jasper now began crying. "My marriage is already shaky."

"I didn't know that."

Jasper held up two fingers. "Two indiscretions. Dumbass mistakes. They meant nothing. But Linda found out. She's fixed on the three strike rule. One more and . . ." He sobbed. "And I'm out."

Martin realized he had now lost all sympathy for Jasper. But he had to stay focused and not tell the man he was a fool. Martin could go down to Anguilla alone, he thought. But he had no first-hand knowledge. Without Jasper there, Dorsey could become prickly, convene a formal inquiry, and haul Jasper down to testify. Then the media circus would ensue. And goodbye chief justice. Seeing Jasper fall apart, crying like a baby, Martin now knew he'd never persuade him.

Minutes later, Jasper was putting on his coat. At the door, he said, "I really appreciate your help and support, Andrew. You're a true friend in my time of need."

Alone, disgusted with the man, he poured himself an Armagnac. The idiot. He'd had enough forever of how they'd been friends since college. Some great friend, dragging him into this. Jasper could have taken the girl to a hotel and done anything he wanted with her there. He kicked the leg of the table so hard that his foot hurt.

Martin thought about how much he had at stake. There was more than the Supreme Court at risk. If the story broke in the press, he feared the impact on his life and career would be devastating. His mind flashed to Burke Marshall, a prominent lawyer and considered a possible Supreme Court nominee, who made a late night call to help Ted Kennedy avoid the consequences of another young woman's drowning in Chappaquiddick. That call ended Burke's tenure as a major company's General Counsel.

Martin couldn't let this destroy him. He had to try to forget about Anguilla and the Supreme Court for a little while, Martin thought, or he'd go crazy. His knee was stiff from sitting so long. He limped to the back door and looked outside. Clouds had broken up. The sky was clear.

He took the Televue NP101 refractor telescope and the mount from the closet in his study and carried them out to a concrete pad in the backyard. While he set up, he recalled his law school roommate Steve had gotten him hooked on astronomy and stargazing. He'd been blown away by the dazzling lights the first time he looked through a telescope. And the concept that he was looking at objects hundreds of millions of light years away was mind-numbing, the immensity of the universe serving to place daily travails into perspective. Martin loved the challenge of finding some of those objects.

This evening, sitting for stability, he wanted to bring into focus the brilliance of the Trapezium star cluster. First Orion. He had it. And Orion's Belt. Great. He adjusted the telescope and moved south and east. Ah, he had it, he thought with pride. The nebulosity. Now he could see all four stars, moving fairly quickly at the high magnification through the field of view, while he nudged the scope from time to time to follow them. But he couldn't find the fainter E and F stars. With this telescope, he'd never seen them. Maybe tonight he would. He refocused, straining his eyes. No luck. They were there, but not visible. They were just beyond his grasp. Would it be the same with the Supreme Court?

He felt a hand massaging the back of his neck. He whirled around to see Francis.

"Hey, Galileo. I'm home."

"Sorry. I didn't even hear you come out. You want to see something incredible?"

"No. I want to know what happened with Jasper."

Reality had come crashing back with a vengeance.

"He refused to budge. He was pathetic, in tears, Linda's already caught him screwing around twice."

She shook her head. "It's the air up on Capitol Hill. First their brains fill with hubris. Then it goes to their dicks."

"Good, Francis, tell it like it is." Martin felt a release from the awful tension.

"And the Supreme Court's up on Capitol Hill. So don't you get any ideas."

"Who has time?"

"What are you going to do?"

"I thought about flying down alone and rejected it."

"You're right. With Wes so scared, he'll turn on you. Make it look like it's all your doing."

Her words jolted him. Yes, he was the one who had engineered the cover up.

"You'll have to leave it alone, Andrew. Hope everybody else does."

Beijing

As soon as Xiang stepped off the plane at Beijing airport, two members of the Ministry of State Security whisked him through back corridors of the terminal, flashing their badges, circumventing security and passport control. A large black Chinese-made sedan with tinted windows was waiting in front of the terminal. "You'll be meeting Minister Liu at headquarters," one of the men said.

Xiang was alone in the back. The driver sped off to Xiyuan, in the West Garden section of Beijing near the Summer Palace.

Soon they were in gridlock. Xiang was not looking forward to this meeting.

He was terrified of Liu.

Xiang had always been terrified of Liu.

He closed his eyes and thought about the first time he had met Liu. He was sixteen years old. Thanks to his father, he had already made a long journey in his life from the remote town in western China where he had been born. When Xiang was five, his father left Xiang and his mother to take a job assembling vacuum cleaners for export in a joint America-Chinese company in an industrial town south of Shanghai.

Xiang didn't see his father, who sent money, for five years. Not until Xiang, a brilliant student, the teachers' favorite, and at the top of every class, was attacked one day after school by resentful classmates. Two pinned him down while a third, holding a hot piece of coal with forceps, touched it against Xiang's left cheek. Xiang was hospitalized and his mother's pleas compelled his father to return to the town for a visit.

When his father heard what had happened, he arranged for Xiang to take a competitive exam for an elite boarding school in Shanghai. Xiang finished first in the exam. Six years later Xiang, who had an ugly scar on his left cheek, repeated that feat in the competitive exam for Beijing University where he planned to study economics and management.

That was when he first met Liu. Ten months before he was to enroll in Beijing University, Liu summoned him to an unmarked building in Shanghai. Without identifying his agency, Liu told Xiang that the government wanted him to go to college in the United States. He was ordered to apply to Carnegie Mellon, Stanford, and University of Illinois to study economics and management. He was admitted to all three.

Liu told him to attend CMU. He didn't know why Liu selected CMU, but it wasn't his to question. The government would fund his education and living expenses. "Understand everything about the United States," Liu told Xiang. "But don't become seduced by the American life or American women. When you return to China after your education, we have plans for you."

But during his junior year at CMU, Xiang fell in love with Kelly Cameron, whose Caucasian American family owned a candy manufacturing plant. He was planning to marry Kelly and remain in the United States.

When Xiang returned to China during the summer before his senior year for a brief visit with his parents, Liu summoned him to Shanghai for a meeting. To Xiang's astonishment and horror, Liu knew all about Xiang's relationship with Kelly and his plans to marry her. Somehow Liu had been spying on him.

Liu told Xiang that unless he broke off the relationship with Kelly and returned to China after graduation to follow the original plan, his parents would be arrested and suffer unimaginable torture.

Reluctantly Xiang complied. Back in China, a year later, Liu enrolled him into a training program for the Ministry of State Security, the Chinese equivalent of the CIA.

Xiang excelled in training. Afterwards, Liu spent ten years in Beijing examining and interpreting American documents. Then he received another summons from Liu, who had risen to deputy minister. This was the time, Liu told Xiang that he was being assigned to the Chinese Embassy in Washington. His cover would be as a member of the economic section of the embassy. He was to learn everything he could about economic and political developments in the United States and forward reports to Beijing via the diplomatic pouch. Meantime, Liu told Xiang, "We will move your parents to a comfortable apartment in Beijing; your father will receive a generous monthly salary without ever working again."

For the next five years, Xiang did his job efficiently. Then Liu, who had been promoted to Minister for State Security, directed him to come to Beijing. That was five months ago.

"We'll be there in twenty minutes," the driver said.

Xiang thought about that Beijing meeting when Liu told him about Operation Trojan Horse, which Liu had conceived. "Our nets have snared an important American. Senator Wesley Jasper from Colorado. You will be responsible for coordinating our activities with Jasper."

Liu told Xiang about his meeting with Jasper in Tokyo in July. Then he said, "You must always keep in mind the objective of Operation Trojan Horse. We are concerned that the United States is shifting its military focus to Asia in order to counterbalance the huge growth of China's military. It's critical for China to know precisely what military moves the United States is planning to make and also which new weapons systems it is developing."

Liu had cautioned Xiang that secrecy was critical. "Trojan Horse is the most important intelligence operation our country has."

"I'm honored to be a part of it," Xiang had said.

Until now, everything had gone smoothly. Xiang was passing valuable information he had gotten from Jasper to Liu in the diplomatic pouch. Xiang didn't have to worry about money flowing from Beijing to Jasper. The process had been established in the Tokyo meeting and was being handled in Beijing, with Xiang being informed when payments were made.

It was all perfect. The ultimate intelligence operation.

Now this!

The car pulled up in front of the Ministry. Two agents led Xiang up to Liu's office where the spymaster was alone, sitting behind an old battered desk that Xiang had heard Liu brought with him from the Internal Subversives Unit where he conducted torture filled interrogations and smoked foul smelling cigarettes.

Liu had a jowly face, lips pressed tightly together. Xiang thought they might be permanently joined because the man never smiled. He was wearing narrow wire framed glasses below thinning black hair and a high forehead due to his receding hairline. Behind those glasses were hard, cruel eyes that had frightened Xiang the first time he met Liu and terrified him when Liu told him to break off his relationship with Kelly.

Liu had asked for the meeting. Xiang decided to wait to tell Liu about Jasper until he heard what the spymaster wanted.

"One of the documents you forwarded," Liu said, "refers to a five-year plan for Asia and Pacific deployment being prepared by the Pentagon.

"Yes sir."

"I want that document as soon as possible. I really want that document. Getting it from Jasper must be your top priority. Do you understand?"

Xiang hesitated. He had to tell Liu and he had to tell him now.

"We have a problem with Jasper."

Liu's eyes were boring in on him like lasers. "What kind of problem?"

Xiang reported, clearly and succinctly, everything that had happened since he had received the call from Jasper in the middle of the night. As he spoke, Xiang observed Liu becoming increasingly agitated. An angry scowl covered his face. Xiang hoped that rage would be directed at Jasper, not him.

At the end, Xiang reached into his briefcase and brought out the *Washington Post* which he had purchased at Dulles Airport, opened it to Vanessa's obit, and placed it in front of Liu.

After reading it, Liu pounded his fist on the desk. "Jasper is a fool," he cried out. "We should cut off his prick. It would be better for all of us."

"I agree with that," Xiang said, relieved he wasn't the target.

"But we can't. The information he has been giving us is valuable."

"I'm happy to hear that. As you instructed, I don't spend time reading the documents. I get them into the diplomatic pouch for transmission to you as soon as possible."

"So, let me give you some idea of their value. The documents supplied by Jasper discuss the technology for a new generation of long-range missiles being developed by the United States. Also, American-Japanese cooperation to thwart our efforts to retake islands which are ours.

"But most important, some documents state that the United States is developing a new military strategy for the Pacific. The Pentagon calls it AirSea Battle, to defeat our technologically enhanced and sophisticated military forces that will prevent the Americans from entering areas which we regard as our exclusive province. To add specificity to the American strategy, the Pentagon is developing a five-year plan to show how many of their warships they plan to move to the Pacific. It will also reveal the timing of the movement of aircraft to the region, how many and where they will be stationed. The documents will also show the anticipated capability of new American ships and fast attack submarines able to operate close to this shoreline."

Xiang was astounded. "That five-year plan would be priceless."

"Precisely. And never forget why we need the information. The Americans claim they are interested in working cooperatively with us. But their true intentions are quite different. They are determined to remain the world's only superpower. They'll do anything to prevent China from growing strong enough to pose a challenge to that position. A decade ago they had a huge military advantage. That has been shrinking. If we have this five-year plan and other information Jasper would be able to give you, we would be able to level the playing field with them. So we may despise Jasper, but we must solve this problem for him with Vanessa and the CD to maintain the flow of jewels from the Pentagon's war chest."

Sounding deferential and respectful, Xiang said, "I would like your advice as to how we solve Jasper's problem with Vanessa and the CD."

Liu ran his hand over his chin, then replied, "Senator Jasper's difficulties with Vanessa and his vulnerability because of the CD presents us with a good opportunity—a way of getting the Pentagon's five-year plan. Do you know what I'm thinking?"

Xiang thought he understood. "In exchange for my solving Jasper's problem with the CD, he should give me the Pentagon's plan."

"Precisely. And the only way you can solve his problem is by finding the CD and destroying it. Nothing and no one can stand in your way. In Washington, only you and the ambassador know about Senator Jasper and Operation Trojan Horse. And no one else can know. Am I making myself clear?"

"Yes sir."

"I will notify Hu, the head of our state security detail at the embassy right now. Tell him that he and every member of his group are to take orders from you."

Xiang knew that Hu wouldn't like it. Too bad, Hu wasn't one of Xiang's favorite people. The man was arrogant and never listened to others. Besides, Hu was twenty years Xiang's senior and had been at the embassy for the last ten years.

As if sensing Xiang's apprehension, Liu added, "If Hu gives you any problem, you let me know."

"Yes sir."

"Now let's talk about where the CD might be."

"I searched Vanessa's apartment. Jasper searched her office. We found neither the CD, nor the key to a bank vault."

"Your search may not have been sufficiently thorough. You may have missed the CD or the key. Go back again to the apartment. Or send Hu."

Xiang didn't think he could have, but he didn't dare argue. "Yes, sir. I'll do that."

"Also, I want you to set up around the clock surveillance on Vanessa's apartment. Perhaps she told someone about the CD. The obit refers to Vanessa's twin sister, Allison. She's a good possibility. When Allison or someone else uncovers the CD, you can seize it from them. Do you understand?"

Xiang nodded vigorously. "Absolutely."

"Should I fly back to Washington now?" Xiang checked his watch. "I can still make a United Airlines plane."

"Yes, but first I want you to do two things. As soon as you leave this office, tell my secretary to give you a secure line into the embassy. Call Hu and have him set up surveillance on Vanessa's apartment. We need it in place immediately."

"I'll do that."

"Then on your way to the airport, I'll have my car stop at your parents apartment. You should have a brief visit with them."

Xiang was puzzled. What an odd request. Why was Liu suggesting this?

"But if I do that, I might miss the plane."

"Don't worry. I'll call the airport. That plane will not be cleared to leave the gate until you are on board."

As Xiang stood to leave, Liu said sternly, "Keep me personally informed of what happens in Washington on this matter."

"I'll do that."

"You must get that CD. Regardless of what it takes. Failure will not be tolerated."

*   *   *

Xiang's parents lived on the twelfth floor of a thirty story high-rise in a middle class area of Beijing. Xiang called from the car to say he was coming, and his father replied, "We'll be glad to see you."

His mother had tea waiting. As Xiang drank it, he asked about his parents welfare. "We have everything we need," his mother said.

Then his father told Xiang, "Let's go outside. I want to smoke. Your mother doesn't let me do that in the apartment."

That surprised Xiang. To his knowledge his father had never done anything his mother wanted.

In the elevator, his father didn't speak. When they were outside on a deserted grassy area, he took out a cigarette and lit up. His hand was trembling. Xiang hoped neither of them was sick. "You don't smoke in the apartment any longer?"

His father looked around anxiously, then said. "I wanted to talk to you alone. Out here."

"Why?"

"This morning, when your mother and I went shopping, I realized that we were being followed by a big man."

"Are you certain?"

He nodded. "If they followed me, I was worried there might be a hidden microphone in the apartment. So I thought it was better to talk here."

His parents had no idea what Xiang did. They knew only that he worked for the state and was based in Washington.

"Are you in trouble?" his father asked.

As the question hung in the air, Xiang put the pieces together. Liu wanted him to visit his parents because he wanted Xiang to know about the surveillance, which had just commenced. Obtaining this five-year plan was vital to Liu. The spymaster knew how much Xiang loved his parents. By exerting control over them with surveillance, he was signaling to Xiang: your parents are my virtual hostages. You do what I'm directing you to do, or they'll suffer. Liu had raised the stakes for Xiang.

"Well, are you in trouble?" his father repeated.

"Oh, no. Not at all. My work in Washington is going extremely well."

He had tried to sound confident and reassuring. He didn't want to worry his father.

Judging from the troubled look on his father's face, Xiang knew that he had failed. But he couldn't say anything else.

Washington

At 7:30 in the morning Martin was in the kitchen, sipping coffee and reading the *Washington Post*, when the phone on the wall rang. Who the hell's calling at this hour? Hope nothing happened to one of the girls. He picked up. "Hello."

"This is Jim Nelson from the *New York Times*, Mr. Martin."

He wondered why the national security reporter for the *Times* was bothering him at home. Having been wounded by his failure to talk to Potts, Martin decided not to stonewall a second reporter.

"Yes," Martin said, trying to sound cordial.

"I'm working on an article about prisoners in Guantanamo who were released. I understand that you represented one of them."

For an instant, Martin didn't know what Nelson was talking about. Then he recalled. A couple of years ago, Paul Maltoni wanted to represent, pro bono, a prisoner at Guantanamo. Martin agreed to supervise him and reviewed Paul's brief in the Court of Appeals in Washington that led to the prisoner's release. Paul had asked Martin if he should put both their names on the brief, and Martin had said, "Sure."

"You can read the briefs in the court file," Martin said to Nelson. "Those are public documents."

"I want to talk to you about the prisoner. What he was like? Did you have any communications with him after his release?"

What the hell was going on, Martin wondered. Nelson was a veteran reporter. He had to know he was out of line. Had a supporter of Corbett or Butler put him up to it?

Calmly, Martin replied, "C'mon, Jim. You know I can't do that. It wouldn't be proper to discuss communications with a client."

"Look here. I'm giving you a chance to help yourself," Nelson said in a surly tone.

"As I said, it wouldn't be proper for me to talk to you."

Nelson gave Martin his cell phone number. "In case you change your mind."

As soon as Martin hung up, he dialed Paul's cell.

"Yes, Andrew."

"Refresh me about the Guantanamo case you worked on a couple of years ago."

"We represented a prisoner in Guantanamo. Khalid was his name. He's an Iraqi who had been arrested near Baghdad after a roadside bomb detonated, killing American troops. He was captured in a roundup of people in the area. There was no evidence he had anything to do with the bomb. You helped me on the brief. I argued it in the Court of Appeals. They agreed, and he was released and sent back to Iraq. That's pretty much it. Why are you asking?"

"I just got a call from Jim Nelson at the *New York Times*."

"Why's he digging this up now?"

"I guess that goes with being on the president's short list for chief justice."

"Wow! That sucks."

"You have an eloquent way of expressing yourself. Can you get together copies of the briefs and all the papers on the Khalid case and meet me in my office this morning?"

Martin heard in the background, "Delta flight 228 to Cincinnati is now boarding."

"Where are you?" he asked Paul.

"Reagan National."

"I didn't know you were going out of town. I thought you were working on my brief in the FCC decency case. 24/7."

"Well, um . . ." Paul stammered. "I'm going to a funeral in Ohio."

"But your family are all from New Haven."

"Yeah . . . well, a woman I dated seriously last year, Vanessa Boyd, died. She was a staffer on Jasper's Senate Armed Services Committee. There was an obit in yesterday's *Post*."

Martin couldn't believe he was hearing this. For a second, he was speechless.

Paul continued, "Actually, I first met her when you sent me up to the Hill a couple years ago to help defeat legislation authorizing arms sales for Taiwan. We hit it off. But this is the damndest thing. She drowned in Anguilla. And she was an excellent swimmer."

"The currents can be tricky in the Caribbean." Martin tried to sound sympathetic. "I'm sorry to hear about your friend. When will you be back?"

"This evening."

"Okay, gather all the papers together on the Khalid case when you return. Come over to my house with them at seven tomorrow morning. I have to get on top of this. And don't talk to Nelson or any other reporters if they call."

When Martin put down the phone, he thought about the coincidence of Paul having dated Vanessa. It wasn't much of one. In many respects, Washington, or at least the Washington world that powerful lawyers, lobbyists, administration, and congressional officials moved in, was like a small community. Paul had said that he dated Vanessa last year. Martin wondered how long Jasper had been seeing her. It was possible his star associate and one of his best friends—or former best friend—were doing this girl at the same time.

Martin knew that Paul had a sharp mind and he could pursue matters when he became curious. He already thought it was peculiar Vanessa had drowned. Martin just hoped Paul would let it rest, get his ass back to Washington, and go to work on the brief.

Hong Kong

Liu looked out of the window of his private plane at the sparkling lights of Hong Kong.

"Fifteen minutes to touch down, sir," a flight attendant told Liu. He handed over his glass, all of the Macallan 10 Years gone.

Liu hated making this trip. His schedule was full in Beijing, but he had no choice.

When Xiang had left his office, Liu had paced back and forth, trying to find a solution to this mess.

To be sure, there was a chance Xiang would find the CD and give it to Jasper in return for the Pentagon's five year plan. But the more he thought about it, the more he realized that was a long shot.

Perhaps there was another way. Small drops of perspiration had dotted his thin mustache. If he didn't supply the Pentagon's plan to Yao and eliminate the threat posed by the CD, the consequences would be severe for him, particularly because any investigation would determine that Liu had caused the problem by permitting Jasper's mistress to record their meeting. Very sloppy on his part. And he knew Yao would never forget about the five-year plan. Once the Chinese president had something in his sights, he never backed away. Unable to come up with another solution, Liu decided he needed advice and there was only one place to turn: Andrei Mikhailovich. The Russian might have an idea.

That meant flying to Hong Kong. He had never wanted the Russian to come to Beijing, where he might be recognized by Russian agents or diplomats. If word got back to Putin of Andrei's location, the Russian President would arrange for his murder.

Liu had called Andrei. "Are you available to meet?"

"For you, anytime. Where and when?"

"Your house as soon as I can get there. I'll fly out of Beijing in thirty minutes."

Liu heard the landing gear going down. He thought about the first time he had met Andrei.

Liu liked to gamble. Initially, he thought that had led to a chance meeting, his first meeting with Andrei. Later, Andrei told him there was nothing accidental about the meeting. "I knew you liked coming to the casino in the Mandarin Oriental in Macau. So I took a room in the hotel for an indefinite stay. Spreading around lots of money. Eventually, I received what I wanted: a tip about your arrival."

That was two years ago, Liu recalled, when he was still deputy director of MSS. Dressed in a suit and tie, accompanied by two security men who were also in civilian clothes, Liu had slipped into the hotel through an unmarked rear door that lead to a small private VIP, admission by invitation only gambling room in the back of the casino. Craps was Liu's game of choice. He spent an hour making large bets with money he had siphoned off from MSS funds, winning a little and losing a little, but essentially staying even.

All that changed when a powerfully built Russian, missing the pinkie on his right hand, picked up the dice across the table. Liu immediately recognized Andrei Mikhailovich, formerly a top KGB agent, then head of its successor, the FSB, rumored to have recently had a falling out with Putin.

Andrei had a hot hand that night. Liu was betting with him as he made point after point, and they were both betting much of their winnings. He sensed the Russian gradually moving around the table, until by the eighth point he was standing next to Liu.

After Andrei made his tenth straight point, he said, "Nyet" to the croupier who offered him the dice. He gathered up his chips and said to Liu in Chinese, "Pigs get slaughtered."

Liu gathered up his as well. After they collected their winnings, Liu said, "Can I buy you a drink in gratitude?"

"No, but you can come onto a yacht I'm using and talk. It'll be worth your while. I promise you."

When Liu hesitated for a moment, Andrei pointed to Liu's two guards. "You can bring them along. Guns and all. It'll only be the four of us. I told the crew to remain on shore until further notice."

Liu and Andrei had gone down to the teak-paneled stateroom while the security men remained on the deck.

Andrei fixed himself a vodka and poured scotch for Liu. When they were seated across a small table and Liu was anxious to hear what Andrei wanted, the Russian began. "I had a falling out with Putin. I told him to go fuck himself."

"That takes guts."

"Or stupidity. Anyhow, I need a new employer and some security. Not that Putin ever plays for revenge." He gave a short caustic laugh.

"And in return for those, what can you do for me?"

Andrei took a long drink of vodka. "Your so-called intelligence agency, MSS, is a joke. Hardly fitting for the world's second most powerful nation on its way to being the top dog."

Liu bristled. "What do you mean a joke?"

"Your primary approach of getting information from tourists coming and going is absurd. You need a comprehensive network of agents in place around the world as we, the Americans, and British all did at the height of the Cold War. I want to teach you how to do that. I know you're close with Yao, and he's likely to be the next president. If you have a plan to remake the MSS according to my plans, and you tell him about it, he's certain to make you director. Once you're in that role, you'll be able to hit the ground running."

"So you want to turn the MSS into the KGB?"

"Why not? Russia supplied you with nuclear technology. Now we'll export our spy craft to you. Or more precisely, I'll export it to you."

"You want a salary?"

"A large one. I have a lavish life style. I'll also want some plastic surgery as well as plenty of security at the right place to live. And two beautiful Chinese women to share it with. Having sex with only one becomes boring. With two, the possibilities are, well use your imagination."

"Beijing or Shanghai?'

"Both are too dangerous. You don't want your Chinese colleagues to know I'm advising you. It's better for you if you make it look like you're doing it yourself. Also, there are too many Russians running around in those cities. If one of them figures out who I am, word will get back to Putin."

"Where then?"

"Hong Kong. Put me up in one of those walled compounds outside of town that British industrialists used."

Liu liked what he was hearing. Perhaps sensing this, Andrei said, "Do we have a deal?"

"Yes."

That was almost two years ago. Each had carried out his end of the bargain.

Operation Trojan Horse had been Andrei's idea. He had taken with him from Moscow his files on important American political figures, including Jasper.

The plane hit the runway with a thud.

Welcome to Hong Kong, Liu thought. Once a jewel in the British crown, it was now under the control of China, as all of Asia would be one day.

*   *   *

When a security man opened the thick metal front gate of the compound for Liu, he spotted in the courtyard the two Chinese women with whom Andrei lived. They were playing a card game. Liu wondered if Andrei took them both to bed together or separately, but he never asked.

Andrei was waiting for Liu in the wood-paneled dining room. The Russian had lost twenty pounds since he moved to Hong Kong. He looked fit and exuded power and self-confidence. He could have passed for an important Central European industrialist. Liu had been paying him well with money siphoned off from the MSS budget. Liu imagined Andrei had been winning at the craps table in Macau as well. And Liu had always thought Andrei had stolen plenty in Russia before he left, which was now stashed in a bank in Singapore or somewhere else in Asia, beyond Putin's reach.

Andrei signaled to one of his servants. Moments later the man carried in plates of roast duck, steamed vegetables, and Cantonese fried shrimp. Another one served Chateau Margaux.

Once Andrei waved them both away, the two men ate in silence for several minutes. Then Andrei said, "What's the urgent problem?"

With Andrei, Liu held nothing back. He laid it all out for the Russian. His meeting with Yao, the Pentagon's five-year plan that the Supreme Leader so desperately wanted, and his conversation with Xiang.

At the end, Andrei was shaking his head, looking squarely at Liu. "You screwed up in Tokyo," the Russian said.

Though Liu knew it was true, if anyone else had dared to say it to the spymaster, he'd be a dead man.

"That's in the past. What do I do now?"

With barely a pause, Andrei fired back, "You have Xiang kill Jasper and make it look like an accident."

"But Jasper is my source for getting the Pentagon's five-year plan for Yao."

"That's the whole point. You'll tell Yao that Jasper is dead and you're starting from scratch to find a new source for the document. That removes his pressure from you. Yao will be unhappy, but he won't be able to blame you for Jasper's death. Also it eliminates the risk of Jasper one day turning on you, which he might very well do because he is under stress due to the CD. Meantime, you'll have Xiang intensify his efforts to get hold of that CD. It's the perfect solution."

"Suppose Xiang doesn't find the CD. What if the media or the FBI gets hold of it?"

Andrei laughed. "Then you will join me in exile somewhere else in the world where neither Putin nor Yao can find us."

"That's a comforting thought."

"Your best move right now is having Xiang kill Jasper."

Liu paused to move food around on his plate with his chopsticks. Then thoughtfully, he said, "Perhaps one day I'll kill Jasper, but I'm not ready to do that yet."

"Because?"

"The intel he is feeding us is so valuable. He's an incredible source. I don't know if I'll ever find another one like him. I hate killing the goose that's laying the golden eggs."

"You don't have to convince me of Jasper's value. I was the one who gave you the file on him."

"For which I'm very grateful."

"You figure that with the intel you're receiving from Jasper, you will continue to rise in the Chinese government."

Andrei was reading Liu's mind. The spymaster nodded. "You could put it that way."

"You're playing a dangerous game. One of those eggs is likely to turn out to be a loaded hand grenade which will explode in your face."

Liu realized Andrei was correct. Xiang was the key to his salvation. Xiang had to locate that CD.

Oxford, Ohio

Riding to the cemetery in the back of the hearse with the windshield wipers slapping away the light drizzle, sandwiched between her sobbing mother and her comatose father, Allison felt as if she were having a nightmare. Nothing felt real. She couldn't believe this was happening. But this was her life. Her family. Or what was left of it.

Unable to sleep, she had cried so much during the night that she didn't know whether she had any more tears. Somewhere about three or four in the morning she redirected her anger away from her mother for destroying Vanessa's life by taking her to New York, to the man who had been with Vanessa in Anguilla. Was he responsible for her death? Or did he merely slip away, leaving her alone on the beach?

And as for her mother, difficult as it was, Allison tried to push aside the bitterness she'd felt, bordering on hatred, for so many years. Her mother's insides had to be ripping apart, Allison thought. She was burying her daughter whose life she'd lived through vicariously. She was misguided, but could Allison say that her own grief was greater than her mother's? Whose grief can ever exceed a parent burying a child? That's not the way it should be.

The black Cadillac passed through the cast iron gates at the entrance to the cemetery, wound around for a few minutes, then began a gradual ascent, coming to rest under a large oak tree close to the graves of Allison's four grandparents. As they got out, a tall sallow-looking man from the funeral home, who was as thin as bamboo, held an umbrella over Allison's head. Allison, her mother, and father moved to one side of the casket, poised above the open grave.

At one end of the gravesite she saw Pastor Barnes, a book in his hand. He was in his sixties, short and stocky, with heavy black-framed glasses halfway down a beak nose too long for his face.

On the other side of the casket were a group of about forty; among them was Sara Gross who was staring at her. Next to Sara was Chuck Burton with a brown crew cut and expensive suit and tie. He had been Vanessa's first boyfriend in grade school, and they dated until she went off to New York. Allison had heard he was now an important lawyer in Columbus, a rising star in the Ohio political galaxy. Beside Chuck were his parents, his mother supported by a cane, his father now with a thick white beard. She remembered Vanessa telling her about Chuck's efforts over many years to hook up with her again and her laughter when she said, "He's as square as a box."

Next to Chuck, she spotted Paul. She felt touched he'd made the trip. Allison recalled arguing with Vanessa after Vanessa broke up with him. Allison had liked Paul and thought he would be good for Vanessa. Allison had told her sister, "He'll be a partner in a law firm and success-ful." But Vanessa aspired to much more than that. She wanted power and wealth.

Close to Paul stood Geraldine Cox. Allison took an immediate dislike to the woman when she came to the house the night before the funeral for a perfunctory visit. In a self-important way she had announced, "I'm the Chief of Staff of the Senate Armed Services Committee." She'd struck Allison as an awkward, slightly overweight brunette with a nervous, restless way, a bad complexion, and an irri-tating laugh that reminded Allison of a machine gun. She constantly twirled the ends of her hair and stole glances at her wristwatch.

Other than Paul, Allison noted, Geraldine was the only one from Washington. And Allison sensed that Geraldine was no friend of Vanessa's. She had said something about having a mother in Cincinnati. She must have volunteered to be the representative of the committee and planned to visit her mother after the funeral.

Although Vanessa attracted men like flies—and perhaps because of that—she had had few female friends.

Vaguely she heard Pastor Barnes reciting a psalm. Not listening, she linked her right arm through her father's. He was so weak and frail. She doubted if he had any idea why he was here. Tears ran down her cheeks, bitter salty tears, mixing with raindrops.

As Barnes was concluding the psalm, Allison thought, I hope he's not going to speak. But he did.

"We are gathered here together in the sight of God to lay to rest a young woman who can best be described as an angel."

Mother obviously got to him, Allison thought.

"I first knew Vanessa Boyd," he continued, "as the most beautiful baby I'd ever seen. She grew up to be a beautiful, very intelligent, and accomplished young woman. She achieved international fame and recognition in her chosen field of fashion. While working hard at that, she made time to earn, with honors, a degree from New York University. Not content to rest on her laurels and retire, she went to Washington to help improve the state of our country. Others talk about doing that, but Vanessa Boyd went and did it. She had an important position on the Senate Armed Services Committee. She was able to influence the passage of legislation, which affects all of our lives and keeps us more secure. Her end was tragic. We can't understand the ways of God. Suffice it to say that he has other plans for this wonderful and talented creature."

More tears poured from Allison's eyes. The pastor began another psalm. Her knees wobbled beneath her black skirt. A bell rang in the tower of Miami at the University of Ohio two miles away. Then they lowered the coffin. And that was all!

Allison's mouth was dry. Her eyes were closing and she was feeling faint. She thought about them being in the womb together. She should be buried with her twin. Allison's body pitched toward the grave. The powerful arms of a young man from the mortuary pulled her back. Then Sara was clutching her.

"I'm fine now," she said.

She noticed the crowd dispersing slowly. A nurse led her father toward a limousine. Its engine was running, foul-smelling fumes belching from its exhaust. "Are you coming?" Mother said. Allison spotted Paul, standing nearby and turned to him. "You have a rental car?"

"Yes."

"Good. Wait here for a minute."

She told Mother, "I'll meet you back at the house."

Then she looked around for Geraldine. The chief of staff was walking rapidly along a path toward her car. Allison cut across the damp grass and caught up with her. "Thanks for flying out."

"I'm sorry for you and your family."

"Are you coming back to the house?"

"Afraid not. I'm due in Cincinnati."

"Before you pull away, I want to ask you something."

Geraldine seemed wary. "Yeah?"

"Who'd my sister go with to Anguilla?"

Geraldine shuffled her feet and twirled strands of her hair. "She told me she was going alone."

"My sister wouldn't do that. Was it with somebody on your committee?"

Geraldine didn't respond.

"You're covering for him?"

"I just know what she told me."

The woman's lying, Allison decided. "I intend to find out. You think I'll let him get away with abandoning my sister's body on a beach? I'll create a scandal. I'll ruin his life, his marriage, and his career."

Geraldine turned away and got into her car.

Allison felt like pelting it with a chunk of sod.

Paul was waiting for her. Walking to the car, he said, "What was that all about?"

"I told you on the phone that Vanessa drowned in Anguilla."

Paul nodded. "That's all you said. Who'd she go with?"

"I've been getting a bullshit story from the police in Anguilla. That she went by herself. That she was swimming alone at night."

"Vanessa?"

From the sound of his voice, Allison knew Paul didn't believe their story any more than she did. "I was hoping that miserable woman from Vanessa's office would tell me who he was. But she's covering for him. He was some scumbag, no doubt married."

"He should come forward."

"And I intend to make sure he does."

Paul and Allison went back to the house where she spoke briefly with friends and neighbors who stopped by to express their condolences. Platters of food were heaped on the dining room table. Few ate anything. After about an hour, people drifted away.

Allison went upstairs and looked in on her father who was resting. In the living room, there were just Paul and her mother. "Will you wait outside for a minute?" she asked him. She wanted to confront her mother.

When he was gone, she said, "You don't believe the story about her death, do you?"

Her mother didn't respond.

"For God's sakes, Mother. Vanessa went off with some guy for the weekend. Probably he was married. When she drowned, the bastard split. Now they're trying to cover it up."

"What makes you so sure?"

"I knew Vanessa. She would never have gone to a Caribbean island by herself. Or anywhere else. When she went on vacation, unless she went with me, there had to be a man."

"Your sister wasn't like that. She was an angel."

"Yeah, well, the angel had marijuana and alcohol in her blood."

"You shouldn't talk that way about your sister."

"I loved her so much. She was wonderful. She was talented. She was gorgeous. And I loved her. But I also saw her for what she was. The real Vanessa Boyd, not some fictional angel you created in your mind. I have to know what happened to her. How could anyone have left her alone like that? Don't you want to know?"

"Some things are better left alone."

"Why? Because you're worried the truth will tarnish her memory?"

Looking at her mother, Allison realized her words had hit home.

"And what difference will it make anyhow? She's gone. Nothing you do will bring her back."

"I want justice, and I need closure."

Allison turned away from her mother, who was still in her fantasy world. Not Allison. As always, she had to learn the truth.

Where should she begin, Allison wondered. Washington or Anguilla?

Washington made more sense. From Vanessa's diary, calendar, and other documents, she'd find the name of Vanessa's lover.

She went outside to Paul. "When's your plane to Washington?"

"I have to leave here in a few minutes."

"I want to come with you."

"Good. I'll call my office and have them get you a seat."

"Give me a couple minutes to pack my things. I'll be right out."

Allison couldn't wait to get to Washington. She was confident she'd find the answers there.

Washington

Tired beyond belief, Xiang got off the plane at Dulles Airport. As soon as he was in his car, he took out his cell and called Hu. "I'm on my way in from the airport. Meet me in my office in forty minutes."

"Get to the embassy first. Then call me," Hu said in a frosty tone, confirming Xiang's apprehension about Hu taking orders from him. Somehow, he'd have to make it work. Complaining to Liu would turn every member of state security in Washington against him.

Next, Xiang picked up the special encrypted cell phone dedicated for calls with Jasper and dialed Jasper's matching cell. The senator immediately answered, "Tomorrow," Xiang said and ended the call.

As he drove, Xiang thought about how difficult his meeting would be the next morning with Jasper in the park. In theory, Liu's idea of using the solution to Jasper's CD problem as a way of getting the Pentagon's five-year plan made sense. But in their last meeting, Jasper seemed to be coming unglued. It would be difficult to strike a rational deal with an irrational man. Somehow Xiang had to find a way to do it.

The Chinese Embassy occupied a large complex in what was the new embassy row in Washington on Van Ness Street, just west of Connecticut Avenue. Its neighbors included such foreign powerhouses as the Pakistani, Saudi Arabian, and Israeli embassies with one important distinction. In size, the Chinese dwarfed all the others. For its construction, Beijing had insisted on using Chinese firms to minimize the risk that listening devices would be built into the walls, floors, and ceilings.

As soon as Xiang reached his office, he called Hu. "I'm ready for you."

"Well, I'm not. I'm finishing up something. I'll be there shortly."

More gamesmanship. Ten minutes later, Hu called. "You better come to my office. I might get an urgent call."

Grin and bear it, Xiang thought when he entered Hu's office, that was much larger than Xiang's. Hu, a tall bean pole with a long narrow face led the way to a table.

Xiang saw a map of the DuPont Circle area spread out.

They leaned over the map. Xiang smelled Hu's garlic breath.

"Here is Vanessa's apartment building," Hu said pointing. "She has a corner apartment with windows to the north and west. Across a narrow alley to the west is a hotel that we're using for surveillance."

"We caught a break.

Hu sneered. "What do you mean *we* caught a break? My men and I carefully canvassed the area. We worked hard to find the hotel."

"Okay. What's the surveillance?"

"We've taken a hotel room which gives us an unobstructed view into the large bedroom in Vanessa's apartment. I've had a man in the hotel room with binoculars for the last ten hours. Nobody has come into that bedroom. I also have two men in a gray Lexus parked in front of Vanessa's apartment building. They're ready to follow anyone if I give the order."

"Good work," Xiang said.

"I know it's good work," Hu said in a haughty tone. "But I'm convinced we're wasting our time. I don't think anyone's coming."

Xiang was ready to slam that one back to Hu. "Surveillance was Minister Liu's idea. Would you like me to tell him that you don't think it's wise?"

Hu reddened. "No, of course not."

"Good. Let's go to the hotel."

"Why do you want to do that?"

"To see the surveillance for myself."

"You don't believe my report?"

Polite wasn't working. Xiang was ready to dig in. "Minister Liu put me in charge of this operation. I have to see it. You can go with me, or I can go alone."

"We'll both go."

They parked two blocks away. When he was in the hotel room, Xiang picked up a pair of binoculars. The set up was perfect. Not only would they see anyone in the large bedroom, but if the visitor turned the lights on and didn't close the curtains, they'd be able to watch what the visitor did. Pluck the CD from a secure hiding place?

The problem, Xiang realized, was that they didn't have cameras throughout the apartment, and they couldn't see into the other rooms from their observation point in the hotel.

Suppose Allison or someone else came into the apartment and uncovered the CD in a room other than the large bedroom. How would Xiang know? How would Xiang get the CD from her?

Xiang Googled Allison Boyd. He studied her impressive academic resume and her athletic prowess on the US Olympic field hockey team. He read about the new project she had undertaken in Israel. One colleague described her as tenacious. He realized she would be a tough nut to crack. He was developing a plan in his mind to take advantage of that tenacity.

*   *   *

Walking into Michel Richard's Central with Paul at eight thirty, Allison noted that the restaurant was crowded. Seemed like mostly young lawyers, briefcases at their feet, BlackBerries and iPhones on the table, stopping for dinner after working late. At the bar, still a score of thirty somethings who hadn't hooked up yet for the evening. Loud, after drinking for a couple of hours, the women's skirts riding high on their thighs, an extra button undone on their blouses. A TV above the bar, showing a Caps game.

Paul, looking self-confident, approached David the maître d', who gave him a big greeting, then led them to a prime table in the back, close to the kitchen, which was visible on the other side of a metal counter where chefs in high white hats left dishes for waiters under heat lamps.

Initially, Allison didn't want to go to dinner, but Paul had convinced her. "You have to eat to keep up your strength. Your investigation can wait for a few hours."

The waiter came by and handed them menus with a wine list. "Something to drink?"

Paul turned to Allison. "I remember from the time we had dinner with Vanessa that you like red wine."

"Right."

Without looking, Paul said, "We'll have the St. Joseph, the only one on your list."

The waiter nodded and rushed away.

"I'm starving," Allison said. "I haven't eaten all day."

"Don't you count the two bags of pretzels we had on the plane?"

"How could I have forgotten?"

"You'll like the food here. It's bistro with creative touches."

"What do you recommend?"

"Mussels first. Then I'm having the rib eye steak. You'll like the lobster burger."

After the waiter returned and opened the wine, he took a pad from his pocket and looked at Allison.

"Mussels to start," she said. "Then the rib eye with fries."

Paul raised his eyebrows. "Whoa. That's a surprise."

He turned to the waiter. "Ditto for me."

Once the server departed, Paul said, "I thought you only eat fish."

"Most of the time, but I like a big juicy steak now and then."

He rolled his eyes. "Okay. If you say so." Then he raised his glass and clinked it against hers. "To being with you again. Despite the awful circumstances."

The dark Rhone, with a full bodied flavor, was delicious, she thought.

"I feel guilty being here and Vanessa's gone," she said. She couldn't bring herself to use the word dead.

"I still can't believe it."

"Why did you two break up? She knew I thought you were good for her. She wouldn't tell me what happened."

"It's not much of a story, I'm afraid. On her birthday I went to her apartment to pick her up for dinner. I had a bottle of Krug and a diamond ring from Tiffany's in my pocket.

"We drank a glass of champagne. As soon as I brought out the ring, she raised her hand and said, 'Stop, Paul. You're a great guy, I don't want to hurt you, but I don't want to marry you.' When I asked her why not she made it clear she wanted to marry a powerful Washington figure. Not an associate or even a junior partner in a law firm."

Allison shook her head sadly. She thought again about how she had urged Vanessa to marry Paul as she worried about Vanessa making a mess of her life. She had been convinced that if Vanessa had settled down with dependable Paul, Allison's worries would be over.

Paul sipped some wine, then continued. "Anyway, I realized arguing with her was futile. We went out to dinner and never saw each other again."

"She had so much to live for. She was beautiful, and . . ."

Allison thought she might cry again. Perhaps sensing it, he put his hand on hers. It helped her regain some self-control.

"When I called you on Tuesday, you told me you had been in Israel when you got the call about Vanessa. What were you doing there?"

Allison was impressed at how smoothly Paul had changed the subject.

"I'm heading up an archeology project with an Israeli partner. We're trying to uncover a town from the time of King Solomon."

"That's good," he said with enthusiasm. "Before we broke up Vanessa told me you'd been promoted to professor, the youngest one ever in the archeology department at Brown. That's quite an achievement. And she also told me you won a bronze medal for field hockey in the Olympics in Barcelona. She was there and so proud of you."

"God, that was almost fifteen years ago."

"Tell me about it."

The mussels came. After eating a few, she said, "I took off a year after undergraduate college to try out for the Olympic team. My dad had been a hero in the Vietnam war and he inspired a love of country in me. I wanted to represent the United States. Somehow I made the team. The brutal training was the hardest part. It included a workout with Navy Seals, which involved 1,000 pushups, 1,000 sit ups, 1,000 jumping jacks, three miles of rowing, lifting a 250-pound log with seven team mates and carrying it the length of a football field, and after all that, a run up a mountain. At the end, I thought I'd throw up and never move again."

"It obviously paid off."

"Yeah. A bronze wasn't bad, but we really wanted the gold. I always play hard to win. In everything. Anyhow, we lost our last match to England. I did something stupid."

"What's that?"

"I injured my leg, but played while hurt, ignoring the doctor's orders. I scored one goal, but my career was over. My limp's gone, but I can't play sports that involve lots of running. I paid a price." She sounded wistful. "I still work out with an exercise bike, weights, and machines. I also do judo. So I keep in shape."

"Would you play hurt again?"

"Of course."

He laughed. "Then it wasn't stupid."

As they finished the mussels and ate their steaks, he asked her to tell him more about her work in Israel. Looking across the table while she spoke, she thought he was genuinely interested.

The waiter cleared their plates and left desert menus.

"Do you have time for dessert?" she asked Paul. "You were working pretty hard on the plane."

"I have to go into the office after dinner to pull together some stuff for my boss, Andrew Martin, but I'm in no hurry for that. The chocolate mousse here is great."

"Count me in on that."

After he signaled the waiter and ordered their desserts, Allison said, "This Andrew Martin must be a tyrant, having you work this late at night."

He laughed. "Actually, I love working with Andrew. He founded the firm, and he's the managing partner. He is the most incredible lawyer, and I always learn so much, not just about law, but how he deals with clients."

Paul was so in awe of Martin, she thought. He had Martin up on a pedestal. "You make him sound like some kind of God."

Paul blushed. "Martin is my patron. He's the reason I came to the firm. And besides, he's a very good lawyer. In fact, right now, he's on the short list to be chief justice. So others agree. The reason I have to go into the office tonight is because Martin has a *New York Times* reporter, Jim Nelson, trying to smear him because of a pro bono case we handled for a Guantanamo prisoner. I have to pull the facts together and meet Martin at his house early tomorrow morning. He has a lot riding on this Supreme Court appointment. It's the ultimate gold ring for a lawyer."

"Do you think he'll get it?"

Paul wrinkled up his nose for a minute. "He should, but he has a big problem. He's very much a Washington insider and a lot of people don't like that. Another reporter, Rick Potts from the *Washington*

Post, did a profile on Tuesday comparing Martin with Abe Fortas. Potts doesn't like Martin, and I'm afraid that may have hurt."

"If Martin leaves, will that affect your chances of becoming partner?"

He shook his head. "I don't think so. Other partners have given me very good reviews. I should know next September." He laughed. "In the meantime, I'm trying to stay out of trouble."

After they finished dessert, the waiter left the check. She wanted to split it. He insisted on paying.

"Thanks, Paul. I enjoyed dinner with you."

"Would you like to stay in my house tonight? I live alone in the poor part of Georgetown."

"You have your own house?"

"I bought it with another associate. He didn't make partner and left town to teach in Austin. I bought him out. I could give you a key while I go back to the office."

"Very nice of you, Paul, but I'll spend the night at Vanessa's. That's where I want to start digging into what really happened to her."

"If I can do anything to help, please call or e-mail." He sent his contact info, including home address, to her iPhone.

At the curb, he told her that his office was only a short walk. He raised his hand and signaled a cab for her.

As she opened the door, he said, "Be careful."

At first, it seemed like an odd comment. But when the cab pulled away, she thought about it some more. If whoever left Vanessa and ran away learned that Allison was trying to find him, he might play rough with her.

*   *   *

Climbing out of the cab and approaching Vanessa's apartment building, Allison noticed a gray Lexus parked in front with diplomatic license plates. DPL6279. One man in the front, behind the wheel. She couldn't see his face.

In the lobby she removed from her bag the key to Vanessa's apartment and her mailbox in the lobby. She recognized the young man sitting behind the reception desk, Fidelis, a Nigerian engineering student.

He greeted her with sad eyes. "So sorry to hear about your sister. She was a nice person."

"I appreciate your saying that, Fidelis. I really do."

"Swimming in the sea can be dangerous," he added.

Allison kept her thoughts to herself and simply nodded.

She stopped at the wall of mailboxes on the other side of the lobby. Vanessa's was jammed with mail, and Allison pulled it all out, glancing through it as she rode up in the elevator. There was nothing of particular interest. Besides bills, catalogues from Neiman Marcus, Saks Fifth Avenue, and Gucci, and junk mail from stock brokers and real estate agents, there were a couple of printed invitations to political fundraisers, equally divided between Democrats and Republicans.

As she opened the door to the apartment, she took a deep breath. She'd never been here without Vanessa before. Well, she didn't have time for emotions or sentiment. She had a mission: somewhere in this apartment there had to be something that would help her identify that bastard Vanessa had been with in Anguilla—the one who cut and ran, leaving her dead body on a deserted beach at night.

She made a beeline for Vanessa's study. The calendar Vanessa always kept on top might tell Allison whom she went with to Anguilla.

It wasn't there!

She checked the desk drawers. *No calendar!*

But what about Vanessa's diary? That would probably tell her about Vanessa's plans for the weekend.

Her sister was obsessive about never taking the most recent volume of her diary out of the apartment, even when she traveled, for fear of losing it. She locked prior volumes of the diary in a bank vault. She told Allison she was guarding her diaries because one day she planned to write a tell-all memoir about her adventures in Washington. "Vanessa in Potomac Land."

Allison looked in all the desk drawers. *No diary!*

Someone must had been in the apartment and taken the calendar and diary.

But maybe she was being too rash, Allison thought. Maybe no one had been here and stolen them. Perhaps Vanessa took the calendar with her. And she could have just finished her recent diary and put it in the bank vault. But then there would be a new one, unless she didn't have a chance to buy a new one.

Allison didn't want to believe that someone had been here and removed these objects. She didn't want to believe that her twin was having an affair with someone so crummy. But if he left her body on the beach, he could easily have done that. Allison, a scientist, couldn't ignore the evidence.

Someone had been there. But her lover might have missed something that gave away his identity.

She booted up Vanessa's laptop on the desk. The password was supermodel. She checked e-mails for the last two months. Nothing about Veteran's Day weekend plans.

She dumped the contents of all of the desk drawers onto the oriental carpet. For the next hour Allison searched carefully through all the papers, and there were plenty, because Vanessa just tossed things in. There were restaurant receipts, movie tickets, Christmas cards, unpaid parking tickets, and tax receipts. But nothing to indicate whom she was dating.

Allison saw a stack of utility bills and bank statements, which she looked through. How sad, Allison thought, that Vanessa, who had made millions modeling, only had about $30,000 in assets. Even the apartment was heavily mortgaged. She had burned through it all.

Allison often wondered how Vanessa had spent so much. She realized her sister was a major shopaholic, constantly buying the designer clothes she had formerly modeled. She had once told Allison, "I'm getting bad financial advice. They put me in a hedge fund that went bust." Allison hoped that's all it was—hoped that Vanessa hadn't gone back to drugs.

Phone bills, Allison thought. That's what she needed. Vanessa might have called the man she was going with to Anguilla, either from her apartment phone or her cell. But she hadn't seen any phone bills. She looked through all the mess of papers again.

No phone bills.

Bastard must have taken those, too.

Allison called Verizon, explained to the customer service rep that her sister died, and asked her to send the current bill with a list of all calls for Vanessa's house and cell phone, as well as the two most recent bills. The Verizon rep, sounding surly, said, "They will be there in a few days."

"Could you please fax or e-mail them to me?" Allison sounded polite, hoping that would work. "These bills are quite important. They have information relating to my twin sister's death."

"You'll need a court order if you want a fax or e-mail."

"I can't believe you're being so unhelpful." Allison was now raising her voice.

"Company policy."

"Get me a supervisor."

"They'll tell you the same thing. It's company policy."

"Well get me one anyhow."

"You'll have to call during normal business hours."

Allison slammed down the phone. She'd have to wait. By the time she got a court order, they would have arrived in the mail.

She went into Vanessa's bedroom. Perhaps her sister hid her diary there because she was going out of town. Or she may have left some evidence of whom she went with to Anguilla. Maybe a note from him.

She looked through the closet. Then the bureau drawers, even the lingerie drawer.

Nothing! Wait a minute, she thought. Her sister kept her clothes in a very orderly way. Every bra and panty part of a matching set; and all neatly arranged—as opposed to Allison, who just tossed clean underwear in a drawer, a habit for which Vanessa constantly berated her.

The lingerie drawer hadn't looked right. She reopened it. Everything wasn't perfectly arranged, as Vanessa kept it. The sets had been disturbed. And wait, that wasn't all. A yellow pair of panties was missing. Vanessa would never have kept a bra if she no longer had the panties. Someone had definitely been in the apartment and taken it.

"Pervert!" she cried out.

She closed all the curtains in the apartment. She walked to the living room and looked out at the street below. The gray Lexus was gone. She breathed a sigh of relief.

Then she remembered Vanessa's bank vault key. Vanessa insisted on putting Allison on the vault box with her. She had told Allison that she had the perfect hiding place for the key. In her pantry, she had a can of

Peets ground coffee she kept three quarters full. Always three quarters full. The key was at the bottom of the can.

Allison raced into the kitchen and checked. The key was still there. She took it out and put it into her bag.

Nothing else she could do here this evening. Tomorrow she'd go to Vanessa's office and talk to some of her colleagues. After that, she'd head to the bank vault.

In the shower she got another idea. American Airlines. She called reservations. From her sister's ticket, which she brought back from Ohio, she read off Friday's date and the originating flight number from Washington Dulles to a sympathetic agent, to whom she explained that her sister had drowned in the Caribbean.

"I want to know with whom my sister was traveling."

"Let me check," the agent said.

Several minutes of canned music followed. Then the agent came back. "Vanessa Boyd was on a single flight record."

"Does that mean she was flying alone?" a disappointed Allison asked.

"Not necessarily. If two people, traveling together, book separately, then their reservations appear on separate records. But our computer does not have that information. I'm very sorry."

Another dead end.

Depressed, she lay down in the small bedroom she always used. She tried hard to sleep. Despite being exhausted, she simply couldn't fall asleep.

*   *   *

In the hotel room across the alley from Vanessa's apartment, Xiang had put down the binoculars once Allison closed the curtains. He tried to evaluate what he had seen. Allison was definitely searching the apartment for something. Information about whom Vanessa went with to Anguilla? The CD? A vault key?

Being able to see only in the large bedroom, he couldn't tell whether she'd found the CD in one of the other rooms. If she had, he'd have to seize it from her. But perhaps she didn't even know about the CD. If that was the case, he'd have to tell her about it. It would whet her appetite so she'd want to find it. She knew Vanessa. She'd have a better chance of finding it. Then if he stayed close to her, he'd seize it from her.

Either way, Xiang had to confront Allison, and he had to do it now.

Prepared to take charge, he turned to Hu. "I'm planning to draw Allison out of the apartment. Talk to her. I'll need Chou's help. Is he still in the Lexus?"

"Yes. I told him to park a block away."

"Good. Give me his cell phone number. I'll dial it myself."

"Whatever you want. I might as well go home."

"No. I need you, too. A soon as Allison is out of the building, I want you to break into Vanessa's apartment. Try to find the CD or a vault key. If she has them with her, I'll get them. Once you've searched, call me on my cell and let me know. Positive or negative."

Xiang put on his tan raincoat. He checked to make sure the gun was in his pocket. He wasn't taking any chances.

When Allison was out of their sight in the apartment, Xiang had watched a video of the last Olympic field hockey match her American team had played against England. She had scored a goal. And she played while hurt. She was one tough woman, he was convinced, and couldn't be underestimated.

After tonight, Xiang wanted to be finished with Allison.

*   *   *

Naked, tossing and turning in bed, Allison glanced at the red digital clock on the night table. 2:50 a.m. Dammit, she thought, she never had trouble sleeping. But her emotions were raw.

Suddenly, the phone in Vanessa's bedroom rang, jarring Allison. She jumped up, ran into the other bedroom, and answered it. "Yes," she said nervously.

"Allison Boyd, I have information about your sister's death and the man she was with in Anguilla."

From the accent, Allison decided the caller was Asian, probably Chinese.

"Give me the information," Allison said.

"Not over the phone."

"Where then?"

"There's a church at 22nd and P. I'll meet you in the grassy area behind the church. Come right now."

"Wait a minute, you can't expect me to . . ."

He hung up the phone.

Shivering, her teeth chattering, Allison clutched the dead phone in her hand, while agonizing over what to do. Meeting a stranger in the dead of the night was a huge risk. But she couldn't turn down an opportunity to obtain information about what had happened to Vanessa.

She could call the police and have an officer accompany her. Even if she could arrange that, it would take too long. More importantly, if the caller saw or sensed a police presence, he wouldn't stick around and talk to her.

Yes, she realized that going was foolhardy and stupid. Somebody had cut out on Vanessa in Anguilla and convinced the Anguilla police to accept a phony story. He or his agents had stolen stuff from Vanessa's apartment. These were determined people. Still, she had to go.

As she dressed, she realized that she needed a weapon. She stopped in the kitchen, pulled a sharp paring knife from a rack and tossed it into her purse.

The open pantry door and the can of Peet's coffee caught her eye. Before leaving the apartment, she put the vault key back in the coffee can and closed the pantry door. Right now, that was the only lead she had. If this was a trap, she didn't want to lose it.

*   *   *

Walking the three blocks to the church Allison was fearful but determined. She tried to steal her courage, but her knees were trembling, her walk unsteady, the briefcase shaking in her hand. Whoever these people were, they knew a great deal. They knew who she was, and that she wanted to find out whom Vanessa had been with in Anguilla. Allison wondered if she was crazy coming to a meeting like this without any protection. No, she wasn't, she decided. She had to see where this lead.

At the curb, in front of the church, she saw a gray Lexus. Plates DPL6279.

She walked to the back of the church. In a grassy area walled off from the street, in the moonlight, she saw two Chinese men sitting on a stone step. Both stood immediately and moved toward her.

"What do you know about Vanessa's death?" she asked in a halting voice.

One of the men, who had a scar on his left cheek, reached into the pocket of his tan raincoat and pulled out a gun. He pointed it at her and said, "Where's the CD? I want it or I'll kill you."

She was flabbergasted. "What CD? I don't know what you're talking about."

"Don't lie," he snapped at her.

"I don't know anything about a CD."

He handed the gun to his colleague, who aimed it at Allison. With her eyes on the gun, she didn't have a chance to react when the man with the scar reached out and grabbed her bag.

"Hey!" she cried out.

Helplessly, she watched him remove a flashlight from the other pocket of his raincoat and use it to search the bag. Not finding anything of interest, he dropped it on the ground.

Then, with the other man still pointing the gun at her, he moved up close to Allison. He ran his hands roughly over her body and into her jacket pockets. She thought of kicking him hard in the balls, but she was convinced his colleague would fire.

When he was finished, she said, "I told you I didn't have the CD. I don't even know what you're talking about."

"Then what are you doing in Washington?"

"My twin sister died, and . . ."

Allison hesitated. She wasn't sure how to play this. She had to assume that these two were working with the man Allison had been with in Anguilla.

Scarface completed the sentence for her. "You want to know whom she was with in Anguilla."

"That's right. And you know. Now tell me."

He stared at her hard. "Mind your own fuckin' business. Leave this alone."

"Whom are you protecting?"

"You have a choice, Allison Boyd. You either leave Washington tomorrow morning, go back to your project in Israel, and forget all this. *Or I'll kill you.* Listen, you're very intelligent. A degree in archeology at Maryland—one of the top schools for that program. You're a professor at Brown, an elite university. Do you understand what I'm telling you?"

"Yes," she said flabbergasted that he knew so much about her.

"Now get out of here and go back to your sister's apartment. We won't bother you anymore tonight. But stay tomorrow, and you're a dead woman."

*   *   *

Xiang took the gun from Chou and put it in his pocket. He followed Allison, with Chou behind him, back to the street. Once she crossed it, heading toward her sister's apartment, they climbed into the Lexus and pulled away.

Seconds later, Xiang's phone rang. It was Hu. "Negative," he said.

"Are you out of the apartment."

"Leaving now."

"Move fast. She's on her way back."

Xiang thought about his situation. Despite his threat, he had no intention of killing Allison. From her bio, he was confident she would never be intimidated. She would stay in Washington and continue digging, now to find the CD as well as to learn whom Vanessa had been with in Anguilla. She might locate the CD; and if he stuck close enough to her, he could grab it. That was why he had told her about the CD. He was convinced she had never heard about it before their conversation. Xiang wanted her to know. If she stayed, he wanted her to become his agent in finding it. She would know Vanessa's possible hiding places that he could never imagine. She would locate the CD. Then he would snatch it from her.

He and Chou would have to park close to the apartment building to pick her up when she left in the morning. He doubted if she'd call the police, but just in case, they would ditch the gray Lexus and use a different car.

*   *   *

Shaken, Allison turned the key, opened the door, and entered Vanessa's apartment. As soon as she did, the scent of garlic hit her. Somebody had been here when she was gone. She reached into the coat closet and grabbed a tennis racket to use as a weapon. Cautiously, she checked the apartment. He was gone. The smell of garlic was everywhere.

Remembering the vault key, she dashed into the kitchen and checked the coffee can. It was still there. She removed it and put it into her bag.

Now she decided to get police help. She called 911 and reported that someone had broken into her apartment. She pleaded with the operator to send an officer even though no one was hurt. The woman said she'd report the request.

An hour later, Allison heard a knock on the door. "DC Police," a man called through the door.

She opened it to see a red, pockmarked, heavyset Caucasian face, dressed in a suit and tie. He held out an ID. "Detective Donovan," she read.

She let him in and they sat down in the living room. Allison told Donovan what happened to her sister and everything that had happened since she entered the apartment the first time. She even gave him the license plate of the Lexus and told him what occurred in the churchyard.

Donovan listened politely, while yawning a couple of times, and took a few notes. She had the feeling he was going through the motions.

At the end, she said, "How can you help me?"

"I don't understand. No one was injured. At least, in Washington. Aside from one pair of underpants, no property was taken."

"But people broke into this apartment twice. Once tonight. Two men pulled a gun on me in the churchyard. Don't you want to find them and arrest them?"

He held out his hands. Sympathetically, he said, "You have to realize it's a question of resources. Do you have any idea how many unsolved violent crimes we had last year in Washington? Even homicides. They'd laugh at me at headquarters if I spent time on this."

"But I gave you a license plate. Doesn't that help?"

"A diplomatic plate makes it harder. It's an unwritten rule: diplomats get away with all kinds of shit unless they kill somebody."

Allison was feeling exasperated. She tried not to show it. "Could you at least find out whose car it was?"

He sighed deeply, pulled out his cell phone, and repeated the license plate.

A few seconds later, he hung up the phone. "The Lexus is registered to the Chinese Embassy. For sure, nothing will happen. Routinely, we have to go to the State Department before we can move up on diplomats. And I know from my own personal experience that they're always trying to placate the Chinese."

"That's terrible."

"I agree. You're obviously an intelligent person. What do you do?"

"I'm a professor of archeology at Brown University."

"Okay, I'm being honest with you. Listen, I know you're grieving for your sister, and you're upset . . ."

"That has nothing to do with it."

"I'm sorry," he said in a kindly voice.

Realizing she was at a dead end, she thanked Donovan for coming. Then she put on the deadbolt and the chain across the door.

She had no intention of quitting. She'd get a couple of hours of sleep and pick up her digging in the morning.

But sleep didn't come. Angry and frustrated from her discussion with Donovan, she had to talk to someone. At six, she decided to call Paul. "Sorry, I woke you."

"No. No. I was up. I have an early morning meeting with Andrew Martin. What's wrong?"

"Do you have time to talk?"

"Sure."

"Before I tell you, I want your promise that you won't tell anyone. Under any circumstances. Agreed?"

"Yes. If that's what you'd like."

She poured out the whole story of what happened since she and Paul split in front of Central. At the conclusion, he said, "Oh my God, that's awful. What can I do to help you?"

"I can't think of anything now, but I appreciate the offer. In a few hours, I'm going to Vanessa's office on the Hill."

"But they said they'd kill you if you continued."

"I won't quit."

"Are you sure that's smart? I'm worried about you."

"I have to do it."

"Okay. But please be careful. And listen, you can't stay at Vanessa's apartment any longer. Stay at my house. You have the address in my contacts. I'll leave a key under the mat in front. Come whenever you want. And call me anytime you need help."

"Thanks, Paul. I feel better having talked to you."

*   *   *

Jasper was already waiting when Xiang arrived at their meeting point precisely at five. Dressed in a navy warm-up suit, the senator was pacing on the path.

The instant Xiang stopped running, Jasper said, "Did you find the CD?"

"Not yet. But I have some good leads. I'm getting close."

"How close?" the senator asked in an anxiety filled voice.

"It wasn't in Vanessa's apartment, but Allison Boyd arrived last evening. She's Vanessa's twin."

"I know who she is for Christ's sake. That's certainly useful information."

Xiang was tempted to say, "Look you asshole, I'm trying to help you." But that wouldn't get him anywhere, particularly today when he had Liu's mission on his mind.

"I'm expecting Allison to lead me to the CD."

"How can you be sure she's looking for it?"

Xiang didn't want to explain to Jasper that he'd told Allison about it.

"From the way she tore up Vanessa's apartment last evening."

"That's all you have? That's what you dragged me out of bed to hear?"

Well here goes, Xiang thought. The approach he had developed to achieve Liu's objective of getting the five year plan.

"Listen, Senator. Allison will be difficult to control. My men and I will be at risk in dealing with her. If I do this for you, I want something in return."

The senator scowled. "What do you mean *if you do this for me*? You have as much at stake as I do."

The senator was staring hard at Xiang, who met his gaze.

"That's not true. If the CD's discovered, I'll slip out of the country or at worst be expelled. The United States would never attempt to try me, but you'll . . ."

Jasper completed the sentence, "Go to jail for a long time."

Jasper looked angry. "Despite all the valuable documents I've given you, now you pull shit like this."

"Don't forget we paid you well for those documents. And getting this CD was never in the deal you made with us."

"Can't trust you fuckin' Chinese. I was a damn fool getting into a deal with you devious people."

Xiang bristled at the slur, but he kept his anger in check. Jasper was totally despicable. No redeeming qualities. Xiang kept focus. "Are you in or out?"

"Okay, what else are you looking for?"

Xiang exhaled with relief. The old politician's instinct for the deal had kicked in.

"One of the documents you gave me discusses a five-year plan for Asia and pacific deployment being prepared by the Pentagon. I want that five-year plan."

"It's not available yet."

"As soon as it is."

Jasper kicked at the ground without responding. Finally, he said, "You're asking for quite a bit. That's a very critical document."

"The CD could destroy your life. That's critical, too."

"You play a hard game."

"We should help each other."

"I don't know."

Another pause. Xiang wasn't sure how the senator would come out.

Finally, Jasper said, "And if I deliver the plan to you, in return you'll do everything conceivable to get that CD?"

"Absolutely. I'll even give the CD to you when you give me the plan. You can be the one to destroy it if you'd like."

"Jasper tapped his foot on the ground, waiting almost a full minute to respond. Finally, he said, "Okay. But you'd better get that CD. Because that's the price of getting the plan.""

*　　　*　　　*

At 6:30 in the morning Martin, dressed in slacks and a shirt, snatched the newspapers from the front of his house.

He waited to open them until he was in the kitchen with a cup of strong black coffee. Every day's papers had been bringing trouble for Martin. It was hard not to be paranoid. As he ripped the plastic bags off the *Post* and the *Times*, he wondered what they were doing to him today.

Nothing in the *Post*. Potts had taken a breather. Hooray.

Martin turned to the *Times*. In horror, he saw his picture at the bottom right of the front page under a large headline. What the hell? He noticed Jim Nelson's byline. Breathing heavily, he read:

Possible Supreme Court Nominee Represented Terrorist

Andrew Martin, one of the individuals being considered by President Braddock for nomination as chief justice represented a terrorist, who was held at Guantanamo. Martin, assisted by Paul Maltoni, a lawyer in his firm, achieved a legal victory last year for Hussein Khalid.

Khalid, despite being on CIA and FBI watch lists, managed to slip into the United States where he was directing a terrorist cell planning an attack on Los Angeles Airport. Khalid, a Saudi national and Al Qaeda activist, was working with a sleeper cell based in southern California when he was picked up by federal law enforcement officials.

Khalid was then sent to Guantanamo where he was being interrogated to determine the identity and location of the other members of this sleeper cell.

Before the CIA had time to obtain this information from Khalid, Martin employed his legal prowess to gain Khalid's release. In order to comply with a court order, the CIA had no choice but to let Khalid leave the country. He was flown back to Saudi Arabia.

To date, no information has been obtained about other members of this sleeper cell. Insofar as authorities are aware, the risk that they will implement their planned attack on Los Angeles Airport remains in place.

Martin and Maltoni were called for their comments. Neither was willing to respond.

The article shook Martin to his core. Could Nelson be right? Had they been responsible for this man's release? If they had, it would end Martin's chance of being chief justice.

The doorbell rang. That must be Paul.

Martin let him in and handed him the article. "Look at this."

As he read, Paul's face turned red with anger. He grabbed a stack of papers from his briefcase. "Nelson has it all wrong. Mohammed Khalid was our client. Not Hussein Khalid; and he was an Iraqi. Not a Saudi. He had no Al Qaeda ties. Nelson's story is completely false."

"You sure of that?"

"Here, I'll show you the documents."

Martin dismissed that suggestion with the wave of his hand. "Did Nelson call you yesterday?"

"It went into my voice mail. I didn't return it. You told me not to talk to him."

"That's right."

"I'm sorry."

"Sorry for what?"

"The Guantanamo case was my idea. I asked you to supervise me."

"That's nonsense. We're lawyers." Martin recalled the cell phone number Nelson had given him yesterday. Martin didn't care that it was early. Livid, he dialed.

"Jim Nelson, here," a sleepy voice answered.

"Damn you." Martin was shouting, venting his anger. "Your article is an outrage. Our client wasn't Hussein Khalid. He was Mohammed Khalid. He was an Iraqi. Not a Saudi. And he didn't have a damn thing to do with Los Angeles Airport. How dare you write an article like that without checking your facts."

"Hey," Nelson shouted back. "Don't you yell at me. I called you yesterday. You wouldn't talk to me. You've got no bitch with me."

"Who was your source?"

"C'mon Andrew. You know we never disclose our sources."

"You didn't dig this up on your own. Somebody fed you this pack of lies. One of Butler or Corbett's supporters. Didn't they? You never got off your fat ass to check. It's sloppy journalism. That's what happened. Isn't it?"

"To use your favorite line. No comment."

"I'll call Bill Devlin. Wait till he finds out somebody's using you. Playing you like a fiddle. Destroying the integrity of the paper. He'll fire you."

"You're a subscriber. You can call anybody you want."

In Nelson's last words, Martin detected a hesitation. The swagger was gone. Yes, of course. Someone fed Nelson that garbage. Operating under a deadline, he didn't verify it. Now Nelson was getting worried.

Francis came into the kitchen. "I heard shouting."

"Show her the article," Martin told Paul.

"Oh, hi, Paul," she said.

When she finished reading, Martin told her, "It's all a pack of lies. We represented Mohammad Khalid. Not Hussein Khalid. A different person."

"You better call Arthur Larkin so he can brief Braddock. Try to head this off."

"Good idea," Martin said. He knew all too well the juggernaut effect on possible nominees when derogatory news breaks.

He had to bite the bullet and call Arthur. As he reached for his cell phone, it rang. It was Arthur. "Have you seen the morning's *Times*?" Arthur sounded grim.

"A total distortion. I did assist Paul Maltoni in representing a prisoner at Guantanamo. But we never represented Hussein Khalid or anyone involved in planning an attack on Los Angeles Airport. Our client was Mohammad Khalid, alleged to have planted a roadside bomb in Baghdad. Big difference. Also, our client ended up being transferred to Iraq, not Saudi Arabia. The *Times* has it all wrong. I intend to call Bill Devlin and get him to publish a correction."

"Good, but those things never get the attention of the original. The damage has been done. It's unfortunate. But send me copies of documents corroborating your representation of this other Khalid fellow."

"You'll have them by noon. Anything else I can do?"

"Well, we clearly have a problem. I spent the last thirty minutes with the president talking about it. He wasn't happy that I didn't know about your representation of a Guantanamo prisoner. As I told you Monday, we don't like being blindsided."

"I should have mentioned it."

"That would have been better. But it's water over the dam. Or under the bridge. Wherever the hell water flows in Washington. Let me tell you where we are."

Martin held his breath.

"First there's the personal perspective. President Braddock believes that the character issue is critical. Nothing in this representation adversely affects your character. We know, and the president agrees, that everyone's entitled to representation. That's what makes our legal system work. If we lawyers had to be personally identified with the people we represent, we wouldn't take half our clients. An argument can even be made that you're admirable defending the underdog—the people who have been arrested, flown off to a strange place, and have no one to speak for them."

Arthur interrupted himself by coughing. "Sorry. Then there's the political fallout, which unfortunately trumps the president's personal views. You've been in this town a helluva lot longer than I have. I'm not telling you anything you don't know."

"Agreed."

"Sometimes an issue like this appears in the press one day and is gone the next. Other times it becomes a snowball rolling down a hill, getting larger and larger, until it knocks the nominee off a cliff. Remember the nominees' problems of tax withholding for nannies and receiving of honoraria from questionable public figures. All sorts of things. We'll just have to wait and see how this plays out."

Arthur paused to take a breath. "What we care about is the public reaction. How much outrage on Main Street and in the media? Even more, the reaction of the senators and particularly the members of judiciary. They have to confirm whoever we select. We won't send up a nominee who's DOA. But for now, you're still alive. Do you have anything else for me? Anything else you forgot to mention on Monday?"

Martin thought of his phone call with Jasper from Anguilla Sunday evening. That would finish him for sure. "Nothing."

Martin next called Bill Devlin, the head of the *Times'* Washington Bureau. "It's a disgrace. All the facts are wrong. I'm sending you copies of court documents, establishing that we represented Mohammad Khalid, who was charged with planting a roadside bomb in Iraq. I want a retraction in tomorrow's paper."

"If the documents back you up, you'll get it."

"And I want the same prominence as today's. On the front page."

"I can't commit to that. Our layout depends on the news we have on any given day."

"That's bullshit. You should be ashamed of yourself."

"Are you finished?"

"No. You should talk to Jim Nelson. Find out who his source was. How he got the facts so wrong."

"You know what'll happen. Jim won't disclose his source to me, and I can't compel him to do it."

In disgust, Martin slammed down the phone.

Martin and Paul gulped down a bowl of shredded wheat and a muffin along with coffee because Francis insisted that they eat. Martin then said, "Let's go," to Paul who had come in a cab.

They climbed into Martin's X-K8 Jag convertible, in British racing green, to go to the office.

As they pulled out of the driveway, Martin asked Paul, "How was the funeral in Ohio yesterday?"

"Really sad. Vanessa's mother was a basket case. And her dad, who had a couple strokes, seemed out of it. He was the lucky one. Nobody should have to bury a child so young. I met her when you sent me up to the Armed Services Committee on that Taiwan arms bill."

"Drowned? I think that's what you told me yesterday."

"Yeah. The story doesn't make sense. The police in Anguilla said she was alone. Vanessa would never have gone by herself. She had to be with somebody who left her dead body on the beach. That's what Allison thinks, too. And she intends to find out."

Martin didn't want to seem too interested, but he had to ask. "Who's Allison?"

"Vanessa's twin sister. Quite a woman. Professor of archeology at Brown. Really smart. She was a bronze medal winner on the US field hockey team at the Barcelona Olympics ten or so years ago. She flew back to Washington with me last evening. We had dinner together at Central."

Martin blasted through a light seconds after it turned to red. Two cars honked at him. He ignored them and glanced at Paul.

"What's Allison doing here?"

"She's hell-bent on finding out whom her sister went with to Anguilla and what really happened."

Oh shit, Martin thought. This gets worse and worse.

*　　*　　*

At nine in the morning Allison stepped out of Vanessa's apartment building with trepidation. She looked up and down the street. No sign of the gray Lexus.

She hailed a cab. "Hart Senate Office Building," she told the driver.

About a year ago Vanessa had introduced Allison to Susan Kramer, another staffer on the Senate Armed Services Committee. Vanessa explained, "She's my closest friend on the committee, which isn't saying much." Allison had to enlist Susan's help. She realized she had gotten lucky because Geraldine Cox was visiting her mother in Cincinnati, as she told Allison yesterday. The chief of staff wouldn't be there to thwart Allison's investigation.

From the cab, she called the committee and was put through to Susan.

"I was so sorry to hear about Vanessa," Susan said, sounding genuinely sympathetic, not like that bitch Geraldine. "I really wanted to come to the funeral, but Kevin, my seven year old, had strep. The nanny was gone and I had to take him to the doctor. Still can't believe it about Vanessa."

"Unfortunately that makes two of us."

"Can I do anything?"

"I'm in Washington. I'd like to come up to Vanessa's office to remove her personal things. And maybe talk with you a little."

"Sure. My nanny's back. I'm on a normal schedule today. When would you like to come?"

"Half an hour."

"Good. I'll be expecting you and alert security to send you up to the committee offices on the fourth floor."

Half an hour later Susan was waiting for Allison when the elevator door opened. She was in her mid-thirties, a bit chunky, with long brown hair that hung down straight, perfect white teeth, and a winning smile. She led Allison into Vanessa's office.

"Can we talk for a few minutes?" Allison said.

"I'm just finishing up something for one of the members. Why don't you gather her things first. Then I'll come back."

That was fine with Allison. She wanted to be left alone. After closing the door and looking over the office, she began to cry. She sat down and pulled together. The time for tears was over. She chided herself. She was up against some formidable people. She had to get her emotions under control.

Allison took down Vanessa's framed NYU diploma and laminated covers from *Vogue* and *Elle* from the wall and piled them on a bookcase. Then she turned to the desk. It looked surprisingly neat with only a couple of committee reports and a hearing transcript on top, which surprised her. Generally Vanessa had small stacks of paper on her desk and lots of little personal notes with "to do" lists. Before leaving for Anguilla, she must have put them in her desk drawer.

Allison opened the center desk drawer. All it contained were more committee reports and hearing transcripts, as well as office supplies: a stapler, pens, pads. No personal papers. She checked the side drawers. Same thing.

After her experience in Vanessa's apartment, Allison understood immediately what had happened. The office had been sanitized. Someone in a hurry, without time to look through Vanessa's papers to pull out the ones which identified her lover, had simply removed everything. These people were always one step ahead of her.

Allison heard a knock on the door. "Who's there?"

"Susan."

Allison opened the door and asked if they could talk in Susan's office. She didn't want Susan to focus on the cleaned-out office and set off alarms. Allison had to do this methodically.

When they were in Susan's office with coffee, Allison, who decided she could trust Susan, said, "My sister drowned in Anguilla. The police down there said she was alone. Knowing Vanessa, I'm convinced she was with a man who ran off and left her body on the beach. I wonder if she told you with whom she was going."

Susan shook her head. Allison's spirits plunged.

"I don't have a name for you, but last Thursday Vanessa seemed happy. She told me she was going to the Caribbean for the weekend. When I asked her with whom, she looked coy and said, 'One day you'll find out. And you'll be surprised.'

"Then she began waving around the ring finger on her left hand. She told me, 'I'm getting married.' When I asked her who the lucky man was, she said the same thing. 'You'll be surprised.' That's all she told me."

"I knew it," Allison said. "She went with a man."

Susan looked thoughtful. "Vanessa was strong-willed. I suppose it's possible he changed his mind about going at the last minute and, furious, she went herself."

Allison thought about that for a moment. "That's conceivable. Do you have any idea whom my sister was dating?"

"About a year ago, a nice lawyer, Paul Maltoni, from Andrew Martin's firm. He picked her up here a few times. I liked Paul and asked her why she broke up with him. She said that she wanted to marry someone very wealthy and powerful. She didn't want just a nice house in Bethesda with a basketball hoop in front and a couple of good-looking kids. 'But hey, that's my life,' I told her. She laughed and said 'it was fine for me.'"

"Whom did she date before or after Paul?"

"She was very secretive about the men she was seeing. She'd go into her office and close the door for personal phone conversations."

"You think they were people working on the Hill? Congressmen or senators?"

Susan looked down and fiddled with her wedding ring. "That was my guess. Probably married. But look, it was none of my business. People can do what they want."

Allison realized she had gotten as much as she could from Susan. "Could you do me a favor? There are a couple of framed magazine covers and a diploma in Vanessa's office. Could you ship them to me in Providence?"

"Sure."

She gave Susan the address and her contact info.

"If you think of anything else, please give me a call."

"Will do."

Riding down in the elevator, Allison thought: Next stop is the bank vault.

Then her stomach growled, telling her to get something to eat. In Vanessa's apartment all she had was yogurt and black coffee. From years of starving herself as a model, Vanessa wasn't big on grocery shopping. Allison decided to make a quick stop before going to the bank.

It was a gorgeous fall day, warm with lots of sunshine. Allison walked along the streets of Capitol Hill, in a neighborhood recently gentrified, until she spotted a small restaurant, the Silver Eagle. Inside, it had a wooden floor, a dozen tables, and a coffee bar on one side. At the midmorning hour, only two of the tables were occupied. At one, a college-age student was working at a computer and sipping coffee. At another, a man and a woman in their mid-twenties were arguing loudly about a movie. Allison sat down at a table against the wall opposite the bar.

A waitress came over, a brunette with a bob wearing braces, with a tattoo on her arm. She handed Allison a menu. She glanced at it quickly. "A tomato and mushroom omelet and a cappuccino."

While waiting for the food, she picked up a copy of the morning *New York Times* abandoned on a nearby table. When she looked at the first page, she immediately saw Andrew Martin's picture. As she read Nelson's article, she understood why Paul was headed to Martin's office early today. If Nelson's right, Martin's selection as chief justice was in deep trouble.

She opened the paper to the continuation of the article. As she did, through the corner of her eyes, she saw two Chinese men enter the restaurant. She spotted the scar on the one's left cheek. Uh-oh, she thought. Those were the two who had been in the churchyard last evening and threatened to kill her unless she broke off her investigation and left Washington.

Allison guessed they wouldn't do anything to her in the restaurant. She looked around anxiously. The bathroom was in the back. Close by was a rear exit. She hoped it was unlocked.

Allison looked down at the newspaper, pretending not to see the two Chinese men.

The waitress brought over Allison's omelet and cappuccino. Without making eye contact with the two, Allison handed her twenty dollars and began eating. When she was finishing the omelet, the waitress returned with her change. "Where's the bathroom?" Allison asked.

The waitress pointed to the back.

"Okay. Don't take my coffee," she said loudly. "I'll be right back."

Carrying her briefcase, Allison headed toward the back of the restaurant, on a beeline for the bathroom. When she was opposite it, she made a sharp right, opened the back door, and charged through it.

She was in a tiny backyard, surrounded by a six foot wooden fence. Damn. She was boxed in. Looking around, she spotted a trash can that she moved next to the fence.

As she did, she heard the Chinese man with the scar shout from the doorway, "Give me your briefcase. Or I'll shoot." She had to take a chance that he wouldn't shoot with so many witnesses in the restaurant. So she ignored him, tossed her briefcase over the fence, climbed onto the trash can and in an instant boosted herself up, while kicking out the garbage can, and she leaped over the fence.

She landed in an alley, rolling to break her fall, but she felt a shot of pain in her left leg, the one she had injured in the Olympics.

She knew she'd have trouble running, but she headed down the alley as fast as she could. She expected the Chinese man to come over the fence and follow. And he did.

He was damn fast.

Glancing over her shoulder, she saw him gaining. Even with a good leg, she'd never outrun him.

Her leg ached. Her breath was coming in short spurts. She would never get away from him. She had to try something else.

She was approaching the intersection of the alley with a street. Allison knew what to do. Still ten yards ahead of her pursuer, she turned right at the corner. He could no longer see her. She dropped down to her hands and knees on the sidewalk, making sure to tuck down her head.

As she expected, he turned the corner at full speed and went flying over her body while smacking one foot against her back. He landed ten yards away in a clump of bushes. He wasn't moving. Must be unconscious. She didn't wait to find out. This was her chance to get away.

She raised her arm. A cab stopped. Trying to shrug off the pain in her back, Allison climbed in.

"Where to?" the driver asked.

"I don't know yet. Just drive."

As he roared away, she was thinking. Vanessa's bank vault might have the mysterious CD these men wanted, but they seemed to know every move she made in Washington. She had to assume they'd be waiting for her when she came out of the bank. She had to get out of Washington, to get away from them.

The bank vault would have to wait, she decided. It would be safer for her to go to Anguilla. She might find some answers there.

"Reagan National Airport," she told the driver.

*   *   *

Xiang wasn't unconscious. Merely dazed. His face scratched, he climbed out of the clump of bushes. He was furious at himself for letting her trick him like that.

He watched her get into a cab and pull away. His eyesight was too cloudy to get the cab's ID or a license plate.

Angry and frustrated, Xiang trudged back to the restaurant where he had asked Chou to wait. He'd have to make up a story for Chou that didn't make him seem like such an incompetent. He didn't want Chou telling Hu what had happened, or Hu might call Liu and ask that Xiang be taken off the case. He'd tell Chou that when he was chasing Allison a police patrol car happened to come along, so he had to let her get away. He'd tell him that to hide from the police he drove into a clump of bushes, and that's how he scratched his face.

He thought about it for a minute. That story would work. As for Allison, Xiang was confident he'd catch up with her again. He'd put two men in front of Vanessa's apartment for surveillance around the clock.

And he had something else. From searching Vanessa's papers in her apartment, Xiang knew where Vanessa banked. If she had a vault box, chances were that's where it would be. He'd put surveillance in front of the bank to snatch Allison after she came out—hopefully with the CD.

When he had been in training, an instructor had lectured Xiang and the other trainees, "Never let your work become personal. You can't be emotional about anyone you're working with or tracking."

Xiang felt himself violating that order. Allison had just humiliated him, and he was becoming emotional about her. Once she got the CD, he vowed to gain revenge.

Meantime, Xiang had another problem. Liu had told Xiang to keep Liu personally informed of what happened in Washington. Xiang, of course, had no intention of calling Liu to report what just occurred and to tell Liu that he had lost track of Allison—his one lead for the CD. But what if the spymaster called demanding a status report before Xiang caught up with Allison again? The spymaster would demand answers. Lying and evasion would never work. Xiang would be in deep trouble.

Alexandria, Virginia

Standing at the American Airlines ticket counter, Allison was dejected once she learned how long it would take her to get to Anguilla. "I'm sorry," the agent said. "It's hard enough getting there in season, but now, you're out of season."

Allison would have to fly to Miami this afternoon, then in the morning to San Juan and connect there for the flight to Anguilla.

With two hours until her flight to Miami, Allison called the Corinthian Hotel in Anguilla where Police Commissioner Har Stevens said Vanessa had stayed. She wasn't expecting any information, but as she learned in her archeological work, there was no harm in trying. Sometimes long shots pay off. She asked to speak to the manager.

A minute later, she heard a man in a British accent say in a quavering voice, "John Burt, here."

"Hello Mr. Burt. My twin sister Vanessa was staying at your hotel when she drowned Sunday evening."

"That's right. I'm very sorry for your loss. She was a very attractive woman and a good guest."

"I want to know with whom she was staying."

There were a couple seconds of hesitation before he said, "Oh, she was staying by herself."

"Are you certain?"

"Absolutely. I keep careful tabs on my guests."

Unlike Stevens, whom Allison thought sounded convincing, Burt was tentative. He's lying, Allison was convinced.

"I'm flying down to Anguilla, Mr. Burt. I'll be there late tomorrow. I want to stay in the same room my sister had."

"Can I ask why?"

"Because we were twins. I have to experience what she did before she died. That's the only way I can get closure."

"Do you really think that's wise? It could be upsetting for you."

"How nice of you to be concerned about me." Her voice was dripping with sarcasm. "But I'm coming."

Her next call was to Paul.

"Are you okay?" he said as soon as he answered.

She considered, but rejected the idea of telling Paul about the Chinese men chasing her. She didn't want him leaning on her to break off her investigation, which she had no intention of doing.

"Completely safe. I'm at Reagan National Airport. On my way to Anguilla. I decided Washington was too dangerous. I'm hoping to get some answers there."

"Makes sense. Call me from Anguilla if I can do anything to help. When you return, immediately come to my house. You have the address and the key will be under the mat."

"Thanks, Paul. I really appreciate it."

"And be careful."

With more time to kill, she went shopping in the airport. She bought a duffel, some clothes, and toiletries.

Before boarding, she had time for another call. It was to Zahava, on the dig in Israel. "I was concerned about you," Zahava said. "But I didn't want to bother you. How are you doing?"

"As well as possible under the circumstances."

"Everyone here said to express their condolences."

"Please tell them I said thanks and that I'll get back when I can, probably in a week."

"We'll be waiting for you."

"How's the work going?"

"We've done a lot more digging, but so far without any result. After what appeared to be our initial success, people are starting to feel frustrated. I'm trying to reassure them that this is the nature of our work."

Allison understood exactly how they felt. She was digging, too, and so far not getting anywhere.

Washington

Martin, in a discussion with Paul, was having difficulty concentrating. So much was happening regarding the chief justice appointment. Arthur had called to say that Martin would soon have a meeting with President Braddock. Martin had always been able to brush aside extraneous matters and deal with the issue at hand. But not now.

Paul cleared his throat.

"Okay," Martin said. "Let's talk about the television decency case."

Paul gave Martin a PowerPoint presentation, outlining the brief, pointing out the difficult issues, and describing the most relevant judicial precedents. Martin felt as if he was grasping only about half of what Paul was saying.

At the end, Martin told Paul, "What this means is that in the next week you have a shit load of work to do. Get on top of every aspect of this case. And I'll need binders with all the important precedents. Also your synopsis for each."

Paul was scribbling. "When do you need them?"

"As soon as possible. Now let's turn to the fact issues. What's the strongest evidence for our argument on the lack of objective standards?"

Paul glanced at one of his pads. "We can point to testimony at the hearing from . . ."

The cell phone on Martin's desk rang. He picked it up and checked caller ID. Gorton in Anguilla. He flipped up the lid, "I'll be with you in a minute." Martin looked pointedly at Paul. "Sorry, I have to take this."

"I'll look through my papers."

"Do it outside the office."

When Paul was gone and the door closed, Martin turned back to Gorton. "What happened?"

"Allison Boyd, Vanessa's twin sister, is coming down here. She's arriving tomorrow and staying at the Corinthian, where the body was moved to Sunday night."

"What's she planning to do?"

"Nobody knows. I heard about it from John Burt, the manager of the Corinthian. He got a call from the sister, who questioned him aggressively. John stuck with the story."

"How'd she respond?"

"She said she was doing it because Vanessa was her twin. And she wants to stay in the same room her sister had. Weird, isn't it?"

"I don't want her to learn anything."

"You don't have to worry. I've got this sealed tight as a drum. John Burt, the policemen involved, and the medical examiner are all old friends of mine. Fortunately, Har Stevens, the police commissioner, was off island when this happened. I wouldn't have been able to control him. I'll have a couple of my guys keeping tabs on Allison from the time she arrives."

Martin recalled that some of those island people played rough. Alarmed he said, "Listen, no violence. We don't want to harm Allison."

"I'll pass the word."

"You better drive it home."

"Don't worry, Mr. Martin. I'll do it."

Martin was worried that Gorton wouldn't be able to control his men.

"If you have any expenses, I want to reimburse you."

"Oh, don't worry, Mr. Martin, my friends all love you."

Martin's mind flashed on his relationship with Gorton over the last two decades—his investing in Gorton's steel band that played at hotels and the man's charter fishing boat service. Then at Gorton's urging, his contributing to a tennis center for Anguilla kids. He'd never imagined any returns from those. But now . . .

"Well, please keep me informed."

Putting down the phone, Martin felt moisture forming under his arms. He recalled what Paul had said in the car about Allison. Damn it, this is getting worse. Who could figure this?

He felt flustered and didn't know what to do. Leave it? Take some initiative? Find some way of heading off this woman? Then, he decided. He picked up his cell phone and called Jasper's office.

"Delores, I have to speak with the senator."

"He's in a hearing now, Mr. Martin. If it's important, I'll send in a note."

"I think you better."

What a miserable fucking complication. Allison must be planning to play private eye. "Always expect the unexpected," Martin recalled Chief Justice Hall telling him when he clerked for the chief. Well, here it was. But he wouldn't just sit back. He was an activist. He'd damn well determine his own fate.

"What's up?" Jasper asked.

"We have to talk in person and ASAP."

"I'm in a hearing now."

"When's it over?"

"Four o'clock."

"I'll come to your office then."

Jasper gave a loud sigh. "Meet me at Camelot at five."

*   *   *

Sitting next to the secretary's desk while she typed, Paul wondered what the hell was happening with Martin. He'd never before asked Paul to leave when he took a call. Even when Arthur Larkin phoned from the White House. It had to be something big. Was the chief justice selection at a critical point?

While waiting to be summoned back into Martin's office, Paul checked his iPad. He had an e-mail from Diane, the associate he asked to help on Jenson's brief. "I'm making good progress," she said. "I will positively have a draft by close of business next Wednesday...Perhaps earlier."

That was good news, Paul thought. It would give him two days to revise it and make Jenson's Friday deadline.

The intercom rang. The secretary turned to Paul. "He's ready for you now."

"Thanks," Paul felt anxious.

Martin, he saw, looked markedly different than the man he'd just been conversing with. Now he seemed tense. His expression was grim, his mouth drawn shut. Beads of perspiration dotted his forehead.

"Are you okay?"

"I'm fine," Martin snapped back. "Now tell me about the evidence linking violence on television with criminal acts in the real world."

Before, Paul remembered, they were on a different issue. Martin must have forgotten. No big deal. He was ready to respond.

"In the hearing, the committee for a Safer America brought in Willie Jones, a prisoner in Maryland. He testified that he'd spent an evening watching violent television shows. And that gave him the idea of robbing somebody at an ATM machine."

"Did his testimony have any credibility?"

"Unfortunately, yes. They fed Jones some good lines. For example—"

Martin interrupted. "Okay. Move on."

Paul was taken aback by this curtness from Martin. Jesus, he's now wound tighter than piano wire.

"There was also testimony from a psychiatrist at the Harvard Medical School. He said that—"

Martin interrupted again. "We better break this off now. I've got something else I have to do. Summarize the evidence on each of the three factual issues. Send it to me by e-mail. I'll study it. Then we'll talk."

Paul hustled out, relieved to away from Martin.

On the way to his office, he thought of how different his life would be if Martin left to be chief justice. Despite the bravado he had shown with Allison at dinner, he was worried his chances of becoming partner would be diminished if Martin left.

Somehow, it would work out, he hoped.

*   *   *

Martin buzzed his secretary, "Google Allison Boyd." He recalled what Paul had told him. "She's a professor of archeology at Brown University. Print what you get and put it in an envelope."

In the cab in a light rain on the way to Camelot Martin opened the envelope. Allison Boyd's academic awards and articles were impressive. She made a real name for herself at a young age. Must be damn smart. Just what I don't need, he thought.

Even worse, she had tenacity. After several years of effort on her part, she had recently received funding to try to uncover a town from the time of King Solomon.

And on top of all that, she had been on the US Olympic team that won a bronze medal for field hockey, scoring a goal in the Barcelona Olympics. So she was physically tough.

Her bio convinced him he had to be firm with Jasper. Not like Tuesday when he'd wimped out because of Jasper's tears.

Martin didn't like Camelot and went there only when someone else selected it. A seedy joint, four blocks from the Capitol, it had opened during the Kennedy Administration. Then and now it was a hangout for lobbyists and congressmen to cut secret deals. And it was used as a rendezvous for men carrying on clandestine affairs to meet their lovers for dinner and dancing.

Entering the octopus-like structure, with alcoves branching out in several directions, Martin looked around, adjusting his eyes to the dim light. Coats of armor, spears, and other medieval paraphernalia were scattered on display. Above the bar, he noticed a painting of a large reclining nude with thick brown pubic hair, a Rubenesque figure extending her arms out toward two helmeted warriors. One of her hands held a red rose, the other a white rose. Next to it was a large painting of a ship partially submerged. A caption underneath said "LOOSE LIPS SINK SHIPS."

He spotted Jasper in a purple velvet booth across the room and hurried over. As soon as he sat down a young blonde waitress, scantily clad in a white diaphanous costume, appeared. She leaned over to place a coaster in front of him, exposing her breasts, nipples and all. "What d'ya want to drink, honey?"

"I'm having a scotch and water," Jasper said.

"Perrier for me, Martin said."

"Pellegrino."

"Whatever."

Martin looked around, feeling nervous. He was relieved that Camelot was largely deserted. No one close enough to hear them.

"I'm busy as hell," Jasper sounded annoyed. "What happened now that's so important?"

The waitress returned with his drink.

Martin began speaking softly. "I just heard from Gorton. Vanessa Boyd's sister is going to Anguilla. She'll get there tomorrow."

"Allison. She's Vanessa's twin."

"You know her?"

"Never met her. But Vanessa talked plenty about her. She said Allison's the smart twin. She's a professor at Brown."

"I pulled up her info on the Internet. She's an archaeologist, used to digging. *She will find out what happened.*"

"No, no. Not if you pay off Gorton. And have him spread money around. I'll ante up the cash."

Martin fumed. "Don't even think about that. I've already done one stupid thing. I won't compound the problem. Besides, you're being absurd. Paying off a few people on Anguilla will not stop Allison from finding out that Vanessa was with you." He paused. "And that her body was moved to avoid implicating you."

"Then I guess I'm screwed." Jasper sounded bitter. "She'll come back and call a press conference, yapping, 'let me tell you what happened to my poor innocent sister.'"

"It does not have to end up like that. You still have a way out."

His face twisted into a snarl, Jasper glared at Martin. "Yeah. What?"

"Go down there with me. Right now. We'll charter a plane. Get there and back before she arrives. We'll straighten it out. Explain to the authorities what really happened Sunday evening. We'll . . ."

Jasper's face was turning beet red. "You're still peddling that shit. I told you Tuesday night . . ." He was raising his voice. "N.F.W. No fuckin' way."

"Shhh. Keep your voice down."

"Then get the hell off this kick."

"Listen, Wes. Think for a minute about what happened. You have nothing to hide. It was an accident. Wasn't it?"

"Of course it was."

"Well, you've been in this town a long time. You know that the cover-up is what brings people down."

Jasper now had a menacing scowl. "It's all your fault."

Martin was incredulous. "You were the one screwing this bimbo. I was home having dinner."

"Don't you get sanctimonious with me. Sunday night you should have told me to go to the police, counselor."

Martin was livid, but he kept his anger in check. "I don't believe I'm hearing this."

"Then keep your ears open. I have something you'll like even less." Jasper locked eyes with Martin. "If I go down, I'm pulling you with me." He was speaking in a voice devoid of emotion, so hard and cold it cut through Martin like a knife. "You're the one responsible for the cover-up. Not me. You made the call to Gorton. I don't even know the man. You arranged to move the body to avoid a scandal which would wreck your chance to be chief justice. That's what I'll tell people."

Martin was so stunned he couldn't speak.

Jasper pointed a stubby finger at him. "Face it. You want me to fly to Anguilla to save your own ass. So you can be chief justice. At least admit it."

"That's ridiculous. I'm trying to help you."

"Are you? Think about it. If the records are corrected, the cover-up *you* engineered goes away. That's the part that's good for you. But my little fun-filled weekend will make huge headlines. Linda will blast me for adultery and divorce me. I'll lose the reelection."

"But it was at my house."

"Nobody will care about that. You lent your house to a friend. You assumed he was taking his wife. Big fucking deal."

Jasper had a point. Martin had made a terrible error, been totally stupid in calling Gorton Sunday night to move the body.

His eyes blazing with hatred, Jasper let out a surly laugh. "You want to throw me to the wolves to save your own hide. Friends don't act like that. And don't you even dream about going to Anguilla on your own. If you do that, or any word of this hits the press because of Allison or anyone else, I'll be the one going to the papers. And you'll be toast. No more chief justice. It'll all go down the drain."

Jasper made a gurgling noise to emphasize the plumbing metaphor, then he rose, left the table, and headed for the door.

Dumbfounded, Martin sat there. He couldn't believe the man. He still had to get through this somehow, but he vowed never to speak to Jasper again.

Gorton was his only chance. Gorton had to prevent Allison from learning what happened. And more than his Supreme Court appointment was at stake. So was his reputation—his ethical, well-respected life and career.

Miami and Anguilla

Allison was fit to be tied. For what must have been the twentieth time, she interrogated the American Airlines gate agent at Miami airport. "Will this plane ever take off for San Juan?"

"I'm very sorry, Miss. But our mechanics are still assessing the problem. We'll have a decision in thirty minutes."

She shook her hand and stamped her foot. "We're already four hours late. A decision? I don't want a decision. I want to get to San Juan so I can make a connection to Anguilla."

"Our agents in San Juan will assist you."

"Yeah right."

To pass the time, she reread the Anguilla portion of a Caribbean guidebook:

> The island, fifteen miles long, in a predominantly east-west direction, and two miles wide, is nestled in the eastern Caribbean close to St. Martin and home to only nine thousand residents. In the 1960s, the Anguillans persuaded England not to confer independence and force them into a federation with St. Kitts and Nevis. So the island still remains a British territory with London appointing a governor, while locals control day to day affairs.

Then she heard the announcement. "Flight 891 to San Juan is now ready for boarding."

*   *   *

As soon as she stepped off the plane in San Juan, there was more bad news. "The last nonstop to Anguilla has been cancelled," an agent told her. "We've rerouted you through St. Martin. Your plane leaves in two hours."

She wanted to scream. Is God sending me a message? Forget about Anguilla and go back to Israel?

No, she wouldn't surrender, she thought with determination. She loved her sister too much for that. Regardless of the obstacles, she'd overcome them.

*   *   *

Finally at ten after eight in the evening, Allison, riding alone with the pilot, took off in a six seater, World War II vintage prop for the ten minute flight from St. Martin to Anguilla. Flying always made her nervous, and small planes even more so.

Terrified, as they tossed around in the wind, she gripped the arm rests with white knuckles.

When the plane touched down at Wellblake Airport, it was night, with a full moon in a sky laced with clouds. Walking toward the terminal she felt the blast of balmy tropical air, still in the low eighties, making her clothing stick to her skin. She was processed quickly through emigration by a young woman with black skin and a bright smile. "Welcome to our island . . . I hope you'll enjoy your stay."

From the back of the taxi, an old beat-up white Chevy, she got her first glimpse of what she recalled another guidebook describing as "the jewel of the Caribbean, with some of the best beaches, best food, and friendliest people of any of the islands." As the cab drove on the left side, it bounced over a deserted and poorly lit road full of pot holes. She passed small houses built from cinder and wood and children playing on the road, illuminated by a light from time to time. She saw an occasional goat or dog in untamed vegetation along the side of the road. She felt very much alone and vulnerable.

The driver, a heavyset man, said, "It's good you didn't come last year on this date."

"Why's that?"

"The big one hit. Hurricane Nellie. Mon, the water six-foot high on dis road. No power. That was the mother. It blew and blew three days. Lost me whole house. Just a pile of bricks and wood. And I got a feelin' another one's gunna hit us again this year. All that global warming stuff. And real soon. How long you plannin' to stay?"

"Just a couple of days."

"Well, if she starts blowin, you take care."

"Aren't there warnings for a big storm?"

"Sometime yes. Sometime no. De biggest ones always fool dem experts. Dey think de'll goin' one direction. Dey turn and go another."

Great, Allison thought. She leaned back on the torn leather seat and closed her eyes, hoping the driver would stop talking. Mercifully, he did.

She didn't open them again until he jolted to a stop, "Corinthian Hotel."

Allison was surprised. In the guidebooks she'd seen the white Moorish Cap Jaluca Hotel that exuded quiet luxury with sweeping lines surrounded by magnificent vegetation. Allison figured her sister would surely have stayed at a place like that. But there was nothing luxurious about the Corinthian. It looked just adequate with three stories, its pink stones freshly painted for the season. The front had sparse vegetation, lit by a row of lights, about half of which were out, running along the path from the driveway to the entrance. Vanessa would never have picked this place. But her lover may have.

As Allison stepped out of the cab, she noticed a man bounding toward her from the hotel almost as if he'd been shot from a gun, short and squat with tan skin, an open mouth, smiling, showing off large ivory teeth.

"I'm John Burt, the manager here."

"How do you do, Mr. Burt. I'm Allison Boyd. My sister . . ."

"I know, Missy. A terrible accident. We spoke yesterday on the phone."

"I need to talk to you some more."

"Sure, sure, but first, I'll get you settled in your room."

While he carried her duffel, Allison followed him inside. Except for the two of them, the hotel seemed empty. She thought of a Stephen King novel about a deserted hotel. Her knees wobbled.

"You still want your sister's room, Missy?" Burt was smiling showing those teeth.

"Please."

"Room six it is. You come with me."

They climbed a wide wooden staircase with a polished railing. Room six, Allison noted, had been freshly painted and had a musty smell. Burt put down her bag on a luggage rack.

"Is there air conditioning?"

"Here it is." He flung open the French doors leading to a wrought iron patio, a breeze blowing in from the Caribbean. Looking out, under the moon, Allison saw lapping waves splashing against the sand.

"You come down when you're ready, Missy."

She surveyed the room. Thinking that Vanessa spent her last days here, she felt a surge of sadness and began crying. Then, seeing the king-sized bed strengthened her resolve. Vanessa hadn't been alone. Sadness gave way to anger.

Who's the bastard who killed her? Or watched her die? Then took off like a thief in the night?

Burt was waiting for her in the dining room, facing the sea, a wall of French doors open to a wooden deck over the sand. He was alone except for a tall thin islander in a white jacket standing behind the bar wiping glasses.

"How about a rum punch, Missy? The specialty of the house."

"That sounds good. Please don't call me Missy."

"Lon, two rum punches."

When seated at a table with the drinks, Allison asked, "Where are the other guests?"

"Our season doesn't begin until the middle of December. Also hurricanes hit now."

"So it's just me in the hotel?"

"For tonight. But I ordered a lobster for you. Cook will grill it in a little while. There's nothing so good as our lobsters."

"Listen to me, Mr. Burt . . ."

"Please, you call me John."

"John, then." Her mouth was dry. She paused to sip the drink. Wow, potent stuff. "Listen, John, I'm not here for a vacation. I want to know what happened to my sister."

"Okay, sure."

"Good, then tell me."

"You know, I really liked your sister. Very classy lady. She called a couple weeks ago. She wanted a quiet place for a long weekend. To relax. Too much tension in Washington. So she came. Arrived Saturday afternoon."

"Who was with her?"

"Nobody, missy. Uh, Miss Boyd."

"You're sure?"

"I met her taxi. Like I did with yours tonight."

"So tell me, what did she do during those two days?"

He waved his arm toward the sea. "Mostly she laid on the beach. 'Working on my suntan,' she said."

That did sound like Vanessa "Did she meet anybody?"

"She ate alone right here. All her meals."

"Did she do anything unusual?"

"Well . . ."

Was he hesitating? "Tell me."

"Both nights she went down to the beach. She said she likes to swim at night. I told her be careful." He paused, then dropped his voice. "She was so beautiful. I watched her from a window upstairs."

"And?"

He looked down.

"Go on."

"The first night she took off her bathing suit. Lovely, lovely body. Truly gorgeous. When she came out of the water, she dried off, put on her suit, and came back in."

"And you were staring at her the whole time?"

He looked at his hands.

Thinking of this creepy man leering at Vanessa infuriated her. But then, wouldn't most men do exactly the same thing?

"You want me to continue?"

She nodded.

"Sunday night, she did the same thing. While she was out on the beach, the phone rang. I was gone maybe twenty minutes." He sounded apologetic. "When I got back to my window, she was stretched out on the sand. Not moving."

"What did you do then?"

"I ran out. She looked like she was dead."

"Why did you think that?"

"I touched her. I mean her pulse. Just her pulse."

"And then?"

"I called the police. They told me not to move her body. Just watch it. They will send people. Then two young policemen came. They took her away in their ambulance."

She slowly sipped up her drink. The story was ludicrous. Vanessa wouldn't swim naked at night by herself. With men, true, she could be reckless and uninhibited. But alone, or even with Allison, she was careful. If she was with a man and high on booze or pot, she might well have gone skinny dipping, as she'd done as a teenager in Hueston Woods Lake. But her being found in the nude, stretched out on the beach, just didn't add up.

"I want to talk to Har Stevens, the police chief. Will you call him for me?"

"Now?"

"Yes, at home if necessary."

He shook his head. "Har went to St. Martin for the evening. You'll have to wait until tomorrow morning."

Now she felt a cold edge in his voice. "What about the two young policemen?"

"They won't talk to you until Har tells them to."

"So I can't do anything else this evening?"

He raised his hand and pointed toward the kitchen. A woman in a black uniform carried out a tray with a grilled lobster, salad, and French fries. She brought another rum punch and a bottle of water.

Burt stood up. "I'll leave you to eat."

She looked at the lobster. "What happened to the claws?"

"Our lobsters don't have claws. Up north, they need them to defend themselves. Ours is a kinder place."

"It wasn't for my sister."

He walked away. She hadn't eaten all day, she realized, and she needed her strength. The lobster was sweet and tasty. But after three bites, the potent rum drink hit her. She couldn't keep her eyes open.

Stumbling up the stairs, she thought about Paul. How terrific her dinner with him had been. And how helpful he wanted to be. Was she crazy coming down here when she could be back with him?

Washington

Xiang liked Italian food. He had never eaten it until he came to the United States to attend Carnegie Mellon, but from the first time that Kelly Cameron took him to Giovanni's in Oakland, he couldn't get enough of it. He was particularly fond of the pastas with shrimp and other seafood, but just about any dish worked for him.

He and Kelly had a plan for one day after his graduation to travel throughout Italy, but the plan for that trip died when Liu squashed Xiang's romance with Kelly.

What didn't die, though, was Xiang's fondness for Italian food. In Washington, he particularly liked Posto on 14th Street near Logan Circle where Massimo, the chef from the high-end, glamorous Tosca, ran a stylish Italian *cucina* with colorful art on the walls.

Xiang had left the Embassy late and at ten o'clock that evening he sat in a corner table in the still crowded Posto with a glass of Chianti munching a pizza while waiting for his seafood pasta.

As he ate, Xiang thought about the call he had gotten late that afternoon from Jasper, setting a meeting for tomorrow at 5:00 a.m. in Rock Creek Park. Xiang wondered what prompted the meeting. Jasper had sounded tense and distraught, but since Vanessa's drowning in Anguilla, that was how Jasper always sounded.

Deep in thought, Xiang, not paying attention to his surroundings, suddenly felt a tug on his arm.

He looked up and saw . . . No it couldn't be. It was an apparition, a trick of his mind, an illusion . . .

He rubbed his eyes. She was still there.

"Xiang, it's Kelly Cameron."

He was too stunned to speak. She was even more exquisite then he remembered. The long blonde hair. The perfectly sculpted face. The sparkling blue eyes.

"Don't you remember me?" she said. "From Carnegie Mellon."

"Of course I remember you. What are you doing in Washington?"

"I'm with the FBI. At headquarters. And you?" She was giving him that gorgeous smile.

"I'm the Assistant Economic Attaché at the Chinese Embassy."

"We're both serving our governments. Are you married?"

"No. You?"

"Married and divorced. I have a little girl. I see you still like Italian food," she said, deftly changing the subject.

"You don't look any different."

"You too."

He held out his hand toward the empty chair at the table. "Would you like to join me?"

She pointed across the room toward the door where a man, tall and muscular who looked to Xiang as if he was an FBI agent, was standing impatiently, holding a woman's coat.

"Thanks, but I just had dinner with a friend. We were sitting over there." She motioned across the crowded room. "I didn't see you until we were on the way out. I had to come by and say hello."

"I'm so glad you did."

"It was nice seeing you."

She turned and gracefully walked away.

I should have asked for her card, Xiang thought. But he didn't need that. He could easily locate her phone number at the FBI.

He watched the brute at the door help Kelly with her coat. Then put his arm around her as they left the restaurant.

Even though Kelly worked for the FBI, she might be willing to see him again. He could easily buy a brand-new cell phone in a shop on the street. If he paid cash for it, the embassy security people wouldn't have any way of finding out.

Sure it would be risky, but he had given enough to China. He was entitled to do something for himself.

Not now, he decided. The time isn't right. With all this Jasper business still unfolding and her at the FBI. But it would be over soon. Then he'd call her.

After dinner, Xiang went home to his empty apartment. He had to be up early to meet Jasper, but he couldn't sleep. All he could think about was Kelly.

I'll call her tomorrow.

He thought about it a little more and changed his mind. No not until he was finished with Jasper and Allison.

*   *   *

Xiang checked his watch. It was ten after five in the morning and still dark. He stood in the bone-chilling cold under a clear sky and a full moon in Rock Creek Park waiting for Jasper to show. Where the hell was he? He'd never been late before. Xiang wondered once more what happened that prompted Jasper to ask for the meeting.

To keep warm, Xiang ran in place on the muddy path, even though his whole body ached, and he still had a headache as a result of his hard landing after he flew over Allison Boyd's body. He had been a fool letting her trip him up like that. When he finally had the CD, he'd get even with her. But first he had to find her.

Xiang saw the senator approaching, breathing heavily.

"Yesterday you told me you expected Allison to lead you to the CD. Didn't you?" Jasper sounded belligerent.

"That's right," Xiang replied warily.

Jasper laughed. "Fat chance of that happening. I'll bet you lost track of her. Am I right?"

"Yes," Xiang said sheepishly.

Sneering, Jasper said, "Would you like to know where she is?"

Xiang realized how much he hated Jasper.

"Of course."

"She's on her way to Anguilla, trying to find out who was with Vanessa."

Xiang was relieved to hear where Allison was. He had been terrified Liu would call him for a status report and he'd have to admit that he had no idea where Allison was. Now he had a dilemma. He could go to Anguilla or send someone there to follow Allison, hoping she'd lead them to the CD. He had a strong belief that this tenacious twin sister would sooner or later find the CD. He figured she understood Vanessa. She'd be able to find it for him.

Perhaps Vanessa had left the CD in Anguilla. Jasper had said he'd searched Vanessa's things after she drowned. But in his state he couldn't be depended on. By checking airplane manifests Xiang would learn when Allison was returning to Washington. If she had the CD, he'd snatch it from her when she was back here. No point going to Anguilla.

If it wasn't there, he was convinced it was in Vanessa's bank vault. He'd follow Allison to the vault and grab it once she returned. Either way, he'd get that CD.

Besides, Xiang doubted there were many Chinese people on Anguilla. He or his men would stand out. No, going there wasn't an option.

Even though all Xiang cared about was the CD, he still had to appear as if he wanted to help Jasper prevent Allison from finding out that the senator had been with her in Anguilla. "I could send people to Anguilla," Xiang said. "To persuade her to come back to Washington before she uncovers your involvement."

After the words were out of his mouth, Xiang held his breath. He had no intention of doing this. If Jasper asked him to, Xiang would lie and say he did and they lost her.

"No need to do that. Andrew Martin, whose house I used, has local contacts. He's already set it up. Hopefully it will work. If not, I'll have a problem. And that means you'll have a problem."

Jasper made it sound like a threat. Xiang didn't like that.

Jasper took a breath and continued. "That's why I wanted you to know she went to Anguilla."

"I appreciate the information. I'll be waiting for Allison when she comes back to Washington. Now let's talk about the Pentagon's five-year plan. When will you have that for me?"

"Are all you Chinese so persistent? Is that why you're getting ahead in the world?"

Xiang kept his anger in check. Jasper frequently made ethnic slurs. Just one more of his disgusting personal characteristics. "I'm doing my best for you to get the CD. I want to know when I'll get the five year plan."

"Goddamn it, Xiang," Jasper hissed in an angry voice. "I'm tired of you harping on the Pentagon's plan. You Chinese are never satisfied. I've given you plenty of good stuff, including data on a new generation of American missiles, the results of our defense planning with Japan, and the plans to increase our Marine contingency in Australia. And lots more."

"For which we've paid you plenty."

"Yeah, but money only goes so far. My neck's on the line. I could get caught. This plan is a very sensitive document. I'm no longer sure that I want to give it to you."

Xiang had a sinking feeling in his stomach. Oh no. Please no. Xiang would be in deep trouble with Liu if he couldn't deliver that document. Jasper was a bully and obnoxious. Xiang decided his best course was to push back on Jasper.

"My neck's on the line, too. I'm doing everything I can to get that CD. If you're not prepared to get me the five-year plan, then all bets are off for the CD. I'll let Allison find it and hang you with it. You'll go to jail alone. Minister Liu and I will be in China. Nobody will be able to touch us there." Xiang was looking right at Jasper. "I can play what you Americans call hardball, too."

Jasper sighed. "Okay. Today's Friday. Monday morning I've scheduled a secret executive session for my committee. The secretary of defense promised to deliver a copy of the plan to my house Sunday evening. We'll meet here Monday morning."

"Bring the document with you."

"I will, but you'll have to deliver the CD to me then. That's our deal."

"Don't worry. I will."

"Good. Now I have to take off."

When Jasper left, Xiang ran on the path while contemplating his next move. Now that he knew where Allison was, he'd go back to the embassy and call Liu with a status report. At least Jasper had been good for something.

As for Allison, eventually she would return to Washington, with or without the CD, he was convinced. And if she didn't locate the CD in Anguilla, she'd go to that bank vault. He simply had to know when she was returning.

Xiang stopped running and picked up a twig, which he snapped into several pieces.

Airline computers. That was the answer. At the embassy they had the technology to hack into those computers.

Sooner or later, she'd book a return flight. He'd keep checking the carriers flying out of Anguilla and into Washington until he obtained her flight itinerary. He'd be waiting for Allison at the Washington airport.

*   *   *

Xiang was in the embassy communications room on a secure phone. Liu answered on the first ring.

"It's Xiang, Minister Liu."

"Yes," was the curt reply.

"I want to give you a status report."

"Do you have the five-year plan?"

"Jasper will have it Sunday evening. He'll give it to me Monday morning at five o'clock Washington time."

"Are you confident of that?"

"Yes, sir. I am."

"I detect hesitation in your voice."

"I had a tough discussion with Jasper. He was resisting giving it to me. I turned him around by threatening to stop blocking Allison from getting the CD. He'll do it now."

"You could threaten to kill his wife and children."

Xiang couldn't believe Liu was raising such a dreadful possibility. How did Xiang end up in this situation?

"As I said, I now believe he will give it to me on Monday morning."

"Well, you better be right. I can't emphasize how important the Pentagon's five-year plan is to us."

Xiang was tempted to remind Liu how much valuable information Jasper had already given them, but he knew Liu would regard that as a sign of weakness that Xiang wouldn't be able to deliver the document. Liu didn't tolerate weakness.

"You will have it on Monday," Xiang said.

"What about the CD?"

"Allison Boyd has gone to Anguilla to try and find out what happened to her sister. Also to search for the CD."

"Are you following her there?"

Xiang took a deep breath. "I thought it made more sense to remain here, keep a close watch on the airplane manifests, and snatch her when she returned. If she has the CD, I'll grab it. If she goes to her sister's bank vault, I'll snatch her and the CD when she leaves the bank."

"Why not go to Anguilla?"

"I'll stand out there. I'll never be able to control the situation. Also Jasper's friend, Andrew Martin, whose house he used, has good contacts in Anguilla. They're committed to making certain Allison doesn't get any information. I think that makes more sense."

There was a long pause.

Finally, Liu said, "Are you too lazy to go to Anguilla? Or afraid of those Island people?"

"No sir. That's not it at all."

"Well, you better get hold of that CD." Liu was shouting now. "If it fell into the hands of the American media, that would do the People's Republic of China enormous damage. Are you too stupid to understand what I'm telling you?"

Xiang struggled mightily to keep his anger in check. This was all Liu's fault. There wouldn't be a CD if he hadn't been careless in Tokyo. Now the Minister was tearing into Xiang about it.

Xiang kept his cool. "As I told you Minster Liu, I believe it would be more productive for me to remain in Washington and move in on Allison as soon as she returns."

"Okay, do it your way, but you better be right about this. If not you'll pay for it."

*   *   *

Showtime, Martin thought. He had to go to the White House this morning for his interview with the president. What would Braddock be asking him? Martin felt nervous. Hell, he was never nervous—not for Supreme Court arguments or client presentations. So why now? But he knew why. The nomination for chief justice meant more to him than anything else in life.

Leaving the office, he stopped in the men's room to straighten his red silk tie with small yellow squares. His good luck tie—he'd worn it to the last six Supreme Court arguments. And he'd won them all. He chose a muted striped shirt, pale green with thin red and yellow strands. I'm like one of those baseball players, he thought, who keeps wearing the same thing when he's in the midst of a winning streak. No oral argument today, but I need all the help I can get.

The *Times* had published a retraction of the Guantanamo article. It appeared on page A7, which irked the hell out of Martin, but it was still there.

Half an hour later, waiting outside of the Oval Office, its door closed, Martin thought about the other times he'd been here. Always representing a client, once the French Government; once the Chinese; other times an American based industrial or financial firm, usually involving serious international or national repercussions. He felt odd today, representing himself.

A buzzer rang.

"You can go in, Mr. Martin," a secretary said.

As he opened the door, it struck Martin how austere this room was, with its plain dignity befitting the power of its occupant. So different from the grandeur and ostentatiousness of the Elysee office of the French President.

Walking on the thick powder blue carpet toward the presidential seal at the center, Martin looked around. Most imposing was the dark wooden desk with thick legs that curled at the bottom which he knew had been used by several other presidents, including Franklin Roosevelt. Two black leather chairs were in front of it. Behind it, was a credenza flanked by an American flag with pictures of the president's family, two married sons and four grandchildren, just in front of the three floor-to-ceiling bulletproof windows facing the south lawn.

He'd read that all the furniture was by American craftsmen in North Carolina. Off to one side was an informal meeting area with an upholstered sofa, four chairs, a coffee table, and a couple of end tables with lamps.

Braddock was standing next to his desk examining a document with Arthur. Then the president glanced up and moved in Martin's direction.

Braddock looked, Martin thought, like the consummate politician. At sixty, he was tall, broad-chested, carrying a few extra pounds, with a warm smile exuding charisma and self-confidence. His hair, still thick, was gray and wavy. The president stuck out his hand, shaking Martin's in a powerful grip, while reaching over and clasping Martin's arm in what had become the Braddock trademark handshake.

"Arthur tells me that you're the best lawyer in America."

"I'm happy Arthur feels that way, Mr. President."

Braddock motioned to the conference area. "Let's sit down over there. We'll be more comfortable."

Martin found himself relaxing. Not too much, he told himself. Have to keep that edge sharp.

The president was looking squarely at Martin. "Why do you want this job?"

Martin felt as if he'd been struck. But he was ready.

"To make a difference for the country. I'm a moderate on political and legal issues, and I worry that a narrow conservative majority has hijacked the court for their social issue agenda. As chief justice, I'd be determined to change this divisiveness. Do I think it will be easy, given the strong views of the members?" Martin paused. "No. Of course not. Will I succeed? Well, I am known for a fair bit of succeeding."

"Have you ever been involved in politics? Run for elected office? Or actively supported any candidates?"

"No, sir. I vote, of course, registered as an independent. And I've contributed money to presidential and congressional candidates from both parties."

Arthur interjected. "An approach which has helped your legal business."

"I won't deny that it has, but it's what I believe. If you ask me how I'll vote on a case involving, say, abortion, I'll tell you, Mr. President, I don't know. It'll depend upon the facts of the specific case. I will try, insofar as possible, to break free of my own personal views. Whether I can do that with a hundred percent rate of success, I don't know. But I promise that I'll try."

Braddock's slightly creased face revealed nothing. God, he's like a sphinx. Martin thought. Looking at him, I have no idea how I'm doing.

"Let me raise a practical issue," the president said. "The choice has come down to you, Judge Corbett, and Judge Butler. They have both been judges in appellate courts for some time. I assume you met both of them somewhere along the way in your legal career."

"Yes, I've argued before both of their courts. They each decided a case in my favor."

"Okay, here's the question. Arthur's impressed with both of their legal abilities, as well as yours. And they've both had experience judging all kinds of cases. You haven't been a judge. Should this experience, do you think, weigh in their favor?"

What a helluva tough question. Martin paused. How to frame his answer? "I don't think so, sir. Judging involves evaluating legal issues and facts, then making a decision based on them. I and other lawyers, and I think Arthur will readily agree, make such decisions every day."

"How about the fact that Butler as chief judge on a federal court of appeals has had experience administering a court system. Should that give him an edge?"

"Let me respond to your question this way, Mr. President. The chief justice has responsibilities within the court that include assignment of opinion writing as well as management of the docket. He's also head of the federal judicial system with a budget in excess of five billion. And he has to set guidelines for all of that. For years, I too have been managing a large organization with several hundred lawyers, perhaps a thousand support people in six offices in four countries. And I've chaired a five-member management committee. Sometimes I love doing it. Sometimes it's frustrating as all get-out. So I think my experience in administration and management far surpasses that of Judge Butler."

Now Braddock nodded his head. Thank God, Martin thought.

"Let's talk about Guantanamo," the president said.

Martin felt a tremor in his gastric tract.

"When I read that story in the *Times*, I didn't think it should be a problem. And I told Arthur that. After all, you're a lawyer. Our system protects accused individuals caught up in that system, whether they're from Iraq or Detroit, by entitling them to legal counsel. Then I received calls from a bunch of senators, including Kendall from Alabama, and some of my own supporters, urging me to take your name off the list. Personally, I'm not inclined to scratch you because of this. But I'm a realist. And I'm practical. I won't nominate someone who can't be confirmed."

Martin's heart was pounding.

"On the other hand, Arthur tells me that it's Kendall who's leading the charge for Butler and the campaign against you based on Guantanamo. Now I've only been in Washington three years, but politics here is not all that different from Albany. I figure Kendall may well be overstating the opposition. So I made some soundings of my own among key senators and members of the Judiciary Committee. I also consulted my party leadership. We had one-on-one frank discussions, away from that horse trading on the Hill."

"And?" Martin couldn't stop himself from asking.

"Well, the *Times* correction this morning did help, even if it was buried in a back page. But to get to the bottom line, I now believe Guantanamo won't preclude you from getting confirmed. So I'm taking the issue off the table."

Martin, who had been holding his breath, finally exhaled. "I'm very happy to hear that, Mr. President."

"Now, let's talk about something I do care about," Braddock said, narrowing his eyes. "Personal character. Integrity. You, Corbett, and Butler all sailed through the FBI interviews, but I fear those aren't worth much. All of you have the top ranking from the ABA review committee. No surprise there. And from what I've learned, the three of you have led unblemished personal lives."

Braddock coughed, cleared his throat and continued. "I've been around enough to know that you, Judge Corbett, and Judge Butler, like everybody else, me included, have some things you'd like to keep hidden. But those are things I want to know about, have to know about, if I'm nominating you to be chief justice. And you've been around Washington a long time. A lot longer than I. Or Arthur, for that matter. You know how brutal the senate confirmation process can be. I don't want . . ." Braddock was now carefully emphasizing each word. "I cannot let myself and my high office be embarrassed by my nominee during the confirmation process. I will not be placed in the position of admitting that I didn't know about these matters and then have to decide whether to withdraw the nomination. Am I making myself wholly clear?"

Martin felt a pang about Anguilla. This was exactly the kind of thing Braddock was talking about. If this came out after his nomination,

Braddock would be furious. But if he were to tell him now, he'd be finished.

He swallowed hard. "I have nothing like that."

"I sure hope not. Arthur tells me you're the most ethical lawyer he's ever met."

"A backhanded compliment if I ever heard one," Martin smiled.

"He says you don't even cheat on tennis line calls." They all laughed. "According to Arthur, unlike a lot of top lawyers, you don't play dirty, don't get down in the mud and get away with what you can, attacking your opponents personally. I gather that you and Arthur were adversaries in a big case."

"That's right."

"And he ended up feeling that way. I like that about an individual. We need more of it."

Arthur interjected, "Let me tell you about the process at this point."

Martin was listening intently.

"We're planning an announcement one week from today. That could change depending on the president's schedule. It'll be accompanied by a ceremony at ten in the morning, here in the White House. I'll let you know. Either way."

Braddock added, "One of my aides told me they're making book on this in Las Vegas."

"That wouldn't surprise me. They do on everything else. What are the odds right now?"

"I don't know what they are in Vegas. Here in Washington, I'd say too close to call."

Anguilla

Knocked out from the potent rum punch, Allison slept until almost ten in the morning. After taking a couple of Tylenols for her splitting headache followed by black coffee, a croissant, and some pineapple, she hardly felt ready to pick up her investigation, but she forced herself to go out.

Half an hour later, she was in a rented gray Ford Escort with a map of Anguilla. How would she find her way? The Hertz agent had said very few of the roads had marked names. Well never mind, first stop, police headquarters.

She found Police Commissioner Har Stevens waiting in his office. He was a tall, heavyset figure in his mid-fifties with light brown skin, a narrow mustache, and a meticulously clean and pressed blue uniform. He offered her coffee, which she accepted, while trying to keep her emotions under check. Can't come on too strong, she told herself.

A window air conditioner was chugging furiously, making noise, and dripping water into a bucket. They must be operating on a tight budget, she thought. Paint was peeling and chipping on the walls. The only furniture was an ancient wooden desk and two straight-back chairs, some British cast-offs old enough to be called antiques. And the odor of cigarette smoke filled the room.

"I'm very sorry about your loss," he said in a kindly voice.

"I still can't believe my sister's dead."

"I gather you came because you suspect foul play."

"I don't know what to think, Mr. Stevens."

He paused to light a cigarette, then leaned back. "You have to understand some things about our island. We have nine thousand people, but only sixty-five police officers. That's because we have almost no crime. I'll bet you can't name another place with a smaller resident to police ratio. Here we all leave our houses unlocked. Still, disputes do arise. Some people drink too much and become violent. We have our share of traffic accidents. Our senior officers, myself included, have all been trained in England. So we consider ourselves professionals."

"That sounds well and good, but tell me what happened with my sister."

He took a puff, then put down the cigarette in an ash tray. Fingering his mustache, he opened a small folder and looked at what had to be a report. "Last Sunday evening when this occurred, I was off island in St. Barts. My deputy, Charles Prince, was on duty. I have his report right here. It says that Sunday evening at 11:46 he received a phone call at home from John Burt at the Corinthian. Burt told Prince that one of his guests had drowned. She was lying on the beach."

"What did Prince do?"

"He dispatched two of our best officers in an ambulance to the Corinthian. They were told to investigate your sister's room and the beach area and then bring her body back to the morgue."

"What'd they find?"

"No indication of foul play. And nothing suspicious in the room."

"Did a doctor examine her?"

"Yes, Brendon McGlothin, our unofficial medical examiner. He concurred that it was an accidental drowning."

Allison pointed. "What's in that folder?"

"Our report." He pushed it over. "You're welcome to examine it."

Allison read through each of the three pages twice. Everything was consistent with what Burt and Stevens had told her. "Can I talk to your two men?"

"Of course. We've nothing to hide. Prince is outside of the office on assignment. If you want to talk to him he should be back in an hour."

"No, I think the two on the scene should suffice."

The two strapping cops introduced as Chester Wells and Malcolm Harper seemed to be around twenty-five and were wearing polished police blues. Harper looked composed and Wells uneasy. Allison would have liked to ask Stevens to leave, but she knew better.

Malcolm politely began, "If I may, when we got to the Corinthian, and we saw your sister on the beach . . ." He lowered his eyes, embarrassed. "We immediately covered her with a blanket."

Allison liked him. "Thank you. I appreciate that."

"We took her body to the morgue. Then Dr. McGlothin came."

"What about her things in the room?"

"We later went back and collected them."

"Did you see anything indicating that a man had been with her?"

Malcolm looked down, shuffling his feet. "No, nothing like that."

"No man's sandals or bathing suit?"

"No ma'am. Just her own stuff, really nice stuff."

Chester Wells, she noted, was looking away, remaining silent. I'm not sure I believe what Malcolm's telling me, she thought.

As soon as the two cops had gone, she told Stevens, "I would like to see Dr. McGlothin."

"You have a car?"

She nodded.

"I'll give you directions."

"Will you please call first and check where he is?"

"I've already asked him to stay at home, unless he has an emergency."

Getting to McGlothin's was a twenty-minute straight shot. A handsome, gray haired, ruddy-faced Scot in his seventies, he was waiting for her at a sleek villa on a slight rise overlooking the most spectacular beach Allison had ever seen. It seemed to stretch on and on. It held soft white sand, shimmering blue-green water, and not more than a half dozen people in sight.

"Bren," as he asked to be called, led her to a veranda with a view of the water. A table was set for two.

"I hope I'm not disturbing you."

"Not in the least. Actually, I'd be grateful if you'd have lunch with me. I don't get many visitors, particularly this time of year."

"And Mrs. McGlothin?"

"She passed about ten years ago. Then I moved here for most of the year. I love this island. Greatest people in the world. They've been here for thousands of years. No one's sure how they got here or from where. Happily, the Europeans didn't put down sugar plantations. The soil's not good enough. And there are no minerals to plunder. So Anguilla never got caught up in that awful slavery business. Its development's been minimal. There are no casinos. You're on one of the few island paradises in the world. But keep that to yourself, or we'll soon be overrun by tourists."

When lunch, a crayfish salad, was served, she asked him about his examination of her sister.

"She was stunning. One of God's finest creations. Her drowning made me so sad."

Allison felt a surge and wanted to cry, but she bit her lip hard and the feeling passed.

"I made only an external exam. There were no wounds or bruises—nothing like that. But I didn't go inside her to check bodily fluids. There was no lab work. It wasn't necessary."

"And?"

"It was an accidental drowning." He sighed. "I've seen enough such cases to recognize one. People don't give the water the respect it deserves." He put his fork down and pointed to the sea to make his point. "Unless there's a storm, we don't get huge surf. So it's easy to delude yourself that it's no more dangerous than a bathtub. Unfortunately, we get powerful riptides."

"Was there a storm last Sunday night?"

"No. It was a fine starry night, but . . ." He hesitated.

"Tell me, please."

"Well, your sister had been drinking and smoking marijuana as well. I could see it in her eyes. I didn't need a blood test. Was she a starlet or a model?"

"She had been."

"I thought so. What about you?"

Allison laughed. "She had all the looks in the family."

"I would not say that."

While he paused to eat, Allison thought about what he'd said. Surprisingly she was believing him. He had sounded sincere, and as he spoke, he was looking at her. Maybe she had been too hard on Stevens and those two young cops. Maybe she was one who was wrong.

"What do you do?" he asked.

"I teach archeology at Brown University in Providence."

"What's your area?"

"The Bible and uncovering facts related to its authenticity. I was in Israel on a dig when your police called me."

"Interesting. Tell me about it, your dig in Israel."

With nothing left to ask about Vanessa, Allison went through the motions while she finished her salad. But her heart wasn't in it. She declined dessert and thanked the affable doctor for his time.

As she was rising to leave, he said, "I doubt there's anything more here for you to learn. You have a wonderful life ahead of you. I hope you'll soon go back and resume it."

Driving to the Corinthian she stopped and pounded her fist on the steering wheel. She'd traveled more than a thousand miles for nothing.

A small boy, around six, darted into the road, chasing a ball. Allison slammed on the brakes. Behind her, a beige van from LIME, the local phone company, screeched to a halt to avoid rear-ending her. The ball had disappeared under her car. She got out to help the child retrieve it. "You a nice lady," he called out.

Approaching the Corinthian, she asked herself whether she could have been wrong. It felt so damn peculiar, Vanessa coming alone. But then she thought about what Susan had said. Suppose Vanessa was planning to come with a man who she expected to marry, and at the last minute he cancelled. If she had the airline ticket, she might have gone alone to show him. And maybe she felt she had to get away.

Allison thought about the Chinese men who had been pursuing her and their desperate search for this mysterious CD. Perhaps Vanessa had been involved over her head in something serious with a Chinese group in Washington and that's why she had come to Anguilla—to escape from them, at least for a few days to regroup.

Definitely a possibility. Made sense.

Slowly, she trudged up the stairs to her room. In the corridor a maid, wide in the hips dressed in a black uniform, was mopping the wooden floor and blocking Allison's way. The disinfectant odor was strong.

Allison waited for the maid to tell her to pass.

"I aired out your room. It was musty."

"I appreciate that, but I'm going home now."

"I hope it wasn't too bad last night."

"No, not too bad." Allison sighed and took out the key.

"Always like that, musty at the beginning of the season. You're the first one since last June."

Allison felt her key drop with a thud on the floor. "What'd you say?"

"You're the first person in this room six since June."

"How do you know that?"

"My sister Rose and I do all the cleaning in this hotel. We know which rooms are taken."

"You're sure?"

"About what?"

"That no one occupied this room last weekend."

"What you mean? Of course, I'm sure."

"Then which room did my sister have here last weekend?"

"Your sister?"

Allison took Vanessa's passport from her purse and showed the picture to the maid, who shook her head from side to side.

"Last weekend there were no guests in the hotel. They were hoping for reservations; and Rose and I were planning to work. But no one booked. On Thursday, Mr. Burt called and told us not to come in. The hotel would be empty over the weekend."

"You're sure?"

The maid, apparently fed up, looked away and resumed her mopping.

Back in her room, Allison went out to the balcony. Staring at the beach and the sea beyond, she tried to sort out what she'd just heard. So then everyone she'd spoken to had been lying. All smoothly orchestrated, but one big lie.

She'd assumed that Vanessa had stayed here, but not alone. So even that was wrong. Then where did they stay?

Eager to confront John Burt, she pounded her fist into the palm of her hand and hurried toward the door. With her hand still on the knob, she caught herself. What could she hope to accomplish with Burt? He'd pressure the maid, who hadn't been clued in, and she'd change her story. Besides, it would be better not to tell Burt. As long as *they* didn't know that she knew, she could still move about freely and maybe track down the bastard. She'd have to make it look as if she'd accepted *their* story. Maybe she'd tell Burt she was staying on a few days to recover.

Then it hit her. Whenever she'd traveled with Vanessa, her sister always insisted on dining in the finest restaurants, a habit acquired in her modeling days.

Allison gathered up the guidebooks and the map and went down to the beach. On a chaise, on the deserted pure white sand, she identified the four top restaurants: CuisinArt Resort, Cap Juluca, Viceroy, and Hibernia. I'll wait until they open for dinner, she thought.

*   *   *

Better for John Burt not to know where she was going. So when he was on the phone, she slipped out a side door. On her way to the car, she noticed a familiar beige LIME van with two men inside who appeared to be sleeping.

CuisinArt reminded her of Beverly Hills transplanted to the Caribbean. She showed the maître d' Vanessa's picture and received only a blank stare. After repeating that scene at Cap Juluca and Viceroy, she felt so tense she had to stop and take deep breaths. Maybe this was not a great idea. But she would not give up, not yet.

Hibernia was about half an hour away, she estimated, on the eastern side of the island. Night had fallen and the wind was whipping up the trees. Without any warning, the skies opened and a torrential downpour pounded on the little car. It rained harder than any time she could ever remember. She slowed to a crawl, the road a watery blur.

Thinking it too dangerous to keep going, she pulled over to wait for a break in the rain. Glancing in the rearview mirror, she saw another set of headlights pull over behind her. After fifteen minutes, the rain still hadn't abated. The wind was now blowing hard enough to rock the car. She hoped to hell this wasn't the hurricane the taxi driver had been predicting. She turned on the radio for weather news. All she heard was crackling static.

Switching on the overhead light, she checked the map. The turn-off should be about half a mile ahead on the left. She decided to chance it. No telling how long the storm would last. Pulling out, she checked the mirror. The vehicle she'd seen behind her was moving, too. Hey, don't get paranoid, she told herself. Another driver could have reached the same decision she did.

Just ahead, she saw a sign with green letters against an orange background. "Hibernia." An arrow pointed left. She exhaled a sigh of relief, her good feeling evaporating when the vehicle behind her turned left as well. They were following her! Shit!

Through the fast moving windshield wipers, she barely discerned a fallen tree in the road. At the last possible instant, she swerved around it. Clutching the wheel, her palms were moist, the defroster and A/C running full blast, her legs shaking. Perspiration dripped from her forehead and soaked her blouse.

At last, she saw it. There's the restaurant, she thought, with sudden relief. It was a small stone house, painted in pastel colors, as if it were in Provence. Allison pulled into the empty parking lot, now a muddy bog with the rain still coming down in sheets.

She parked adjacent to the building and dashed from the car. By the time she reached the door, her clothes were soaked. Immediately she pivoted, looking back toward the parking lot. The van from LIME was pulling in.

Will they stay in their vehicle, she wondered, at least until she spoke to whomever's inside. After that, God only knows what.

Allison rushed into the ladies room to dry her face and hair. Above the sink, she noticed photographs of a horse named Mary Pat in a winner's circle. Emerging, she smelled the aroma of roast duck. An attractive dark haired woman in her late thirties was waiting. "I'm Mary Pat," the woman said in an Irish accent. "May I help you?"

Allison took out Vanessa's passport and showed her the picture. "I'm Allison Boyd. She's my twin sister, Vanessa. Have you ever seen her?"

Mary Pat studied the photo. "Yes, she was here last Saturday for dinner. Wearing a yellow print dress with blue butterflies. And thin straps."

Vanessa had a dress like that. She'd bought it when they were in Italy last summer.

"Whom was she with?"

Mary Pat hesitated. "Will I create problems for myself? Is this a marital situation?"

"Please. My twin sister died the next day. When she was still here in Anguilla."

"She died!" Mary Pat sounded incredulous. "You said she died?"

Allison nodded.

"What a pity. Oh, I'm sorry. Why didn't I hear about it? This is a small island."

"That's what I need to know. Please, will you help me?"

Mary Pat appeared to be studying her. "At first, I couldn't believe she was your sister. You look so different. But now in the lines of the face I see the resemblance."

"Please help me. Tell me everything you can about her."

"She was here with a man. Just the two of them. They sat there." She pointed to a table next to the wall. If the wind hadn't been blowing away from it, the table would have been drenched.

Finally she was cutting through all the bullshit.

"Who was he?"

"I don't know. I got a call from him that afternoon for a reservation. He said he was John Smith and he was calling from a boat. But I don't believe that was his name because when he got to the restaurant, he said the reservation was for Richard Smith."

"What about a credit card receipt?"

Mary Pat shook her head. "He paid with cash. They seemed romantic together."

Mary Pat paused.

"What else?"

"He had a wedding ring. She didn't. I notice that sort of thing."

Allison took a small pad and pencil from her purse. "Can you describe him?"

Mary Pat closed her eyes. "An American. White. In his fifties. About six one. Maybe one hundred and eighty pounds. Short dark brown hair, graying on the sides. A pleasant round face. No mustache or beard. No eye glasses. Dressed smartly in a blue blazer and white slacks. He acted like he was powerful and important. He complimented the staff and me. Picked two very good wines. Both burgundies. A white and a red. Corton. He asked me to tell my husband, who's in the kitchen, how much they enjoyed the meal, particularly the duck from France."

Allison carefully wrote everything down. "Did they drive or come by cab?"

"I watched them leave in a big car. An SUV."

"Did you notice the license plate?"

Mary Pat shook her head.

Outside, it was still pouring. No one else had arrived. The lights flickered momentarily, but stayed on.

"Don't worry about the power going out in here. We have our own generator."

Allison now thought about the van that had followed her. "Do you have any idea why a van from LIME is parked outside?"

Mary Pat looked into the parking lot. "All that's out there now is a little gray car, which I assume is yours. This time of year, rain like this can last for hours. You're welcome to stay here, inside with me. We live upstairs. My husband, my daughter, and I. I could lend you some dry clothes. You could even sleep here tonight."

Her offer was enticing, but Allison had been busy formulating a plan. The van might be coming back. So before that happened, she would drive as fast as she could to police headquarters. She could get there, hopefully, before the van caught up. Then she would confront Stevens with what Mary Pat had said. Now he'd have to tell her the truth.

Mary Pat insisted that Allison change into dry clothes, going upstairs and returning with a pink cotton blouse and khaki slacks. "They'll be a little large for you, but if you tighten the belt, the trousers should stay up." She handed Allison an umbrella. "Please drive carefully."

Allison gunned the engine and shot out of the parking lot, hunching over the steering wheel, driving as fast as she could. Every few seconds she glanced back. Nobody there. So far, so good.

Five miles later, she spotted headlights, approaching from the rear. The van? She couldn't tell. God, what should she do? She'd stop, see if it passed. She pulled over. The headlights pulled over, right behind her. It was the van!

In the mirror, she saw a man getting out on the passenger side, walking toward her. She thought about flooring the accelerator and racing off, but they'd still come after her, and they knew the roads better. This crap has to end, she decided.

She got out of her car and moved toward him. He kept coming, the outline of his body glowing in the van's headlights. At maybe ten yards, she saw him reach into his pocket and pull out a knife.

He extended his right arm closing in and eying her.

She wanted to scream, to run, to flee, as she watched him raise his arm. Then she darted to one side and grabbed his arm. Taking advantage of his surprise, she swung him by the arm over her body, and thank God, heard the crunching sound of his arm breaking. He lay on the ground, writhing and screaming in pain, the knife next to him. She picked it up and charged the van.

Again, she counted on surprise. Ferociously, she slashed two tires on the right side. The driver, cursing through the open window, tried to drive right at her. But with two flat tires, his van leaned to one side and could barely clunk forward.

She grabbed a rock and tossed it at the front windshield. Flying glass and the rock made him lose control. The van careened into a ditch.

Heart pounding, almost totally out of breath, she got back into her car and roared off. Now what? Go to the police? Bad idea. Better if she left all her stuff in the hotel room. She had her wallet, Vanessa's vault key, and their two passports in her bag. That was all she needed. She'd drive to the dock in town. Find somebody with a boat to take her to St. Martin, and get the hell off this island.

*   *   *

She checked into The Palms, a small hotel near the airport in St. Martin. Her teeth chattering, goose bumps on her arms, she turned the deadbolt and put the chain on the door. After a long shower, she fixed hot tea from a machine on the counter.

To warm up, she climbed under the covers.

One thought kept racing through her mind: *My God, they were trying to kill me.*

What in the world was happening? she asked herself.

But it was a rhetorical question. She was getting close to learning whom Vanessa had gone with to Anguilla and they were determined to kill her rather than have her discover that information.

Thinking about her experience that evening made her whole body shake.

She had to talk to someone about what had happened.

Paul. He was her only choice.

She reached for her cell phone.

"Where are you?" he asked.

She was unbelievably relieved to hear his voice. "St. Martin. I'm flying back to Washington in the morning." Her voice was coming out in short bursts.

"Are you okay?"

"No. I'm terrible. On Anguilla some men followed me and tried to kill me. I managed to escape."

"Holy shit! Did you go to the police?"

"They're running the cover-up. Vanessa had to be involved with a man who's getting support from the police."

"Did you get any information on his identity?"

"I'm getting close. I have a description."

"What's he look like?"

She read him her notes from the conversation with Mary Pat.

"That description fits lots of men in Washington. Let me think about how we can narrow it down. As soon as you land in Washington, come right to my house. You'll be safe here. I'll be at the office. Call me on my cell and I'll come home."

Allison had no intention of doing that. The first thing she had to do when she returned to Washington was go to Vanessa's bank vault.

Washington

Martin came home at nine in the evening. To his surprise, he found Francis there and in bed.

"Hey, I thought you were going to the Kennedy Center for chamber music with Sharon."

"Stomach virus," she muttered. "Leave me alone."

And he did until almost eleven thirty in the evening when she called to him. "I've rejoined the living."

He went upstairs and found her in bed, propped up against the headboard.

"Wow! It just hit me all at once. Sorry to kick you out, Andrew."

"You okay?"

"For sure. Now I want to hear about your meeting with President Braddock and Arthur. And I want the whole nine yards."

For the next half hour he reported while she interrogated like a trial lawyer about small details. When he was finished, she said, "I think it all sounds positive."

"I didn't mention Jasper and Anguilla to Braddock. You think I should have?"

While she thought about it, he added, "It's not too late. I can call Arthur first thing in the morning and inform him."

"No, no. You made the right decision. I know Arthur. You'd be out. He'd tell the president. And Braddock would turn on you, concluding that he didn't want someone sleazy on his short list."

Martin winced.

"I didn't say *you* were sleazy," she continued, as if reading his mind. "What I said was Braddock might jump to that conclusion. No, no. You were smart. You had no choice."

Later asleep, next to Francis, Martin dreamt he was walking through a field. He saw an electrified fence in the center with yellow neon lights on top. He knew he had better stay away from it, but the light became dim. Then, a searing jolt like electricity shot through his body.

The cell phone on the night table rang. It was Gorton. "You don't have to worry about Allison Boyd. She never learned what actually happened."

"What about Har Stevens? I was afraid he'd be a problem."

"Fortunately, he was off island the night Vanessa drowned. His deputy and the two officers stuck with the story I created for them."

Martin let out his breath in a sigh of relief. "Good work, Gorton."

"But I have to tell you. She is one tough lady. Roughed up a couple of my guys."

"I told you no violence," Martin said sharply.

"She came after two of my men who were following her. They had all they could do to defend themselves. One has a broken arm and the other one cuts on his face from a broken windshield."

Martin had never dealt with violence like this. Sure, he had represented criminals who were connected to violent crimes, generally in court appointed cases. But not in his own life. He felt as if he was rapidly losing control of the situation. "What about Allison?"

"I don't think she had a scratch."

"Has she left Anguilla?"

"She took a boat to St. Martin about an hour ago. My nephew's. While she was on the boat, he heard her booking a plane on American Airlines to Washington for the morning."

Great, Martin thought, she was coming back here to resume her investigation. But meantime, he had dodged a bullet in Anguilla.

Gorton added, "Good luck to you in dealing with that hellcat, Mr. Martin."

"Thanks for everything, Gorton."

Once Gorton clicked off, Martin decided to call Jasper. He didn't want the senator doing anything foolish. Martin called him at home, waking Jasper.

"Good news, Wes. Anguilla was a dry hold for Allison."

"How do you know that?"

"Gorton just called me."

"Okay," the senator said and hung up

"Thanks for the show of gratitude," Martin said into the dead phone.

*   *   *

Xiang was in the computer room in the Chinese Embassy watching a technician deftly hack into airline computers. She started with United. "No record of Allison Boyd." Then moved on to American.

Xiang was looking over her shoulder. He saw the name Allison Boyd appear on the screen followed by a flight number: American 220 from Miami. It showed an arrival time of 2:55 p.m. today into Reagan National.

Xiang decided that he and Han would wait at the exit for American on the lower level in a dark blue Civic, with Han driving. He expected Allison to take a cab. It would be too difficult to channel her into a cab with a driver working for him since it was impossible to control those cab lines. So he'd follow her cab.

If Xiang were a gambler, he'd bet heavily that if Allison hadn't found the CD in Anguilla, she would immediately go to the bank and Vanessa's safe deposit box before the bank closed. So if she didn't go to the bank, that meant she had the CD. He'd follow her cab and when she came to her destination, probably Vanessa's apartment, he'd pull up behind her, jump out, and grab it. With the element of surprise that should be doable.

But suppose she retrieved the CD from the bank vault?

He tried to put himself into her mind. She would undoubtedly place the CD in her briefcase. He could try to snatch it from her on the street as she left the bank, but that would be too risky in broad daylight. Besides, as he learned two days ago, Allison was tough. She'd fight back and bystanders or a passing policeman might intervene.

He didn't know where she'd be going with the CD, but suppose he arranged to have a cab waiting in front of the bank, with the driver working for him, and hopefully that was the cab Allison got into. That would be easy to arrange in front of the bank. Then it wouldn't matter where Allison planned to go. The driver could take her to a destination that Xiang selected.

Getting control of a DC cab was easy. For enough cash, he was confident he could borrow one from a cab company. But the driver couldn't be Chinese. Xiang was convinced Allison would never get into a cab with a Chinese driver after what she'd been through the last couple of days.

He came up with an idea for the cab and driver. Xiang had become friends with Kiro, a Nigerian intelligence agent attached to their embassy. The Nigerians were courting China for a large new trade agreement. Xiang was confident Kiro would help.

Xiang called Kiro. Half an hour later he was seated in the Nigerian Embassy telling Kiro, "I need a favor."

"I'm listening," the tall, thin Nigerian responded in English, spoken with a British accent, the result of four years at Oxford.

"You once told me that a number of Nigerian cab drivers in Washington were on your payroll."

"That's right. They supplement their income with drop-offs and pickups for me."

"Can these men be trusted?"

Kiro's head snapped back. He was scowling. I've insulted him, Xiang thought. Before Xiang had a chance to say anything, Kiro interjected.

"Apology accepted. But whatever you're planning, I don't want to risk my driver being arrested."

"Don't worry. He won't be. I promise you that."

"Okay. Tell me what you want him to do."

When Xiang finished, Kiro was shaking his head. "It's too risky. I don't want to lose a good man. Besides, my government doesn't hold most of the American debt as yours does. They don't treat us with any deference."

Xiang viewed Kiro's comment as an offer to negotiate. He had come expecting it. So, casually, he reached into his jacket pocket and removed an envelope which contained ten thousand dollars in US currency. He laid it down on the desk without saying a word. Kiro's superiors might have bugged his office. He didn't want to get the Nigerian into trouble.

"Our two governments are currently embarked on a cooperative approach in many commercial activities. I view what I'm asking as part of that cooperation,"

Silently, Xiang slid the envelope toward Kiro.

"When you express it that way, it is something I can do. But I don't want my man arrested."

"I assure you. He will not be."

As Xiang left the Nigerian Embassy, he considered another possibility: suppose that Allison didn't have the CD and after all this she didn't know where it was. What to do about her then?

He thought about it for a few minutes and decided he'd have the cab drive them to a remote location in Rock Creek Park. There he'd rough her up and threaten to kill her in an effort to intimidate her into leaving town before she found out that Jasper had been with Vanessa.

*   *   *

Allison's plane landed ten minutes early. Seated in the bulkhead in coach, on the aisle, she raced through the first class cabin as soon as the door opened, nearly crashing into a gray-haired man who shouted, "What's the hurry lady?"

She was the first one off the plane.

Without any bags, ten minutes later, she exited the terminal on the lower level and headed for the cab line.

A light rain was falling. She gave the driver the bank's address on Connecticut Avenue, a little north of Vanessa's apartment. Anxiously, Allison checked her watch. She would make it well before four o'clock when the bank closed.

Getting access to Vanessa's safe deposit was easy for Allison. When Vanessa opened the box, she had sent forms to Allison to sign, putting her sister on as a co-lessee.

In the bank, Allison took the gray metal box to a booth, closed the door, and opened the lid. Inside were four volumes of Vanessa's diaries—substantial books, but each one with a different cover—and a stack of hundred dollar bills. That was all.

No CD.

This was the last place Allison thought Vanessa might have hidden the CD. Not finding it here, she was rapidly coming to the conclusion that there was no CD and that the Chinese were mistaken about its existence. Perhaps Vanessa had led them to think she had a damaging CD. But why? Did Vanessa have a powerful Chinese official as a lover and she was blackmailing him? That was possible.

Allison put the diaries into her bag. She'd look at them later when she got to Paul's.

She counted the money. Twenty thousand dollars in hundreds. She put it in her bag.

When Vanessa had opened the box, soon after she moved to Washington, she proudly told Allison, "I believe in keeping cash. You never know. I have a million dollars in cash left over from my modeling days in the bank vault I just opened."

Amazing how Vanessa burnt through money. Not just spending it, but she had lost so much with managers and financial advisors who had either made bad investments or stolen it. Allison had recommended wealth managers she knew, but Vanessa had said, "They're too boring."

And when Allison suggested putting it into US government bonds, Vanessa replied, "I might as well be stashing it under a mattress. I want to make money with my money."

Allison exited the bank and looked around for a cab. The rain was coming down harder. A cab was parked at the curb. Allison signaled to the driver; he waved his arm, motioning her to get in.

He was a Nigerian, she guessed from his name and looks, and this was confirmed by the small Nigerian flag hanging from the rearview mirror. He was a muscular man, wearing a dark green t-shirt which showed off his biceps. Music in an African language was playing in the cab.

She gave him Paul's address. He turned off the music and pulled away.

Exhausted, she had trouble keeping her eyes open as the wheels turned.

Dozing, she noticed the driver turning into an alley. "Shortcut," he said. "We'll miss some traffic."

Not knowing Washington that well, she didn't protest.

Seconds later, he made a sharp turn into a rear loading dock for a building, stopped the cab, and turned off the engine. Now Allison was alarmed. Two Chinese men sprang up from behind a dumpster. She recognized them as the two who had confronted her in the churchyard and then came into the Silver Eagle restaurant.

One of them, the one with the scar on his cheek who had chased her over the fence behind the restaurant, opened the back door of the cab. The other one was holding a gun aimed at her. "Get out of the cab," the first man said.

She was convinced they'd shoot her if she didn't obey. Besides, the driver was obviously working with them. She got out.

The man with the scar grabbed her bag and rifled through it.

"Fuck," he said. Then dropped it on the ground. He ran his hands over her body.

Frowning, he said, "Where's the CD?"

"I don't know what you're talking about. I swear it. I've never heard of any CD my sister had."

"You're lying."

"I'm not. Ever since you told me about it in the churchyard, I've done everything I could to find it. I searched her apartment. Her office. Her bank vault. No CD. Either she didn't have it, or it doesn't exist. Why would I possibly lie to you? I'm not stupid. I wouldn't give up my life to protect some CD I've never even heard of. You have to believe me."

He closed his lips, pressed them together, and stared at her. "I believe you," he said.

She picked up her bag. "Good. I'm leaving now,"

She turned to walk away, down the alley. He grabbed her arm to stop her. "No. Get back into the cab." She didn't move. He let go of her arm.

"Why won't you let me go now? Please. I have no idea where the CD is even though I did everything I could to find it. I'm no use to you."

"That's certainly true, but you know too much. So now stop stalling and get back into the cab."

The other man raised the gun. She was convinced they planned to kill her if she got back into the cab. Or on the loading dock if she didn't. Still, she held her ground.

"Wait a minute," the first man said. "What are those books in your bag. I want to see those."

His colleague lowered the gun again.

The first man reached for her bag. As he did, he was leaning forward, arm outstretched. That was the break she needed. She swung the bag with all her might against his face. It smacked him in the nose. She heard the sound of bones breaking as the diaries struck him. The man screamed.

Before his colleague with the gun had a chance to react, she raced toward the end of the alley. She was still gripping her bag.

Over her shoulder, she saw the second man, gun in hand, running after her. She reached the sidewalk on Massachusetts Avenue, which was crowded with pedestrians. She wove in and out of people, many of them were holding umbrellas, so her pursuer couldn't get off a shot.

At the corner, without waiting for the light to turn green, she raced across R Street. The driver of a white van slammed on the brakes, narrowly missing her, while honking his horn and shouting, "You stupid idiot." She glanced over her shoulder. Her pursuer was gaining ground.

He was not nearly as fast as his colleague, but with her bad leg, still faster than she was. Soon, she'd be in trouble, she realized. Pedestrians would thin out and he'd get off a clear shot. She had to change the dynamic.

Up ahead she saw a Metro sign—the DuPont Circle station. She raced toward it then tore down the long, steep escalator crowded with people leading into the station, almost knocking over an elderly woman. A couple of men in suits and ties screamed at her and grabbed the side rail to avoid being pushed over. She could sense he was behind her.

She had a substantial lead. If she could get into a train, she thought, and it pulled away before he could get in, she'd be safe. At the bottom of the escalator, she leaped over the turnstile, still clutching her bag while a startled station manager yelled, "Hey Miss." Then down a short escalator, which ran to the train platform below.

Desperately, she looked down the tracks for an incoming train. Dammit! No such luck! No train!

She tried to hide behind a dark brown square trash bin that said, "NEWSPAPERS ONLY," close to a group of about ten people waiting for a train. For an instant, the gunman didn't see her and he stopped, looking in every direction. Then he spotted her and ran toward the trash bin.

She was on the verge of panic. What else could she do?

Climbing down on the tracks was suicidal. She'd be hit by the next train or electrocuted by the current on the third track. Instinctively, she was moving forward, toward the far end of the platform, escaping from him, but at the same time boxing herself in as she approached a stone wall.

"Okay, you miserable bitch," he shouted, waving his gun at her. People on the platform screamed and got out of the way.

As he came closer, she could see saliva, dripping from his mouth. His unshaven face looked like black sandpaper. His eyes were bloodshot.

It was just the two of them at the end of the platform.

He raised his gun, aiming at her. Before he had a chance to fire, she tossed her bag at him, hitting him on the forearm, knocking the gun from his hand. The gun and her bag fell harmlessly onto the burnt red tile platform.

He gave a bloodcurdling cry and came after her with his fists clenched. She realized that he had her backed up to the edge of the platform, above the tracks. She had to watch her footing or she'd fall onto the rails.

At that moment, the small white circular lights along the edge of the platform were flashing, signaling an oncoming train.

Face red with anger, he swung at her with a broadside and missed. He reached for her, trying to grab her neck, but she ducked away at the last instant. He was too far committed to pull back and recover his balance. While waving his arms helplessly, he fell on the tracks in a jumbled heap just as the train barreled into the station. She watched the train smash into him.

People screamed.

In the pandemonium Allison picked up her bag and ran toward the nearest exit. She tore up the moving escalator, heading toward Connecticut Avenue.

As she reached the street, rain was coming down in sheets. A torrential downpour of cold pelting rain. She saw three DC police cruisers descending on the area. She crossed the street and went into a Starbucks to hide until the policemen disappeared down the escalator. Then she was back on the street. She had to get to Paul's house. She'd be safe there. She didn't run for fear of attracting suspicion. As she walked, she kept looking for an empty cab—a near impossibility in Washington on a rainy afternoon.

"Don't be stupid," she muttered aloud. A cab driver would be a witness who could tell the police where she had gone. She had to get to Paul's house on foot. She figured it was only about thirty minutes. Maybe a little more.

As she walked, her shoes sopping with water, she periodically glanced over her shoulder. No one was following her. The frigid rain drenched her hair and soaked her clothes. She shivered, but she didn't care. She was safe.

*   *   *

Bleeding profusely from the nose, Xiang asked the Nigerian to give him something to stop the flow of blood. The driver found an oil-stained cloth in the trunk. Xiang decided that would have to do. He asked the Nigerian to drive him to the Chinese Embassy. "I'll do that, man, but then we split. I didn't bargain for shit like this."

Xiang couldn't argue.

In the embassy, he immediately went to the medical office. A nurse asked him, "What happened?"

"I'm with MSS. You don't ask me questions."

"Yes, sir, Mr. Xiang."

She went to work on his nose.

"It's broken," she said. "You'll need some stitches to stop the bleeding and a bandage. It won't look pretty."

"Stupid cunt," he cried out.

The nurse pulled away, "What did you call me?"

"Not you. Someone else."

He checked his cell phone. No messages. By now Han should have called to let him know what happened with Allison. He hadn't told Han to chase her. He should have let her run away, but Han was a hothead. He was acting on his own. Xiang hoped that Han didn't kill Allison. That would create more problems for them.

*   *   *

Paul lived in a small red brick townhouse on the northeast edge of Georgetown. Looking at the dark house, Allison decided Paul wasn't home yet. Which made sense. It wasn't that late. Vanessa had told her that Paul worked insanely long hours, like most young lawyers in large Washington law firms.

Allison climbed three cracked, wobbly cement steps and walked up to the front door. She reached under the mat, picked up the key, let herself in, and closed the door.

"Anyone home?" she called out.

As she expected, no answer.

Not wanting to spread water around the house, she left her bag and shoes next to the door, then peeled off her clothes and underwear and picked them up. Naked, she carried them up the stairs and into a bathroom. She dropped them into the bath tub. Then she grabbed a towel from a closet and dried herself.

A white terrycloth robe was hanging on the back of the door. She put it on, then went down and yanked her cell phone from her bag. The house was warm. She sat down next to a vent blowing hot air and called Paul's cell. He answered immediately. "Where are you, Allison?"

"Your house. I'm terrified. I just arrived."

"I expected you much earlier. I've been worried sick. What happened?"

"I'll tell you when I see you."

"I'm on my way."

"Oh, Paul, that would be wonderful."

Forty-five minutes later, he arrived.

"Sorry it took so long. When it rains, getting around this town is impossible."

"I'm just glad you're here."

"On the phone you said you were terrified. What happened?"

"It was awful. When I got off the plane I took a cab to Vanessa's bank to check her vault box."

"Did you find the CD?"

She shook her head. "Just a few of her old diaries and some cash. When I left the bank, I got into a cab on Connecticut Avenue. I gave the driver your address. But it was all a set-up."

"What do you mean?"

"The driver took me into an alley and pulled into a loading dock. Those two Chinese thugs were waiting for me. One had a gun."

"Did you get the number of the cab?"

"C'mon, Paul. Who looks at cab numbers?"

"What about the cab company?"

She was becoming annoyed. He sounded like such a lawyer. "I don't know. Maybe it was a blue or green. I was tired. About all I remember is that the driver was Nigerian."

"Which describes about half the cab drivers in town. So what happened in the alley?"

"They grabbed my bag and searched me, looking for the CD, I guess. When they didn't find it, they tried to force me back into the cab. I think they planned to take me somewhere to kill me."

"My God."

"I smacked one of them with my bag. Probably broke his nose. Then I ran. The one with the gun chased me. We ended up in the DuPont Circle Metro Station where he tried to attack me on the platform. I ducked and he ended up on the tracks. An incoming train killed him. I got the hell out of the area. And I walked to your house in the rain. Nobody was following me."

"You're safe here."

"But what do I do now?"

There was a long pause. Finally, Paul said, "I need a few minutes to think about it. Why don't you go upstairs and take a shower. I'll get together some dinner for us. When you come down, I'll have a plan."

Allison was finally feeling relief, knowing that Paul would help her.

"I better dry my clothes."

"I'll find some clean clothes of mine that might fit. I'll leave them on the bed."

"That'll be a good trick, considering you're six two and about one eighty and I'm five eight and one thirty."

He laughed. "I'll do the best I can."

After showering, she found a blue Yale Law sweatshirt he left and work out pants that tied with a drawstring.

She came downstairs to find two plates of pasta with tomato sauce and an open bottle of Barbara d'Alba on the battered butcher block kitchen table. It looked good. She was starving.

On the counter a small television was playing.

"Can we turn that off?" she said.

He shook his head. "We have to hear what they're saying about the Metro incident."

As they began eating, Paul said, "Before we decide on our next move, tell me what happened in Anguilla."

She relayed everything that had occurred from the time she arrived in Anguilla until she boarded the plane to fly back to Washington.

At the end, she said, "Bottom line. I'm getting close to learning whom Vanessa was with in Anguilla. I have Mary Pat's description as well as Vanessa's diaries. I'm hoping I can get there. I'm going to nail that bastard."

"Together, we'll do it," Paul said. "I know the territory. I'll be able to help."

Suddenly, Paul pointed to the television. He raced over and increased the volume.

"Again, the hour's top story. There was an incident at the DuPont Circle Metro station this afternoon. During a struggle between a man and a woman on the platform, the man was either pushed or fell onto the tracks where he was hit and immediately killed by an oncoming train."

Allison saw her picture flashed on the screen.

"Oh no!" she cried out, horrified.

The announcer continued. "This picture of the woman involved was taken by one of the people on the platform with a camera on his cell phone. The woman's identity is not known. She fled the scene. The dead man's identity has not been released by the police.

"One witness told reporters that the woman was acting in self-defense. Another disputed that account. The police have not issued any statement. A gun was involved."

Upset, she said, "I'm in deep trouble, Paul."

"We need a plan. It's only a question of time, and not much, until somebody recognizes you. That means your name will be in all the papers and on television. The mystery woman the police are looking for."

"I don't want to turn myself in. The police might hold me indefinitely."

"You're right. It seems crazy but some zealous prosecutor might even charge you with manslaughter. You never know. Here's what I think you should do. Tonight, don't leave my house. Tomorrow morning, I'll buy you some clothes. Funky ones. Change your look. Then I'll take you to a nearby hair salon. Friend of mine runs it. He'll change your appearance and color your hair. He'll dye your hair blonde. Make you look like Vanessa. You're already pretty close except for the hair. After that, we'll look at Vanessa's diaries. Those may give us an idea of how to proceed."

"Why can't we start tonight?"

She yawned.

"That's why. You hardly slept last night. You have to be fresh for this."

"What about your firm work?"

"I'm drafting a brief for Andrew Martin. I can do it at home."

She looked at him skeptically.

"Don't worry, I have it under control."

"You're taking a risk helping somebody the police are looking for."

"I'll take it. You've been swept up in something horrible. You need help. You can't fight this alone. Besides, I like you, Allison. And when I like people, I want to help them."

Thank God, she thought with relief.

When they finished eating, Allison said, "I'll clean up. You did all the cooking."

"No. You're exhausted. Go to sleep. We'll get to work in the morning."

"Okay."

She stood up and as she did, the drawstring gave way. His warm-up pants dropped to the floor, exposing her naked bush.

She blushed.

He smiled. "Well. Well."

Embarrassed, she pulled up the pants, held them, and said, "Good night, Paul, and thanks for everything."

*   *   *

Xiang's bandaged nose ached. He was sitting in his office in the Embassy, anxiously waiting for Han to call when a secretary burst into the room. "The ambassador wants to see you immediately."

The ambassador, a trim gaunt man, a supporter of Deng in his youth, was sitting behind his desk with a scowl on his face. As soon as he saw Xiang, he shot to his feet and shouted angrily, "What are you trying to do to me and our country? You useless piece of dog shit."

"What do you mean?"

"Your assistant, Han, was killed. He was chasing a woman on a Metro platform. When he caught her, they were fighting. She pushed him onto the tracks and an incoming train killed him."

Xiang couldn't believe this.

"He was chasing this woman on assignment for you. Wasn't he?"

"Yes," Xiang said weakly.

The ambassador pointed to Xiang's face. "I assume you were injured in the same operation."

Xiang nodded.

The ambassador shook his head in dismay. "You're both incompetent. Han stupidly had his ID in his wallet, showing him to be a member of the embassy staff. Don't you tell your people anything?"

"That was a mistake," Xiang conceded.

"Everything you do is a mistake. The only good news is that after talking with the state department the Washington police refused to release Han's name or to inform the press he was a member of our staff. Even that is not so good because I have been summoned to the state department tomorrow for a meeting at two in the afternoon with Secretary of State Jane Prosser herself. What would you like me to tell her? That I have this fuckup Xiang on my staff who has embarrassed me and the Chinese government? Should I kiss her ass and ask her to convince the Washington police to call off their investigation?"

Xiang didn't know what to say.

Red-faced, the ambassador continued his diatribe. "I intend to use my secure phone which runs directly to Beijing and call Minister Liu. I will ask him to order you back to Beijing before the Americans find out about you. Liu will throw you into one of his prisons for enemies of the state."

Xiang was shaking with fear as he watched the ambassador reach for the red phone, embodying the latest encrypted technology, which they were confident the Americans could not break. When he got Minister Liu, he put the phone on speaker.

In succinct sentences, the ambassador explained what happened at the Metro station and his summons to the state department. At the end, he said, "I want you to recall this fool Xiang immediately, before the Americans grab him and imprison him."

Xiang held his breath, waiting to hear what Liu said.

After a moment, Liu replied, "Xiang, was Han's work concerned with the matters you recently discussed with me in Beijing?"

"Yes, sir, it was." Xiang decided to keep his words vague. He was aware that the ambassador knew in general about Operation Trojan Horse, but perhaps not about Jasper's supply of information, or Vanessa's death. "The woman involved was the sister of the dead woman."

"Did you order Han to pursue this woman?"

"No sir. I didn't. She ran away and he went after her before I had a chance to stop him. It's my fault. I'm truly sorry."

Liu then said to the ambassador, "Xiang is acting as my personal representative in a matter of extreme importance to the People's Republic. How dare you question his actions? By questioning him, you question me."

"But . . ." the ambassador said.

"Don't you dare question me."

Xiang understood what was happening.

He was a pawn in one more incident in the never-ending conflict between the Chinese Foreign Ministry, for whom the ambassador worked, and MSS, Liu's agency. The latter almost always had the upper hand.

"It is your job as ambassador," Liu continued as if he were talking to a child, "to deal with the American State Department to avoid any damage. And to avoid having Xiang arrested in the United States. Now

Xiang, tell me what has happened on this matter since you returned to Washington from Beijing."

Xiang told him in detail, ending with the Metro incident. Though his nose ached, Xiang was embarrassed to tell Liu that Allison had broken his nose. Instead, he reiterated that Han raced after Allison on his own and again said, "I'm very sorry for this entire incident."

"Han behaved foolishly," Liu said. "But the ambassador will find a way to smooth it over with the Americans. Won't you?"

"Yes," was the grudging response.

"Now Xiang," Liu continued, "I want to come back to the important issue—Jasper and the CD. What is the status?"

Xiang selected his words carefully, dropping them like pebbles into a lake.

"I now believe there is no CD. That mentioning it by Vanessa was a bluff to blackmail Jasper. To force him to marry her."

"How sure are you there never was a CD?"

Xiang hesitated for a moment while he thought about the facts. Both he and Allison had looked everywhere Vanessa might have concealed it.

"I'm certain," he said.

"Would you bet your life on it?"

Xiang didn't dare show weakness, or it would undercut his position.

"Yes sir," he said with a confidence he didn't feel.

"Your parents' lives?"

What a question. Liu was a monster. Still, he couldn't bend. "Yes sir."

"For your sake and theirs, I hope you are correct."

Xiang didn't respond.

"And if you are," Liu continued, "that changes the dynamic. I do not want you to pursue Allison any longer."

That disappointed Xiang. He wanted to get even with her for what she had done to him. How to express his disagreement with Liu without appearing to challenge the Minister?

"But if we continue pursuing Allison, we might be able to stop her from finding out whom her sister was with in Anguilla. If she does and reveals it, Jasper could lose his reelection, and that would cost us a valuable asset."

"True, but with everything that's happened, working with Jasper is too risky. Once he gives you the five-year plan, I'll want you to terminate Jasper."

Xiang didn't know what Liu meant by terminate. End the relationship or kill the senator. Expecting Liu to clarify, Xiang didn't ask.

Liu continued, "Besides, we're not hurt unless the CD appears. Jasper would go down alone. Suppose the press gets hold of his weekend tryst with Vanessa. He wouldn't dare disclose what he has given us. That would lead to life in prison for him. So, he wouldn't drag us down with him. This Allison is tough. I don't want to risk having a second agent—you or one of your other people exposed like Han. That would create a much more serious problem for us. Do you understand?"

"Yes, sir."

"Good. Now, let's talk about Jasper. You told me that he promised to give you the plan on Monday, the day after next."

"Correct. When he hands it over to me, he expects me to deliver the CD to him."

"So *you* have a problem because the CD doesn't exist."

Now it's *my* problem, Xiang thought. "One possibility when I meet Jasper on Monday is to persuade him that with all my efforts, I established the CD doesn't exist. He should be sufficiently relieved that he'll still give me the document."

"But he might not."

"I could offer additional money. An extra payment."

"And if that still doesn't work, I want you to seize the document from Jasper by force if necessary. Do you understand?"

"Yes, but doing that could effectively sever our relationship with Jasper."

"Of course, I realize that. You insult me."

"I didn't mean . . ."

"Getting the five-year plan is critical. As for Jasper, the man's such a fool that continuing to work with him is a questionable decision at best. Now, are you prepared to do what I said? Even use force with Jasper if necessary?"

Xiang would do anything. A few minutes ago, he thought he faced imprisonment and torture in China.

"I'll do it," Xiang said with conviction.

After hanging up the phone, Xiang went home. He slept for a few hours, then checked online news sources to see what spin the news was putting on the DC Metro killing. Not surprisingly, Allison Boyd had been named as the woman who was involved in the struggle with the unidentified victim. Someone had recognized her picture. Allison's impressive bio was given. The police said, "She isn't being charged, but is wanted for questioning. Anyone who knows her whereabouts should notify the police."

Xiang felt as if the whole business was spinning out of control.

*   *   *

Martin and Francis were having breakfast in the kitchen with the television tuned to CNN. Normally, she would never have permitted that, but with the chief justice appointment so close, she even suggested it. "We don't want to miss any news."

As Martin picked up a spoon with shredded wheat and skim milk and put it into his mouth he saw a picture of the Supreme Court building. Then the announcer said, "Judge Mary Corbett from the US Court of Appeals in New York has withdrawn from consideration for chief justice for personal reasons." Martin pumped his fist into the air. "Yes," he shouted. The announcer continued, "There are unconfined reports that Judge Corbett's withdrawal is related to a failure to file tax returns. That leaves Judge Butler and Andrew Martin as the two remaining candidates on the president's short list."

"Oh, Andrew, that's great," Francis said.

"Agreed. But I always thought Butler was the more formidable of the two."

She laughed. "Wow. You can't please some people. We're almost . . ."

He stopped her in midsentence, pointing to the screen with a woman's picture and the name, Allison Boyd.

"The DC Police have now identified the mysterious woman in the DuPont Circle Metro incident who fled the scene as Allison Boyd, professor of archeology at Brown University. They have still not released the name of the dead man. Miss Boyd's twin sister recently died in Anguilla. There is speculation that the two incidents are somehow related."

The news went on to other stories.

"Oh shit!" Martin cried out. Then he turned to Francis. "A full-scale investigation of the Metro incident would zero in on Vanessa's death in Anguilla. I thought we were out of the woods with Gorton's call, but not now."

Francis looked puzzled. "It's all so peculiar. Who could have been chasing Allison with a gun? You think your friend Jasper could have decided that the only way to end this was by hiring thugs to kill Allison?"

Martin respected Francis's ideas, and he never dismissed anything she said out of hand, but this one seemed a bit farfetched. He wrinkled his forehead. "Wes hiring thugs?"

"You said he sounded desperate at Camelot. Desperate people do bizarre things. And hiring killers in our great city is almost as easy as buying a cappuccino."

He laughed. "That's a helluva comparison."

"Then who was chasing Allison?"

"Damned if I know."

"You could give Police Chief Bradley a call and ask him the identity of the dead man. Remember he presented you with an award for your contributions to the police department's youth clubs."

Martin shook his head. "It's tempting, but Bradley's savvy from being a longtime NYPD cop. We've had so little contact that he would likely be suspicious."

"Just trying to be helpful."

Francis stood up. "Faculty meeting. Have to get going."

Martin was still in the kitchen, sipping coffee and thinking about Allison when his cell phone rang. It was the Chinese ambassador.

"I have to speak with you about an urgent matter," he said. "Are you available this morning?"

Martin had represented the government of China for eight years. He had an annual retainer of one million dollars. For that, he was consulted about various matters, always high level, from time to time. Also he made calls to American officials to break bureaucratic log jams or to reverse decisions that had gone against the Chinese. In the past, the ambassador always called Martin's office and scheduled an appointment through his secretary.

"I'm leaving the house in a few minutes, Martin told the ambassador. Let's meet at my office in an hour."

"Could I possibly come to your house?"

"Certainly, I'll give you the address."

"I recall it from the wonderful dinner party you invited me to last year. I'll be there in about thirty minutes."

*   *   *

When the ambassador arrived, Martin was dressed in a suit and tie. He offered coffee or tea, which the ambassador declined. He was all business. His face was wrinkled with concern. Martin led him into the first floor study, the same room in which he had spoken to Jasper when the senator called from Anguilla. They were seated in leather chairs across a coffee table.

"I'm sorry impose on you," the ambassador said.

"Please, it's never an imposition. I'm always happy to talk with you."

The ambassador cleared his throat, then said, "You've no doubt heard about the DuPont Circle Metro incident."

Martin straightened up with a start. "Yes, of course. Involving the woman Allison Boyd."

"Well, this is extremely awkward and sensitive. The dead man's name is Han Shi. A member of my embassy staff in the economic section. Once the police saw his embassy ID, they called the state department. The secretary's office directed them to withhold his name until I've had a chance to meet with Secretary of State Prosser. We have a meeting scheduled for two o'clock this afternoon. I don't have to tell you that now is a tense time in relations between our nations with economic, trade, and currency issues."

"I'm well aware of that."

Martin wanted to scream. "Why in the hell was Han Shi chasing Allison with a gun?" But he waited for the ambassador to continue.

"This was a lover's quarrel," the ambassador said.

He told the blatant lie with a straight face. "Really," Martin said, deadpan himself.

"Yes, it got out of control, and it would be very unfortunate if those facts became public."

"What would you like me to do?"

"I understand you are friendly with Secretary of State Prosser."

"That's correct. I've known Jane for a long time, since she was a senator from Indiana."

Martin recalled that Jane had been in his dining room at the time he received the call from Jasper in Anguilla.

"I'd like you to meet with the secretary of state and ask her to persuade the Washington police to halt their investigation of the Metro incident. Please explain to her this was a lover's quarrel. You may tell her that it is important for my government to avoid this embarrassment."

Martin took a deep breath and thought about the request. He had always prided himself on his ethical standards. Moreover, he had cultivated good relationships with top officials like the secretary of state because they knew he was honest. "A straight shooter," Jane had once told him when he presented to her a complicated issue for the French government.

Now, he was being asked to make representations that he knew were totally false. Normally, he would never have done it, but this was a special situation. He knew that somehow Han Shi's pursuit of Allison Boyd was related to Allison's effort to discover the facts about her sister's death. A police investigation of the Metro incident would lead back to the Anguilla drowning and the danger of exposing Martin's role in moving the body.

He should be grateful to the ambassador for giving him a way to block the investigation. At the same time, he recognized he would be starting down a slippery slope of immorality and unethical conduct. Hell, he had already started down that path when he made the call to Gorton Sunday night, asking him to move Vanessa's body. Having taken that step, he had to take this one.

Martin thought about other famous Washington lawyers, such as Clark Clifford, Abe Fortas, and Burke Marshall—all revered for decades as he was, whose reputations and careers were destroyed by ethical lapses. He had to be very careful or he'd end up like them. But he had to do it.

"Okay, I'll meet with the secretary of state. I can't promise you success. Jane can be unpredictable. But I will try and report back to you."

"That's all I'm asking."

"If I succeed, you won't need your two o'clock meeting with her."

The ambassador thanked Martin and left. When he was gone, before reaching for the phone to call Jane, Martin paused to contemplate what was happening.

Had Jasper hired Han Shi to do his dirty work and kill Allison as Francis suggested? Was Han Shi moonlighting as a hired thug? Was that what the ambassador was trying to cover up? It seemed too farfetched. There had to be a better explanation, but Martin couldn't think what it was. He had decided not to press the ambassador and he didn't want to call Jasper.

As he thought about it some more, it occurred to him that the Chinese might owe Jasper a favor, and Wes had called it in to help protect him from Allison's snooping. If that was what was happening, Martin didn't want to know about it.

He'd do what the ambassador wanted because if he succeeded, it would help him. At least he hoped so.

*   *   *

"Excellent dinner Sunday evening," Jane said, when they were alone in her spacious office in the state department. "All the wines were superb, but the '90 Clos La Roche was ethereal. It may be the best wine I've ever drunk."

"Having seen your cellar, that's quite a compliment."

"Yeah, but unfortunately, I'm stocked too heavily in Bordeaux. I like those wines, and many are outstanding, but there's nothing like a fabulous aged Burgundy for an incredible soft, velvety taste."

"I couldn't agree with you more."

"I never realized Francis played at Aspen. If she ever gives a performance, be sure to invite me."

"Will do."

They were seated at the small conference table in a corner of her office. Jane was sipping water. Martin had a cup of coffee. I'm drinking too much of this stuff, he thought, but he couldn't cut back.

"I'm almost afraid to ask you about the chief justice nomination," Jane said. "I'm amazed you can do anything else."

"It is a tense time."

"I'd love you to get it. Well, anyhow, what's on your mind this morning?"

"I'm here at the request of the Chinese ambassador.

"The Metro incident?"

"Exactly."

"What's this all about, Andrew?"

Martin hated lying to her. Damn it, he had no choice.

Calmly and coolly, he laid out the lover's quarrel explanation, embellishing it with details he made up from Allison's background to make it sound more believable.

When he was finished, Jane was smiling. "Oh Andrew, that is so boring. I envisioned all sorts of exotic explanations. A fight between an archeology professor and a Chinese diplomat over terra cotta warriors. Or maybe valuable relics from the Ming Dynasty. When I was at Yale, the Italian government sought to recover a large number of antiquities. Wow, that was a nasty battle. Here I was imagining fascinating scenarios."

"Such as?" Martin held his breath, hoping she didn't mention Vanessa.

"Allison had stolen valuable artifacts from China during a trip there. She had smuggled them out in her luggage and now the Chinese were trying to recover them."

"That would be much more exciting."

"Someday, I'd like to meet Allison Boyd, the archeology professor. She must be one tough cookie."

I hope you never do, Martin thought.

Jane paused to sip some water, then continued, "Tell your client, the Chinese ambassador, he can relax. For a lover's quarrel, I'll persuade the DC Police to back off. To close the investigation and treat it as an unfortunate accident. Besides, the dead party is a Chinese national in this country on a diplomatic passport. If they want to close it out, we shouldn't object."

"I think that's right."

"You can tell the ambassador I'm canceling our two o'clock. We don't have to waste our time on nonsense like this. All of us have too much to do."

Martin started toward the door. As he did, Jane said, "Did you know the twin sister of Allison Boyd died in Anguilla about a week ago?"

Martin tried to act natural, though he felt tension and moisture forming under his arms.

"I heard that."

"Odd, isn't it?"

"I learned long ago that life is full of coincidences."

"I guess so. See you soon, Andrew. And good luck with the Supreme Court."

*   *   *

When Allison woke up, she found a note from Paul on the kitchen table. "I went shopping for clothes for you. Help yourself to breakfast."

She scarfed down some cereal, then grabbed a cup of coffee and began reading Vanessa's diaries, starting with the most recent.

After an hour, Allison was feeling sick to her stomach. She knew Vanessa had been no virgin, but my God, she had slept with so many different men that Allison's head was spinning. Except for Paul and a finance man, Jim Conway, a few months before she began dating Paul, all of them were congressmen or senators. In her diary, Vanessa didn't give them names or physical descriptions. Simply referred to them as Congressman A or Senator B. At the time the most recent diary had broken off, Vanessa was dating Senator Q. Perhaps he was the man she went with to Anguilla.

Vanessa described in detail what they did on their dates and in bed together and the gifts they gave her. She discussed the likelihood they would marry her, and if they were married, the possibility of their leaving their wives for her. It gave Allison a sad and sordid picture of Vanessa.

Allison came to the realization that she had failed in her effort to pull Vanessa away from her self-destructive way of life. The old Vanessa, influenced by the modeling career Mother had pushed her into, had reasserted itself. She couldn't escape, in spite of Allison's influence. In the end, this led to her death. Sadly, Allison thought, as she flipped through the diary, Vanessa could not have been saved.

Allison heard the front door open and Paul shout, "I'm home." She closed and put away the diaries.

Paul bounded into the kitchen with two shopping bags filled with funky clothes, as promised. There were walking shoes, as well as sunglasses, and a large brimmed hat to cover her face until the beauty salon went to work on her.

That occurred half an hour later. When Allison was finished and she studied herself in the mirror, she was convinced she looked so much like Vanessa that even Mother would have thought her daughter had returned to life.

It occurred to Allison that maybe Paul, who had been so much in love with Vanessa, was trying to recreate her, like Jimmy Stewart in Vertigo. He was being so nice to her that she didn't share the thought with him.

From the beauty salon, they returned to his house.

"Now let's figure out whom Vanessa went with to Anguilla," Paul said.

"He has to be a member of Congress."

"What do you base that on?"

"Vanessa's diaries. When you were shopping, I went through them. She dated a number of members of Congress. But she didn't mention any names. She just referred to them as Congressman A or Senator B."

"I should read the diaries. I might be able to figure out who they are."

Allison shook her head. "Vanessa didn't include descriptions of them. And I'd rather you didn't."

Allison didn't want to hurt him. She hoped he wouldn't press her. But he continued.

"When you said she was dating those guys in Congress, you mean she was fucking them."

"C'mon Paul. Leave it alone."

"Was she doing them while she and I were going together?"

"Paul, believe me, the diaries won't help."

Paul looked as if he'd been kicked in the teeth. She couldn't blame him. "So, I guess that means yes. Hey, no big surprise. Once when Vanessa came over she insisted on showering immediately. I was suspicious and now I understand."

Anxious to move away from the diaries, Allison reached into her bag and took out the notes she had made when she had been with Mary Pat at Hibernia in Anguilla. With careful emphasis on each word, she read Mary Pat's description. "Is there any way we can use this?"

"I have an idea," Paul exclaimed, now snapping out of it.

"Okay, what is it?"

"I can get pictures of all the members of Congress. With this description, we should be able to narrow it down to a reasonable number. Then forward pictures of those to Mary Pat for an ID."

"I like it."

"Right off the bat, we can eliminate the women, the non-Caucasians, and lots of the others."

"How do we get all their pictures?"

"Easy. I'm hooked up to my computer at the office. Same Internet access. I go online with a legislative service. I can pull up pictures and backgrounds of all the senators and House members."

"Great."

Paul rushed into the den. With Allison looking over his shoulder, he booted up the computer. Minutes later, the printer began spitting out five hundred thirty-five pages. On each, in the upper left hand corner, was a color picture. In the text below there were physical descriptions, bios, and committee assignments.

Paul split the pile in half and handed one to Allison. After only the first cut, they had reduced the possibles to seven—two senators and five congressmen.

For two of those, Paul knew staffers well enough to find out where their bosses had been Veteran's Day weekend. Hal was someone he played tennis with from time to time. And Bruce had been a law school classmate he saw at alumni functions and lunched with periodically. He asked each of them in an offhand way, where their bosses had been on Veteran's Day in an otherwise general conversation. Both had been in Washington. "Okay. We're down to five."

Paul restudied those. "Two," he said, "are too old and feeble to make a jaunt like that. And I doubt Vanessa would climb into bed with them. So that leaves us Congressman Wayne Pelston, upstate New York, Senator Dave Wolcott, North Carolina, and Senator Wesley Jasper, Colorado. Both Wolcott and Jasper are on Vanessa's Senate Armed Services Committee. Jasper is the chairman."

"Paul, you're fantastic." She felt as if they were almost there.

She watched him pick up Jasper's sheet and stare at it. His hand was shaking. What's going on, she wondered. "Time to call Mary Pat," Allison said.

With Paul listening, she took out her cell and called. "Hi, this is Allison Boyd. I spoke with you two days ago about my sister who drowned in Anguilla . . . I'm back in Washington . . . Yes, I got back without any problem. And thanks so much for the clothes. I'll return them to you. Now I have a favor to ask. I'd like to e-mail you photos of three men who might have been with Vanessa. Would you let me know if one of these is the guy? . . . Thanks so much. What's your e-mail address? I'll have them to you in a couple of minutes."

Paul scanned the three bio sheets. Then he typed a cover note. "Here are the three. Were any of these men with my sister, Vanessa, at your restaurant last weekend? Thanks for your help. Best regards, Allison." He hit the send button.

While they waited for a reply, Paul paced around the room, looking anxious as hell. "What's with him?" Allison asked herself.

"Could you please stop pacing? You're driving me crazy."

He sat down, staring at the computer. Five minutes later, Mary Pat's reply appeared on the screen. "It's Senator Wesley Jasper from Colorado."

Before Allison said a word, Paul replied by e-mail. "Are you certain?"

In an instant came Mary Pat's response: "Quite certain."

"Thank her," Allison said.

Paul typed that and hit the send button.

"Oh, Paul. We have our man. And it makes sense. He was the chairman of her committee."

"I guess so," he said glumly.

"What's bothering you?"

He hesitated for a minute. Then he said, "Jasper is a good friend of Andrew Martin's. I wish it were someone else."

"Listen, Paul, You've been so great to help identify that scumbag Jasper. Now I'd like you to stay out of this. I can't let you do anything to endanger your job."

"Don't worry about that. What are you planning to do now?"

"I'm going to confront Senator Jasper face-to-face in a public place—probably in a restaurant."

"Why? What do you hope to accomplish?"

"I want to find out what happened to Vanessa in her last days? And how she died?"

"You really think he'll tell you?"

"I'll threaten to go to his wife. And the *Washington Post*."

"If he tells you, will you still go to his wife and the paper?"

"I don't know. But Paul, I can go on now by myself. I can't put you at risk. And Jasper's relationship with Martin does that."

"No. We're in this together," he said emphatically.

She didn't want to hurt Paul's career, but he wasn't accepting that. So she changed her approach. "I'm not sure you have anything to add."

"You'll need a witness when you confront Jasper to avoid ending up with a he said/she said."

"I have to do this alone."

"I think you're wrong."

"Tell you what. If you want to help, come along and wait outside the restaurant. Hide across the street or in an adjoining doorway. If you see any hostile looking Chinese people approach, call me on my cell and let me know."

"Okay. Will do."

She recalled the sound of bones breaking in the nose and face of one of her assailants on the loading dock. She expected him to be trying to find her. "Oh, and one of them may have a bandage on his nose. He's angry and dangerous."

"The guy you hit with your bag?"

"Yeah. How do I get Jasper's office number?"

"Once Martin asked me to deal with him. I kept it."

Paul punched keys on his computer, printed out a page, and handed to her. "All of his contact info."

She called his office and said to his secretary. "I want to talk to Senator Jasper. Tell him that Vanessa Boyd asked me to call."

Seconds later, she heard, "This is Senator Jasper, who's calling?"

In a calm, clear voice, she responded. "Vanessa Boyd asked me to give you something."

"Who are you?"

"Meet me at noon at Bistro Francais in Georgetown. A booth in the back."

Allison hung up.

Paul said to her, "You think he'll show?"

"Damn right. He sounded scared to death."

*   *   *

As Allison left Paul on M Street and walked into Bistro Francais she wondered what the hell she was getting into.

Don't lose your courage, she told herself, shrugging off fear. She owed it to Vanessa to find out what happened. And she owed it to herself. Then she had to punish Jasper. He shouldn't get away with it.

Maybe she was jumping to conclusions, she thought. She better let him talk. Start with an open mind.

Allison walked past the bar and the wooden tables in the front of the bistro to the booths in the back. The restaurant was nearly empty. Dinner was their main business.

She spotted Jasper in a booth in the rear, his back to the wall. With determined steps, she headed that way. Across the room, she saw two elderly, gray-haired women eating salad.

"Senator Jasper," Allison said.

He stood up and looked at her with a petrified expression. "My God. You startled me. You look just like Vanessa."

"I'm Allison, Vanessa's twin."

"What did Vanessa give you to pass along to me?"

"Sit down, Senator. We have to talk."

Despite her intent to let him talk first, she was about to unload, but Jasper preempted her. "I knew your sister professionally at the Senate Armed Services Committee. We all liked her. I, of course, learned about her death, and I'm very sorry."

Astounding, Allison thought. He *learned about her death*.

"I believe you knew her a little more than professionally." Allison forced herself not to raise her voice.

"No, you're mistaken. Whoever told you . . . "

"Senator, I have an eyewitness who saw you with Vanessa last weekend in Anguilla."

"That's not possible. Last weekend I was in Colorado."

"Her name's Mary Pat, the proprietor of the Hibernia. You ate there with my sister Saturday evening. You had the duck and ordered two expensive bottles of wine, a white and a red Corton. You sat along the wall. At the end of the dinner, you told Mary Pat to tell her husband in the kitchen how much you enjoyed the duck. Is that enough for you?"

Allison, even in the dim light, could see the color draining from Jasper's face. He leaned forward and whispered, "What do you want? How much?"

"You're contemptible."

"Well then, what do you want?"

"First, to know what happened to my sister. All the details."

Jasper sat back up, seeming to recover.

"I wasn't with your sister. I already told you that."

"Give up, Senator. If not, I'll go to your wife with the e-mails I have from Mary Pat. Your wife knows you weren't in Colorado. After I talk to her, I'm going to the *Washington Post*. Then the *Denver Times*. I won't stop until I ruin your life."

Jasper sucked in his breath. "And if I tell you, just assuming that I do have something that would satisfy you . . . then how do I know you won't go to my wife and the papers anyway? All I'll be doing is giving you rope to hang me."

"To continue your metaphor, it doesn't take much rope to hang a man, and I already have plenty. So a little more won't matter."

Jasper's mouth hung open as if frozen.

While the Senator pondered this, a young waitress came over, placed two glasses of water on the table, and held out menus. "Would you like to look at these now?"

Allison wanted her away fast. "Pick your best fish dish. Bring two of them with ice tea."

Jasper looked beaten. "What do you want to know?"

"What happened Sunday evening?"

"Your sister was a wonderful woman. We were having a terrific weekend . . ."

"No, no, not now. I don't want to hear any of that." Her voice was quavering. "Sunday night, what happened? And the truth. No more idiotic stories."

"Okay. Okay. We were having a blast, living it up in a private villa on the beach."

"You weren't staying on a boat?"

"No, I hate those things. We had a great dinner Sunday evening at a place along the water. Then we went back to the villa. We stretched out on some chairs on the beach, sipping wine. She'd concealed a joint in her purse. She smoked that."

"What about you?"

He shook his head. "I don't do that."

"Oh I see. You're a boy scout. An adulterous boy scout."

"Anyhow, she said, 'It's time for a swim.' That was insane. With all the drinking we had done. And then the pot. I told her that. She laughed. Said 'you sound like my sister, Allison. Always worrying about me.' She stood up and pointed out to the sea. 'Look how calm it is. There's nothing to worry about. Come in with me,' she said. 'C'mon Wes.' But I refused. 'You're an over–the–hill creep,' she said. She pulled off her clothes and ran into the water. When it was up to her waist, she dove in and began swimming out. I watched her, following her bobbing head getting smaller and smaller, hard to see even with the moonlight. I thought I heard a noise, but I couldn't see a thing. I got up and looked around. Nothing there. Must have been a dog, I decided.

"Then I looked back toward the water." His voice dropped to a frightened whisper. "At first I couldn't see her. Then I did. Little sticks, must've been her arms waving wildly. Her head, I could see it, then I couldn't, then I could. A faint shriek. 'Help me . . . help me.'

"I peeled off my shirt and pants and ran into the water. In college I'd been a lifeguard at a resort during summers. 'I'm coming,' I shouted. 'Just hold on. I'm coming.' I swam as fast as I could, but it was tough going, even with the current pulling away from the shore. Remember I'd had a lot to eat and drink. I focused on her head bobbing up and down and moved on a straight line toward her.

"I thought I was only a couple of yards away, but suddenly I couldn't see her. Her head must have gone under. And this time it didn't come up. I dove down, swam madly to where I'd last seen her, found her, grabbed her around the waist and pulled her up, choking and gagging. I turned her onto her back. With one arm around her chest, I swam sidestroke, kicking hard as I damn well could, fighting the current back to shore. In the first couple of minutes, I couldn't make much progress. My whole body inside and out hurt like hell. I thought I'd never make it back with her. For an instant, I thought of leaving her and trying to save myself. But I couldn't do that.

"Finally, I could stand up. I placed her over my shoulder, face down, hoping she would start coughing. That water would come out of her mouth. But her body was totally limp. I plowed on through the sand with her over my shoulder."

Allison's teeth were clenched so hard her jaw ached.

"Once we reached dry beach, I placed her on her back and put my mouth over hers. Blew as hard as I could to force air into her lungs. All the while, praying, pleading silently. Don't die on me. Oh please God, don't let her die on me. Dammit, breathe. Please breathe. But it didn't happen. She didn't breathe. She didn't move.

"Then I turned her head on the side hoping the damn sea water would trickle out, but nothing. Not even a drop. I punched down on her stomach. No response. I looked into her eyes. Not even a flicker of her eyelids.

"I felt her pulse. Nothing. He shook his head. "Believe me. I did everything I could."

"What happened next?"

"I rolled away and fell exhausted on to my back, on the sand. I shut my eyes tight imagining that this last half-hour was all a terrible dream. A nightmare that would pass when I opened them. But I knew it wouldn't. A naked dead woman, who wasn't my wife, was lying there next to me."

Oh, you poor philanderer, Allison thought. *Was she supposed to feel sorry for him?* "So what did you do?"

"Well, I couldn't leave her on the beach. I picked her up and carried her up to the villa. Placed her down on a bed. Covered her body. Not her face."

"And then?"

"A lot of pacing around trying to decide what to do, spinning out possible scenarios. Each one worse than the other. Then I started shivering despite the balmy air. Well, my life's over, I thought. I'm fucked. Totally fucked! How could I ever have been so stupid? Why did I ever come here?"

"For some great sex," Allison softly responded. "That's why."

Jasper ignored her and ranted on. "What the hell had I been think-ing? To put my whole life on the line for this? 'Idiot,' I shouted out loud, pounding my hand against my forehead.

"Desperate, I decided to call the owner of the villa. I grabbed a cell phone and dialed him. He told me to come home. He'd take care of it."

"So how'd my sister's body end up on the beach in front of the hotel Corinthian?"

"I don't know. I swear. I left her on that bed in the villa and took off . . . Ms. Boyd. I'm not a bad person. I did all I could." Jasper began to sob. "He said he'd take care of it."

"You miserable bastards—'take care of it'—that's my sister you were talking about. Not a dead fish that washed up on the beach. She was left to rot. Or be eaten by animals."

The waitress came over with their food, set it down, and departed. Neither of them touched it.

Jasper said, "You may not believe this, but not an hour has gone by that I haven't been haunted by that night. That I haven't regretted running away. I'm not offering that as an excuse. Just an explanation."

"The hell with that. I want to know who told you he'd 'take care of it.' Who left my sister's body on the beach and created a bullshit story that she stayed alone at the Corinthian Hotel?"

"Ms. Boyd, I told you everything I know. Isn't that enough?"

"No, not for me. I have a right to know who the SOB is."

"Why?"

"He has to pay for what he did."

"He didn't do anything. It was an accident. She drowned."

Looking at him, she decided he wouldn't bend on this issue.

"Now I've told you everything about my relationship with your sister."

"Not everything. You didn't tell me that she expected you to marry her. Did you?"

"I never once said anything to her about marriage."

Relying upon what Susan had told Allison, but not wanting to involve Vanessa's committee colleague, whom Jasper could punish, Allison said, "Really. Before the weekend, she told me that she expected you to ask her to marry you."

"If she said that, she was unfortunately mistaken. I would never have left my wife and kids."

Allison decided to try a shot in the dark. The Chinese had been so anxious about the mysterious CD they believed Vanessa had possessed. She wanted to gauge Jasper's reaction.

"What about the CD?" Allison asked.

Jasper sat up with a start. He looked white as a sheet.

Pay dirt, Allison thought.

"What CD?" he asked weakly.

"The one my sister had." Allison was flying blind. Going on instinct. "The one she told you about."

"There never was a CD." He looked terrified. "It was all fabrication on her part."

"Why? To induce you to marry her?"

"No. Nothing like that."

"What then?"

"I have no idea what she was talking about."

She guessed that under the pressure of the moment, Jasper had told her too much, and he realized it. But he couldn't take it back.

"This discussion is over," he said. "I've told you what you wanted to know. Go now and leave me alone."

She got up and left the restaurant.

*   *   *

As Xiang sat in his office in the Chinese Embassy, Liu's words, telling him not to pursue Allison any longer reverberated in his brain like an old vinyl record that was stuck in one place.

Xiang had never disobeyed an order of Liu's, but this time he had to. The continual pain in his nose left him with a burning desire for revenge. But even more than that, he had bet his own life and those of his parents that the CD didn't exist. What if he was wrong? The three of them would die, he was convinced.

Even if there was a CD, he could emerge unscathed if he found it and destroyed it. That was easy to say, but he'd been searching without success for days for that damn CD.

At this point, he was convinced Vanessa had not hidden it. He had looked in every conceivable place.

If she didn't hide it, what did she do with it?

Then it struck him. Vanessa and Allison were more than twins. They had an incredibly close bond. Allison was risking her life to avenge Vanessa's death.

That must be the answer. Vanessa sent the CD to Allison for safekeeping.

He was also convinced that Allison hadn't seen the CD. In fact, she didn't even know about it until he had told her about it.

He went on line and checked Allison's Facebook page. She said that she had taken off from teaching this semester to work on a dig in Israel. Probably she had flown from Israel to Ohio for her sister's funeral. And from there to Washington. Never stopping in Providence, where she lived and taught at Brown. So if Vanessa sent the CD to Allison in Providence, it would be waiting for her there. At her home or office.

He searched some more on the Internet until he had a home address for Allison and the address of the department of archeology at Brown. Then he checked airline schedules. It was too long until the next plane to Providence. He decided to fly to Boston and drive down. There was no late evening plane back to Washington, but he could drive to Washington from Providence.

He'd have to leave enough time to get back to Washington for his five o'clock meeting with Jasper in Rock Creek Park tomorrow morning. Regardless of what happened in Providence, Xiang had to make that meeting. Jasper had promised to bring the Pentagon's five-year plan.

Nothing could stop Xiang from being there.

*   *   *

From Bistro Francais, Allison and Paul went back to Paul's house where she told him what transpired in her conversation with Jasper. When she was finished, he asked. "What do you intend to do now?"

"Take the story to the *Washington Post*?"

"Why? To destroy Jasper?"

"Not just that. He refused to tell me who arranged to move the body. If the *Post* gets on the story, they'll dig that out."

"They might not believe what you tell them about Jasper. He is a powerful man in this town. They won't just take your word for it."

She took out her cell phone and held it out. "They'll hear it all in Jasper's own words. I had my phone recording."

His head snapped back. "Wow! I'll never underestimate you."

"Jasper's a miserable disgusting sleaze bag."

"That may be, but there are risks for you in going to the press."

"What do you mean?"

"They always put their own spin on stories. I loved Vanessa, but as you know, she slept with many senators and congressmen. They'll focus on her sexual activities. After all, this was a weekend tryst between a senator and a very sexually attractive aide, and presumably one of many such adventures. I don't want you to be hurt."

As she weighed what Paul said, he continued. "I've had a few experiences of my own with the press which haven't been so good. Hell, look at what the *New York Times* did to Martin and me about our Guantanamo case. They totally twisted the facts. Martin was furious and he got a retraction, but still—hey! That's an idea. Why don't I set a meeting for you with Andrew Martin. He's had lots of experience dealing with the press. He'll be a good sounding board. You don't have to listen to him."

Allison was skeptical. "I know you have a high opinion of Martin, but what can he do for me?"

"He has superb judgment. He gives people advice in tough situations. And he's dealt with the Washington press a lot. What can you lose? Just an hour of your time."

She thought about what Paul had said. She had no doubt that he had her best interests at heart. Perhaps she was acting rashly. Talking to Martin would be a sanity check. She was at a critical juncture. She didn't want to overlook anything.

*   *   *

Martin was sitting at his desk, trying to concentrate on a brief, but all he could think about was being chief justice.

His phone rang. He could tell from caller ID that it was Paul on his cell. "Yes, Paul."

"I wonder if I could ask you a personal favor."

"Sure."

"Remember I went to Ohio for a funeral?"

"Yeah. Vanessa Boyd. A Hill staffer you dated."

"That's right. Well anyhow, her twin, Allison, is in Washington and she needs some advice. I told her you're the one I always turn to. And I was wondering . . ." Paul sounded nervous. "I was wondering if I could impose on you to meet with her this afternoon. I know it's a bad time for you with the Supreme Court, the FCC decency case, and everything else. But she won't take much of your time. I mean as a favor to me."

Martin abruptly felt vibrant, alive. This was a gift from the gods. He'd convince Allison to get off this kick and go back to her own life. Having Paul there would be a huge plus.

"Of course. I'll do it. What time?"

"We can be there in an hour."

"I'll be expecting you."

Martin placed down the phone, wondering if he should level with Allison. Tell her what happened Sunday night when Jasper called. He paced, weighing the pros and cons. No, too risky, he decided. He didn't know Allison and what if she were to take this story to the press? It all seemed so unfair, he thought. Sure he had been wrong to have made that stupid call, but Vanessa was already dead. It was an accidental drowning he had nothing to do with on a faraway beach. Why should he have to pay such an incredibly high price for one mistake with all the good he'd done?

And the consequences for Jasper? Hell, after what Wes threatened, why should he give a shit about Jasper? No, the only way was to persuade her to back off. But no threats or rough talk. He would appeal to her intelligence. And there was something to be said for leaving it alone. She couldn't bring her sister back. And it had been an accident.

He walked over to the credenza, picked up the family picture, taken on the beach in front of the house in Anguilla, and placed it in a drawer.

*   *   *

Allison followed Paul into Martin's office. Paul made the introductions.

"You're a busy man, Mr. Martin," Allison said "I appreciate your taking the time to meet with me."

"For a friend of Paul's, I make time."

"He tells me you're a legend in the legal world. That you should become chief justice. From the *Wall Street Journal* profile of you, I have to agree."

"What did you particularly like in that article?"

Without hesitating, she responded. "Three sentences. 'He's a pragmatic idealist.' 'He's apolitical, but public spirited,' and 'Under that thick head of brown hair lies a steel trap of a legal mind.'"

"Hey, you remember that article better than I do. The one Potts wrote in the *Post* wasn't nearly as flattering. In fact, not flattering at all. And the *Times* has been beating me up about Guantanamo." He laughed. "You read the right article. What do you do, Allison?"

"I'm on the faculty at Brown University."

"Specialty?"

"Why do I feel as if I'm being cross-examined?"

"Sorry. Too many years in the court room."

"The Middle East. Specifically biblical sites. I've taken off this semester to work on a dig in Israel."

"Let me show you something."

Martin led her across the room to a cabinet with thick glass doors. Inside were two jugs of dark orange pottery. And a metal knife. Identification cards underneath.

"Where'd you get these?"

He smiled. "You know they're from the Megiddo excavation, and it's illegal to take them out of Israel."

"Well, yes."

"Many years ago, I represented the Government of Israel in a border dispute with Egypt over the Sinai. And spent a lot of time with General Dayan. As you perhaps know, he was passionate about archeology. When I had been at Oxford on a Rhodes, I studied Middle Eastern history. So General Dayan and I had long talks on the subject. We were fortunate to get a good result in the dispute, so in addition to my fee, the Israelis lent me these artifacts, to keep during my lifetime. Then they go back to Israel. It's all documented in proper legal form."

"I'm impressed. Do you have any special security for them?"

"Our firm has guards around the clock."

Paul chimed in. "And when you move to the Supreme Court, you'll take them with you?"

"If I do. We're still a way away from that." He shrugged. "It's Washington."

Martin led them to the conference table.

"Anyhow. Enough about me. Paul said, I might be able to help you."

Allison leaned forward, looking at him. "Veteran's Day weekend, my twin sister, Vanessa, who worked for Senate Armed Services, went with a man to Anguilla and she drowned."

"Oh, I'm so sorry to hear that. So sorry for your loss."

"Thank you. Well, anyhow, perhaps it was an accident. Perhaps not. At any rate, they were staying in a villa, and the man she was with arranged for the owner of the villa to move her naked body to another beach so he wouldn't be implicated. Then he cut and ran."

"The guy sounds despicable."

"You're right, Mr. Martin. He's just scum."

"Please call me Andrew."

"At any rate, Andrew, I did a lot of digging here and in Anguilla . . ." She decided to omit mention of Paul's help to avoid creating a problem for him with Martin because she had taken him away from his work at the firm. She also decided not to mention the CD or the Chinese chasing her. At this point, she had no evidence that the CD and the Chinese had anything to do with what happened to Vanessa in Anguilla. Besides, she didn't want Martin to become distracted from the main issue, which was whether she should go to the *Post* with the Jasper story.

Martin was on the edge of his chair, listening intently.

"Bottom line," she continued, "I identified Senator Jasper from Colorado as the man my sister went with to Anguilla."

"Are you sure of that?"

"I confronted him a couple of hours ago at a restaurant, and he admitted it." She pulled out her cell phone and held it up. "I recorded the whole conversation. What he wouldn't tell me though, was whose villa it was. The man who arranged to move the body. So I told Paul I want to take my story to the *Washington Post*, and he told me to talk to you before I did that."

"What do you hope to accomplish by going to the *Post*?"

"I want to punish Jasper. And I figure the *Post* reporter will uncover the name of the villa owner which I haven't been able to do. What do you think?"

"First of all, let me tell you again how sorry I am about your sister. Not being a twin, I can't even imagine your grief. But . . . I assume you want my honest opinion."

"Of course."

"I think you'd be making a mistake going to the press. If you do, you'll suffer more, far more than you can imagine. The media will pounce on you, your sister, your parents, her high school classmates, her former lovers. Face it. This situation has all the ingredients of a lurid, attention-grabbing, story. Former super model. Sex with a Senator. Nude swimming. Alcohol, no doubt. Perhaps drugs."

"Look. I know my sister was no innocent."

"They'll dig out almost every man she slept with. If any others were in Congress, they'll particularly focus on them and name them. They'll trash her and tarnish her reputation. And the story will go on and on."

Waving his hands for emphasis, he continued. "Television crews will camp out on your parents' lawn in Oxford, Ohio. I assume they're still alive."

She nodded.

He continued. "Every time your mother or father comes out, they'll shove microphones in their face. You want to bring this down on them, too?"

She was biting her lip. She hadn't considered this might happen. Her poor dad was in bad enough shape without any of this. She closed her eyes and buried her head in her hands.

After a long minute, she looked up and said, "I just don't know. I owe it to my sister to expose what happened. And what about the man who arranged to move her body? It would be terrible if he got off scot-free."

"I agree, but what difference does it make? You can't bring your sister back. But your parents are still alive. What about the shame they'll feel? And you must have loved your sister. Look what you'll do to people's memory of her and how people will think of her for years to come."

"I don't know," she repeated.

"Tell you what, Allison. I think you should take twenty-four hours and think it over. The time won't matter. I always find that a decision like this needs thought."

He picked up a card from his desk. "This has my office, home, and cell numbers. Feel free to call me anytime."

"Thanks. I appreciate your taking the time to talk to me."

"Again, I am sorry for this tragedy. Now if you don't mind, I'd like you to step outside for a few minutes. I have to talk to Paul about one of our cases."

"No. Of course not. Paul, I'll meet you out on the street, on Pennsylvania Avenue in front of the building. I need some air."

*   *   *

Waiting for Allison to leave, Martin studied Paul. How in the world am I going to do this, he thought. Obviously Allison's emotional about her sister, and Paul's emotional about her. Still, I have to persuade him to get her to back off. If this went to the *Washington Post*, they'd pursue the story. His involvement would come out.

"Paul, let's look at this like a couple of lawyers. According to Allison, what are the facts? Her sister went off to Anguilla with Senator Jasper, a married man, for a weekend tryst as two consensual adults. Do I have that right?"

Paul nodded. "And her sister drowned."

"Right. No evidence of foul play?"

"Correct. But the body was moved."

"So what? It didn't disappear. And it wasn't mutilated. I assume it was shipped back home for a proper burial."

"Yeah. I was there."

"So now Allison wants to punish Jasper by wrecking his life."

"Something like that."

"But here's my problem. Beyond everything I told her about hurting herself, if she succeeds, she'll be hurting others too."

"So what if Jasper suffers? He . . ."

"Not just him. His wife and kids. They'll be hurt. And other people. When these things blow up in the press, lots of people get hurt. That's what I was telling her. Allison's parents and Allison will pay a heavy price."

"Jasper shouldn't have gone to Anguilla," Paul said stubbornly.

"No, of course not. And Vanessa shouldn't have gone either. But you know Washington. A psychiatrist ran a study a couple of years ago showing that it's no coincidence many of the people who make it big here have the type of personality leading them to extramarital affairs. We're not psychiatrists, but you and I have lived here long enough to know that's what happens. And had Vanessa not died, they'd have both flown home, sated from sex and happy, and making plans to do it again."

"So what are you telling me?"

"I don't see Allison accomplishing anything positive. She can't bring her sister back. All she can do is cause a lot of pain to other people, particularly her parents, and she'll tarnish her sister's image."

He couldn't tell if he was getting through to Paul.

"I don't know, Andrew. You make some good points."

"Then try to persuade Allison not to go to the press for her own sake. And for the sake of everybody else involved."

"I'll think about it and talk to her, Andrew."

Martin was convinced he hadn't gotten anywhere with Paul, who was clearly aiding Allison. Without Paul's help, Allison would never have fingered Jasper.

This wasn't over yet. So what could he do about Paul? His best course was to get Paul out of town and isolate Allison. She didn't know her way around Washington like he did. On her own, she might not get the attention of the right people at the *Post*.

"Okay, enough about Allison, Paul. I want to talk to you about the FCC decency case. The CEO of Global Media was the most effective witness for our side at the hearing. Rather than rely on cold transcript, I want you to get on a plane this afternoon, fly to Los Angeles, and spend some time with him. I'll set it up. That'll make the brief come to life."

"Can I wait a couple of days?" Paul asked.

"So you can help Allison? Is that it?"

Paul didn't respond.

"Now, you listen to me," Martin told him in a stern voice. "You're up for partner in less than a year. You've worked damn hard for that prize for eight years. Do you really want to blow your chances by wasting your time on a dead girl when you should be going all out on one of the most important cases you've ever worked on? If I leave to be chief justice, this could be your case and your client—a huge source of billable hours."

When Paul didn't respond, Martin continued, "I like you, Paul. I want you to be a partner in the firm whether I'm here or chief justice. But if you don't get your priorities straight, you'll never make it. Am I making myself clear?"

"Yes sir. You can call the CEO. I'll fly out this afternoon."

*   *   *

Allison was sitting on a bench on Pennsylvania Avenue letting the cool breeze whip through her hair. She found it refreshing and mind-clearing.

When she had been in Martin's office, listening to him talk, all of the disparate pieces of what had happened to Allison since she had received that call in Israel came together. Actually the process started in her meeting with Jasper.

The senator nearly blew a gasket when she mentioned the CD. So it did relate to him and his affair with Vanessa. Also the Chinese had been after this mysterious CD. Susan had said Vanessa expected Jasper to ask to marry her. And Vanessa's diaries all pointed to her desire, almost obsession, to marry someone powerful in Washington.

Allison knew her sister. Vanessa would be willing to use any tool at her disposal to get what she wanted. Even blackmail.

So what must have happened was that Vanessa threatened Jasper with disclosure of what was on the CD if he didn't marry her. But before he decided, or afterwards, she drowned. Perhaps, he killed her. Allison realized she had no evidence to support that supposition.

On the other hand, one thing was clear: if the CD existed, it contained potent information because the Chinese had done everything conceivable to get their hands on it. And Jasper was terrified about the CD.

Vanessa could have been bluffing, Allison thought. Perhaps there was no CD, but suppose it existed. Vanessa couldn't have taken it to Anguilla or Jasper would have it. So Vanessa had hidden it. But where? It was not found in her apartment or office, and was not in the bank vault.

Allison knew how her sister thought. She tried to put herself into Vanessa's mind. Where would she hide it?

Think, she told herself. Think.

In a moment, she had the answer. Vanessa always turned to Allison when she got into trouble or needed help. So it made sense that Vanessa would have mailed it to Allison in Providence, either to her apartment or her office at Brown. Being in Israel, Allison wouldn't have seen it.

That must be what Vanessa did.

Allison had to fly to Providence that afternoon. With the DC Police after her, she'd have to be careful. The disguise would help. For the airplane, she could use Vanessa's name and passport for ID.

No, that would be stupid. The airplane ticket agent might have seen Vanessa's picture and *Post* obit. Also, at airports, there were those pesky TSA security people. But this did not occur on Amtrak. The train was a much safer choice.

At Brown, she'd have to slip into her office at night when the building was deserted. She'd need to do the same when going to her apartment. She'd have to be very careful.

She wasn't sure whether she should tell Paul what she planned to do. She'd wait to hear what Martin told him and then decide.

A few minutes later, she saw him coming through the revolving door. As he approached the bench, he looked worried.

"What'd Martin say to you?" she asked.

"He told me to urge you not to go to the *Post* for your sake and your family's."

"What do you think?"

"I don't know. He made some good points,"

"I agree. I'm tossing them around as I think about what to do. What about your case?"

"He wants me to fly to Los Angeles this afternoon to meet a witness. And I have to go." Paul sounded dejected and resigned.

"I understand."

"I'll only be there twenty-four hours. I'll take the red-eye back tomorrow."

"Don't worry about me. I'll be fine."

"I want you to stay in my house until I return."

"But I don't look like Allison Boyd any longer."

"You can't take a chance. Please, Allison. Don't leave the house."

"Okay. I hear you."

She had no intention of telling him she was going to Providence. All he would do was argue with her about it. And she had to do it.

*   *   *

Fifteen minutes after Paul left the office, Martin's phone rang. He saw from caller ID it was Arthur Larkin.

Martin didn't wait for his secretary to answer. He picked up himself. "Yes, Arthur."

"I shouldn't be making this call, but you're my friend."

"And?" Martin was holding his breath.

"Braddock has decided to nominate you. Announcement is in three days because of his schedule."

Martin was so excited he wanted to scream.

Arthur continued. "Other than Francis, don't tell a soul. Not even your daughters."

"I understand and thanks for the call."

"One other thing."

"What's what?"

Arthur laughed. "Stay out of trouble for the next three days."

On the Rails and Providence

With Allison sitting in the quiet car, no cell phones or talking, the Acela train pulled out of Union Station in Washington. She took out her iPhone and was pleased to see a message from Zahava.

"Great news!!! The last couple of days we discovered objects which might be from King Solomon's time. Everyone here is singing your praises for not giving up in the face of adversity. We know that you have serious personal matters to resolve, and we don't want to rush you, but we were wondering if you have any idea when you'll return. The editor of the London based *Archeology Magazine* would like to send a team down to do a piece on the dig. But, I won't schedule it until you're back. You're going to be quite famous when this article appears."

The message excited Allison and buoyed her spirits. She replied. "What wonderful news. Thanks so much for sending it. I expect to be back within a week. As soon as I'm there, we can schedule the magazine visit."

Allison put away her iPhone and looked out of the train window. The Maryland countryside was passing by. I'll finish this and get my life back, she thought.

In Philadelphia two Chinese men boarded the train. As they moved along the aisle toward Allison, her heart was pounding. She didn't recognize either of them, but the man with the scar on his face could have sent them to follow her. They would call and tell him she was en route to Providence. He'd be waiting there to kill her as he had threatened. And that was before she broke his nose.

Don't be paranoid, she chided herself.

They walked past her and sat down, two rows behind. They'll probably get off in New York, she told herself.

They didn't. When the train pulled out of New York's Penn Station, they were still there.

*　　　*　　　*

Arriving in Providence, Xiang decided to go to Allison's apartment first. He thought it more likely that Vanessa would have sent the CD there.

He parked two blocks from her apartment building, a dilapidated three-floor wooden frame building with peeling gray paint, and made his way along the sidewalk, careful to avoid patches of ice and snow. The directory listed Allison's address as second floor. That meant other people lived in apartments on the first and third.

Though it was only ten minutes to seven in the evening, all three units were dark. That made Xiang's job easier.

He didn't see any cars driving on the street or other pedestrians, but he didn't run. Anyone who suddenly came along would think he lived there.

It took him thirty seconds to unlock the front door which led into a hallway and staircase shared by all three apartments.

Inside the door, he saw the entrance to the ground floor unit on the right. He didn't hear any noise coming from inside. On the left were three mail boxes and mail was piled on the floor. He pried open Allison's mail box, pulled out all the mail, and gathered up the pieces on the floor which were addressed to Allison.

He climbed the uncarpeted wooden stairs softly, cursing under his breath because they creaked. On the second floor he glanced around quickly, but didn't see anyone. So he put down the mail and used his tool to open the door. Once inside, he looked around quickly for a security system. There wasn't one. He imagined that university professors didn't have much worth stealing.

He turned on a lamp on the end table and studied the apartment. It was a two bedroom furnished modestly in what was old furniture, none of it matching, which Allison might have picked up at used furniture shops. The professor had lots of important things on her mind. Furniture and living conditions weren't two of them. Quite a contrast from her twin sister.

Xiang cleared Allison's desk by dumping everything but the computer on the floor. He dropped the mail on the desk and carefully went through each piece. Most related to her teaching, including journals and letters from other professors. After he examined an envelope, he tossed it onto the floor.

Nothing at all from Vanessa. He'd go to Allison's office in the archeology building next.

After Xiang left the apartment building and walked to his car to drive the ten blocks to the archeology building, he glanced back at the apartment and realized that he hadn't turned off the lamp. Well that didn't matter. After he was finished in Allison's office, whether he found the CD or not, he planned to come back to her apartment and wait there as long as he could, until he had to leave to drive back to Washington, in the hope that Allison might be in Providence and coming home—perhaps with the CD.

After parking a couple blocks away from the archeology building, he turned the corner and looked up at the imposing four-story gray stone structure. There were only a couple of lights on inside which he would have expected on a Sunday evening. Also, as he expected, the front entrance was locked. It was on a main thoroughfare.

Xiang decided the chances were too great of being spotted if he tried to work at that lock. So he walked around the building. In the back he found another door, that was metal. The lock looked tough to open, but he was confident he could do it.

Xiang removed the tools from his briefcase and went to work on the lock. As he did, he heard a window open on the third floor.

A young man with a black beard and curly hair leaned out of the window and called down to Xiang. "Hey, what are you doing? I'm calling the police."

Xiang was furious at himself for getting caught. He had to get away from the archeology building now. His only option was to go back to Allison's apartment and wait there, hoping she came before he had to leave to drive back to Washington. Maybe she'd have gone to her office and picked up the CD. Then he could snatch it from her. It was admittedly a longshot, but his only chance now.

Racing to his car, Xiang wasn't worried the police would track him to Allison's apartment. He had parked around the corner from the archeology building; he was confident the man in the window hadn't seen his car. And no one was chasing him.

As Xiang got into his car and pulled away, he heard police sirens headed to the archeology building. He drove in the other direction, making a circle to get back to Allison's apartment. He parked in an alley in the back. If he saw her, besides grabbing the CD, he'd scare her or even put her into the hospital.

Climbing the stairs to Allison's apartment, he checked his watch. He could stay in the apartment for no more than an hour. He had to leave enough time to drive back to Washington tonight. He couldn't miss his 5:00 a.m. meeting with Jasper tomorrow. The senator would be giving him the Pentagon's five-year plan.

Providence

As the train approached the station in Providence, Allison stood up and moved to the front of the car. Through the corner of her eye she watched the two Chinese men and held her breath. They didn't move. They must be going to Boston.

It was five minutes after nine in the evening when she stepped out of the station in Providence. Two cabs were parked at the curb. She was the first in the cab line, but she motioned to the two students behind her to take the first cab. She took the second one. She had read about that in a novel called *Spy Dance*. It was a good safeguard if a spy was worried someone was trying to abduct him.

She asked the cab to drop her three blocks from the archeology building— another bit of tradecraft from *Spy Dance*.

As she got out of the cab, she was careful to avoid the ice at the curb. It had snowed a couple of days ago and a cold breeze was whipping off the ocean. In her thin jacket, it cut through Allison like a knife.

Approaching the archeology building, she was astounded to see three police cars parked in front, the lights on their roofs flashing.

She removed her key to the front door from her bag. A policeman, tall and heavyset in his forties, stopped her in front of the door.

"Who are you?" he asked.

Act natural, she told herself. The Metro incident may have been big news in Washington, but Providence was a long way off. "Allison Boyd, archeology professor."

"ID?"

She removed her university ID from her wallet and held it out. He glanced at it and looked quizzical.

"I decided to bleach my hair," she said. "A woman's prerogative.'"

He smiled. "Yeah, my wife does it all the time. She's a redhead this week. You can go in."

"What happened here?"

"Some Chinese guy was trying to break in. A grad student upstairs saw him and called us. Strikes me as an odd place to break in."

"Maybe he wanted to get a copy of an exam."

He laughed. "You're funny, Blondie. You know that."

"People tell me all the time. So what happened to the Chinese guy?"

"He got away before we arrived."

She guessed it had been her assailant from Washington, and he was looking for the CD. She would have liked to ask the cop whether the Chinese man had a scar on his left cheek, but she realized that would get her a ride to police headquarters for interrogation. Besides, she was convinced he was the one.

After Allison used her key to open the front door of the building, the cop handed her a card and said, "This has my office and cell phone. Call me if you hear or see anything about this Chinese guy."

Allison thanked the policeman and put it into her bag.

Before going to Israel, she had asked the secretary to the department chairman to place all of her mail on the desk in Allison's office. As she entered her office, she saw three good sized piles. Allison had no interest in reading her mail. She was on a mission: to find an envelope from Vanessa.

Nothing in the first two piles. Her hopes sagged. Was this all a wild goose chase? Still, Vanessa might have mailed it to her apartment.

Midway through the third pile, she saw it. A plain brown envelope. The return address had no name, simply Vanessa's home address in Washington. She checked the rest of the third pile. There was nothing else from Vanessa.

Allison opened the plain brown envelope carefully. Inside she saw a CD in a case, covered by bubble wrap. No markings on the case or the CD. No note.

Allison eyed the CD player on a credenza against the wall. She was tempted to play it immediately, but thought better of it.

She recalled that her department head and other faculty members had seen Allison's name and picture in the Washington press after the Metro incident and had sent her e-mails asking what was happening, all of which she had ignored. She had better take the CD, get the hell out of the building, and play it in her apartment.

She made certain to turn off her office lights and lock her door as she exited the building.

The policeman said, "Done so soon?"

"I just had to pick up some papers."

"Well, have a nice night, Blondie," he said and laughed.

She set off on foot. With the collar pulled up on her jacket, she covered the ten blocks to her apartment quickly. Only a couple of cars passed. They didn't seem to pay her any attention.

Two blocks from her building, she saw that the apartments on the first and third floors units were dark. But *there was a light on in her apartment.*

She had remembered to turn off all the lights when she had last been there four weeks ago. She was now convinced the Chinese man had been in her apartment. Or was still there, alone or with others.

If he was still there, she could have him arrested for breaking and entering. That would get him out of circulation while she listened to the CD and acted on what she learned. She took out her cell phone, then searched her bag for the policeman's card.

As she did, she saw a Chinese man with a bandage on his nose race out of her building and toward the alley in the back. He had to be the man she smacked with the diaries on the loading dock.

She had no time to call the policeman. Her only option was to stop him herself.

She reached down to the ground and grabbed a tree branch that had fallen in the recent storm.

"Hey," she cried out and chased him.

By the time she reached the alley, he was in his car and the engine was on. Tree branch in hand, she ran toward his car. He gunned the engine and drove toward her. When he was almost at her, she flattened herself against a garage door. He narrowly missed her and continued driving. She expected him to turn around and make another pass at her.

As he did that, she dropped the tree branch and her bag on to the ground. She grabbed her cell phone in one hand and with the other frantically searched her bag for the cop's telephone number.

That must have frightened her assailant because he executed another U turn and roared away from her.

No point calling the policeman, she decided. She let herself in the front door of the apartment building and noticed that her mail box was open, but there was no mail inside or on the floor. He had undoubtedly taken it all. Hopefully, he left it in her apartment.

When she entered her apartment, she saw her mail and papers from her desk scattered on the floor and gasped. "Holy shit!"

She realized that she should call the police, but that wouldn't accomplish anything. The man was already gone.

She looked through the mail tossed on the floor and glanced at the envelopes. Nothing from Vanessa. She hoped he hadn't taken away something else Vanessa had sent, but at least she had the CD.

She walked over to a small portable CD player. She carried it to her desk and inserted the CD, moving her chair close to the machine so she could keep the volume low to avoid waking anyone in the building.

She hit play and heard:

"This is Vanessa Boyd, a staff member of the Senate Armed Services Committee. On July 26th of this year, I was in the Tokyo suite of Senator Wesley Jasper from Colorado in the Okura Hotel. What follows is a recording of a conversation between Senator Jasper and Minister Liu, the director of the Ministry of State Security for the Chinese government."

Liu (in English): Thank you for agreeing to meet with me, Senator Jasper.

Jasper: Your ambassador in Washington told me that you would like to discuss a matter of mutual interest. I was curious. Would you like something to drink?

Liu: Scotch. If you have it. Cool.

Jasper: That's my drink of choice. The Japanese government left me a bottle of Macallan 18.

Liu: Good.

A pause.

Liu: Salute . . . Do you mind if I smoke?

Jasper: No. Of course not.

Pause.

Liu: Let me come right to the point. I understand that for various reasons, you have financial concerns at this critical time with a reelection next year.

Jasper: I have always been able to raise money effectively. I have a number of large donors who will contribute and raise money. As the incumbent, I have an enormous advantage. I am not concerned.

Liu: Of course not. I simply wish to make matters easier for you.

Pause.

Jasper: How much easier?

Liu: Five million US dollars deposited monthly into a numbered Singapore account whose undisclosed Chinese owner would assure strict confidentiality.

Jasper: You're asking me to violate the law by taking money from a foreign government. I won't do that.

Liu: I will structure it in a way that no one else will ever know.

Jasper: People always find out.

Liu: Not if we're careful.

Jasper: I don't know.

Liu: If you're not interested, I'm sorry I've wasted your time.

Jasper: I'm not saying I'm not interested. Suppose . . . just suppose I am. How would I access this money?

Liu: By inserting the account number into your cell phone, you will be able to transfer electronically as much of the funds to an account anywhere in the world. If we reach an agreement this evening, when you return to Washington one of my people at the embassy will arrange a meeting and explain the logistics to you. They are quite simple.

Jasper: They will have to be because I am not strong in technical matters.

Laughter.

Jasper: And what would I have to do in return for the money? Block my committee from approving armed sales for Taiwan?

Liu: For five million a month, I want something more than that.

Jasper: What?

Liu: My government is interested in your military's developing presence in Asia and the Pacific. We want to know which troops and equipment are being moved to various Asian and Pacific locales. Second, we want to know what new weapons are being developed by your defense contractors. Third, we're interested in knowing what military commitments the United States has made to Japan, South Korea, and other nations in Asia.

Pause.

Jasper: You're asking me to commit treason.

Liu: I prefer to think of it as friends helping each other.

Jasper: A rose by any other name is still a rose.

Liu: I don't care what you call it.

Pause.

Jasper: If I'm caught, I'll go to jail for life. Maybe to the electric chair.

Liu: You won't get caught.

Jasper: You can't guarantee that.

Liu: You'll be safe as long as you behave wisely.

Jasper: I love my country.

Liu: Of course you do. None of this will damage the United States. It will merely insure that both China and the United States understand each other's capabilities. That way there will be no chance of a miscalculation that could lead to war.

Jasper: Do you honestly believe that?

Liu: It happens to be true.

Jasper: I don't know . . . If I agree to this, how would I hand over the information?

Liu: You would make copies of the relevant documents. Your contact in Washington would tell you how to deliver them.

Jasper: I don't know. You're asking quite a bit.

Liu: And giving even more.

Jasper: If I'm caught, my name will be vilified. My wife and children will become hated.

Liu: You won't get caught.

Pause.

Jasper: The money's not the issue. I won't do it.

Liu: Too bad. Sorry, I wasted your time. I'll find someone else. I'm leaving now.

Pause.

Liu: Goodbye.

Jasper. No. Don't go. Tell me again. Do you really believe you can make this foolproof so I won't get caught?

Liu: Absolutely. Our interest is identical to yours on this point.

Pause.

Jasper: Okay, I'll do it.

The CD ends.

As Allison replayed the CD and listened to it for a second time, everything fell into place.

Jasper had killed Vanessa because he knew she had the CD. Unquestionably, Jasper and the Chinese would have killed anyone to get their hands on the CD. For Jasper, it would mean life in prison. For the Chinese, it would mean a serious international incident and a poisoning of relations with the United States.

As she turned off the machine after listening the second time, she was outraged at what her sister had done. Vanessa had learned that Jasper was willing to betray his country. She should have reported this to the FBI. But, no, she didn't want to turn in her lover. Indeed, she wanted to use what she had learned about his treason to her own advantage—to compel him to marry her. She wanted to join him in his treason—to become a partner.

Allison felt sick. This was worse than Vanessa sleeping around with different men. This was being a traitor.

Their father had taught them to love the United States. Vanessa was willing to betray him as well as her country.

Horrified, Allison thought about Jasper. She knew he was scum for leaving her sister's dead body in Anguilla and running away, but now she realized he was even worse than she had thought: he was a traitor who could do incalculable damage to the United States.

Jasper had to be stopped. She had to get the CD to the FBI fast. Paul might be able to help her do that.

She checked her watch. By now he should be on the ground in LA, probably in his hotel room.

She called him on his cell. "Hope I didn't wake you."

"No, I was just revising a draft brief for Jenson that Diane, an associate, gave me. What's up?"

"The most incredible thing."

"What happened?"

In describing the CD to Paul, she identified Jasper but referred to the other man only as an intelligence agent of another nation. She had no reason to believe anyone was listening on her phone, but instinctively she felt using Liu's name subjected her to great risk. She was relieved that Paul didn't ask her the identity of the other man. She wondered if he had the same concern for her.

When she finished, he said, "This is unbelievable. Far worse than I ever imagined."

"Agreed. What I plan to do in the morning is go by train back to Washington. Then take the CD into FBI headquarters."

"Wait a minute. You can't do that. First, you're wanted by the police. Second, you look funky, and third, you can't just walk into the FBI building. You have to get to the right person."

"Can you find out who that is?"

"I can't from here, but Martin will know immediately. Maybe he'll even go with you. Jasper has to be stopped. I'll have my meeting tomorrow and take the red-eye home, but you can't wait. In the morning you should take the first train to Washington. From the train, call Martin and get on his calendar tomorrow afternoon. When you meet with him, tell him about it. He'll be able to advise you."

"Why Martin?"

"As I said, he knows the top FBI people. He deals with high-level Washington stuff all the time. Also, he obviously likes you. He gave you all his numbers and told you to call anytime. Use his cell and call between seven and eight in the morning. That's what I do when I really have to talk to him. He's at home having breakfast. You can always get through. Don't tell him what you want. Just that you want to meet. It'll be easier in person."

"Okay. I'll do that," she said.

"And be real careful. Wear a hat or something to cover your face. Remember, there's a warrant out for your arrest."

When Allison hung up the phone, she thought about her situation. It really was precarious.

There was a limited amount she could do to protect herself. But one thing she could do was ensure that the contents of the CD were published and Jasper destroyed even if she were killed.

And she knew exactly how to do that. She went to a nearby office supply shop which catered to Brown students and was open all night. There, she made a copy of the CD. She put it into an envelope addressed to the foreign editor of the *Washington Post*, added stamps, and put that into a second envelope addressed to Sara Gross in Oxford, Ohio.

She began filling out a FedEx form to send it to Sara. Then it occurred to her that was stupid because she'd be leaving a trail that would lead to Sara. The best was plain old US Mail. No express, no certified, and no record of it being sent.

She addressed it and added stamps. On her way to the mail box at the corner she called Sara on her cell. "Sorry to call so late."

"No problem. I'm on call tonight. They've been coming about every fifteen minutes."

"I need a favor."

"Hey, wait before you get to that. What's happening with you? We heard all about that Metro incident. We're all scared for you."

"Don't worry. I'm okay. But here's what I want. I'm mailing you a brown envelope to your home. Ordinary mail. Put it in a safe place. If anything happens to me . . ."

"Like what?"

"Like I'm killed."

"Oh my God."

"Then I want you to open the envelope." Allison was cold. She was talking fast. "Inside you'll see another envelope stamped and addressed to the *Washington Post*. I want you to mail it. Got that?"

"Allison, what's this about. What's in the envelope?"

"You don't want to know. Please just do what I asked. Promise?"

"I promise."

"Thanks."

Allison went back to her apartment, slept a couple of hours, then caught the 6:50 a.m. train to Washington.

She used Martin's cell number to call him at 7:15 a.m., just as Paul suggested. He didn't ask her what she wanted, but he simply said, "Come to my office at nine this morning."

"I can't make nine. I'm on a train on my way back from Providence."

"Then come as soon as your train arrives."

/

Washington

Driving from Providence to Washington was tough for Xiang. The first part of the trip was in sleet and freezing rain. The rest of the way just rain. At least the traffic was light. All the while Xiang kept his eye on the clock. He had committed the route to memory.

He planned to arrive at his Connecticut Avenue apartment at 4:15 a.m.. He pulled up in front of the building at three minutes after that. Just enough time to change clothes and set off for Rock Creek Park to meet Jasper.

Xiang decided that the rain and mud on the jogging trail would be an advantage. In all of their meetings to date, Xiang had never seen another jogger on the trail at five in the morning. For today's meeting when he expected Jasper to turn over the five-year plan, anything to ensure their privacy was an advantage.

When Xiang reached the meeting place, he found Jasper already there holding a black Chevy Chase Country Club umbrella over his head. He was wearing a wind breaker with a pocket large enough to hold a document. Hopefully, the plan.

Water was running down Xiang's head and into his eyes. He moved close enough to Jasper to get under the umbrella.

"What happened to your nose?" Jasper asked .

"I was in a boxing match with one of my colleagues. You should have seen what he looked like."

"Now tell me about Allison Boyd," Jasper asked anxiously. "She's all over the news. Was the man she killed at the Metro station one of yours?"

"You don't have to worry. Everything is taken care of."

"It doesn't seem that way to me."

"The secretary of state persuaded the Washington police to close their investigation."

"That's good news."

"Do you have the document for me?"

Jasper shook his head. "The secretary of defense asked for a two-day delay in the hearing. The military people couldn't complete the five year plan and be ready to testify until Wednesday morning at ten. They'll deliver the document to my house Tuesday evening. I'll bring it to a meeting with you here Wednesday morning at five."

"Okay," Xiang said softly.

Xiang was disappointed, and he knew Liu would be upset because of the delay, but nothing he could do about it. The important thing was that Jasper was still planning to turn the document over to Xiang.

"Now what about the CD?" Jasper asked.

Xiang realized he couldn't tell Jasper there was no CD and that he was in the clear. If he did that, Jasper might not turn over the document. He had to stall and maintain his leverage over Jasper.

"I'm getting close."

"You told me that the last time we were together."

Xiang had to string Jasper along until Wednesday morning when Jasper had the five-year plan. "I expect Allison to go to Vanessa's bank vault today. Chances are that's where Vanessa hid it. Once she gets it, I'll snatch it from her and deliver it to you Wednesday morning."

That seemed to satisfy Jasper. He was smiling. But as soon as the words were out of Xiang's mouth, referring to the bank vault, he realized he had screwed up. He had left one loose end: those books in Allison's bag that he had never examined at the loading dock. Those could be earlier volumes of Vanessa's diaries Allison found in the bank vault box and might have mentioned Jasper. Well, it was too late to do anything about it now. Besides, they didn't involve the CD. They could only hurt Jasper.

But if Allison exposed Jasper's affair with Vanessa in Anguilla before Jasper delivered the plan to Xiang, Jasper might be too angry to turn it over. Damn. Xiang felt inadequate for the role Liu had thrust upon him. He was too inexperienced. Like a boy, unaccustomed to water, he was thrown into a lake. Sink or swim. He was thrashing, but he made up his mind not to go down.

"You might be right about the bank vault being the place where Vanessa hid the CD," Jasper said thoughtfully.

The rain was letting up. Jasper paused to put down the umbrella. Then he continued, "Allison's a tough little wench, and she's used to digging. That's her job in archeology."

"I know that. I did research on her. That's why I'm confident she'll lead me to it in the next two days." He thought of Providence. He was angry at himself for not being able to break into the archeology building. That must have been where the CD was: in Allison's office.

"I hope you're right."

Xiang saw a jogger approaching on the trail. "We better split," he said and took off running away from the jogger at a much faster pace.

Over his shoulder, he watched Jasper raise his umbrella and use it to conceal his face.

As he ran, Xiang thought about his meeting with Jasper. When he got to the embassy, he had to call Liu, who wouldn't be happy that Xiang didn't have the plan. He'd curse and yell at Xiang. But at the end of it, he'd have to wait two more days for something that valuable.

*   *   *

Allison took a seat in front of Martin's desk.

"What have you decided about going to the press?" he asked.

"I was trying to make up my mind. Then I found a CD that puts a whole new light on the incident."

"What CD?" Martin sounded puzzled.

"When I put together all the pieces of what happened in Anguilla, I decided Vanessa wanted Jasper to marry her. To convince him to do that, she threatened to disclose a damaging CD."

Allison took it out of her bag and held it up.

"Where did you get that?"

"Vanessa mailed it to my office at Brown."

"Do any other copies exist?"

She decided to lie. She had to protect her insurance policy until she needed it. With Martin. Even with Paul. With everyone except Sara. "To my knowledge, it is the only CD. There are no copies."

"What do you mean the CD is damaging?"

"Do you have a CD player?"

He pointed to a machine on the credenza. Allison inserted the CD and hit play.

As it did, she watched Martin's face. What she saw was stunned disbelief.

Paul had told her that Jasper was a friend of Martin's. She was sure he never expected this from the senator.

At the end, he said, "This is very serious."

"I realized that so I called Paul in LA about it last night. I told him that I wanted to take it to the FBI. He said you could help me. Tell me where to go in the FBI."

"I don't think you want to do it yourself. You're wanted by the DC Police. That will affect your credibility."

"Then how should I get it to the FBI?"

Martin walked over to the window overlooking Pennsylvania Avenue. He appeared to be deep in thought. After a minute, he sighed, turned around, and said, "Leave it with me. FBI Director Jim Forester is a former judge and someone I've known a long time. I'll take it to him. Jasper may be my friend, but he can't get away with treason. You've done the country a great service."

"You want me to go with you to see Forester?"

"No offense, Allison, but your presence will only complicate things with that arrest warrant for you. When I talk to Forester, I can sidestep all that stuff. Ultimately the CD speaks for itself."

She handed him the CD. "I guess you're right. How soon will you be able to get the CD to the FBI?"

Martin asked for her cell number and said, "Stay in Washington. The FBI doesn't move real fast, particularly with something like this where a member of Congress is involved. They may want to talk to you. Meantime, keep out of sight so you're not arrested."

When Allison left Martin's building, the sun was shining. She decided to walk to Paul's house. It would take her about an hour, but she hadn't exercised in days and she needed it.

As she walked, she felt very pleased with herself. This was all turning out so much better than she expected. Rather than simply disclosing Jasper's weekend trip with Vanessa in the media and destroying his marriage and his political career, she would be responsible for Jasper going to jail for treason for a very long time. She would gain her revenge over Jasper for what he had done to Vanessa in Anguilla.

*   *   *

After Allison left, for a full two minutes Martin sat dumbstruck at his desk. He asked his secretary to hold all his calls. He had to think this through.

He played out in his mind what would happen if he took the CD to Forester. The FBI would initially schedule an interview with Jasper. Since he was a US senator, they wouldn't immediately arrest him. Jasper might try to argue that the CD was a phony, fabricated by his lover to force Jasper to marry her. But the FBI technical people would cut through that. They'd establish the CD was authentic. Jasper was going down. No doubt about it.

Martin recalled Jasper's harsh words at Camelot. "If I go down, I'm pulling you with me."

He had no doubt that Jasper meant it. He would trumpet Martin's involvement in Vanessa's death. The chief justice nomination was practically his. Arthur had told him that. He couldn't let that snake Jasper, an adulterer and a traitor, disrupt what he had worked for all these years.

As Martin rehashed the Anguilla events in his mind, he wondered if Jasper was responsible for Vanessa's drowning. The man was a superb swimmer. He could have found a way to kill her, which would make him a murderer as well. And if that was the case, Martin thought, he would have, unwittingly, been an accessory after the fact. My God. He'd never thought of his possible involvement in a murder until now. But this CD was so explosive that Jasper could have killed Vanessa because of it.

Since Allison's visit, the stakes for Martin had increased exponentially. He had to act to save not only his chief justice nomination, but his career—indeed his life.

He had to find a way out of this quagmire.

One possibility was to hold up turning the CD over to Forester for a brief period of time—long enough to disclose the CD to the Chinese ambassador and determine whether it was a forgery or something else was happening. Perhaps this CD wasn't what it seemed.

Martin realized doing that would be a dangerous move. He was a private citizen, not part of the United States law enforcement. He had already intervened for the Chinese in misleading the secretary of state in connection with the Metro death. People could argue that Martin's talking to the ambassador about the CD would make him complicit in Chinese espionage. That would be far more serious than moving the body of a dead woman.

How could he possibly justify that?

"Well, Mr. Prosecutor, I wanted to make certain the CD was authentic."

"That wasn't your responsibility. Was it, Mr. Martin?"

"No, sir. It wasn't."

That rationalization just wouldn't fly.

But on the other hand, if the CD was a forgery or if something else was involved, Martin had to know before he turned it over to Forester. Martin had so much riding on what happened with this CD. He had to remain in charge for as long as he could. To control his own destiny.

What should he do?

Call the Chinese ambassador or not?

Martin honed in on the tough decision.

I can go either way.

That's bullshit.

Having come so far down the slippery slope, you know damn well what you're going to do.

Martin thought about his schedule for this evening. Francis would be at the Kennedy Center for dinner and a concert with a colleague. He would be alone in the house.

He called the Chinese ambassador.

"I would like to meet with you this evening at eight at my house. Can you do that?"

"I'll be there," the ambassador replied.

*   *   *

Martin knew the ambassador liked good scotch. He had a bottle of aged Glenlivit on the tea wagon in the den.

"I think you will need this," Martin said as he fixed them each a drink. "And you had better sit down."

When they were both seated, Martin said, "You have a very big problem." He didn't say "we" because the ambassador would have no idea Martin was involved in Vanessa's death.

The ambassador took a gulp, then said, "More about the Metro matter?"

"That would be easy. I want to play a CD for you."

As it played, Martin watched the ambassador. His face turned pale. He was trembling. Martin thought he might have a heart attack.

At the end, after Martin hit the stop button, the ambassador said, "Is this a privileged conversation?"

"Absolutely. I am the lawyer for your embassy and country."

"Then I want to ask you how you got the CD?"

"Allison Boyd, the woman who pushed your man onto the Metro tracks, gave it to me."

"Are there any copies?"

"She told me, 'no.' I believe her."

"What do you intend to do with this?"

"Take it to Jim Forester, the FBI director."

"I see."

"In view of my long relationship with your government, I am willing to wait until ten o'clock tomorrow morning to take it to Forester. Perhaps, before then, you can persuade me that the CD is a forgery or give me some other reason not to turn it over."

*   *   *

Xiang was in his apartment cooking dinner when he received a call from the ambassador, "Come back to the embassy now. Meet me in my office as soon as you can."

The frantic tone in the ambassador's voice informed Xiang that something serious and terrible had occurred. He immediately guessed: someone had found the CD, which he had told Liu didn't exist. His heart was pounding.

Xiang drove at breakneck speed to the embassy and immediately went to the ambassador's office.

The grim-faced ambassador told Xiang, "Vanessa's CD has been located, exposing Operation Trojan Horse."

"No . . . how could that be?"

246 THE WASHINGTON LAWYER

"The girl Allison found it."

"Where?"

"I wasn't told."

"You heard the CD?"

The ambassador nodded. "Unfortunately, it's exactly as Vanessa represented to Jasper in Anguilla. It exposes operation Trojan Horse and Minister Liu's recruitment of Jasper. It's a disaster."

Xiang was thinking about what he could do now. The ambassador interrupted him. "We'll call Minister Liu in Beijing on the secure phone. The three of us have to be on the call."

"Of course," Xiang said weakly.

Moments later, with the call on speaker, the ambassador reported on his meeting with Martin and what he had heard on the CD. As he spoke, Xiang heard Liu curse from time to time. At the end, Liu asked the ambassador to leave the office and close the door, "So I can talk to Xiang alone."

When the ambassador was gone, Liu told Xiang, "Pick up the phone and get it off speaker."

"Yes sir."

His hand was shaking so badly he could barely hold the phone.

"Now listen, Xiang. You assured me on your life and that of your parents' that the CD did not exist. You said it was all a bluff by Vanessa to induce Jasper to marry her. Correct?"

"Yes, sir. I'm prepared to come home and accept my punishment."

"I would enjoy that, but I have an alternative. A way for you to redeem yourself."

"I'll do anything you ask."

"Good. I want you to meet Jasper tomorrow morning and kill him."

Liu said it coldly, in a voice devoid of emotion, as if he were asking Xiang to close the door.

Xiang was stunned. He wanted to serve his country, but this wasn't what he had signed on to do. He realized he was being stupid and naive. Though it was risky for him, he decided to make a pass at persuading Liu to change Jasper's death sentence.

"But tomorrow evening Jasper will have the five year plan. Wednesday morning, he'll give it to me."

"Perhaps he will, or perhaps he's just stringing you along as you are with him and the CD."

That stopped Xiang for an instant. He reddened and said, "I've spent enough time with Jasper to know when he's telling the truth."

"I doubt that. But don't be such a fool. Even if what you are saying is correct, that he expects to have the five year plan tomorrow evening and to give it to you Wednesday morning, that will never happen now. If Jasper is alive tomorrow morning, he'll be arrested before noon. He'll never even get his hands on the five year plan. Jasper can't possibly help us anymore. The only chance we have of persuading Martin not to turn over the CD to the FBI is if Jasper is dead. Do you understand?"

Reluctantly, Xiang now agreed with Liu. "Yes sir. That's correct."

"Let me ask you, Xiang, have you ever killed a man?"

"No, sir."

"And you don't want to kill Jasper. Do you?"

Xiang steeled himself to reply in a firm voice. "I am prepared to kill Jasper. That's what's required."

"Are you certain? If not, I'll have somebody else do it."

"I am certain. This is my project."

"Well, you had better mean it because your parents will pay the price if you don't do it in a manner that avoids any possible responsibility falling upon you or the People's Republic of China. Am I making myself clear?"

"Yes, sir. It will be done."

"When?"

"Tomorrow morning at five."

"You better not mess this up."

Xiang staggered out of the ambassador's office and left the embassy. He decided to leave his car and walk home. As he moved up Connecticut Avenue toward his apartment, he was in agony. He had always considered himself a good person, a super achiever in school, a respectful son, and loyal to his nation. At Carnegie Mellon as a student, he had been respected, a recipient of a number of top honors.

Even after he joined, and was in the intelligence service, he believed that he was serving his nation, not compromising his moral standards. He had been a fool to have believed that he wouldn't have to do something like this while working for the MSS.

He had also been a fool to have left his village to go to Shanghai. One thing led to another and, blindly, he'd ridden the train up and up the mountain until now when he suddenly felt as if he were hurtling into a moral abyss. How could it have come to this? To his contemplating the murder of another human being?

To be sure, Jasper was a despicable person, a traitor, and an adulterer, but Xiang couldn't rationalize killing him.

He had his own ineptitude to blame for being in this position. If only he had found the CD, it would never have come to this.

He passed shops and small restaurants filled with people talking and laughing.

He wasn't Liu's slave, he decided. He still had control over his destiny. He didn't have to kill Jasper.

A plan was taking shape in his mind. As soon as he returned home, he would call his parents and tell them to leave immediately for the countryside where they'd lived before they moved to Beijing. They still had friends and relatives in the town. Most of the people hated the government in Beijing for arbitrarily dictating living conditions and favoring the cities at the expense of rural areas. They would provide his parents a place to hide from Liu's agents.

As for Xiang, he knew the United States very well. It was a huge country. He could disappear into the American west somewhere in Oregon or California and become one more of the millions of illegals residing in the United States. He'd take on another name. Most Americans lumped all Chinese, even all Asians, together. No one would notice or care. Yes, that's what he would do. He wouldn't kill Jasper. He'd run away.

When he entered his apartment, he smelled the peppers and eggplants he had been cooking before the ambassador had summoned him to the Embassy. He couldn't think about eating.

He sat down at his desk, grabbed his cell phone, and called his parents. The phone rang three times. Then, horrified, Xiang heard in Chinese, "This number has been disconnected."

In his haste, he must have dialed incorrectly, Xiang thought. He ended the call and dialed again. Same message.

He felt as if he'd been hit in the gut with a two by four. He felt sick to his stomach as the realization of what had happened took hold.

While he was walking back to his apartment along Connecticut Avenue, Liu, one step ahead of Xiang, had concluded Xiang might want to disobey his order to kill Jasper. So Liu had moved quickly, cutting off his parents phone service, probably even arresting them, or at least having tight surveillance placed on them around the clock. There was no way Xiang could talk to them. There was no way they could escape.

Liu had thwarted his plans for disobedience. Xiang had no doubt that unless he murdered Jasper, Liu would kill his parents.

Sadly, he realized he was no match for Liu.

In grim resignation, he thought about how he would kill Jasper and avoid having the murder attributed to him. He also had to eradicate Jasper's connection to him.

As Xiang picked up the special encrypted cell phone to call Jasper, he realized he would have to ask Jasper to bring his phone to their meeting tomorrow morning so he could take it before it was found by the FBI or police. He had an easy way to do that: he would tell Jasper he was upgrading their phones to a newer model.

Before the call, he went over the plan in his mind several more times. He couldn't leave any loose ends in this operation. Not only his own life, but his parents' were on the line.

Satisfied, he picked up the phone and called Jasper. "Tomorrow morning," he said. Then anxious to make certain Jasper would come, he added, "Good news." That way Jasper would think Xiang had the CD.

"I'll be there," the senator said, sounding elated.

"And bring your phone with you. I want to exchange it for a newer model. See you then."

*   *   *

Xiang arrived at their meeting point in Rock Creek Park fifteen minutes before five.

Jasper always jogged toward the meeting point from a southerly direction. Xiang didn't want it to look as if Jasper had stopped for a meeting. He wanted to kill the senator when he was still running. So Xiang found a spot fifty yards south of the meeting point with thick shrubs on one side of the trail.

He crouched down behind the shrubs and waited.

Xiang was wearing tight black leather gloves. He pulled out the gun with a long silencer. Then he put on a ski mask, showing only his eyes.

At five minutes to five, Xiang saw Jasper approaching.

Xiang waited until the senator, jogging, was almost even with the bush. Then he stood and raised his gun hand.

Before firing, Xiang saw surprise on Jasper's face. Then recognition. He knew.

Xiang pumped a single bullet into Jasper's chest. The senator dropped to his knees, then collapsed onto this back.

They had taught Xiang well in shooting school. He was confident a single shot was all it would take to kill Jasper.

Calmly, he walked over. The senator's body shook in a spasm. Then stopped moving. Xiang checked Jasper's pulse.

He was dead.

Swiftly, but methodically, he removed the senator's wallet and cash to make it look like a robbery. He lifted the encrypted cell phone from Jasper's pocket and put all those items in the pocket of his windbreaker along with the gun.

He raced away from the scene in the direction of his car. Then he drove home. Disgusted with himself, he peeled off his clothes and soaked under a hot shower as if that would purge his guilt for Jasper's murder. Then he put the gun, two encrypted phones, and Jasper's wallet and cash into a brown supermarket bag.

He drove to the Embassy where he placed the items in the bag into a box marked "CONFIDENTIAL EMBASSY PAPERS."

He personally carried that box down to the basement of the embassy. There, he instructed the clerk on duty, a young woman, to lock it in the secure vault. The embassy, by international law, was Chinese government property and could not be searched by the Americans.

No one could ever tie Xiang or the Chinese government to Jasper's murder.

To the world, it would look as if one more jogger had been robbed and killed in Rock Creek Park.

Xiang took the elevator back to his office. There he called Liu and reported. "It was done."

"Okay," Liu replied tersely and hung up the phone.

No praise from the spymaster.

Xiang went up to the ambassador's office and reported to him Jasper's murder. "This better not be traced to you," the ambassador responded.

Not much support there, either.

Xiang returned to his office. All he thought about now was his parents. He hoped he'd saved their lives.

He waited a full hour before calling Beijing. This time his father answered immediately.

"How are you and Mother?" Xiang asked.

"Both fine."

"Anything I can help you with?"

"We are both fine. Thanks to you."

Relieved, Xiang put down the phone. Of course, Liu would take good care of them now that Xiang had killed Jasper. They were a valuable asset for Liu. As long as he had control over them, Liu could make Xiang do anything he wanted.

*   *   *

At six thirty in the morning Martin was on the treadmill in the exercise room in his house unsuccessfully trying to blot out thoughts about the CD, Allison, and Jasper, when the doorbell rang. He raced to the door to answer before it woke Frances, still sleeping upstairs.

Opening the door, Martin saw the grim-faced Chinese ambassador. "Can I come in?" he asked.

"Sure."

Martin led him to the study.

"Sorry to bother you so early," the ambassador said.

"What happened?"

"Senator Jasper's dead. He was jogging in Rock Creek Park and was killed in a robbery. A soon as I heard about it on the news, I rushed right here."

How convenient, Martin thought. He had no doubt one of the ambassador's colleagues at the embassy working for MSS had killed Jasper. It was obvious to Martin from the discussion on the CD that Jasper had supplied information to Liu, but he was no longer of use to the spymaster. Indeed, after Vanessa's death, Jasper was a liability to Liu, as he was to Martin.

The Washington lawyer could guess what the ambassador would say next.

"In view of Senator Jasper's unfortunate death, I would like you to reconsider submitting the CD to the FBI and instead to destroy it."

Martin had guessed right. "You're asking quite a bit from me. That would be hard to justify."

"We're your client. Isn't that justification?"

"I didn't receive the CD from you in a lawyer client communication. I received it from Allison Boyd."

"True. But with Jasper's death, his espionage has ended and he can't be punished."

"That's certainly correct."

"Now let's talk about the consequences of your turning it over. Minister Liu and his colleagues aren't subject to American law. There will be no one to punish. All it will do is inflame and poison relations between our two great nations for a long period. That will hurt both of us. So it would be in your national interest, as well as ours, to destroy the CD."

It was a clever argument, Martin thought. "There's merit in what you say. But I'm a private citizen. That's a decision to be made by the officials of the American government. They have to balance the issues that you raised."

The ambassador smiled. "With all due respect, Andrew, you know much better than I that a critical decision like this will never be decided rationally. The press will get hold of it. Congressmen will call press conferences and Sinophobia will have a field day in the media. That public outcry will preclude your government from making the choice which is in your country's best interest. Only you alone can make that choice now. You know I'm correct."

As Martin thought about his response, the personal issue for him weighed heavily. Disclosing the CD was virtually certain to bring to the forefront Vanessa's death and Martin's role in covering up what had happened in Anguilla. His nomination as chief justice, a virtual certainty at this point, would go down the tubes.

Martin sighed. Once again, he was faced with a moral and ethical dilemma. And once again he would do whatever was necessary to preserve his chance to be chief justice. By acceding to the ambassador's request and destroying the CD, would he be an accessory to murder? Of course not, he tried to rationalize. He had no real knowledge that the Chinese had murdered Jasper. Merely supposition. He also tried to tell himself that the ambassador's argument had merit: what he would be doing was in the best interest of the United States. But Martin was too smart to accept any of those rationalizations for a moment.

"I'll destroy the CD," Martin said in a barely audible voice.

The slippery slope had now plunged him through the gates of hell.

When the ambassador left, Martin focused on Allison. He'd still have to deal with her. But he had a way to do that.

*   *   *

When Allison woke up at seven in the guest bedroom in Paul's house, she immediately checked the online *Washington Post* on her iPhone.

"Oh my God," she cried out as she saw Jasper's body on the small screen and under it an article entitled, "Senator Jasper apparent victim of a robbery."

In stunned disbelief, she read, "Senator Wesley Jasper from Colorado, who frequently jogged in Rock Creek Park in the early morning, was fatally shot at around 5:00 a.m. this morning in an apparent robbery.

"In view of Jasper's status as a US senator, the FBI has assumed control of the case. Kelly Cameron, an FBI special agent on the scene, issued a statement: 'At this point, we have no basis to believe this was anything other than a robbery. However, our investigation is still in its very early stages, and all possibilities will be considered.'

"Senator Jasper was 55 years old. The senator is survived by his wife, Linda, who was in Colorado at the time of his death, as well as two children."

Allison's cell phone rang. It was Paul. "Hi. I'm at Dulles I just got off the red-eye."

"Have you seen the news?"

"Not this morning. Why?"

She told him about Jasper's death. "Jasper was murdered!" Paul cried out. "He wasn't one of my favorite people, but still. One thing it does is give finality to your investigation of Vanessa's death."

"What do you mean?"

"It's over now. Jasper's dead."

Paul couldn't be more wrong, but she didn't want to argue with him over the phone. She would do that in person.

"I'm on my way to the house," he continued. "I'll see you soon."

Once she hung up the phone, Allison focused on what Paul was overlooking.

It wasn't over.

She still had to find out whom Jasper called from Anguilla. The villain who arranged to move her sister's dead body.

With Jasper now dead, she wondered if she had lost any chance of finding out who that was. There had to be another way.

Think, she told herself. Think.

Wait a minute. She had one slender ray of hope.

Jasper had told her at Bistro Francais that once he brought Vanessa's body to the villa he grabbed a cell phone and called the owner of the villa.

Perhaps he had reached for the nearest cell and it was Vanessa's. If that was the case, and Allison had the cell, she could check it for past numbers called. But Vanessa's cell never came back with her from Anguilla. Jasper or someone else must have discarded it.

But there might be another way. The first evening at Vanessa's, Allison had asked Verizon to send copies of phone bills with the most recent statements. She had done it hoping this would lead her to the man Vanessa had been with in Anguilla. Well, now she knew he was Jasper. But if the senator had grabbed Vanessa's cell to make his call, then the number of the man he called, the owner of the villa who moved Vanessa's body, would show up on Vanessa's Verizon statement on the list of most recent calls made from that cell.

By now, the Verizon bills should be in the mailbox at Vanessa's apartment.

Excited, Allison burst out of the house. In the street, she flagged a passing cab. She gave the driver Vanessa's address and said, "I'll only be a minute. If you want to wait and bring me back here, I'll give you a generous tip."

The cabbie willingly obliged.

As he navigated his way through heavy morning traffic, Allison thought this could be the break she needed. But she cautioned herself that it was a long shot.

The instant the cab stopped in front of Vanessa's building, Allison was out of the door, practically flying into the building. The man at the desk pulled back with a start. She guessed he thought dead Vanessa's apparition had just flown through the door. She was already past him to the mailboxes in back of the lobby.

She opened Vanessa's box, saw a Verizon envelope, and yanked it out. Back in the cab, she ripped open the envelope.

Recent cell phone calls made from Vanessa's cell since the last bill were arranged on one sheet. At the bottom was the last call made.

She checked the date and time. It was precisely when Jasper said he called the owner of the villa. So he must have used Vanessa's cell. Her eyes ran over to the number called: a 202 area code. A Washington DC number.

The cabbie slammed on his brakes and shook his fist at a driver who ran a red light. Allison's head almost hit the partition, blocking off the front of the cab. "Sorry Miss," the driver said. "Some people shouldn't drive."

Allison turned back to the Verizon bill. Her eyes ran across the rest of the line to the number called. It seemed very familiar. She knew that number.

It was Andrew Martin's cell! She had dialed it yesterday morning from the train. To confirm, she checked recent calls on her own cell. There it was.

That dirty bastard. He had not only helped Jasper cut and run in Anguilla, but he was responsible for moving Vanessa's body. And then lying and manipulating Allison.

She was beyond livid. She was more angry than she'd ever been in her life. If she could get her hands on Martin, she'd strangle him.

She wanted to confront him. Immediately!

She'd go anywhere she could find him.

How could Paul have been taken in by him?

As the cab pulled up in front of Paul's house, she looked at the meter which read $22, handed the driver $40, and said, "No change. But hold on a minute, we may be going somewhere else."

Still in the cab, she tried Martin's cell. Got voice mail.

Maybe he went to the office early. She tried that. A secretary answered in a crisp British accent, "Mr. Martin's office."

She tried to sound calm. "This is Allison Boyd. I'd like to speak with Mr. Martin. Please tell him, it's urgent."

"I'll check to see if he's available."

After a pause, the secretary said, "He's in a meeting. Can I take a message?"

S.O.B. won't talk to me. "Tell him I want my CD back and I'm on my way to his office."

"I'll tell him that when his meeting ends."

"No. You'll tell him that right now. I'll hold."

Another pause.

Then the secretary was back on the line, "Mr. Martin said that he returned your CD to you yesterday."

What an outrageous lie, Allison thought as she left the cab and walked into Paul's house. Why would Martin do that? He could have said he'd given it to the FBI, but he didn't do that. He still had the CD she gave him or destroyed it. The only explanation she could think of was that he was somehow mixed up in Jasper's death. Nothing made sense. All that was clear was that Martin thought he had the only copy of the CD and he wasn't giving it back to her. He thought he was depriving her of it.

For now, she couldn't worry about the CD. She had a more pressing objective: destroying Martin for what he did by taking away Vanessa's dignity in death and for lying to and manipulating her. She knew how to get even with Martin. She would destroy his chance to be chief justice.

She fixed a pot of coffee while thinking about the best way to accomplish that. Suddenly she heard the front door open. She held her breath until she heard Paul's voice. "Allison, I'm home."

"I'm in the kitchen."

When she saw him, she said, "Don't even take off your coat. I have the most incredible thing to tell you."

"What happened?"

"When Vanessa drowned, Jasper called your boss Andrew Martin from Anguilla. Martin's the low-life who arranged to move the body and let Jasper race off into the night."

Paul dropped his bag with a thud. "That's ridiculous. The silliest thing I ever heard. Everything that happened must be getting to you."

"C'mere. Look for yourself."

She put the Verizon bill on the kitchen table and with a pencil circled the call made from Vanessa's cell to Martin's cell.

She watched all of the color drain from Paul's face. In a state of shock, he collapsed into a chair.

As he did, she stated the obvious, "Jasper used Vanessa's cell to make the mystery call. The time and date match exactly."

"But . . . but . . . there must be another explanation. Not Andrew, I don't believe it."

"The phone records don't lie. There is no other explanation."

"How the hell could Andrew have done such a thing?"

She imagined this must be hard for Paul. The man was his demigod whom he had placed on a pedestal.

"Easy. He was covering up for his buddy Jasper. And he was worried that disclosure of Jasper's weekend with Vanessa at his house and her drowning would derail his chance to be chief justice. How inconsiderate of my sister," Allison said caustically.

"Of course," Paul continued, "it fits for another reason. I'd forgotten about it, because I don't think he's used it for years, but Andrew has a house in Anguilla. Or at least he did years ago. When his daughters were young, the family used to go down there. So he probably has influence in Anguilla which he used to engineer the cover-up. I should have realized all this, particularly because Jasper was Martin's friend. I'm sorry I was so blindsided by Martin."

"Don't give yourself a beating. You were very helpful in getting me to focus on Jasper."

"I'd like to go in and confront Andrew. Tell him I can't believe he did this."

She shook her head vigorously. "I think the time for confronting Martin is over. He already sweet talked me and conned me twice. You once."

"Then what do you intend to do?"

Before she had a chance to answer, her cell rang. She glanced at caller ID. It was Har Stevens, the police commissioner in Anguilla. She answered.

"This is Allison."

"Har Stevens here."

"Yes, Mr. Stevens."

"We've had a new development in your sister's case and I'm rather embarrassed about it."

"What's that?"

"A witness, a twelve year old boy who lives on the island has come forward. The boy was playing with his dog on Shoal's Bay Beach the night your sister died. He was too frightened to tell anyone what he saw. Finally, today, he told his mother, and she came to see me."

"What did he say?"

Allison held her breath.

"The boy said a woman, must have been Vanessa, was with a man on the beach sitting in a chaise. They were drinking something. She left the man, took off her clothes, and swam out into the sea. A few minutes later, the man swam out to her. They embraced romantically, and then he pushed her under the water, holding her there. She was screaming and waving her arms. He held her there until she stopped moving and shouting. Then he swam back with her still body and carried her up to the villa they were staying in. I am absolutely convinced the boy was telling the truth."

It all fell into place for Allison. Jasper murdered Vanessa. He had no intention of marrying her, and he couldn't let her disclose the CD.

"I'm so sorry," Stevens continued. "As I told you, I was off the island when this occurred. I have questioned my deputy and the two officers who were responsible for moving the body to another beach adjacent to the Corinthian. They admitted what they did, corroborating the boy's story. All three have been suspended and will be disciplined. This is not how we do things on Anguilla."

"I appreciate you calling, Mr. Stevens."

"Please, if there's anything I can do to soften your pain."

"Let me ask you one question."

"Certainly. Anything."

"Who's the owner of the villa they were staying in?"

"Andrew Martin. An important lawyer in Washington, DC."

"That's what I thought."

She hung up the phone and reported on the call to Paul.

At the conclusion, she said, "I'm not a lawyer, but doesn't this make Martin an accessory to murder?"

"Probably not. If he didn't know Jasper murdered Vanessa. But apart from the legal issue, his conduct was totally reprehensible."

"And somebody like that shouldn't be chief justice of the United States."

"How do you intend to use this to stop him?"

"Listen, Paul, from this point on, I don't want you to be involved. He's your boss. You have a partnership on the line, which you've worked damn hard for eight years to achieve."

"But I want to help."

"Really, I insist."

He sighed with resignation. She knew he'd back off and let her take it from here.

"Thanks for all your help and moral support," she said.

Out on the street, she hailed a passing cab, located the address of the *Washington Post* on her iPhone, and told the driver to take her there.

She was no Washington expert, but she knew exactly what to do. Rick Potts hated Martin, she realized from reading his profile when Martin was placed on the president's short list. He would devour her story about Martin's involvement in her sister's death like a hungry little pig at a feeding trough. She had the facts to back it up: The tape of her discussion with Jasper at Bistro Francais, the Verizon phone bill, and what Har Stevens had told her. Also, that Martin owned a house in Anguilla. She would omit any mention of the CD or the Chinese involvement. Those would just complicate a clear story of Martin's culpability.

*   *   *

After Paul watched Allison's cab pull away, he returned to the kitchen, poured a cup of coffee, and slumped down at his kitchen table. He had been in Washington eight years, and he had studied American history at Yale. He knew that in Washington the mighty so often stumbled and were brought down. Men revered for their integrity, and women too, frequently sold out when the price was right.

He had thought Martin was above this. He would have bet most of his meager assets on it. How could he have been so wrong?

Didn't he know Martin well enough? Or did the prize just have to be large enough: such as the Chief Justice of the United States.

Was that what caused Martin to rationalize his behavior? To justify what he clearly knew was abhorrent?

This isn't over yet, what happens between Allison and Martin, he thought. They still had another act to play.

She was damn smart. He was convinced that she had a copy of the CD somewhere, which she refused to disclose to Martin or even to him. And Martin, somehow caught up in all of this, didn't realize there was another copy. Paul was persuaded of this because Martin's one flaw was that he sometimes underestimated other people.

Allison was someone never to be underestimated.

*   *   *

Allison spent almost two hours with Rick Potts in his office at the *Post*. Afterwards, he told her she should remain incognito until this was all over.

He arranged for her to use one of the hotel rooms the *Post* maintained for confidential sources and those wanted by the police, across 15th Street in the Madison Hotel, so she wouldn't have to register.

He promised to call her on her cell if he needed anything else.

When he didn't call by six in the evening, she ordered dinner from room service. At eight she went to sleep and got the first solid night's sleep she had gotten since the first call from Stevens.

*   *   *

At eight thirty in the evening, the phone rang in Martin's house. With so much happening, he didn't wait for the housekeeper to answer, but grabbed the phone on the first ring in the den. It was Rick Potts.

"What do you want?" Martin asked in a surly voice.

"I'd like to read you the draft of an article I'm finalizing for tomorrow's paper."

Martin's heart was pounding.

Francis came into the room, sat down on the sofa, and was watching him.

"At the end," Potts continued, "I'll give you a chance to deny any statements, to offer proof that I'm wrong, or to comment."

"Go ahead," Martin replied softly.

As Martin listened, he realized that Allison had gone to Potts with the story of his complicity in Vanessa's death. Also, that Jasper had murdered Vanessa.

Allison had given the story to Potts in detail. His chances to be chief justice were over. At least, for some reason, she hadn't told Potts about the CD which would have involved him in Jasper's murder.

When Potts was finished, Martin tried to sound indignant. "What's your source for this outrageous pack of lies?"

"You know I can't tell you that."

"I'll call Bill McCormick. He'll fire you."

"Bill's already read and approved it. Any specific points you'd like to challenge?"

"No comment."

"I want you to be aware that I'm calling the White House to see if they have any comment."

Martin hung up the phone. He looked at Francis.

"Allison went to Potts."

"I gathered as much." She began to cry. "I feel sorry for you, Andrew. You've done so many wonderful things. And to be brought down by a phone call to Anguilla to help a friend."

"I was stupid to make the call. Stupid not to have gone to Anguilla, even without Jasper, and straightened it out."

"You were helping your friend."

He refused to attribute it all to that. "I wanted the gold ring. I lost my moral compass."

"Well, so what? You'll still be the Andrew Martin I love. A powerful Washington lawyer, if not chief justice."

He didn't have the heart to tell Francis that while he would continue at the firm, his reputation would be tarnished. He could have avoided that had he gone to Anguilla even without Jasper. Well should have—could have—it was too late for that.

"It seems unfair, Andrew. You've done everything right for many years and then you made one slip."

He shook his head in dismay. "I deserve to be chief justice. Everybody agreed. Including the president, and now this."

"C'mon over here," she said.

The two of them stretched out on the sofa. He held her in his arms. "We'll go on from here," she said.

They remained like that for about half an hour when the phone rang. Martin got up and answered.

"Andrew Martin," he heard in a man's voice he didn't recognize.

"Yes. Whose calling?"

"My name is Henry Young. I'm the president's Deputy White House Counsel."

"You mean Arthur Larkin's assistant?"

"You could say that. Arthur asked me to call and tell you that the president was withdrawing your name as a possible nominee for chief justice."

Martin was furious. Arthur didn't even have the decency to call himself. Well, he'd better get used to the fact that people would no longer treat him the same as they had before.

*   *   *

Across town, in his Connecticut Avenue apartment, Xiang was sitting in front of the television with his eyes glued to the screen. CNN was about to broadcast a statement from the FBI about Senator Jasper's murder.

To Xiang's astonishment, he saw Kelly Cameron, his Kelly Cameron, identified as the FBI spokesperson, on the screen, for an interview by Bruce Newman, a CNN reporter.

She now looked grim-faced.

Xiang listened intently.

Newman: "Thank you for joining us Miss Cameron. I gather that you are in charge of the FBI's investigation of Senator Jasper's murder?"

"That's correct, Bruce."

"Do you believe this was a simple robbery, or was there some political issue that led to the senator's death?"

"At this point, we don't know. We're not ruling out any possibilities."

"We were informed that the senator's wallet was missing. Doesn't this indicate that robbery was the motive?"

Kelly smiled lightly. He remembered that smile. She gave it whenever she heard something that sounded stupid. Or knew somebody was hiding something from her.

"The killer may have wanted it to look that way. Our investigation is still in its initial stages."

"Can you tell our viewers anything else?"

Kelly stared directly into the camera, narrowed her eyes, and said, "You can be certain that we will catch the perpetrator of this terrible crime."

Beijing

At his desk in Beijing, Liu was surprised to see that he had an e-mail from Andrei. The Russian preferred to communicate only in person.

Liu opened it and read: "It took you a few days, but I'm pleased that you finally got there."

Liu smiled. Andrei had learned of Jasper's murder and couldn't resist reminding Liu it had been his idea.

Liu typed his response: "Thank you."

Now for the hard part. President Yao must not have heard of Jasper's murder or he would have called Liu over to his office. Liu picked up the red phone in his office and called President Yao's secretary to arrange an urgent meeting. "Come now." The secretary said. That made Liu happy. He liked having that kind of influence with the Supreme Leader.

On the other hand, the Chinese President wouldn't be getting the Pentagon's five-year plan immediately. Though many would have been content to wait patiently for what they wanted, Yao wasn't one of them. He always wanted everything right now.

As soon as he was alone with Yao, Liu said, "As you're aware, violent crime in the United States, including robberies and murders, are practically an epidemic."

"Of course I know that. It's a consequence of their so-called democracy. It's disgusting that those people lecture us about our human rights violations. But why are you telling me this?"

Liu took a deep breath and tossed it out. "Because only days before Senator Jasper promised to deliver the Pentagon's five year plan to us, the senator was killed in a robbery in Washington."

"Have they found the killer?"

"They're still searching."

Yao was frowning. "I assume you had nothing to do with his murder."

Though he was startled by the question, without flinching Liu replied, "Of course not. Why would I do anything to interfere with our getting the Pentagon's document?"

"I don't know all the games you people in MSS play. I just hope this isn't one of them."

"I assure you it's not."

"Good. Then tell me how you're going to get the Pentagon's plan for me."

Liu was ready for that one. "I intend to recruit another high-ranking American government figure with access equal to or better than Senator Jasper. We'll get it from him."

"How long will this take?"

"I have some very good candidates. It will be my top priority."

"Humph. It had better be."

"It will be."

"And keep me informed."

"Of course."

Leaving the office, Liu breathed a sigh of relief. Andrei would have been proud of how he had manipulated the Chinese President. Of course, he didn't have any candidates to replace Jasper, but he was expecting Andrei to help him, drawing on his KGB information.

In the back of the car, returning to his office, Liu opened the window, lit a cigarette, and thought about the two loose ends that he had with what had transpired: the Chinese Ambassador and Xiang.

Yesterday, after Liu had given Xiang the order to kill Jasper, he had spoken with the ambassador, told him what Xiang was doing, and directed him to pressure Martin not to turn over the CD. Liu had been relieved to receive the ambassador's call an hour ago telling him that he had succeeded.

The problem for Liu was that the ambassador not only knew that Liu had arranged Jasper's murder, he had also heard the CD, which meant he knew of Liu's carelessness in letting Vanessa record his conversation with Jasper.

Liu would have preferred to arrange the ambassador's death to eliminate the threat of him telling Yao about the CD and Jasper's murder. The trouble was that the ambassador was well regarded among members of the Central Committee. Even the Supreme Leader had said complimentary things about the ambassador to Liu. If he were to die mysteriously, there would be a full-scale investigation which Liu could not control.

Liu thought about the ambassador some more and finally came up with a solution. Liu kept personal files on many of the top leaders. He knew that the ambassador's only child was a daughter whom he cared deeply about. She was married to a French man and living in Paris with two children. On the ambassador's next visit to Beijing, Liu would have a chat with him. He would explain to the ambassador that Liu had made arrangements with an MSS agent in Paris to kill the ambassador's daughter and grandchildren if he dared to mention anything about the CD or these events. And Liu wouldn't be bluffing. He would make all the arrangements for the three Paris murders so all he would have to do was make a single phone call.

Then there was Xiang. He could destroy Liu as well as the ambassador. Arranging Xiang's death would be an easy matter. No one cared about Xiang other than his parents. But Liu didn't want to do that. He viewed Xiang as a valuable asset in the United States to do his bidding. And as long as Liu had Xiang's parents under his control, Xiang would do what he wanted.

He realized he was taking a risk leaving Xiang alive, but he was prepared to do that . . . at least for now.

Washington

Allison awoke at five thirty. Potts had said he'd make sure a copy of the morning paper would be at the front desk in the hotel, held with her room number. No name.

It was there. She picked up the paper and a cup of coffee in the lobby.

In the elevator, returning to her room, she glanced at the upper right hand corner. She saw Martin's picture and the headline: "WASHINGTON LAWYER INVOLVED IN CONGRESSIONAL STAFFER'S MURDER," and under that, "WHITE HOUSE WITHDRAWS ANDREW MARTIN FROM CONSIDERATION AS CHIEF JUSTICE."

Back in her room she read the article. Potts laid out the whole story, beginning with Jasper's murder of Vanessa and his Sunday night call to Martin. He had it all right. Within the body of the article he quoted a criminal law expert saying, "It is extremely unlikely that Martin would be charged with any crime."

At the end, Potts quoted an unnamed White House source stating that, "In view of these facts, the president withdrew Martin's name from consideration as chief justice."

Allison didn't care about the criminal charges against Martin. She was just pleased that she had knocked him out of the running to be chief justice.

She read the article again. Potts, as promised, didn't mention Allison by name or as a source. There was no reference to the CD or to the Chinese chasing her—topics which Allison hadn't discussed with Potts.

But now that she had gained revenge for what happened to Vanessa, Allison turned her attention to those topics—the CD and the Chinese.

She felt as if she were trying to solve a complicated puzzle: the Chinese had desperately wanted the CD; she gave the CD to Martin;

Jasper was mysteriously and coincidentally murdered the next morning by an unidentified killer.

She felt as if she had to find a way to fit these pieces together or she would still be at risk because she had listened to the CD even though Martin didn't think she had a copy. Most importantly, she knew about Liu's meeting with Jasper at which Liu recruited the senator.

She closed her eyes and moved the pieces together in her mind, the same way she solved a complex archeological issue. Finally, something clicked.

Question: Who would have wanted Jasper dead at that point?

Answer: The Chinese. Jasper had become a liability now that the CD had been discovered.

Question: How could the Chinese have known that the CD had been discovered?

Answer: Andrew Martin, because Allison gave it to Martin.

Conclusion: Martin had to be working with the Chinese. She recalled that the first time Paul had met Vanessa, Martin had sent him to the Hill as a representative of the Chinese government to oppose an arms sale to Taiwan.

The Internet was wonderful. Allison accessed the government files for registration of foreign agents, all public information, for Andrew Martin. Sure enough, he was registered as an agent for the governments of France, China, Brazil, and Australia.

So Martin must have tipped off the Chinese about the CD rather than taking it to the FBI director as he promised, which was why he lied to her and said he returned it to her.

Allison now knew what she had to do with this information to protect herself.

Using Madison Hotel stationery, she wrote a letter to Rick Potts explaining about the CD; the conversation between Jasper and Liu; how the Chinese had chased her; how she had given it to Martin, who was registered as a Chinese agent; and how Jasper had been murdered only hours later. "From all of this," she wrote, "the inescapable conclusion is that Andrew Martin was a conspirator with Chinese officials in the murder of Senator Jasper."

She reread her letter, placed it in an envelope addressed to Rick Potts and put it into a second envelope addressed it to Sara Gross.

Inside she added a note: "Sara, when and if you have to mail the prior package I sent you, before doing so, please open that package, insert the letter inside this envelope addressed to Rick Potts, reseal it and mail it. I am doing well and hope you will not have to mail it. Allison."

She got stamps at the desk and dropped the letter to Sara into a mailbox at the corner.

Back in her room, she checked the time: 7:15 a.m. She called Martin's cell.

"Are you proud of yourself?" Martin said.

"I called because we have to talk."

"I have nothing to talk to you about."

"Oh, I think you do. You shouldn't have believed me when I told you that you have the only copy of the CD."

"You're a liar, too."

"Coming from you, that's quite a compliment."

"I'll meet you at the Cosmos Club in an hour."

"It'll have to be in the dining room. Not a private room."

"Fine. And I'll want to see your cell phone to make sure it's not in the record mode. As I've learned, you have a tendency to do that."

*   *   *

Allison met Martin in the reception area of the club at the bottom of the grand circular staircase running to the second floor of what had once been the most ornate mansion in Washington.

"Where's your cell phone?" he asked.

She showed it to him, placed in her bag, and checked that in the cloak room, along with her coat.

"Do you want to frisk me, too?" she asked. She was wearing a skirt and blouse. "Maybe do a strip search in the ladies room."

"That's funny."

The maître d' led them to a table facing the garden in the wood paneled dining room. Only a few other tables were taken—none close to them. They could easily talk.

Martin ordered a blueberry muffin and coffee; she did the same.

"You wanted this meeting," he said tersely. "Tell me about the other CD."

"I will, but first I want you to know that Paul had nothing to do with my going to Potts with the story or what I'm about to tell you. All he did was print for me copies and bios of the 535 members of Congress so I could zero in on Jasper, based upon what an eye witness in Anguilla told me. He has a great deal of respect for you and your firm, and I hope he doesn't suffer because of me."

"You could have come to me with your story rather than going to Potts."

"I tried that a couple of times. You manipulated me to try to save yourself. I went to Potts because he knows what you're really like."

"You have a vivid imagination. I want you to know that I had nothing to do with you being attacked in the Metro station. You can believe it or not, but it happens to be true."

"I'll give you that, but . . ."

"And I had no idea Jasper murdered Vanessa."

"I think that's probably true."

"All I was doing was trying to help a friend. I didn't know about the CD. Jasper was responsible for everything that happened. I became collateral damage because of your digging and that unfortunate CD."

"Just an innocent victim in all of this. Is that what you tell yourself? Is your capacity for rationalization that great?"

"Now what about the other CD?"

The waitress was approaching with the coffee and muffins. Allison waited until she was gone to continue in a soft voice. "I've deduced that you were responsible for Jasper's death."

Calmly, Martin replied: "That's the most absurd thing I've ever heard. What could possibly lead you to that conclusion?"

"I gave you the CD. You lied about giving it back. Jasper was murdered hours later. You represent the Chinese. The Chinese had been trying to kill me to get their hands on the CD. Jasper was only a liability to them now that you, their representative, had possession of what you thought was the only copy."

"But you made another one and lied to me about that."

"It was my insurance policy."

"I hope you're not expecting me to respond to these ridiculous charges."

"No, of course not."

He paused to pick off a piece of the muffin top.

He's stalling, she thought. Washington's top lawyer is stumped. He doesn't know what to say. Still, she had to admire his calm veneer.

"What will you do with this fairy tale you've constructed? Take it to your friend Potts?"

She shook her head. "No, I'm not interested in damaging you any further. You got lucky."

"I don't understand."

"I've laid out in a letter to Potts the whole story of your involvement in Jasper's murder, which is a crime, unlike what happened in Anguilla. I've given that letter and the CD to a third party. Not Paul. Someone you don't know or have ever heard of. If anything happens to me, that third party will mail the letter and the CD to Potts. So you will be charged with murder. Your Chinese clients will be charged with spying in the United States. Some of them will be banished from the United States. The scandal will adversely affect American-Chinese relations for years to come.

"So the point is," she was talking slowly, articulating clearly, making certain he understood exactly what she was saying, "both you personally and the Chinese government would suffer mightily if anything were to happen to me. Then you would lose your powerful law practice and your fancy lifestyle. So don't even think about having me murdered."

"You flatter yourself," he said in a barely audible whisper, "if you think anyone would want to kill you."

"Perhaps, but I won't end up like Senator Jasper. I want to make certain you and those Chinese agents don't come after me."

She gave Martin a moment to respond. When he didn't, she stood up, turned, and left the dining room.

Israel

One Month Later

Allison was relieved and happy to be back on the dig. Not only was she among friends, but she was doing what she loved to do. They were uncovering new objects almost daily. The results of the dating tests on the objects confirmed her belief that this was a town from the time of King Solomon.

Tomorrow, a reporter from the prestigious London based *Archeology Magazine* would be coming, with a photographer to interview Allison and her coworkers for an article about the dig.

Allison was in her small, wooden-framed, makeshift office, reviewing her notes in preparation for the interview, when Zahava came into the office.

"You have a visitor," Zahava said.

"But I thought the London people weren't coming until tomorrow."

"No. Someone else. From the United States."

Allison walked out of the office and saw Paul Maltoni standing there, dressed in khaki slacks, a polo shirt, and a Washington Nationals cap. He was holding another identical cap in his hand.

When he saw her, he stepped forward, smiled, and handed the cap to her. "I figured you could use this with the hot sun."

She put it on. "What are you doing here?"

"I happened to be in the neighborhood."

"You don't look like a lawyer with a prestigious Washington law firm."

"I'm not. The day after you left my house, I went into Martin's office, seeking some explanation for what he had done. And he told me to get the hell out. Then and there I told him I was quitting. I couldn't stand to work for him after everything he did."

She was pleasantly surprised. She wouldn't have guessed that. "Good for you."

"Oh, and he had a message for you."

"I can imagine."

"He said to tell that nosey bitch Allison he hopes you're happy."

"As a matter of fact, I am. I hope he was damaged by what happened."

"Well, he didn't get to be chief justice."

"I hope he'd suffer more than that."

"I don't know what happened to his law practice. I've stayed as far away from the firm as possible."

"What will you do now?"

"I've taken a job as a trial lawyer in the Civil Division at the U.S. Department of Justice. I want to use my law degree to do some good, which was why I went to law school. I start next week."

"That's great. I'm happy to hear it."

"If you ever come to Washington, I hope you'll let me know. I'd like to have dinner with you."

"We'll do it," she smiled, "on one condition. You get to pick the wine, but my turn to pay. I insist."

He laughed. "I would never argue with you, Allison. When you want something, I learned that you get it."

About the Author

Allan Topol is the author of ten novels of international intrigue. Two of them, *Spy Dance* and *Enemy of My Enemy*, were national best sellers. His novels have been translated into Chinese, Japanese, Portuguese, and Hebrew. One was optioned and three are in development for movies.

In addition to his fiction writing, Allan Topol co-authored a two-volume legal treatise entitled *Superfund Law and Procedure*. He wrote a weekly column for Military.com and has published articles in numerous newspapers and periodicals, including the *New York Times*, *Washington Post*, and *Yale Law Journal*.

He is a graduate of Carnegie Institute of Technology, who majored in chemistry, abandoned science, and obtained a law degree from Yale University. He became a partner in a major Washington law firm. An avid wine collector and connoisseur, he has traveled extensively researching dramatic locations for his novels.

Since his graduation from Yale Law School, Allan Topol has been a Washington lawyer.

For more information, visit www.allantopol.com.